BLACKMAIL WAS JUST
THE BEGINNING...

Dr. Stern tore open the envelope. It contained four photographs of his daughter. She was naked. Her hair was in wild disorder and her mouth was open in a scream of agony. A man stood behind her. His face did not show, but the shiny jackboots and death's head insignia of the SS were clearly visible.

Stern collapsed into a chair, trembling.

In the morning there was another envelope. It contained a single unspeakable photograph.

He sat waiting, listening to the pounding of his heart. He knew when the phone rang he would agree to anything.

The end might be the ultimate betrayal!

THE EINSTEIN PLOT

THE EINSTEIN PLOT

Basil Heatter

A DELL BOOK

For Connie,
now and always

Published by
Dell Publishing Co., Inc.
1 Dag Hammarskjold Plaza
New York, New York 10017

Dell ® TM 681510, Dell Publishing Co., Inc.

ISBN: 0-440-12385-2

Printed in the United States of America

First printing—March 1982

BOOK I

1941

ONE

Jens Larsen got out of Norway in May 1941, thirteen months after the German invasion. Along with Konrad Torsten and Vidkun Helberg, two friends from Rjukan—the last town to surrender in southern Norway—he escaped in a rotten old trawler which had to be pumped for twenty minutes every hour. Crossing the North Sea in such a tub was no joke, but on the night of May tenth they anchored in the Thames Estuary. London was taking one of the worst poundings of the war from Luftflotte 2. Hundreds of searchlight beams lit up the sky, providing a frantic backdrop against which swam the motes of the barrage balloons, the exclamation marks of bursting shells hurled from thousands of antiaircraft guns, and the ranks of the German bombers being harried by the British night fighters.

From the deck of the trawler it looked as though the whole of the great city was going up in flames.

Helberg, pipe clamped grimly, tilted his head back and muttered, "Looks as though we've jumped from the pan into the fire."

Larsen did not answer. He was trying, with small success, to distract himself from the nightmare scene around him by thinking of other things. He thought of Michelle Stern and the level gaze of wide-spaced dark eyes set in a delicate heart-shaped face. It had been more than two years since he had last seen her, but he had forgotten nothing of her appearance.

Was Michelle still in London, and if so how would he find her? The British SOE, the security operations executive, might be able to help. They would consider him a romantic idiot looking for a girl he had met only briefly two years before at an otherwise dry-as-dust scientific meeting in Copenhagen, and he probably was. Rjukan had fallen to the Germans on May third the year before. Since then Larsen had concentrated on getting away to England with his information. Only now and then did he permit himself the luxury of remembering Michelle.

Overhead there was a sudden explosion of light as one of the bombers burst into flame and tumbled out of the sky like a burning leaf.

"Good," said Helberg. "Kill the bastards."

At that same moment, three hundred miles north, Rudolf Hess, number two man in the Nazi hierarchy, was sliding back the canopy of his Messerschmitt and preparing to jump into the night sky over Scotland. In the darkness below nothing was visible, but in fact he was within twelve miles of his intended target.

Hess grunted as the parachute straps bit into his shoulders.

Despite the severity of the raid Captain Peter Guthrie was asleep in his flat in London when he was awakened by the insistent ringing of the phone. He groped for the instrument on the bedside table and finding it at last muttered sleepily, "Guthrie here."

"This is Jock Coleville, Peter."

Guthrie opened his eyes. Coleville was an aide to Churchill. "Yes, Jock?"

"PM would like you to be ready to leave for Scotland in fifteen minutes."

"Christ, Jock, it's two in the bloody morning."

"Three, actually. You'll be picked up by limousine in the street in front of your flat. Be there."

Guthrie listened to the click as Coleville rang off. He turned to the girl who slept beside him. "Zofia, love."

"Not again, darling."

Guthrie grinned. "You're safe as far as that goes. I'm leaving for Scotland."

She murmured something he could not quite hear.

"Leave the key above the door, love," he said as he left.

The Rolls stood waiting in the street, engine purring softly. The great car appeared like a fairy-tale apparition amid the glittering fall of broken glass which littered the streets. A weary air-raid warden in a white helmet stood on the corner surveying the Rolls doubtfully. In the rear seat the diminutive figure of Lord Beaverbrook sat with head slumped and eyes closed.

As the driver opened the car door for Guthrie, his lordship opened his eyes and grunted, "Morning."

"Guthrie, sir."

"General Guthrie's son?"

"Yes, sir."

"Knew your father. Very sorry to hear of his death. Arras, wasn't it?"

"Yes, sir."

"Quite a brilliant action considering how little he had to fight with."

The Rolls, almost soundless at sixty, was speeding through the deserted streets heading north.

"What were you doing before the war?" Beaverbrook asked.

"Schoolmaster."

"What subject?"

"Physics." Beaverbrook's half-closed eyes opened wider. Having attended a rural school in Canada, England's greatest press lord—and now the legendary head of aircraft production who was miraculously providing Spitfires at the rate of more than two hundred a week—still had a farm boy's respect for higher education.

"You don't look like a schoolmaster."

Guthrie chuckled. "No, sir? What should I look like?"

"Don't know. Spectacles, probably."

"I have those, sir. Just not using them at present."

"What's your job, then? Something to do with intelligence?"

"You might say that," Guthrie answered cautiously, suspecting that Beaverbrook already knew more about him than he was letting on.

"Maude Committee?"

Guthrie nodded.

"I suppose that explains what you're doing here?"

"What exactly am I doing here, sir?"

"They told you nothing over the phone?"

"Only to be in the street in fifteen minutes."

"Well, it seems that the number two devil, Hess, has parachuted into Scotland. Landed adjacent to the

Duke of Hamilton's castle. Regards himself as some sort of peace emissary. We don't know yet if the man is really Hess or a trick double. I knew Hess in Berlin before the war, and so the prime minister has asked me to go up to Buchanan Castle to have a look at him."

"What has that to do with me, sir? I wouldn't know Hess if I met him on the street."

"Professor Lindemann, the PM's scientific adviser, put your name forward. I suppose because of your association with the Maude Committee."

"I still don't understand, sir."

Despite the fact that the sliding glass window separating them from the driver was fully closed, Beaverbrook lowered his voice. "I know it sounds fantastic, but there is reason to think that Hess's journey to Scotland—if it really is Hess—is somehow associated with Germany's effort to secure a uranium bomb. Have you ever heard of a certain Professor Hauser?"

Guthrie nodded. "Karl Hauser. German physicist. Geopolitical expert. Second rank but well known for his racial theories."

"Well, it seems that Hess was carrying a card from Professor Hauser inscribed with a message apparently intended for the Duke of Hamilton. In view of Hauser's association with the Institute of Physics in Berlin, Professor Lindemann suggested that someone from the scientific end—more exactly, that is, from the Maude Committee—should come along."

"I see."

"They tell me Scotland is quite nice at this time of year," Beaverbrook added dryly, closing his eyes. In a moment he began to snore gently.

They were out in the country now and in the sky

there was the first faint hint of dawn. It was hard to
say exactly where they were, the road signs having
been taken down so as not to provide information
for German parachutists. Beaverbrook's driver, a former racer, took the road with a combination of skill
and abandon, hurling the car straight through inter-
sections."

Guthrie let his mind drift back to the girl he had
left in his bed. At the thought of her warm, full
breasts and the way she had circled his back with her
legs, he found himself stirring restlessly.

It had all seemed casual enough at the start. Doesn't
it always? The shared intimacy of sudden danger.
Huddled forms under blankets. A woman moaning.
Hurt? Well, no, not really. Fornicating, actually.

Do you come here often? To this shelter, that is?
Perhaps we'll meet again. I say, would you care for
a glass of champagne? There's a place I know just
around the corner. . . .

Banal beginning. Now he could hardly do without
her.

The Rolls swept onward. A startled farmer carting
manure barely got his rig out of the way. Shook his
fist. They must be doing close to a hundred. His lordship seemed relaxed enough. Nothing fazes these old
boys.

Guthrie slept.

The commandant of the military prison at Buchanan Castle gave Beaverbrook a brisk salute and then
led the way along a series of narrow stone-flagged cor-
ridors lit by naked bulbs. In the cold, damp air of the
castle their breath was visible. At the head of a flight

of steps guarded by a military policeman who stood rigidly to attention was a wooden door so low that they were forced to stoop to enter.

As the door opened another guard inside the room sprang to attention. The German, dressed in expensive leather flying clothes, was asleep on a narrow iron cot.

"Shall I wake him, sir?" the guard asked.

Beaverbrook shook his head. For a moment there was no sound in the room but the German's heavy breathing.

"All right," Beaverbrook said. "Wake him now."

At the touch of the guard's hand on his shoulder the German opened his eyes. The heavy brows creased in bewilderment, but then as his gaze fastened on Beaverbrook, he jerked himself upright.

"Hello, Beaverbrook," he said in a guttural voice. "I see they have sent you to greet me."

Beaverbrook said coldly, "Well, Hess, what exactly are you doing here?"

"I have come on a mission of peace. The Fuehrer wants only peace with England."

"He's left it a bit late, don't you think?"

The German regarded them sternly. He had the self-righteous look of a fanatic. Crackers, thought Guthrie. "It is never too late for peace," said Hess. "The Fuehrer does not wish to destroy England. We are of the same race, the same blood. The Fuehrer wishes to have the British Empire and the Royal Family remain intact. The Fuehrer wants . . ."

"To hell with what the Fuehrer wants!" Beaverbrook interrupted. "Listen, Hess, we've already taken the worst you can throw at us. We took it again last night in London. Why should we quit now?"

"Because there is worse to come, Beaverbrook. Much worse. Weapons of unbelievable ferocity. *Brighter than a thousand suns*. I swear to you England will be destroyed. Believe me . . ." Carried away by the urgency of his message Hess was spouting a flood of words.

Beaverbrook looked at Guthrie and motioned toward the door. They stopped outside.

"He's certainly Hess, no doubt of that," Beaverbrook said.

"Is he as mad as he seems?"

"What do you think?"

Even through the closed door they could still hear Hess ranting. He was demanding that he be treated with ambassadorial rank and taken to meet Churchill immediately.

Guthrie shrugged.

Beaverbrook frowned. "This superweapon he's yelling about. I suppose that's the same thing your people are working on?"

"Perhaps."

"Anything to it?"

Guthrie said, "Hard to say, sir. Naturally we don't know very much about what the German physicists may be up to. Since Hahn and Strassmann first split the atom, very little additional information has become available."

"As I understand it some of your refugee scientists in London worked in Berlin before the war."

"One in particular. Dr. Stern. He was Professor Einstein's assistant at the Kaiser Wilhelm Institute."

"You might want to have a word with him. Find out if there's anything to Hess's ranting."

"Certainly, sir."

Beaverbrook led the way back along the narrow corridor.

TWO

In Berlin Captain Karlheinz Pintsch, Hess's adjutant, came to see the Fuehrer. It was three o'clock in the afternoon, Hitler's lunchtime, and Pintsch trembled at his own temerity. But the matter was urgent.

"Who is Pintsch?" Hitler asked.

Bormann had recognized the name. "He works for Hess."

"Bring him in." The Fuehrer was wearing his usual plain gray uniform without decorations. His eyes were deep-sunk and his skin looked waxy. Beside him sat Eva Braun in a tweed skirt and woolen sweater. Also at the table were Bormann, Ribbentrop, Air General Udet, and Dr. Todt, architect of the Siegfried Line.

Hitler's guests were allowed meat, but the Fuehrer stuck to his regular diet—mushrooms, curds, and yogurt topped off with tomato catsup. As was customary with Hitler at mealtime, he had been delivering a monologue on Frederick the Great. His guests had heard it all before.

Pintsch was shown in.

"Well?"

"Mein Fuehrer—"

Hitler glared.

"—the *Stellvertreter* has flown to Scotland."

"The Deputy Fuehrer has flown to Scotland?"

Pintsch nodded.

"Insane," said Hitler.

Pintsch stood dumb.

Hitler said something to Bormann in a low voice. Bormann left the table and returned with two SS officers. "Karlheinz Pintsch," Bormann said, "you are under arrest. You will be held at Obersalzberg until a court of inquiry can be convened to look into your part in the events of today. Heil Hitler!"

Pintsch, almost fainting, managed to bow to Hitler before he was marched away between his towering guards.

"Get me Goering," Hitler ordered.

"Yes, mein Fuehrer."

Bormann made the call to Goering from an anteroom. One of the SS officers stood waiting for him.

"What do you want done with him?" the SS man said, referring to Pintsch.

"Make sure I never see him again."

That weekend Churchill spent at Ditchley Park with several members of his staff; among them Professor Lindemann, General Hastings Ismay, and Brendan Bracken. Churchill was able to put the war out of his mind long enough to attend a screening of *Go West*, with the Marx Brothers.

The movie ended at midnight and the Prime Minister put on his mandarin dressing gown with the red and gold dragons and lit up a fat Romeo y Juliet. His aides were slumping with fatigue.

"What's first, Jock?"

"The Duke of Hamilton is here, sir."

"The devil he is."

"Yes, sir."

"Blasted young fool." Churchill and the duke had encountered each other on several occasions in the House of Commons when the duke had been a member of Parliament. And then there had been that rather nervy stunt, flying a light plane over Mount Everest. "All right, dammit. Show him in."

The duke, a good-looking young man in RAF uniform, was ushered into a room already blue with cigar smoke.

Churchill said, "Where's that Cognac, Jock?"

"Here, sir."

"You'd better have some, Hamilton. You look worn."

The duke, who had been driving for hours over blacked-out roads, accepted gratefully. "You've heard about this business in Scotland, sir?"

"Hess? I understand he dropped in to have tea with you."

"That seems to have been his intention."

"No warning?"

"None."

"Why you, Hamilton?"

The duke took out a visiting card and handed it to Churchill. On one side was engraved "Dr. Karl Hauser." On the reverse side, written in ink, "$E = MC^2$."

"So that's the famous calling card. Who the devil is Hauser anyway?"

"A scientist. Rather distinguished. Member of the staff at the Kaiser Wilhelm Institute."

Churchill turned the card over and looked at the back.

"That's Professor Albert Einstein's formula for the equation of energy," Hamilton volunteered.

"Anything secret about it?"

"Not particularly."

"Then what does it all mean, Hamilton?"

The duke took another swallow of brandy. "I met this chap Hauser about six months before the war. He was climbing in Katmandu. I was doing some flying."

"I heard about that. Damn fool stunt."

The duke nodded. "The Nepalese put us up for the night in a guesthouse and we shared a bottle of whiskey and had rather a long chat."

"Geopolitical?"

"Something like that. England and Germany united against the Bolshies."

"That was all?"

"I never heard of him again until now."

"And so when Hess thought of going off on this so-called peace mission, Hauser suggested your name."

"It would seem so, sir."

Peter Guthrie rang the bellpush at David Stern's flat. Stern answered the door. The scientist did not fit the academic mold. A tall, lean man, he had the kind of wide-shouldered athletic frame that never seemed to put on weight. His fair hair as yet showed no touch of gray, and although he had spent most of his adult years in laboratories his blue eyes could still capture the smallest print without benefit of glasses. It was ironic, Guthrie thought, that this Jewish scientist should look more Aryan than most of the Nazis.

"You're looking well, David."

"You too, Peter."

"Michelle not home?"

"Not yet. She's over at the BBC this afternoon."

"I'll be sorry to have missed her. She's the prettiest girl in London."

Stern smiled. "If you will do me the honor of staying to lunch, you may see her yet."

"I'd be glad to, David, but I'm afraid it'll have to be another time." He could see the framed photo of Stern's dead wife. Their daughter, Michelle had inherited her dark good looks from her mother. "In fact I came to talk to you about this Hess matter."

"The radio has been full of it. Unbelievable."

"Did you know Hess?"

The ghost of a smile touched Stern's lips. "We moved in different circles."

"It's said that he's had some interest in the sciences."

"If he did I don't think it extended to theoretical physics. Perhaps, like Hitler, he has been concerned with astrology."

"What do you know about Dr. Karl Hauser?"

Something flickered in Stern's candid blue eyes. He dropped his glance briefly. When he raised it again there was just a hint of grimness on his lean features. "Are you investigating me, Peter?"

Guthrie smiled. "As a member of the Maude Committee you have already been thoroughly investigated."

"So?"

"We're interested in the connection between Hess and Hauser."

"And the connection between Hauser and myself?"

"If there was one."

"There was, but I am afraid it will not do you very much good."

Guthrie drew out a packet of cigarettes and offered one to Stern, who declined with a shake of the head. "Do you mind telling me about it, David?"

"Not at all. For what it's worth, I knew Hauser in Berlin, along with many others who worked there—Hahn, Meitner, Pritsch, Strassman, Einstein."

"The card Hess was carrying had Hauser's name on one side and Einstein's equation for the measurement of energy on the other. Do you understand the connection?"

"Not really."

"Are you still in touch with Einstein?"

"Not so much anymore. He does not approve of the work we are doing here. He would prefer to see the war won by some other means. He wrote to me, of course, when he heard about the death of my wife—he was very fond of Denise—but we have all lost someone. Since then there has been perhaps a card at New Year's, that sort of thing."

"Would the Einstein equation have some particular significance for the Germans at this time?"

"Lise Meitner used the Einstein equation to measure the release of energy. Perhaps Hauser intends it now as a warning to England. . . ."

The scientist broke off at the sound of a key in the front door. Michelle Stern came into the room. She was bareheaded, and her long dark hair and piquant face glistened with drops of moisture. The English air had touched her ivory complexion with a hint of rose. She bent to kiss her father, then turned with a smile to Guthrie.

"How are you, Peter?"

"I didn't expect you home so early," Stern said. "Nothing wrong, I hope."

"Nothing at all. In fact it went very well. They tell me I'm getting quite professional. Did I interrupt something?"

"No, no. We were talking about an old friend of yours, Dr. Einstein."

Michelle's large dark eyes gleamed. "Uncle Albert. Hair in his ears and those awful carpet slippers and a moth-eaten sweater, and of course the violin. They say only twelve people in the world were capable of understanding what he was talking about. I like to think I may have been one of them. At least when he was telling fairy stories. He told the most beautiful tales imaginable. I have stolen most of them for my broadcasts. When the holidays came he used to give me extravagant presents. I think," she said wrinkling her small up-tilted nose at Stern, "that the Herr Professor may have been a little in love with my mother. Every now and then he used to pull that lofty mind of his down out of the clouds. Like you, Peter, and that Polish countess."

Guthrie pretended more discomfort than he felt. "So you know about that, do you?"

"Among refugees there are no secrets. Norwegians, Danes, Dutch, Poles, Jews, we are all in the same soup. Except the French, the French have secrets from everyone, even from each other. But come into the kitchen and tell me about her while I put the kettle on for tea. What is her name?"

"Zofia. Captain Lesniowska, to be more exact."

"Oh, but I know her. So that's the one. We met at the BBC when she came there to make Christmas recordings for the Polish Army in Exile. Very nice, too. Full of schmaltz. All that Warsaw Concerto background music. And then her father, the colonel . . ."

"General. General Sikorski."

"Would you believe he had the nerve to pinch my bottom?"

"Did you slap his face?"

"A general? Certainly not. But what a sly dog you are, Peter. Where did you meet her and how long has this been going on?"

She was setting the table while she talked, seeming to mesmerize cups and saucers out of the air with her long tapering fingers. Both men were captivated by her vivacity. Her father's eyes never left her while she moved about the room.

THREE

At his home in Oranienburg, twenty kilometers north of Berlin, Dr. Karl Albert Friedrich Hauser dressed himself that morning with unusual care. He had been invited to visit the office of Admiral Canaris, head of the Abwehr, and the foxy little admiral was known to be a stickler for formality. Hauser wore a custom-tailored dark blue suit and a wing collar with black bow tie. He felt a little nervous—the appointment with Canaris had come as a surprise. He considered taking something to calm himself but decided against it. He would need all his wits about him.

Before leaving the house to walk the four short blocks to the train station he went out to the greenhouse to check the air temperature. A bachelor, he had one great passion, his orchids. Despite wartime restrictions he was able to maintain the greenhouse at the proper heating level, and his blooms flourished.

Returning to the house he picked up his walking stick and black homburg, regarded himself in the mirror set above the coatrack, and decided he looked fit. Not too much point in speculating what Canaris had in mind. Probably Hess. There were bound to be repercussions. It was said that Hitler had frothed at the mouth.

He returned once more to the bedroom for the gray kidskin gloves he kept in his bureau drawer. Everything in the room was a model of neatness. Above the bureau was a photo of Denise Stern.

Beside the portrait of the dead woman was a smaller framed snapshot, this one of a child who was unmistakably Michelle.

He walked from the train station to the Abwehr headquarters at 76/68 Tirpitzufer. It was a pleasant walk past the chestnut and lime trees of Berlin's Tiergarten. Typical of Canaris that a man who enjoyed such enormous power—as head of the Secret Intelligence arm of the German High Command, he directed the activities of agents in every country in the world—should continue to maintain his offices in the old converted townhouse he had occupied for many years.

Hauser was shown in after a short wait. The admiral's office was a small cluttered room, kept just as it had been when Canaris had first occupied it in 1934—the same old Persian carpet and the same untidy nineteenth-century desk ornately bound in bronze, its surface ink-stained and unpolished. An iron cot covered with army blankets stood in one corner. On the cot lay the admiral's constant companion, the fat old dachshund, Seppl, who alternately snored and grumbled.

On the admiral's desk was a model of the light cruiser *Dresden* and a file of letter paper bearing the insignia of the Abwehr—three brass monkeys, one cupping its ear, another looking over its shoulder while the third held its hand over its mouth. Above the desk was a curious drawing of a fork-tailed devil, presented to the admiral by the Japanese ambassador, and an enlarged photo of Hitler in the act of boarding Canaris's former command—the old battleship *Schlesien*. It might have been the office of a provincial boy's-school headmaster rather than that of the world's most powerful spymaster.

"My dear Dr. Hauser. Please do come in." The admiral swept up a file of papers from one of the chairs. "Forgive the confusion."

Canaris was physically unimposing, a small white-haired man with a melancholy expression and a slight lisp, which had impelled the head of Britain's secret service to label Canaris an "intriguing, traitorous, lisping old queer."

"It was good of you to take the time to come to see me, Herr Doctor," Canaris said.

"Not at all, Herr Admiral."

"Let me see," Canaris rifled through his papers in absentminded fashion, "what it was I wanted to talk to you about."

What a smokescreen, thought Hauser.

"Oh, yes." Extracting a sheet of paper from the file Canaris peered at it closely through his thick-lensed glasses. "It has come to my attention that some years ago you were associated in Berlin with a certain Dr. David Stern, a protégé of the Jewish physicist Einstein."

Hauser felt a ripple of anxiety along his backbone. His hands had gone clammy. "That is true, Herr Admiral."

Canaris had detected the flicker of fear in the other man's wide blue eyes. He did not like Hauser very much—an overdressed pedant—but he was beginning to see how he might be useful. What had started only as a wisp of an idea in the admiral's devious mind was now beginning to take shape. It was complex, perhaps fatally so, but the complications were the sort that lent zest, and they were undoubtedly necessary to kill a man like Adolf Hitler.

"Stern and his family left for England in 1937," Canaris began. "As Jews their position in the Reich was untenable. Yet one year later Frau Stern returned to Germany. One wonders why." The admiral had swiveled his chair to the left. His gaze appeared to be directed toward the portrait of the Fuehrer.

Hauser coughed nervously and withdrew a peppermint lozenge from his waistcoat pocket and popped it into his mouth.

"Her mother was dying," Hauser said. "She returned to Germany to be with her at the end."

"And was then arrested and placed in one of the camps for Jews, where she later died."

Hauser's courage was returning. Canaris, with his pink complexion and shining white hair, was not a menacing figure. "May I ask, Admiral, if a discussion of Stern and his family was the purpose of this appointment?"

Canaris appeared not to have heard the question. "Shortly before she was arrested Frau Stern visited your home in Oranienberg."

"We had been friends before the Jewish . . . problem became a threat to the fatherland." So the foxy little bastard knew of Denise's visit. And if he knew that, he knew the rest. But what did it matter now? And in any case why was it the business of the Abwehr and worth this much of Canaris's time?

"Of course," Canaris said. "The situation was not

unusual. Her presence was reported to the authorities and she was arrested and removed."

Hauser unwrapped another lozenge. He had decided to say as little as possible. It had all happened a long time ago. Still one could not help but feel upset when the past was raked over. He regretted that he had not taken something to steady his nerves before leaving the house.

Canaris was leafing through another file. "Professor Stern and his daughter are now living in London, where, it has been reported, he is engaged in research on the uranium bomb."

"I have no knowledge of that," Hauser said.

"Of course not," Canaris said smoothly. "How could you? But I suppose you do have some knowledge of this unfortunate Hess affair?"

Hauser had gone pale. "Only what is generally known."

"Yes?"

"That Herr Hess suffered a nervous breakdown during which he flew to England in a misguided effort to bring about peace."

Canaris looked more than ever like a benign grandfather. "I think, my dear Dr. Hauser, that you and I are after the same thing."

"Which is?"

Canaris smiled warmly. "A just and lasting peace for Germany."

"Of course, Herr Admiral. But how is that to be obtained?"

"You may have opened a path in the right direction. Let us return for a moment to the nature of your dealings with Hess. I gather you and he were friends before the war."

"Our relationship goes back to university days in Munich. Hess, along with other students, shared some of my geopolitical theories."

Canaris nodded. "The Fuehrer himself has indicated a desire for peace with England. The terms he has offered are extraordinarily benign. The British would be fools not to accept. But since the mission has apparently failed the Fuehrer has of course chosen to disassociate himself." Canaris picked up an official-looking document bearing the imprint of the Fuehrer's headquarters. "All photographs of Hess are to be removed from party and government offices and all accomplices to this act of insanity are to be mercilessly punished."

Canaris let his voice trail away. Hauser sat in silence. He was aware of the unpleasant dampness of his palms, but to wipe them on his trouser legs would be too revealing.

Canaris replaced the document on his desk. He removed his glasses and began to wipe them with a crisply folded handkerchief, meanwhile studying Hauser with candid blue eyes.

"The office of Deputy to the Fuehrer, formerly held by Hess, has been abolished," Canaris went on, "and is henceforth to be known as the party Chancellery. Its chief executive officer will be Reichsleiter Martin Bormann. I do not believe, my dear Doctor, that Martin Bormann may exactly be counted as a friend of yours. In fact I think it is safe to say you may be in extremely hot water. I would suppose it is only a question of time before Bormann issues an order for your arrest."

"What are you suggesting, Herr Admiral?" Hauser could barely speak.

"I am suggesting that you be arrested by the Abwehr instead of the Gestapo. A matter of form of course. You will be detained for a week or two for questioning and then released. All very innocuous of course, my dear Doctor, but I think it will do to satisfy the Fuehrer, who is, in any case, very busy at the moment. My excuse for taking an interest in this matter will be that Hess carried your message abroad, which brings it into the province of the Abwehr."

"I meant it only for the good of Germany, Herr Admiral. A warning to our friends in England that they had better make peace before it is too late."

"Of course," said Canaris soothingly, "but you realize that Reichsleiter Bormann might look at it another way, that you were providing secret military intelligence to the enemy."

"That is untrue."

"Untrue or not, the suggestion alone will be enough to hang you. The main thing, my dear Hauser, is to proceed in an orderly fashion. First to this uranium bomb. The idea has been kicking around for some time now, I gather."

Hauser nodded.

"Without gaining very much official support," Canaris went on.

"That is so. The Fuehrer has never displayed an interest in such matters."

"But I think I know someone who will have both the interest and the prestige required to see it through. I am referring to Reichmarshal Goering."

Canaris leaned back in his chair. His smile was gentle. He had replaced his glasses and stared through them with an expression of owlish satisfaction. "I think it is time, my dear Hauser, to take you entirely into my confidence. What I am about to tell you remains of course a secret between us. If you were to reveal it to anyone, we would both be hanged for treason. You for having encouraged Hess in his flight, myself for having conspired to overthrow Adolf Hitler."

Hauser felt the blood leave his cheeks. Despite the overheated room he found himself shivering.

"My loyalty," Canaris went on, "is like your own. It is to Germany first rather than to any political party. Hitler, against the advice of the General Staff, is planning to invade Russia. It is clear that a two-front war would mean the destruction of the fatherland. It must be stopped at all cost. To that end I have been in touch with certain high-ranking officers on the other side. Among them the Englishman, Menzies. Menzies, as you may know, is the head of MI-6. We are old friends—and enemies. In the First War he made a journey to Spain with the express intention of assassinating me. That he failed was due more to my own good luck than his poor judgment. Since then, and more particularly since the start of this war, we have often communicated."

Canaris paused as if to collect his thoughts. There was no sound in the room but the heavy breathing of the old dog. Hauser was motionless.

Canaris resumed. "My last communication from Menzies came just two weeks ago. It conveyed very bad news indeed. His government has decided against seeking terms with Germany. They will insist on a policy of unconditional surrender. Germany will be forced to fight to the end; the war will go on for years. Unless . . ."

"Yes, Herr Admiral?" Hauser's voice was hardly more than a whisper.

"Unless we can force them to change their terms."

"How can that be done?"

Canaris smiled. "Basically it was your own idea, Hauser. A brilliant idea."

"I don't understand."

"This uranium bomb. Once we have such a weapon they will be forced to the negotiating table."

Hauser shook his head. "I am sorry to disappoint you, but we are a very long way from achieving such a weapon."

The admiral's ordinarily dour features were still wreathed in a smile. "Whether we have the weapon or not is unimportant. What matters is that they should *think* we have it."

FOUR

Torsten and Helberg remained on board while Larsen went to the head of the dock to use the phone. It rang for what seemed a very long time. At last a man's voice said, "Yes?"

"I was given this number to call. My name is Jens Larsen."

"Where are you calling from?"

"A public phone at the dockside. I have just arrived by ship."

There was a longish pause. "Can you give me the name of your cousin Arne's eldest son?"

"I beg your pardon?"

The request was repeated. "And has the boy been ill recently, and if so, what was the matter with him?"

Larsen chuckled. "You English. The name of Arne's boy is Claus, and he was in hospital a month ago to have his appendix out. Also Claus has a birthmark on his rear end."

"Quite. Well look here, Mr. Larsen, would it be convenient for you to come by for a chat?"

"When?"

"Now. Look for Commander Richardson."

"Half an hour?"

"That will do nicely. Oh, and leave your friends at home, if you don't mind."

"They won't like that."

"Won't they?"

Larsen replaced the receiver and walked back. From a distance the old trawler looked even more decrepit. A miracle that they had managed to nurse her across. He shivered slightly at the memory of the great gray seas.

Helberg, with the ever-present pipe in his jaw, said something to Torsten, and they both laughed.

"What's so funny?"

Torsten shook his big head with its mop of blond hair. "You are. You still look like a kid. How do you do it?"

Larsen smiled. He did look like a schoolboy alongside these two large, powerful men. They were good fellows, a little rough sometimes, but well intentioned.

Helberg said, "What did he say? Are they making us generals?"

"Very likely, but until then you are confined to the ship."

"What! I'll give them bloody confined. Why do they think we risked our necks getting away from the Germans? If we wanted confinement we could have stayed in Norway."

"He told me to remind you there is a war on."

"Shit!"

All right," Torsten said, "but don't be long. We want to get ashore to have a drink and look for a tart."

"What tart would have you the way you smell?" Larsen said.

* * *

Commander Richardson was an imposing figure over six feet tall, with a carefully trimmed nautical beard. His uniform had a Bond Street flair. Larsen, unshaven and still wearing his heavy turtleneck sweater and rubber boots, felt grubby by comparison.

"Please sit down, Mr. Larsen. You must be tired after your long voyage. How was the weather?"

"Rotten."

The commander took a pipe from the rack on his desk and lit it with an air of great deliberation. He clicked the gold lighter shut and leaned back in his chair.

"Meet any Germans?"

"There were plenty of German patrols around Trondheim, but the ship was lying to the west, at Hitra. In bad weather the Germans prefer to stay inside in the shelter of the fjord."

"You had good luck."

"Enough, I think, for one lifetime."

"We were thinking of asking you to return to Norway."

Larsen shook his head and grinned. "Not today. Maybe tomorrow." Fatigue had poisoned his system; he was having trouble holding himself erect. Helberg had the right idea, a few drinks and a woman. This foppish Englishman depressed him. "I suppose you're serious," he said in a tired voice.

Richardson nodded.

"I'd like a bath first."

"I should think it would be several months before we can set up the operation. We'll try to make it for a period of good weather on the Hardanger Plateau."

Larsen's head came up with a jerk. He had been

nearly asleep in his chair. "There is no good weather on the Hardanger."

Richardson said, "You had better come with me."

They went down a flight of steps and across what appeared to be a parade ground that was littered with the impedimenta of the balloon barrage. In the center of it all was a statue of Captain Cook. Larsen chuckled.

"What's so funny?" Richardson said.

"I was thinking of something I saw walking over here," Larsen said. "A hat maker's shop. They had a sign in the window advertising specially reinforced anti-shrapnel bowler hats." He shook his head. "You English."

Richardson raised an eyebrow. "Quite. You'd better stretch out for an hour or two." He opened the door to a small room which contained a cot and a chair. There was a pillow at the head of the cot and a blanket folded neatly at the foot.

"I'll send someone for you in two hours," Richardson said.

Too tired to kick off his boots, Larsen fell instantly asleep.

His rest was wracked by ugly dreams, a familiar nightmare from his childhood dating from his first visit to the Hardanger Plateau, the loneliest and largest mountain range in northern Europe. In his dream he was pursued by an invisible presence. Moving with him through the blizzard was a herd of reindeer. He was glad of the warmth provided by their packed bodies. The herd surged forward. Suddenly, above the clutter of beasts and through a partial clearing in the snow, he saw that they had reached the edge of a great cliff. Beyond, there was nothing. He attempted to fight his way free, but the animals in front were already tumbling over the edge, twisting in space as they fell thousands of feet to the rocks below. He fought to free himself from the tight-packed bodies, but it was hopeless.

"Are you all right, sir?" A young woman in uniform was bending over him.

The nightmare had been very real. "Just a bad dream."

"Commander Richardson is waiting for you in room thirty-nine."

He followed the Wren along the hallway. When she opened the door he had the impression that she had led him into some kind of newspaper office. There were fifteen or twenty uniformed people arguing, dictating, telephoning, or writing on what appeared to be legal documents consisting of pale-blue paper tied with string. Through the windows could be seen the branches of trees in St. James's Park. Richardson sat at a desk in the far corner of the room. Behind him was a green baize door.

"There you are. Feeling better?"

"I don't know yet."

"Tea?"

Anti-shrapnel bowlers and silver tea services. "Please."

Richardson poured. "This is where it all happens. What we like to call Intelligence."

"I thought you were with the SOE."

"I'm really part of Naval Intelligence, but we

overlap from time to time. This Vemork thing will be a sort of combined operation. I'd like to ask you a few questions."

The tea was bringing him back to life. "I don't suppose you have some whiskey to put in this?"

"As a matter of fact I do. How's that?"

"Better."

"A few formalities for the report. Name?"

"Jens Anton Larsen."

"Age?"

"Thirty-four."

"Profession?"

"Chemical engineer."

"Employed at the Vemork plant of Norsk Hydro?"

"Yes."

"How long have you been employed there?"

"I think you must surely know all this already."

"We do," Richardson acknowledged, "but it's routine to go back over the questions before preparing a formal report."

Larsen shrugged. "Five years."

"And during that time the plant has been engaged in the production of so-called heavy water?"

"Yes."

"What is the present annual rate of production?"

"Between three and four thousand pounds a year."

"All of which is sent to Germany?"

"Yes."

"For what purpose?"

"It can have only one purpose. Nuclear research."

"Has the long-range program been discussed?"

"They want to raise the Vemork output to ten thousand pounds a year."

"Can that be done?"

"Given enough water and enough electrical energy, it can be done. But it takes seven tons of water and thousands of kilowatt hours to make a single ounce of heavy water, even at Vemork, and Vemork is the largest plant of its kind in the world."

"Was the reason for this increased need discussed?"

"Not with me, but of course we all know what they have in mind. They are attempting to produce atomic weapons."

"How far along are they?"

Larsen shrugged. "I have no way of knowing. I was told only to manufacture the heavy water, nothing more."

"And if the supply of heavy water can be stopped?"

"Then I would suppose that work on the atomic bombs would be stopped."

Richardson nodded. "Which brings us to the crux of the matter. We have been informed that it would be extremely difficult to knock out the Vemork plant with a bombing raid from the air. Correct?"

"The plant is situated in a cleft between high mountains. It would be very difficult to bomb with any accuracy. In addition, it's heavily fortified with anti-aircraft weapons. Worst of all, a bombing run on the Vemork plant will place the civilian population of Rjukan in the gravest danger. A stray hit on the liquid ammonia storage tanks will destroy the town."

"We have considered that, Mr. Larsen, but we must also consider that the Germans may be much closer than we know to achieving an atomic chain reaction. The SOE and Combined Ops are of the opinion that we cannot wait very much longer before shutting off their supply of heavy water. A decision has been made to land a commando force by glider on the Hardanger Plateau."

Larsen pursed his lips.

"You don't like the idea?"

"I don't know. I am not a military man. But I can tell you the Hardanger is a rough place. It will be very difficult to provide a smooth landing area for your gliders."

"Do you have any other suggestions?"

"A small team of saboteurs could be sent in by sea to work their way overland or even be dropped by parachute."

Richardson shook his head. "The plant at Vemork is enormous—seven stories high and well guarded. Even if a sabotage team were to get through it is unlikely they could do enough damage to halt production permanently. It will need a sizeable strike force to overcome the German resistance and cripple the plant."

Larsen sighed. The hour or two of restless sleep had done little to repair the ravages of five days at sea. "What is it that you wish me to do?"

"You and your two friends have lived in Rjukan and worked at Vemork. You know the hydro plant and the best way to reach the heavy-water cells. In addition you are all three experienced skiers and mountaineers."

"You want us to go in with the gliders?"

Richardson shook his head. "We want you to go in before the gliders. That will give you a chance to set up a camp and establish radio contact with the commandos. After the strike you can make your way overland to Sweden."

Larsen thought of Torsten and Helberg. They would kill him. And if they didn't, the Germans surely would.

A gentle spring rain gave Hyde Park the soft quality of a Japanese painting. Children ran across the grass while young lovers strolled hand in hand. For the moment the scars of war were forgotten. Although the Germans had been overhead in force again last night, the raid had seemed to lack conviction. Londoners were beginning to speculate that the worst might be over. The Luftwaffe no longer attempted daylight raids, and it was said that even at night their losses were becoming prohibitive. Michelle Stern tried to remember what it would be like to live in a city that had not been under constant threat of attack. Perhaps more striking than anything else would be the sudden quiet. Only the hum of traffic and the laughter of children.

It would be, she decided happily, very much like today.

But today was a special day, a day that was hard to believe. She had finished her recording session and had been about to leave the building when the receptionist had said, "There's a phone call for you, Miss Stern."

"Michelle?" A man's voice, one she did not recognize.

"Yes, this is Michelle."

"I don't know if you will remember me after all this time. I am Jens Larsen. We met in Copenhagen. . . ."

"Jens! Is it really you?"

He chuckled. "Yes, Michelle."

"But where are you? Where are you calling from? Surely not Norway."

"No, no. I am right here in London."

"How is that possible?"

"I thought it might be fun to sail over just to see how you are getting on, and so here I am."

"Jens, stop that. Don't tease me. How did you get here?"

"Tell you all about it when I see you. If you do want to see me, that is."

"But of course."

"Say ten minutes? At the corner of Hyde Park?"

"You must be close by."

"Very. I can almost see you."

"Tell me where you are."

"Can't. Military secret. Look for me at the gate."

She was walking more rapidly now, her slender figure very erect in the belted raincoat, the beret tilted rakishly over her dark hair. She told herself to slow down. It was not ladylike to be early. One must not appear too eager. Oh, the devil with it. She was eager to see Jens Larsen and there was no point in concealing it. The funny part was that she might not even recognize him when she saw him. They had only known each other a short time—those few days in Copenhagen. He had seemed so boyish to be part of that company of distinguished graybeards gathered to discuss the properties of fissionable matter.

She had asked him if he wasn't there under false pretenses, and he had laughed and said, Yes, in a way, he wasn't really a physicist at all, just a chemical engineer at a hydro plant. He had described the wild country of the Hardanger Plateau and the herds

of reindeer. "You must come to Norway someday," he
had said, "and I'll show it to you."

They had walked together in the Tivoli Gardens,
taking a kind of childlike delight in the shops and
restaurants, the ice cream vendors, the swan boat
rides on the lake.

That was all there had been to it really, nothing
more than those few days in a happy, fairy-tale city.
He had written to her when she had gone back to
England, and she had answered; but then suddenly
German troops were overrunning Norway, and there
had been no more letters.

Had he survived up there among the wild gorges?
She had thought of him often.

A crowd milled around the Hyde Park gate, but
she was able to pick him out almost at once—a thin
young man, not very tall, wearing some kind of rough
seaman's sweater that came right up under his chin,
his reddish gold hair shining with damp, his lips
pursed in a soundless whistle.

She quickened her pace as his eyes lit up in recognition.

As they walked together in the park she said, "I
still don't know how you found me. Don't tell me
they are broadcasting my children's stories to Norway."

He shook his head. "No, but if they did, it would
be worth your life to listen."

"Would the Germans regard me as a dangerous
enemy agent? I find that very exciting."

"The truth is that it was a man named Richardson
who told me where to find you."

"Max? Max Richardson?"

"That's the one. Commander. Bit too elegant for my taste." Larsen raised one eyebrow and his voice took on a supercilious drawl.

Michelle smiled. "I don't really know him all that well. I've met him a few times with Peter Guthrie."

"He mentioned Guthrie. What's he like?"

"Peter? Smashing. I'm mad about him."

"Are you?" Larsen said, a note of jealousy creeping into his voice. "That's nice."

Michelle laughed. "Only as a friend. Actually he's very much involved with a beautiful Pole. But what were you doing with Max? And how in the world did you get here?"

"All top secret," Larsen said with a broad wink. "Have to get to know you a great deal better before we can discuss such matters. Shall we say dinner to-morrow night?"

"That would be lovely."

"Where and when?"

Michelle smiled. "This one will be on me. I am, after all, a working girl. Come to the flat. I'm a superb cook."

"Will your father be there?"

"Yes. I know he'll want to talk with you."

"I'm not so sure about that."

"Why ever not?"

"I had the feeling he took a poor view of me that time in Copenhagen. Thought I was paying too much attention to you."

"Come off it, Jens. Are you serious?"

"Absolutely."

"Well, I won't stand for petty jealousies," she said firmly. "If you want to be a friend of mine, you had better start off by being a friend of my father as well."

"I do want very much to be your friend, Michelle."

Her hand had slipped down into his as they walked. "Then come to dinner tomorrow night like a good boy," she said. "And shut up about it."

Having left the park they found themselves in the ruins of a bombed-out section of flats where rescue workers still struggled among the debris. Two wardens dug into the rubble. They were gaunt-faced, middle-aged men covered with dust, obviously close to exhaustion. Around them glittered shards of broken glass. They were digging at the base of a massive timber.

Jens said, "Wait here."

He walked rapidly over to the two men. "Can I help?"

The older of the two wardens, his face gray under its coating of dust, handed Jens the shovel and said, "I could do with a rest, mate."

"What are we looking for?"

"There's a report of a little girl missing. Could be under that lot there."

"If she is, she couldn't be alive."

"We don't know that, do we?"

They found the child after twenty minutes of digging. She was still clutching her doll. Her thin, sticklike limbs were hardly much bigger around than those of the doll. The warden who had relinquished his shovel climbed down into the hole and carefully lifted out the body and covered it with a blanket. The corpse made a pitifully small shape under the blanket.

"Direct hit," the warden said. "Couldn't have known anything. Dug her folks out earlier."

When Jens returned to Michelle he saw tears running down her cheeks.

"This wretched war," she said in a broken voice. "This rotten war."

FIVE

Reichmarshal Goering washed down his fifth para-codeine with a swallow of Moselle. He was up to thirty tablets a day. Aggravations. That swine, Gunsche, had arrived with the newest uniform. Magnificent sky blue with facing lapels of raw silk. But the trousers refused to close, and Gunsche had the temerity to suggest that the Reichmarshal might have gained a few pounds. Goering weighed 380, but he would not admit it; instead he muttered darkly that all tailors had Jewish blood in them somewhere.

Gunsche had turned pale. Goering grinned to himself. He had been eating pâté by the bucket. He would let Gunsche sweat.

He hid a smile behind another swallow of wine and glanced briefly at the old fox sitting across the table from him. Three for luncheon today—Canaris and the two Herr Professors.

Apart from running the Luftwaffe, Goering was also head of the Forschungsamt, the Directorate of Scientific Research, a largely meaningless title devised to cover the methods by which he spied on his fellow Nazis. He had formed an intelligence service within the Landespolizegruppe which now had three thousand agents. Only the Fuehrer was safe from the

Forschungsamt's listening devices. Goering began each day by browsing through the transcripts which kept him informed of the sexual peccadilloes of the party leaders.

Today's luncheon had been arranged by Admiral Canaris to discuss a more serious matter. Dopel, the younger of the two scientists was, Goering decided, a most boring individual. He was already bald and had the waxen complexion of one who spent most of his time indoors.

"We have a complete grasp of the principle," Dopel was saying. "In 1938 first Hahn and Strassmann and then Meitner and Frisch succeeded in splitting the atom. It was done also at around the same time by Fermi in Italy and Joliot-Curie in France. However, no chain reaction was achieved. U-235, the essential ingredient, is extremely expensive and difficult to obtain. But we have been able to extract small amounts of it from heavy water, and the power thus produced has been used in experiments in Hamburg, Oranienburg, Berlin, Leipzig, Heidelberg, and Munich."

"Then why are you taking so long to get a damned bomb out of it?" Goering's patience was running thin.

"With all respect, Herr Reichmarshal, it is not easy to achieve something the world has never seen before."

Fearing that the pedant would launch into another lecture, Goering cut him off with a muttered *"Scheiss."* Dopel looked stunned. Goering attempted to fill Canaris's wine glass, but the admiral put his hand firmly over his glass. Goering shrugged. Canaris was a dry stick. Always had been. He looked regretfully at the shafts of sunlight pouring through the windows. A day to be out in the hills hunting.

"Spare me your lesson in elementary physics," he said. "I don't really care if the basic ingredient is U-235 or horseshit. We have been hearing about this damned bomb for years now. I demand facts, not theory."

"We believe that when the Herr Reichmarshal comes to Leipzig he will see . . ."

Goering gulped another pill. His mind was already on dinner. The pâté he had brought back from Paris? And with it the different-colored vodkas from Poland. Roast salmon done in the Danzig style with a Moselle from his own cellar in Trier. A goose from the Schorfheide with Château Haut Brion followed by a light Viennese torte with Château Yquem. And when the cigars had been passed Napoleon brandy for the gentlemen and a Danziger Goldwasser for the ladies. He would wear the beautiful gray-blue uniform with the collar tabs of ivory-colored raw silk and the gold-embroidered marshal's batons on a silver brocade base. . . .

"The appointment in Leipzig . . ." Canaris was saying.

Goering nodded, compressing his great jowls. "Shall we say ten A.M.?"

"As the Reichmarshal wishes."

Goering sat on after the others had left, plucking now and then with stubby fingers into the silver bowl of hothouse grapes. He was puzzled by several aspects of the conversation, not the least among them the presence of Admiral Canaris and the tight-lipped Dr. Hauser who had maintained a rigid silence all through the meal. It was true that the presentation of the project belonged to Dopel, but then how did Canaris enter the picture? Certainly the wily little chief of military intelligence was no scientist, nor was he responsible for security within the borders of the Reich. That was Himmler's job. Goering doubted Himmler was even aware of the progress being made in the development of the remarkable new weapon. Hauser, in his brief introductory remarks before lunch, had hinted at a lack of top-level support.

In theory their approach should have been through Fritz Todt, minister of armaments. Perhaps Todt was too conventional in his thinking to see the possibilities of this atomic fission project. It required someone with style and verve. Someone very much like himself.

Canaris and this fellow Hauser had been quite right to bring it to his attention. Things had not gone as well in the skies over England as Goering might have hoped. The bombing of London had, if anything, hardened the British resolve to continue the war. In addition, the British fighters plus their damned radar, which seemed able to pick up the German bombers from the moment they left their airfields, were taking a heavy toll from the Luftwaffe. At present the Fuehrer did not appear too concerned, but the time would surely come when the failure of the Luftwaffe to bring England to her knees would be charged against Goering. When that time came it would be well to have another iron in the fire.

A gray day in Leipzig. Gray university buildings overwhelmed by an even bleaker sky. As the Reichmarshal plumped his massive hams onto the chair that had been brought for him, Canaris regarded the opéra-bouffe figure with distaste. What a crew these Nazis were: Hitler with his pasty face and mad eyes.

Goebbels the wizened dwarf with the gimpy leg. Chinless, goggle-eyed ex-chicken farmer Himmler and this great pink pig Goering. Clowns all of them, but they would be the death of Germany.

Hauser called their attention to the pile. For twenty days L-IV, the spherical atomic pile, had been immersed in its tank. Now it simmered like an old stewpot. A stream of noxious bubbles came to the surface. Atomic reaction? Canaris thought not. There was a leak somewhere, most likely a chemical reaction between the uranium core and the water.

An official photographer appeared, dancing like a monkey around his apparatus. Goering inflated his chest and thrust out his chin, a pose reminiscent of photographs taken when he was the dashing young commander of the Richthofen Squadron in the First World War.

Goering eyed the pile narrowly. "Is the damned thing about to go up?"

"I think not, Herr Reichmarshal," Hauser answered.

Goering said nothing, but left his chair.

The sphere appeared to be swelling. Was that possible, Hauser wondered, or was it a trick of refraction? He gave a signal and the sphere was withdrawn. A technician unscrewed one of the inlets. There was a whistle of air filling the vacuum inside. Seconds later a stream of hot gas filled with particles of burning uranium powder shot upward.

Goering backed away.

The sphere was thrust back into the cooling water. Hauser made a dive for the shelter of the retaining wall. There was a sound like a muffled drumbeat. Debris from the shattered pile rained all around him.

He was still lying there with his arms over his head when Goering touched him on the shoulder with the tip of his baton and said, "I think you can get up now, Herr Professor. And it might be a good idea to call for the fire brigade."

The Reichmarshal lumbered into his Mercedes and was whisked away.

The brigade chief, a ruddy-faced dolt in high boots and shiny helmet, surveyed the dripping ruins with satisfaction. "My compliments, Herr Professor, on a superb explosion."

Only Canaris smiled. He was remembering how the Reichmarshal's fat face had dropped a foot.

SIX

The short, golden English summer had given way to
the gales of winter. With the advent of bad weather
David Stern grew more morose. He thought of his
dead wife, and his heart gave its familiar lurch.
He still could not remember her without pain. Michelle, who so resembled her mother, was a daily
reminder of his loss.

When the word had come that it would be safe
for Denise to slip back into Germany, he might have
stopped her. But he had not been strong enough.
The weakness of the intellectual. Einstein, Peierls,
Bretscher, von Halban, Kowarski, Frisch—all had
fled. Then Hauser and his reassurances that he stood
in well with Hess. Perhaps he had been sincere, but
none of it had helped Denise. And in any event her
mother was already dead when she got there.

He beat his fist against his brow.

Darkness enveloped him. He ought to close the
blackout curtains and turn on the lights but he hated
the feeling of being shut in; it seemed to emphasize
his loneliness.

Quiet in the city. For the moment, only the subdued
hum of sparse traffic.

He remembered a time in Berlin when that big

city, too, had seemed to hold its breath. Meitner and Frisch had already gone to visit Bohr in Copenhagen. Lise Meitner's letter: "Your results are really very disconcerting; a process using slow neutrons that yields barium? At present it seems to me very difficult to accept that there is such a drastic breaking up of the uranium nucleus but we have experienced so many surprises in nuclear physics. . . ."

A thin veil of snow along Unter den Linden. Peace on earth, good will to men . . .

The Duke of Windsor and his duchess touring Germany in a black Mercedes along with that swine Ley. Lunch at Berchtesgaden and the duke giving Hitler the full Nazi salute while the duchess courtseyed as if to royalty.

Everyone talked about how lovely the weather had been that year. The perfect white Christmas, joy, oh, joy. Only a month after lovely Crystal Night with the diamonds of shattered glass in the streets and the bloodied heads.

In some ways he had always felt that fission by atomic weight as outlined in the Einstein formula was not the answer. Might it not be more appropriate to think of fission by atomic number? The uranium nucleus (92) would fission into barium (56) and then into krypton (36). A simultaneous discharge of neutrons?

He looked down from the window hoping to see Michelle coming along the street, but there was no sign of her. Why was she late? Was she with that fellow Larsen?

He had a headache. It was stuffy in the flat. Perhaps he ought to go out into the city to find a woman. Despite the blackout streetwalkers still practiced their trade, carrying tiny flashlights which they shone over their bodies.

The brief copulation would be meaningless but might help to relieve his anxieties. But the London police did not take kindly to aliens roaming the streets. Despite the fact that he was working on a top-secret project of the highest priority, he had not, until recently, been allowed even to own a bicycle. For that matter he could not possess a map of England or travel from one area to another without official permission. In London the fist thumping on the door came at seven in the evening; in Berlin at four in the morning.

"Silly bastards," Sir John Cockcroft had said of his own security people, "they see spies behind every bush. Why, they're even searching nuns to make sure they're not wearing German boots and trousers under their habits. Damned awkward for the nuns, eh, Stern?"

His headache was worse. He took two aspirins and lay down.

Michelle hurried home through the dusk, smiling at strangers, enjoying the overcharged sensation of champagne bubbling in her veins. Jens Larsen had been in London for more than a month on this most recent leave, and during that time they had managed to see each other almost every day. Jens was involved in a training exercise of some sort, but they always managed to find a little time together—a walk in the park, tea at Brown's, meetings that were all too brief. Jens had not appeared at the flat again since the night she had first invited him home to dinner. That had been a disaster. Her father had behaved abominably. As the evening wore on his jealousy of the young Norwegian had become more apparent, his questions and comments more caustic.

Jens excused himself and left early. Michelle had walked with him as far as the corner. The silence of shared embarrassment hung like a curtain between them. She felt the blood stir in her cheeks.

"I am so sorry, Jens," she said.

"It's all right, Michelle."

"No, it's not all right. I never thought I would have to apologize for my father."

Jens smiled. "Please. No apologies are necessary. I came prepared. You will remember that I told you I thought he did not like me."

"But I know he does. He expressed a great deal of admiration for that paper you read in Copenhagen."

"That was before I began to pay too much attention to his daughter."

"I know you think that, but I can hardly believe it."

"You have a real problem on your hands, Michelle."

She felt a pang of anxiety. "Does that mean we won't see each other again?"

Larsen chuckled. "Of course not. It would take a thousand fathers to keep me from seeing you again. Tomorrow night?"

"Yes. Oh, yes."

"But this time we go *out* to dinner," Jens added firmly.

They parted on the corner, and he kissed her lightly, just brushing her lips. Her heart sang. She watched his short erect figure go striding off.

She had walked slowly back to the flat, her mind in a turmoil.

That night she had quarreled bitterly with her father. The next morning he apologized. "Please invite him again," he said, referring to Larsen. "I would like to make amends."

"Some other time." She had answered vaguely, not wanting to put him to the test.

Zofia cocked her uniform cap at a rakish angle and winked at her reflection in the mirror. It had been a trying day, but in a little while she would be free for her date with Peter. Sleeping with Peter was quite the nicest thing that had happened to her since the start of the war. Before that, however, it would be necessary to prepare her notes. Regardless of the fact that he was her father, or perhaps particularly because he was her father, the general would tolerate no slackness, and she knew he would want a summary of the meeting. She sighed. Peter would have to wait. Quickly she sat down at the desk and began to transcribe her notes.

The meeting with de Gaulle had taken place in his apartment at No. 6 Seamore Place. The Frenchman did himself well in a sumptuously furnished flat owned by one of his wealthier supporters. General Sikorski and his daughter were ushered into a vast room where de Gaulle sat as stony and remote as a military statue.

There was little love lost between these two leaders of armies in exile. But the awkward moment was broken by Sikorski, who rendered the Frenchman a smile and a salute. Moments later they were seated across from each other at a small round table where tea was served. De Gaulle, Zofia thought, was one of the strangest-looking men she had ever seen—the heavy-lidded eyes almost like those of an elephant, the great nose, the almost nonexistent chin, and the small, pursy mouth under a toothbrush moustache.

More than anything he reminded her of a very tall boy scout; she could imagine him sitting around a campfire with the same grave air, bony knees sticking out of his khaki shorts. But it would not do to underestimate him. A man who was so full of himself could easily be turned into an enemy. Particularly since the Free French and the Polish Army in Exile were more or less working the same side of the street.

The word for him, she decided, was the French word *gonflé*. He was inflated. Stick a pin into him and there would be the hiss of escaping air. It was rumored that he was presently engaged in a power struggle within his own ranks and that strange things went on in BCRA headquarters in Duke Street. Officers who volunteered to fight with the Free French were asked to sign an oath of loyalty, not to France but to de Gaulle. An officer named Dufour claimed to have been tortured in the Duke Street basement because he had refused to turn over a list of resistance leaders. It was common knowledge that Churchill could hardly bring himself to be civil to de Gaulle.

Speaking of Churchill, Sikorski had told a little story of how the PM's servant had stolen his shoes in order to keep him from prowling the streets while air raids were in progress and how the great man had responded by saying, "Damn you, Ives, my nanny

couldn't keep me in when I was ten and Adolf Hitler
certainly won't now that I'm grown."

Sikorski smiled as he told the story, but de Gaulle
maintained his air of unshakable gravity.

"Churchill," said de Gaulle, "is reported to have
said that he would sleep with the devil if it would be
of benefit to England."

"Which particular devil do you think he was referring to, General?"

De Gaulle pursed his lips. "One that may not be
overly fond of you, General Sikorski."

Before the subject could be pursued the Frenchman
had risen to his feet like some lumbering camel. The
audience was over.

As they motored back to the hotel Sikorski was
silent; de Gaulle had given him much to think about.

Peter Guthrie was a passionate small-boat sailor.
He kept a little green sloop in the river near Lyming-
ton. The yacht had been laid up for the duration of
the war, but in fair weather Peter and Zofia often
went down to visit her for a few hours. On this clear
November day, Guthrie sat in the cockpit wearing old
flannel trousers and a seaman's sweater. The tide was
going out and the boat lay over on her side in the
mud. Wintry sunlight bathed the river in a clear light.
Old men wandered around the yacht yard with metal
cages on the end of poles sifting at the creamy edges
of the mud and lifting out carpet slippers or discarded
cooking utensils which they regarded with interest
before consigning them once again to the endlessly
devouring mud. Peter, dreaming of long voyages, was
content to sit in the cockpit while Zofia, covered by a

heavy woolen blanket, slumbered on one of the precariously tilted bunks.

He looked down at her through the open hatch. Her shining brown hair was spread out on the cushion and she lay with one hand pressed against her brow. He felt lazily content, supremely happy.

She opened her eyes and looked at her watch. Then she glanced up at the hatchway and saw him looking down at her.

"What are you smirking at?" she said.

"You're enough to make any man smirk."

"Where are Jens and Michelle? I thought they were coming to join us."

"You know how it is with young lovers."

"How is it?"

"Glorious. Best thing that ever happened to me."

"You mean that, don't you?"

He smiled down at her and nodded. "With all my heart."

"Tell me, young lover, what do you think of Jens?"

"I like him very much. Why do you ask?"

"I like him, too. I also like Michelle. I would not want to see her hurt. She seems terribly vulnerable."

"To Jens?"

"To the situation with David. You know how jealous he is."

"David is a thoroughly civilized man," Guthrie said. "He'll come around."

"And what if Jens goes off somewhere? What will happen to Michelle then?"

Guthrie looked thoughtful. "I see what you mean. Perhaps I'd better have a word with Max Richardson. Find out what they intend for him."

*   *   *

Richardson leaned back in his chair, lacing his fingers together, showing his starched cuffs. He raised a quizzical eyebrow. Visits from Guthrie were rare.

Peter hesitated. Although they had known each other for years he and Max had never been close. There were times when he had actively disliked Richardson. His queerness? That dandified air? The cold objectivity with which he manipulated people? Part of the job, no doubt, and Max was good at his job.

"What are your plans for Jens Larsen?" Guthrie said.

"Why do you ask?"

"I've been seeing a good deal of him. I like him. Also he's a close friend of Michelle Stern. In fact, that was how I got to meet him. I don't have to tell you how important Dr. Stern is to our program."

"Yes, I quite see that." Richardson looked thoughtful. "What I tell you now is of course to be kept under your hat."

"Of course."

"Security Operations are planning to send him back to Vemork."

"Why, in God's name?"

"Planning to blow the place up."

"When?"

"Can't say."

"What are his chances, would you think?"

"None at all," Richardson answered.

After Guthrie had gone Richardson reached into his desk drawer for the flask of brandy. It would not do to be seen nipping too often, but the shop was virtually empty at this hour. Evening shift would be coming on shortly, and they would not think it unusual to find Richardson still at his desk. He was known to do twice the work of all the rest. Hitting the Cognac again? Well, why not? There was strain enough in the job without having old school chums like Guthrie reminding him of how empty his life had become.

Max the rock. Carved of granite. Sends people off to die without a quiver. Trained for the bar, you know. Bloody lawyers are all the same. Never get involved. You may get the chap off or on the other hand he may go straight to the hangman. Can't afford to show emotion.

What was the war after all but a bloody great balls up. First there had been that ass, Chamberlain, giving bloody Hitler everything he bloody wanted, and then finally going to war at the wrong time and in the wrong place. For bloody Poland, for God's sake.

Perhaps it was because he had been a lawyer and was accustomed to dealing ruthlessly with people that they had given him this bloody job. Whatever the reason, he would do it as well as it could be done. There would be something in it for him when it was over. A ribbon or two. With a decent war record behind him, he might enter politics. The fact that he had spent the war in London wearing fresh linen and with well-polished shoes would not be held against him.

Would anyone ever ask if Max Richardson had shed a tear over the men he sent out to die? Not bloody likely.

Meanwhile he was getting a little drunk.

And damned lonely.

SEVEN

Hauser had been summoned once again to Canaris' office. There had been no meeting between them since the dismal experiment at Leipzig. To Hauser's surprise the admiral was in a distinctly affable mood.

"Come in, my dear fellow. Come in. I have something to show you. But first, what can you tell me about a certain Professor Paul Harteck of Hamburg?"

"He is a chemist."

"Any good?"

"I believe so, yes. He appears to have an intuitive grasp of complicated technical problems."

"Including our own little project, the uranium bomb?"

"Yes," Hauser admitted. "I believe he's done some work along those lines."

"Well, you might be interested in this letter Harteck recently sent to the War Office. It was obtained by one of my agents. It appears he has come up with a revolutionary new type of ultracentrifuge for enriching uranium. If it works, it will greatly increase the supply of heavy water obtained from the plant at Vemork."

Hauser studied the letter. It explained in simple terms the types of reactors which might be used for the final step in the fission process. Simple enough, he reflected, as he read, for even those blockheads in the War Office to understand.

> As is well known, two methods can be adopted for building a uranium reactor:
>
> Reactor Type I consists of natural uranium and about five tons of heavy water.
>
> Reactor Type II consists of uranium metal enriched in uranium-235 and consequentially smaller in quantity, together with smaller quantities of heavy water.
>
> Our research group has been following the first method while the Americans and British will probably have adopted the second. Only experience will show which of the two is the more practical in the long run. In any event the second method will result in significantly smaller reactor units and is, furthermore, more akin to the manufacture of explosives.

"I intend," Canaris said, when Hauser looked up, "to see that a copy of this letter is sent by courier to Lisbon. From there it will be passed on to General Menzies in London. He should find it most interesting. Now, what is your opinion of the Harteck ultra-centrifuge, Hauser? Do you think it will succeed?"

"I think it is committed to the wrong principle," Hauser said carefully.

"Which is?"

"The continuous and immense production of heavy water. As yet the Vemork plant has not come even close to providing the five tons which Harteck thinks will be required."

"This second method, then, that Harteck mentions —the reactor Type II that he believes the Americans may be working on?"

"It is quite a different approach—one that might be called the plutonium alternative. It is based on an Einstein theory dating back to the early thirties. Namely, that fissionable matter such as uranium might decay into a new element—number 94, or plutonium. Einstein guessed that energy could be extracted from uranium by the production of this stable new element and that if alpha particles were emitted, their half-life would be on the order of a million years or more."

"What would be needed then for Germany to beat the Americans to the punch on this so-called plutonium alternative?"

Hauser allowed himself the luxury of a half smile. "What I would call the X factor. The genius factor, if you will."

"An Einstein, is that it?"

Hauser nodded.

"Perhaps something can be arranged."

This time Hauser did not smile. The admiral seemed quite serious.

"I have devised a plan," Canaris went on. "A key figure will be a former associate of yours, this fellow Stern in London. I will require a good deal of information regarding Stern and his daughter—psychological profiles, if you will."

Hauser frowned. "I am afraid I still do not follow. What exactly is this scheme of yours?"

Canaris leaned back in his chair. "Nothing more nor less than to bring your X factor to Germany to give us the bomb."

"Surely you can't be serious."

"Never more so. But first we must do our home-work. The plan will not be presented to the Reich-marshal until every detail has been ironed out. When the time comes I will let you know. I want you to be absolutely confident in your presentation."

"I? But surely it is your scheme. I could never have imagined anything so fantastic myself."

"No one but you and I will ever know that, Hauser. Think of it. The greatest scientific brain of all time brought back to Germany to give the fatherland the greatest weapon the world has ever known. Not even Bormann will be able to touch you after that. Think of it as your insurance policy, my dear fellow."

EIGHT

"I think," said Michelle, "that this might be one of the five best days of my life."

Larsen smiled at her. "I'm jealous. What were the other four?"

"I can't remember. Possibly Christmas when I was nine, that sort of thing."

They had spent the day walking in the park, a late November day of crystalline brilliance. Although it was Sunday, no church bells rang. The bells would ring again only in the event of an invasion.

Michelle unwrapped the food parcel she had brought and handed Larsen a sandwich.

"I think I love you," she said.

"Only think? Not sure?"

"Yes, I'm sure."

"How can you be sure of anything at nineteen?"

"That's when you're sure of everything. It's only when you get old and cynical like you that you begin to have doubts. How old are you anyway?"

"Thirty-one."

"You're a liar. I happen to know you're thirty-four."

"How do you know that?"

"From Peter Guthrie. He knows everything about you. Even your tattoo."

"Is nothing sacred?"

"Not in wartime. You might easily be a German agent sneaking around me just to find out what my father is working on."

Larsen lay back against the small sloping hill, the sun on his face. He closed his eyes. "I wish Berlin would give me more assignments like this one."

"Peter not only knows you're an enemy agent; he told me you were once married. Is that true? Why did you never tell me?"

"It didn't seem important."

"Not important! Are you mad?"

"I'm an old man. I'm entitled to be alone with my memories."

"Did you love her?"

"In the beginning. At the end we hated each other."

"That's the part I want to hear about. Where you hated her. What was she like?"

"Medical technician. Very self-disciplined. Once the initial excitement wore off, we found we had nothing in common."

"How would you like a little initial excitement with me?"

"That might be nice," he said without opening his eyes.

She bent down to kiss him. It was a long kiss. Larsen let himself flow with it. Her breasts were soft against his chest. He slipped his hand underneath her blouse and felt the sweet warmth of her skin. When at last she pulled back he said, "I'm old enough to be your father."

"Do they start that young in Rjukan?"

"The winters are long. There's not much else to do."

"I think I'd like it in Rjukan. Will you take me?"

"I'll think about it. Perhaps we ought to try that kiss again."

"I'll think about it."

Larsen opened one eye. "So you have claws, eh?"

"Of course. Just like your ex-wife?"

"Did we come here to talk about her?"

She shook her head. "We came for two reasons. First so that I could tell you I love you and second so that I could tell you what I don't like about you."

"I brush my teeth regularly. I try to please."

"Your teeth are fine. It's the way you keep disappearing. Three times you have gone off without a word."

He sat up, his expression suddenly serious. "I'm sorry about that, Michelle. Truly. It's not something I can talk about."

She nodded. "I know. I was only teasing."

Three times in the course of the summer Larsen, along with Torsten and Helberg, had been alerted to stand by for the attack on Vemork. Each time they had traveled up to Wick Airfield in Scotland and had boarded the aircraft. Each time the operation had been scrubbed. The explanation had been bad weather over the target area, but Larsen had begun to wonder if the entire mission had not been ill conceived. When he expressed his doubts, Richardson had answered, "It's out of our hands. Combined Ops will handle it as they see fit."

Now he had been summoned to Wick again. This time—the fourth time—it might turn out to be the real thing. There was barely time to say good-bye to Michelle.

"I tell you it's nothing to worry about," Larsen

said, standing and reaching out to help her to her
feet.

Michelle shook her head, the dark glossy hair flung
across the ivory forehead. "Don't treat me like a
child."

"Why do you say that?"

"You've told me you will be away for four weeks,
somewhere out of England. Do you think I don't know
what that means?"

"It means only what it says. They're sending me
on some sort of research project. It's not all that mysterious, but you know how they classify everything as
secret these days. The time will pass quickly, and I'll
be back safe and sound before you know it."

"I hate it when you talk to me this way. I could
hit you."

"Go ahead."

"Stop playing the fool. Do you think I don't know
where you're going? They're sending you back to
Norway."

"What makes you say that?"

"Because it's the place you know. Oh, don't worry,
I'll keep my mouth shut. I don't even discuss such
matters with my father."

"Michelle, look at me. Please, Michelle, darling."

She threw her arms around his neck, and he felt
her tears against his face. "Michelle, listen to me. I
swear to you it's not what you think."

"You're lying." Her voice was muffled.

"Please, Michelle." He fished his handkerchief out
of his pocket and dried her tears.

"I'll be good now," she said. "How much time
do we have?"

"An hour or two."

"Then let's get out of here."

He shook his head. "Where do you want to go?"

"To a hotel."

He stared at her. She was very pale. "Are you sure?"

She nodded and said in a low voice, "Can't we?"

"Of course."

Michelle was halfway across the graveled path. He hurried to join her. There was a seedy-looking hotel across the street, a gray façade in the fading light of the wintry afternoon. Her hand in his was like a chip of ice.

"Wait here," he said in the lobby.

She gave him a small smile. God, she looks fifteen, he thought. "I'm not very experienced at this sort of thing," she said. "Should I try to look married?"

"Can you?"

She reached into her pocket, pulled out a gold band, and slipped it over her finger.

"Do you always come prepared?"

"No," she said. "Just today."

"Why today?"

"I had a feeling."

"I love you."

"You don't have to say that."

"I want to say it."

The room was worse than he had supposed. Gray sheets and wallpaper that had peeled from the dampness. He slipped in beside her and held her naked body against his own. She was trembling.

"It's all right," he whispered. "We don't have to do anything."

She was silent for a moment and then said, "Oh, you great fool," and turned and put her mouth against his.

He had hurt her. She cried out. Good God, they'll think I killed her. Her body arched against his.

"Am I hurting you?"

"Yes. No. Oh, my God!"

She clutched him tighter. "Don't stop," she whispered. "Please don't stop!"

In the street she kissed him once, held him tightly for a moment, and said, "Take care of yourself," and ran off.

I am the victim, Larsen told himself later in the train to Scotland, of middle-class morality. He was experiencing a mixture of remorse, guilt, pride, and love. Who would have supposed she was still a virgin? A child. No one who was nineteen and in London in 1941 was a child.

He would come back to her.

He was sure of it.

Torsten and Helberg snored beside him on the seat, Helberg with his collar open. For a man like Helberg life was so much simpler. No Hamlet soliloquies after the fact. Like that day on the trawler when Larsen had entered the forward compartment and surprised him with a woman, her head turned on the pillow, sweater rolled up around her neck, sturdy legs around Helberg's back. Face burning, he had retreated.

From the wheelhouse he had seen Helberg pay her off, a jolly-looking English blonde with immense breasts. Showing plenty of leg as she stuffed the notes into the top of her stocking. Looked up at him in the wheelhouse and said something to Helberg, and they both laughed. Blew him a kiss as she went off swinging her hips.

"She liked you," Helberg told him with a friendly leer. "She said next time she'll do us both for the price of one."

"No, thanks."

"You don't know what you're missing. Tits like footballs. And these English tarts know their stuff. She told me you came in while we were on the job. Too bad you didn't stay for the rest of the show." Larsen had felt the blood move in his cheeks. "Wanted to know who's the kid? Said you were the skipper, and she roared."

Now the darkened train ran fast through the blacked-out countryside. Larsen closed his eyes, but sleep eluded him. Torsten, his body adjusting to the motion of the train, slept with his long legs stretched from one seat to the other. They knew the secret of happiness, those two. Sufficient unto the day. Seize the moment. Don't fuck up your life with romantic blather. Who the hell knows what tomorrow will bring?

Tomorrow would bring the Hardanger.

At the airfield at Wick in the freezing dawn they saw the rows of Horsa gliders standing two abreast waiting to be hitched by their towlines behind the Halifaxes. Richardson was there waiting for them, immaculate as ever in his navy greatcoat. He wore gray kid gloves.

"Bloody cold," said Richardson.

Larsen nodded.

"I have good news for you. They've switched it all to the Riviera. Two weeks in the sun, expenses paid, courtesy of His Majesty's government. Meanwhile this."

"What's that?"

"A commission for you. Here are your pips, Major Larsen."

"What about the others?"

"Sergeants."

"I see."

"Don't sound so dreary, old man. Come to the mess, and we'll have a drink on it." Richardson was as cool as ever, his dark saturnine features well set off by immaculate linen. He said lightly, "By the bye, you're on your own. They've turned me down. I won't be going with you."

Larsen felt a sense of relief. He did not think he could tolerate Richardson for the long run. "Does that change the mission?"

"Not at all. You'll carry on as before. Radio contact remains the same. You'll be outranked when the glider forces arrive, but until then you'll be in command. Best tell your other chaps about it now."

Helberg chuckled when informed that Richardson had backed out. "I asked him once what they did in the SOE, and do you know what he told me? He said they make plastic shit."

"Eh?"

"S'truth. Plastic turds. Yak, buffalo, camel, elephant, you name it. Man in charge goes around to the London Zoo some mornings to collect the shit. Exact copies stuffed with high explosives scattered over the landscape. Chap steps on elephant dung and loses both legs."

"You believe that?"

"S'what he told me, What about it, Jens?"

"*Major,* for God's sake," said Torsten.

"What about it, *Major*?"

"Commander Richardson has a British sense of humor."

"What about those cyanide pills? Is that part of his British sense of humor, too?"

"I'm afraid not. Got yours?"

Torsten reached into his pocket and took out the capsule containing the brown, rubbery-looking pills. "Not much to look at, are they?"

"What did you expect," said Helberg, "bonbons?"

"Well, they might at least have coated them with sugar. Make it easier going down."

"Ten seconds and you'll never know the difference. It's better than being left to the tender mercies of the Krauts."

"Let's get off the subject," Larsen said. "You've had thorough training. You know what to do."

Helberg stared disapprovingly at the plywood gliders. "I don't think much of those egg crates. The Hardanger will make matchsticks of them."

"That's not our worry."

"Right. All we've got ahead of us is a nice clean jump."

"Lucky us."

Richardson came out of the Operations shack. "Be a few hours yet," he said. "There are some cots inside for the air crews. Put your heads down for a while if you like."

"Not a bad idea," growled Helberg.

"Major Larsen, if you'll come with me we can go over it once more with Operations."

Larsen followed Richardson into the Quonset hut. The interior, lit only by two small windows at either end and a series of weak electric lights, was gloomy. The Operations officer, a balding man sporting an oversize RAF-style moustache, said, "We've been advised of a last-minute change."

"Oh?"

"It's been decided that the transport aircraft should not pass anywhere near the Rjukan valley or the Mösvatn dam. A new dropping point for the gliders has been selected. Lake Skryken."

"That's thirty miles away," said Larsen. "Over rough terrain. It will take them two days to get down to Vemork from there."

The Operations officer shrugged. "Direct orders from London. Nothing to do with us."

"But it doesn't make any sense."

"To the troops in the field it never does."

"Well, then, dammit, let's speak to someone who is not in the field."

"We're only the export airfield, old man. Limited authority. Simply the shipping agents, so to speak."

"There are more than one hundred and fifty men involved in this besides myself. They're not sides of beef, you know."

The Operations officer raised an eyebrow but said nothing. Larsen turned to Richardson. "Can't you do something about this? I know that Lake Skryken area. Impossible country for any kind of landing. And even if they do land safely they could be caught in a blizzard. It might take as much as a week to establish contact."

"I'm afraid it's out of our hands. Anyway, it's too late to change things now. We can't possibly make the drop without some kind of visual sighting, which means moonlight. If we miss this moon period we'll have to wait weeks for another, and who knows what the weather may be like by then? The whole thing might drag on for months. You know what happens to operations like this when you start postponing them. The men lose heart. As it is, they're worked up to a nice pitch of fitness. Sorry, Major. Everything has been laid on, and this is the time to go."

Larsen frowned. "Then why wasn't I consulted? Presumably we're being sent in first because we know the ground. Why make a decision of this kind without talking to the people involved?"

"As a matter of fact, old boy, we did try to reach you."

"When?"

"Yesterday. Staff meeting in the late afternoon. Had calls out for you all over the place but no luck. Simply had to proceed without you."

"What time was that?"

"Fourish."

He had been in bed with Michelle at four o'clock. Lord. Now the success of the mission and, quite possibly, the lives of all concerned were at stake. Perhaps he would not have been able to alter their decision even if he had been available. The tricks fate played.

Once again his Hardanger nightmare came back to him. The drifting snow, the reindeer. The icy cliffs. The abyss.

But it was, as Richardson had pointed out, too late to change things.

NINE

As the "jump" light flashed, Larsen hurled himself through the open doorway of the Halifax. His heart hammered against his ribs. The night air was like a knife blade across his face. The chute popped behind him and he was brought up with a jerk. Below him a limitless expanse of icy, moonstruck whiteness; above, the fading image of the bomber, engines drowned by the roar of the wind, and then his two companions outlined briefly against the moon.

He was a little drunk. They were all a little drunk. Standing on the icy cold tarmac Richardson had offered him half a bottle of black rum. He had declined, but Richardson pressed it on him. "Go on, take it."

"They'll court-martial you for this."

"More than likely. Don't be a fool. Go on, man, take it."

He was surprised. It was the first sign of humanity Richardson had shown.

"Share it with the sergeants," Richardson had said with a smile. "Do you all good."

They had shared it on the plane. The rum had lit a fire of false courage in their bellies. Now, hurling himself out into the howling gale of the slipstream, he was terrified, but the rum helped. He heard Helberg singing as he floated down.

"Shut up, you fool," Larsen shouted.

The dim whiteness of the ground was rushing up at him. He bent his legs in preparation, and then did the tumble and roll. He felt a sharp pain in his ankle and thought for a moment he might have broken it (God, that would have been all they needed), but then he came up standing with the chute dragging him downwind and finally managed to collapse the silk long enough to wriggle out of the harness. Someone else had come down close by.

He looked up, searching for the canister that would contain food and explosives. He saw it floating down and scuttled in that direction, sliding on an icy patch and falling heavily on his shoulder, but then picking himself up and collaring the second chute. One of the other men pounded toward him and he called, "Give me a hand with this thing."

Torsten whipped out a knife and said, "I've got it." He cut the canister loose.

"Where's Helberg?"

"Over there, I think."

"Let's find him."

"Right." He had observed Larsen's limp. "You all right?"

"Sure."

"You hit hard. Is your leg okay?"

"Yes, come on."

They found Helberg in a shallow ravine. He was lying on his back looking up at the sky, laughing.

"Drunken sot," said Torsten.

"Get him on his feet."

They hoisted the giggling Helberg out of the ravine. He seemed steady enough once he realized he was alive.

"Round up the other canister while I set up the radio. We'll try to establish contact to let them know we're on the ground and then we'll make for the hut at Skryken," Larsen said.

The training period at Cambridgeshire had been exhaustive. They had been made to set up the receiver and transmitter over and over again in darkness. But no training program could possibly have simulated conditions on the Hardanger—the freezing wind and driving snow, the clumsy mittened fingers. Everything took longer than he had expected, but at last he was able to receive a weak signal. Using code he informed SOE that his party was safely on the ground and prepared to undertake the second stage of the operation. London's answer was lost in static. Cursing, he packed up the gear and then with the experienced mountaineer Torsten leading the way, they set out for the refuge on the shore of the lake.

The collapsible sledge that held their supplies was easy enough to tow, but even so it was well after dawn before they reached the hut. Larsen's ankle had swollen and his limp was more pronounced, but he struggled on, trying to make the best of it. As they topped the last rise before the lake they could see mile after mile of fresh snow with no living creature in sight. The unpainted, weatherbeaten hut lay below them. Lying on his belly in the snow Larsen studied the cabin through his glasses. Nothing, no tracks or wisp of smoke rising from the chimney. Torsten and Helberg were anxious to get into shelter, but he held them back. He, too, was freezing, but one could not be too careful. At last he said, "I'm going down. You two wait here. If anything happens don't make a fight of it. Leave me. Establish contact with London on the agreed-upon frequency."

"Let me go," said Helberg.

Larsen, buckling on his skis, shook his head. "No."

"Bucking for a medal, eh?"

"Something like that."

"Goddam hero."

"Degenerate bastard," said Larsen, giving him an affectionate punch on the shoulder.

He skied down in long curves, the rifle over his shoulder, feeling naked and exposed, waiting for the sound of the shot. But nothing came. There was no sound but the slither of the skis on fresh snow and the keening of the wind. When he was twenty yards from the hut he dropped flat and waited. He was a little warmer from the exertion of skiing, and in his white parka he must be almost invisible. After five minutes he got up again, skied down the rest of the way, and peeked through the frosty window. The hut was empty. Raising his ski pole he signaled to the others on the ridge, then opened the door and went into the hut.

The place was musty, mouse droppings in the corner. No warmer inside than out, but at least it offered protection from the wind. There was a stack of wood and an iron stove, but they could not light a fire during the day; the smoke could be seen miles away.

Larsen took off his wet mittens and began to flex his frozen fingers. There was hardly any feeling at all in his feet; he would have to get his boots off.

There was a clatter of gear and voices outside as Torsten and Helberg arrived.

"What a dump," Helberg said.

Torsten grinned, blue eyes blazing above reddened cheeks. "Looks like the Palace Hotel in Oslo to me. Anything to get out of that damn wind."

"From the look of it it's been a hell of a long time since anybody's been here."

"Only the chance hunter," said Larsen, "and no one at this time of year."

"No one in his right mind, anyway."

"I could do with a drink," Helberg said.

"Hot soup is more to the point. What about it, Torsten? Set up the Primus while I fiddle with this radio."

Torsten primed the little stove with alcohol and then pumped until he was rewarded with a hissing blue flame. The steaming soup was poured into aluminum mugs. Larsen savored the last drop. It was unfortunately true that one had to undergo privation in order to appreciate the simple comforts. With food in their bellies and a roof over their heads, what more could a man ask?

By midnight they had established radio contact with the approaching Halifaxes. Flares had been set out for the glider landing, but as Larsen listened to the exchange of signals he realized with growing horror that the planes were lost. For several hours the Halifaxes had been groping through heavy clouds which had moved in from the west. Aware that the Germans, too, must be listening, he had attempted to guide them in without success. Outside the hut the wind howled; a rising gale was in the making. The entire operation was now in danger. Even if the aircraft were able to locate the landing area, it would be extremely risky to cut the gliders loose in such conditions.

The group captain on board the lead aircraft had apparently come to the same conclusion. He announced with regret his decision to turn back; fuel was running low, and they had no choice; they would make another attempt when conditions improved. With a heavy heart Larsen accepted the decision. He was about to shut off the set when he heard a sudden garbled conversation between the lead aircraft and its glider. They were somewhere to the west of Rjukan and running into heavy cloud and icing conditions. Then all communication with the glider suddenly ended. The Halifax reported to London that the glider had fallen into the sea. There was no word at all from the second Halifax.

Torsten and Helberg sat in glum silence as Larsen shut down the set.

"Those poor bastards," Torsten said at last.

"What now?" Helberg asked.

Larsen sighed. He felt a hollowness inside, as if he had been gutted. "We'll have to see what London says."

"Fuck London," Helberg growled. "A fucked-up plan from the start. Bastards like that Richardson, what do they know of conditions here? They sit there sipping tea while better men go out to die. I tell you it stinks."

"All the same it had to be tried," said Larsen, not really believing it, thinking again that if they had been able to reach him that afternoon when he had been with Michelle, he might have been able to talk them out of it.

"Tell that to those poor bastards who are down in the sea."

"Why not try calling London again?" Torsten said.

"Why not just forget those fuckers altogether?" Helberg said. "There's nothing they can do for us now."

Larsen listened to the shriek of the rising wind. Conditions on the plateau were even more brutal than usual. One good thing about it, it would be safe to show a light or even a bit of smoke from a fire. The only living things out there in this kind of weather would be the reindeer. Helberg, in his rough way, was right. The operation had been badly planned from the start; the idea of using gliders in that kind of weather and across such terrain was insane. And there was in fact nothing London could do for the advance party. They would have to make their own decisions. And each radio contact increased the chance of their being tracked by the Germans.

The choices were simple: They could stay where they were, but not for very long; with winter coming on they would soon starve or freeze to death.

They could try, while they were still in good shape, to get away to Sweden. By hiding during the day and traveling across country at night they might just make it. Perhaps one chance in a thousand.

They could surrender to the first Germans they came upon and hope not to be shot out of hand.

Or they could proceed with the mission on their own.

"So?" said Helberg.

"I think we ought to go ahead with the attack as planned," Larsen replied.

"What, the three of us? Are you crazy?"

"Perhaps."

"It's suicidal."

"It was suicidal from the start," said Torsten. "What's the difference now?"

"I'm not ordering you to do anything," Larsen said. "If you want to make for the Swedish border on your own you're free to do so."

"Meaning what?" said Torsten. "That you'll attack the plant by yourself?"

"Yes."

"You are one crazy little fucker," said Helberg.

Torsten grinned and ran a hand through his shaggy mop of hair. "What an idea. You might just have something there, little Jens."

"Oh, shit," said Helberg. "One grave is as good as another. Let's do it."

Torsten turned to Larsen. "What I don't see is how in hell you propose to go about it."

"I don't know yet." He was silent for a while, thinking. "What I do know is that three armed and determined men can do a lot of damage. I think the key is to move fast. Once the Germans begin to figure out where those gliders were headed, they'll rush in all kinds of reinforcements to Vemork."

Helberg, listening to the wind rattling the windows, said, "I hope you don't propose to move on a night like this."

"No, we'd freeze to death before we were halfway there. But at this time of year a northeast gale ought to blow itself out pretty fast. If the storm eases off within the next few hours we'll start at first light for Rjukan."

"Sounds good. We can stop in at my Uncle Paal's to warm our asses over his fire and drink his schnapps."

"That's exactly what we won't do. If we succeed in blowing up the plant the Germans will be looking for us, and if they find out we got any kind of help they'll shoot every man, woman, and child in Rjukan."

"You're serious? We go it alone?"

"Absolutely alone. Except for one thing."

"What's that?"

"Information. We'll have to get some idea of when the shifts change now. I was thinking of Einar Skinner."

"That old drunk!"

"No one will suspect him. He makes deliveries regularly with his bread cart, which means he passes through the guard lines every morning. He'll know when the shifts change. And there's another thing. He lives alone, has no wife."

"Except for the bottle."

Larsen nodded. "To be cold blooded about it, if the Germans do shoot him he'll be no great loss."

"Well, you've got a point there," Helberg said.

"If you're lucky enough to catch him sober," Torsten said. "Otherwise forget it."

"We'll have to chance that."

"And what if we're seen and recognized in Rjukan?"

"We'll have to chance that, too."

They came to Skinner's hut at dawn after a bitterly cold night in the mountains. The old man was asleep. He was sober, although shaky. He stared at Larsen in amazement.

"Jens Larsen. What are you doing here? They told me you got away to England."

"Be very quiet, Einar, and listen."

"I need a drink, Jens."

"Later. You have any coffee?"

The old man indicated the pot on the wood-burning stove. Larsen took off the cover. Inside was a disgusting mixture that resembled tar. He thrust a few sticks of wood into the stove and lit a fire. Through the window he could barely make out the hillock of snow behind which Torsten and Helberg were hidden.

The coffee was terrible, but after a few sips the old man's voice strengthened and his hands no longer trembled so violently. He regarded Larsen shrewdly and said, "Have you come from England, Jens?"

"Yes."

"Ah. You had better be careful then of these goddamned Germans. Look what they did to the others."

"What others?"

"The ones who came two nights ago in the gliders."

"They were supposed to have gone into the sea," Larsen said.

"No, no. They crash-landed near Egersund."

"Alive?"

"They were then, but the Germans shot them. Said they were spies and saboteurs, and that it had something to do with the plant at Vemork. They were here yesterday to search the village. A good thing you didn't come yesterday."

"But the troops in the gliders were in uniform. Why weren't they taken prisoner?"

"The Germans kill whom they please." The old

man's bloodshot eyes squinted up at Larsen. "Were you with those others?"

"In a way, yes."

"And you are going to Vemork?"

"Yes. But I need your help, Einar."

"Right." The old man responded immediately. "If it has to do with the fucking Germans you can count on me."

"Then, this is what I want you to do, Einar. . . ."

The hydroelectric plant at Vemork, only five miles from Rjukan, lay deep in a rocky gorge that was untouched by sunlight. The only approach was over a narrow suspension bridge that crossed the tumbling river. No more than two sentries, one at either end, were required to guard the bridge. Not only the bridge but the road winding down from Vemork to the plant was brilliantly floodlit at night. A cat could not have crossed the bridge without giving the alarm. Heavy machine guns had been set up on both ends of the bridge, and fifteen German troopers lived in a barracks hut between the turbine hall and the electrolysis building. In addition there were two Norwegian night watchmen inside the compound with two more on the main gate and the penstocks. All doors leading in and out of the electrolysis building were kept locked except for one that gave access to the yard. Each supply truck entering the plant was carefully checked at both ends of the bridge.

Einar Skinner had a horse and wagon, both, like himself, almost in the final stages of decrepitude. Drunk as he might be when he went to bed, he still managed to hitch up the rig every morning and drive to the bakery in the predawn darkness to pick up his load of bread. The old horse, arthritic bones complaining, knew the way so well that Einar was often able to doze off.

The shambling horse, the creaking wagon, and the sleepy old man were too familiar to require inspection. The first sentry at the bridge waved Einar on and the second simply nodded. With methodical slowness, iron-shod wheels clattering on the metal, the wagon crossed the bridge. Clouds of icy vapor from the roaring river rose into the still air and Einar held his collar tighter and shivered. He kept his head down and his eyes half closed. Any undue curiosity or alertness might arouse suspicion.

The sentry sniffed appreciatively at the odors of warm bread rising from beneath the canvas that covered the heavy wicker baskets. He shouted, "Halt!"

The old horse slowed from a shuffle to a stop. Skinner, giggling drunkenly, glanced up at the German.

"What have we here, old man?"

"Bread. As usual."

The German cast off the lashings of the canvas. He reached under the canvas and into the basket. Einar Skinner's heart thumped. Christ! He passed this way every day with his innocent load, and no one paid him any attention. Now, when he was carrying the explosives and weapons Jens Larsen had given him, he was being stopped and searched. What had made the bastard suspicious?

The loaves of bread were in a tightly packed layer above the three machine pistols and the boxes of plastique. The detonators were in separate cartons. The sentry broke off a corner from one of the loaves and thrust it into his mouth.

"You Norwegians are not much good for anything

else, but you do know how to bake bread," the German said.

Einar, his knees shaking, managed a foolish grin.
"Pass!"

Einar clucked to the old horse. The wagon rolled forward and down the rocky path to the cookshed. Still no lights showing in the barracks hut. So much the better. Fucking Germans slept late. Tomorrow they might be awakened early with a little surprise.

The sky was turning gray in the east, but in the gorge it was still dark. Even so, he could make out the precipitous walls rising almost straight up. Einar Skinner had lived in Rjukan all his life, and he could not remember having heard of anyone climbing the gorge. Now Jens Larsen and his two companions proposed to do so. They had about as much chance, thought Einar, as rabbits in a cage of wolfhounds.

They waited in the hut. Einar Skinner's few grubby articles of clothing hung suspended from nails driven into the raw wood. In one corner were a dozen or so empty liquor bottles and piles of girlie magazines. The magazines had been published in Stockholm and showed naked blond women being mounted by men and animals.

"Wow!" said Helberg, "the old man has weird tastes."

Jens Larsen did not consider himself a prude, but he found the comment disturbing. Whatever Einar Skinner's sexual fantasies might be, the old man was entitled to some privacy. He had accepted without question the dangerous job Larsen had given him.

"Shut up!"

"Oh, hell, Major, would you deny a condemned man a few last pleasures?"

It was true. They were condemned. This time tomorrow morning . . . Even if they succeeded in conquering the gorge, there would still be the Germans to deal with. And the explosives. And the getting away. The British had sent two planeloads of commandos for the job and failed. Here they were, three civilians-turned-temporary-soldiers, trying to pull it off. And if by some miracle they succeeded, there would still be the hard slogging over 350 miles of rough country to the Swedish border with every German in Norway on the lookout for them.

"Why not try to get some sleep?" he said roughly. "Einar should be back soon, and then we'll know what's what."

"Good idea," Helberg said. He leafed once more through the magazine, grumbling, "What cows!" then tossed it back onto the pile. He and Torsten both settled down with their parkas under their heads. Soon they were snoring. Larsen, eyes open, waited.

When they heard the wagon creaking along the road, Larsen signaled to the others to remain quiet. He peeked over the sill and saw that Skinner was alone. The old man unhitched the horse and led him into the shed and fixed a nosebag of oats for him. When he came into the house he was grinning.

"Well?" Larsen asked in a tense voice.

"In a minute, boys. Let's have a drink first."

The old man uncorked a bottle, passed it around, and then finished most of it himself. When he put it down his eyes were shining. "That's better! It went like a dream, boys."

"No trouble?"

"That bastard at the bridge reached into the basket. I thought my heart would stop. But all he wanted was a free hunk of bread, blast him!"

"And the stuff?"

"Behind the cookshed under the garbage pit as agreed."

"Wonderful, Einar."

"I could do with another drink," the old man said.

Larsen considered. Skinner certainly deserved another drink after what he had been through, but if he gave him the money for another bottle, the old man might wind up boasting of his exploits. "Not until we leave. There'll be a little something for you then. I want you to stick to your regular routine. What do you usually do after feeding the horse?"

Skinner's faded blue eyes twinkled. "I feed myself and then I sleep."

"Good."

Skinner had brought in with him three of the fresh loaves. They tore into the bread, then sat down to wait. Skinner slept. The hours dragged by.

The Vemork operation had been of particular interest to Peter Guthrie not only because of the enemy's use of heavy water but also because of the firm friendship that had grown up between himself and Jens Larsen. He could not conceal his dismay when Richardson informed him the attack had failed.

"We're genuinely sorry," Max said.

Everyone is always sorry when these things go bust. "How did it happen?"

"We're not sure. We thought at first one of the gliders had gone into the sea, but it appears now that they both crash-landed. Probably iced up and got too heavy for the tow rope."

"Survivors?"

"Some, but they were picked up almost at once and executed. Even the wounded were shot." Richardson paused. "SOE Norway intercepted a report from Reich Commissioner Terboven to General Rediess, chief of the secret police. Rediess sent this telegram to Berlin. As you can see, he was none too pleased about it."

Guthrie studied the green slip of paper:

A BRITISH TOWING AIRCRAFT AND ITS GLIDER CRASHED NEAR EGERSUND AT ABOUT 3:00 A.M. ON THE 20TH. CAUSE OF ACCIDENT NOT YET KNOWN. AS FAR AS HAS BEEN ASCERTAINED, TOWING AIRCRAFT'S CREW IS MILITARY, ALL DEAD. THERE WERE SEVENTEEN MEN IN GLIDERS, PROBABLY AGENTS. THREE OF THEM KILLED, SIX BADLY INJURED. GLIDER'S CREW WAS IN POSSESSION OF LARGE QUANTITIES OF NORWEGIAN MONEY. UNFORTUNATELY THE MILITARY AUTHORITIES EXECUTED THE SURVIVORS. EXPLANATION SCARCELY POSSIBLE NOW. REDIESS.

"In other words it would have been perfectly all right to shoot them after questioning," Guthrie said bitterly.

"Yes."

"What about the advance party? Larsen and his friends?"

"No word."

"But they did get down all right?"

"So far as we know. A weak signal was picked up

and then lost almost immediately. Rotten weather."

"Then presumably they're still up there on the Hardanger."

"Running for their lives, I imagine."

"What are their chances?"

Richardson shook his head. "Not a prayer. The Germans are on the alert now."

"I see."

Richardson studied his fingernails. "I suppose it will come as a shock to the Stern girl. I believe they were quite friendly."

"Yes." Guthrie had seen Michelle the day after Larsen's departure, and although she had put on a brave enough front, it was obvious that she was distressed.

"She'll have to be told."

"I'll do it," Guthrie said.

"One other thing. This morning we heard through Stockholm that a false air-raid alert had been sounded in Rjukan. While it was on, two hundred German troops entered the town and searched every house. If our friends were in the neighborhood, they were almost certainly picked up."

TEN

The wind was down, the gorge bathed in moonlight. The hydro plant could be heard before it was seen, a thin humming sound as if thousands of bees were at work. The humming grew louder, and then at last they could look into the gorge and see the flat, snow-covered roofs of the two main buildings, immense concrete structures. The suspension bridge was barely visible, no more than an airy tracing in the moonlight.

No words passed among the three men; everything had been discussed beforehand. A shallow hole was dug in the snow, and all extra equipment—skis, parkas, knapsacks—was buried to be collected on the way out if they survived the assault.

Torsten, the most experienced climber, led the way, with Larsen next and Helberg bringing up the rear. It had been agreed that being roped together would slow them down too much; their only hope lay in speed and mobility. If a man fell, he would have to take his chances. It had been further agreed that if any of them was injured or wounded he would be left behind.

The night had grown warmer, and what little wind there was had shifted to the southwest. They were at

the beginning of a period of thaw. Dangerous conditions for the descent of the gorge and the climb up
the other side. The snow was loose and shifting, and
they could be caught in a slide. At least the drone
of the generators and the rush of water through the
gorge might cover the thunder of dislodged snow
tumbling off the rocks.

Torsten disappeared over the edge. Larsen gave him
a few seconds, then followed. The rocks were slippery
under their covering of snow. With freezing hands
Larsen edged himself down, planting each foot solid-
ly before moving the next. The slope was even more
precipitous than he had expected. No wonder the
Germans didn't bother to patrol the gorge. Even in
daylight it would have been a hell of a job to get
down one side and up the other.

Despite the cold he was sweating inside his wool
uniform jacket. Once Helberg crashed into him from
above and nearly dislodged him. He clung on with
both hands until Helberg had regained his feet.

The pitch was too abrupt for a straight descent.
Torsten had begun a traverse off to the side. Larsen
followed, trying to keep close to Torsten's steps. In
the moonlight Torsten was clearly visible. Larsen felt
as exposed as a fly on a sugar bowl. He expected at
any moment to hear a cry of alarm from the guards
and to feel the hammer blow of a bullet in the back.

Water vapor rose around them in clouds. They
must be approaching the river. Suddenly Larsen was
knee deep in freezing water. Torsten started across.
Larsen felt his feet sliding out from under him and
struggled to regain his balance. A heavy hand took
him by the back of the collar and forced him upright.

Helberg said in a whisper, "Steady!" Larsen, regaining his feet, nodded his thanks.

The river, although wild, was not very deep. At no
point did it rise above their knees. Then they were
across, and Torsten halted them for a brief rest.

"Ready?"

"Yes."

Going up was, in a way, easier. They moved more
slowly and felt themselves to be in better control.
They stayed closely bunched up.

When they were halfway up the shift changed. Two
busloads of workers passed over the bridge. A twenty-
four-hour-a-day production schedule was being maintained. According to Intelligence the Germans had
insisted on an increase to over five thousand pounds
of heavy water a year, and there was no way that
could be done except by working around the clock.

As the buses crawled over the bridge their head-
lights swept across the cliff face. For a moment the
three Norwegians were exposed. They flattened themselves against the rocks. Then the light was gone. Helberg exhaled noisily. The climb went on.

At a few minutes before eleven they topped the rise
and lay panting in the snow. They had been climbing
steadily for more than two hours. Larsen's legs were
trembling with exhaustion. The prospect of the return journey did not bear thinking about.

He was tempted to race straight across the narrowest
part of the shelf to the protection of the factory buildings, but Einar Skinner had warned them against
that; only two weeks before the Germans had sown
mines over almost every foot of open space. The only

way through the minefield would be along the road-bed of the narrow-gauge railway that ran along the edge. There was a wire fence and locked gate where the tracks entered the compound, but the lock was on a short length of chain; heavy wire cutters should be able to deal with that.

Crouching low, aware of the drop to one side and the minefield on the other, they scurried along the roadbed to the fence. It had suddenly occurred to Larsen that in the months he had been away from the plant the Germans might have electrified the fence. If that were so, the man holding the wire cutters would be fried. Even if Skinner had known about it he might have failed to mention it. There might be a switch in the guard tower. He took the wire cutters from Helberg and gingerly, feeling like a man about to vanish in a puff of smoke, touched the tip of the metal to the chain. Nothing. With a sigh of relief he applied the cutters and then with both Helberg and himself pressing the grips they sheared through two of the links and swung the gate back far enough to slip through. Once they were inside they closed the gate again and hung the broken chain back around the post.

Ahead was a low side tunnel leading into the electrolysis plant, but first they would need the explosives Einar had buried behind the cookshed. Although the windows had been painted over, a small amount of light shone from within the shed. Like animals on the prowl they began digging into the pile of refuse and empty tin cans. In a moment they had unearthed the tarpaulin containing the Sten guns and the cartons of explosives. The Stens were quickly loaded, and then with each man carrying his own weapon they ran for the low entrance to the side tunnel, Tilfluktsrom 7.

It was black inside. Larsen led the way over a tangled web of pipes and cables. There was no room to stand, and it was difficult to crawl carrying the weapons and explosives. A glimmer of light ahead from a screened vent. Through the vent they could catch a glimpse of the high-concentration room. It was brilliantly lit and there appeared to be only one man on duty, a Norwegian whom Larsen recognized. Motioning to the others to follow, he unfastened the catch to the connecting door and stepped into the room, weapon at the ready.

The Norwegian worker had been bent over one of the concentration cells. He looked up in astonishment. The sudden appearance of Larsen wearing the uniform of a British major and carrying a submachine gun had unnerved him completely. Mouth agape, the man said nothing. At last he muttered, "Is that you, Jens Larsen?"

"Yes. I don't remember your name."

"Kjelstrup, Arne. But how—"

"No time for explanations. Are there any Germans on this level?"

"Only the sentry at the main door."

"Good. We are here to blow up the place. You will remain here until I give the signal, and then you will open the door and run like hell. Understood?"

"Yes, but . . ."

"Now, just shut up. The less you know about it the better. If you're questioned afterward, tell them the truth; you were held at gunpoint."

Torsten and Helberg had begun to lay charges around each of the eighteen heavy-water cells. Each charge was connected with a high-speed fuse which in turn was attached to a slow time fuse. If all went well, they would have just enough time to escape from the building before the explosives went off.

"Ready," Torsten said.

"How long?"

"Three minutes."

"All right, Arne. You get out of here."

Kjelstrup looked confused. He had removed his glasses and was vigorously wiping them. "But . . . but what will I tell them?"

"The truth, damn it. You were held up by armed commandos. Now, unless you want to go up with the rest of the place, you'd better get the hell out of here."

Kjelstrup replaced his glasses and ran for the door. Larsen ventured a last look around the electrolysis room before leading the way back into the cable tunnel.

No longer worried about noise, they scrambled through the darkened tunnel, cursing as they fought their way past obstructions. Surely it had been more than three minutes. Was the fuse defective? It was a simple mechanism that depended on the corrosive action of acid eating through a bit of copper wire, but the acid might have been weakened by the intense cold. What if, after all this and the deaths of so many good men, the damned thing didn't work? There was no time to brood about it. They were out of the tunnel and running for the gate when the first charge, curiously muffled, went off. It was followed almost immediately by a much louder explosion. Helberg shouted with excitement. Every light in the electrolysis building had gone off. Out of the blackness searchlights probed suddenly, pinning them to the wall.

They heard the sound of shots. Helberg responded with a burst from his Sten that knocked out two of the lights. Larsen had opened up now with his own weapon. No time to aim, just spray the damned thing. The gun jumped in his hands and he was aware of the acrid stench.

"Come on!" Torsten shouted. "Make for the ravine!"

They ran along the railway bed and kicked open the gate. A German sentry was beyond the fence, down on one knee and firing his rifle. A burst from Torsten's Sten stitched across his middle, seeming to cut him in two. Helberg had turned to fire at the remaining light. He made a strangled sound and toppled over clutching his throat. A gout of blood welled from between his fingers. Larsen came back to kneel beside him, but then Torsten's hand was on his shoulder and the blond giant was bellowing at him, "Come on! There's nothing we can do!"

They ran for cover, bending low, dodging. Larsen did not look back. He was almost at the edge of the gorge before he realized he was alone. The firing from the Germans was heavier now, and above the racket came the scream of a siren. In one swift glance he took in the situation. Half-dressed Germans were running out of the barracks hut. Streams of tracers were pouring from the machine gun nest at either end of the bridge. And Torsten was down, motionless in the snow, the Sten still gripped in one hand.

Larsen felt a push against his shoulder as though he had been jostled in a crowded bus. He slipped and fell sideways over the edge of the step and down into the gorge. All around him were rocks and snow and rubble tumbling downward. He struggled to right himself, to hold on, but his arms had no strength. He was brought up short by a head-first collision with something hard and immovable. Darkness washed over him.

He had no way of knowing how long he had been unconscious. The searchlights had evidently been repaired and were still sweeping the area, but the sirens no longer howled.

He lay head downward in a mass of snow and rubble, almost all of his body buried except for his head. Certainly the Germans must have searched the gorge with their lights and concluded that he had been buried in the avalanche. Some small miracle had kept his head above the surface. He had collided with one of the sparse trees growing below the lip of the gorge. If it had been a rock his skull would have been smashed. As it was, he was conscious of intense pain in his shoulder and arm. Had he broken something in the fall? Then it came to him that he had been shot. There had been that curious pushing sensation just before he went over the edge. He had felt nothing at the time but now it hurt like hell.

Gingerly he moved his left arm. The pain stabbed at him. How much blood had he lost? Possibly being buried in the snow had slowed the bleeding.

By wrapping his good arm around the tree trunk he was able to drag the upper part of his body out of the snow. As the wound in his shoulder was exposed to the air, he felt such pain that it was all he could do to keep from crying out. He must not think about the wound or about his two dead friends. His only hope was to concentrate on one thing at a time—getting the rest of the way down the gorge and then somehow up the other side. What then? He could not return to Einar Skinner's hut, the Germans would be searching every house in Rjukan. Perhaps they had already taken hostages, perhaps Einar Skinner was dead.

With a struggle he hauled himself a little higher until his legs were free. He could see now that he had fallen almost halfway down the side of the gorge, and that the steepest part was already behind him. He waited for the wave of giddiness to pass. He must move quickly but carefully. At first light the Germans would begin to search for his body. He must be well away by then.

The moon was still up, and by its light he picked his way down the side of the gorge, moving from tree to tree, trying not to start another snowslide. As the grade lessened the snow grew deeper but firmer. Suddenly he was on level ground at the bottom and once more up to his knees in the rushing water. There was no sensation of cold. Had his feet already frozen? He might survive a gunshot, but frostbitten feet and gangrenous toes would mean his finish.

He began to work his way up the far side of the gorge, moving crablike from one handhold to another, knowing he could never make the top. Something in him resisted the idea of dying in that dismal ravine. He struggled on, the cold night air rasping his lungs, his grip on handholds growing ever feebler.

As he reached the top he lost consciousness for the second time. When he came to again he was aware of something soft and warm touching his face. A heavy breath and slobbering lips. Angels?

If so, they knew damn all about kissing in heaven.

An immense head outlined against the moon and two great holes of darkness for eyes. Something huge hovering over him. A horse. And then hands under his armpits. Too weak to protest at the pain, he was only dimly aware that he was being dragged up onto a wagon. A voice whispered, "Lie still." Something— was it hay?—was being dragged over him and then the rough feel of canvas. He was being buried. A rough shroud and an undertaker's wagon.

ELEVEN

Michelle's face was pale, but her eyes were steady. "There is no hope then for Jens?"

"There is always hope," Peter Guthrie said.

"But not much."

If she would cry, it would be better. Her dry eyes and quiet voice worried him. The war eventually touched everyone, but Michelle's reaction was not what he might have expected.

"We're not sure what happened," Guthrie said. "The report was from a clandestine station some distance away, and their information was secondhand. The two men with him were killed by the Germans, and their bodies were identified, but Jens disappeared. They think he may have been lost in an avalanche."

She nodded. "He told me once about a bad dream he'd had. It was something like that. Did he at least do what he was sent for?"

"Yes. He did that all right."

"I'm glad."

David Stern came into the room and looked at Michelle's face and then turned and went out again.

Guthrie said awkwardly, "I'd better be going."

"Thank you for coming to tell me." Her voice was still composed, but when she reached out to touch the back of his hand, her fingertips were icy.

The wagon bounced over the dirt road. Each bump sent a shaft of pain through Larsen's wounded shoulder. Someone was singing, croaking rather. It was Einar Skinner singing an American jazz tune.

The wagon had stopped. Skinner's voice could no longer be heard. Then from somewhere behind came the sound of doors swinging shut. The tarpaulin was drawn back and a lantern was thrust down into the bed of the wagon, dazzling his eyes.

"Is that you, Einar?" Larsen said.

The old man gave his characteristic dry chuckle. "Were you expecting Heinrich Himmler?"

"Where are we?"

"A little place I know. The house burned down years ago, but the barn is still in good shape. Come on, now, let me help you out of there."

Larsen groaned when the fingers touched his shoulder.

Skinner said, "All right, I know you're hurt. But we've got to see to that shoulder and get you warm. Too bad there's no way we can fetch a sawbones, but they're the first ones those German bastards will be checking. You'll just have to trust old Dr. Skinner."

"What happened at the plant?"

"You don't know?"

"I'm not sure."

Skinner chuckled again. "Why, you just blew the shit out of it, is all."

"The electrolysis cells?"

"Whatever they were, they are not anymore."

"How do you know?"

"It was all over town in ten minutes. Even the fucking Germans can't keep a thing like that quiet."

"And the others?"

Skinner shook his head.

"How did you know where to look for me?"

"If you were coming out at all it had to be somewhere along that road. It was just luck that I happened to be where I was. There was so much firing going on I thought at first the damned Germans were shooting at me. I can tell you I nearly crapped my pants. Easy now. Can you stand?"

"Not very well."

"The shoulder is clean. A lot of blood, of course, but those things always look worse than they are. I believe the bullet went right through. But we've got to get those wet boots off. Christ knows what shape your feet are in."

The boots came off followed by the wet socks.

"Holy mother," Einar Skinner said.

Larsen looked down. His frozen feet were dead white.

"Feel that?"

"No." His feet were like chunks of wood. The toes would rot and turn black and have to be cut off.

"It may not be too late," Einar said, "but first the shoulder. Hang on, now. This will hurt like hell." He had pulled a bottle of brandy from his pack and, uncorking it with his teeth, poured it over the wound.

Jens felt as though his arm had been raked with a hot iron. He groaned through clenched teeth.

"What a waste of good booze," Einar said. He raised

the bottle and took a swallow, then offered it to Larsen. Larsen raised his head to drink.

"Stay drunk," Skinner advised. "It won't hurt so much."

Larsen took another gulp of the brandy.

"I knew a man once who cut off his own toes," Skinner said.

"Yes?"

"That was in the north, at Tromsø. His feet were frostbitten like yours, and he was stranded alone in a hut in the mountains. When his toes turned black he tried to cut them off with his knife, but he was too weak and the blade was too dull."

"What happened to him?"

"Oh, he died."

Jens managed the ghost of a smile. "You're a real comfort, Einar."

"In your case it may be different. I think your feet are maybe not so bad as his. We may yet be able to save them. But when the circulation begins and the blood comes back, you will wish they had fallen off. If you want to holler, go ahead; there is no one to hear us. Now we must begin to get you warm. Hot water is what we will need and plenty of it. I have a tin in the wagon; we can melt snow in that."

Skinner searched under the straw in the back of the wagon and produced a five gallon can. He took it outside and packed it with snow, and then returned and piled a heap of small rocks together in one corner of the barn. Using hay and bits of wood he soon had a fire going. Almost at once the snow began to melt. When the water in the tin was steaming, Skinner dipped Larsen's wet socks into it, then draped them over Larsen's feet. Larsen felt nothing. Skinner repeated the process every ten minutes.

Larsen looked down at his feet. The dead look was gone; the feet were beginning to turn red.

"Feel anything?"

"Christ, yes," Larsen said, gritting his teeth.

"That's enough for now. We don't want to burn them. There's another swallow of the pain-killer left. Want it on your shoulder or inside?"

"Inside."

Skinner held the bottle for him while he drank off the last of the brandy. A dirty-looking dawn was beginning to filter through the barn's single window. As the blood returned to his feet, it brought with it unbelievable pain. The old man had not been exaggerating when he said he would want to holler. The bullet wound in his shoulder was bad enough, but it was nothing compared to his feet. Sweat bathed his neck and forehead, and Einar wiped it off for him.

Larsen said, "Won't the Germans be expecting you?"

Skinner shook his head. "No bread on Sunday. Anyway, they will be too damned busy searching the ravine for your carcass. You and your friends gave them a real surprise last night. They'll be running around like bedbugs when the mattress is on fire. The best thing is for you to stay quiet here for the next few days until the excitement dies down."

"And what about you?"

"I'll go to work tomorrow just as though nothing has happened. The only thing is I may be a little drunker than usual. I may be so drunk that no one will think it worthwhile to ask questions, and they won't be particularly surprised if I don't show up the next day or the day after."

"And if they come looking for you?"

Skinner shrugged. "They'll figure I fell into a snowbank somewhere and froze to death. Meanwhile, you'll have nothing to do but to lie quiet and enjoy yourself. A real holiday. After a few days we'll try to get you over to Kongsberg. I know a doctor there. He's a good man, that one, and he knows how to keep his mouth shut."

Larsen looked at the old man with increased respect. He might be a souse, but his brain was still sharp, and when it came to saving Larsen's life he had shrugged off the danger to himself. All the same, he could not expect Einar Skinner to look after him indefinitely. As soon as he was physically able, he would have to part company with the old man and try to get away to Sweden.

Larsen slept fitfully, slipping in and out of delirium. At times he was aware of the old man coming and going, but he could not be sure if it was real or another hallucination. His dreams were peopled with familiar faces. His father, who had been a surgeon in Oslo, but who had died young of heart disease; his brother Britt and his little sister Julia. She had been only eight when their father died, and Jens had been forced to play a difficult father-brother role with her. Now Julia was mixed up in his fantasies with Michelle, Julia's form with Michelle's face. He was making love to Michelle, and in fact it was his little sister Julia.

He awoke sweating.

"Can't say I like the look of that shoulder," Skinner said. "It's beginning to puff up."

"Are you sure the bullet isn't still in there?"

"Feels that way, does it? No, it went clear through, but it must be sore as hell, and you may be starting some infection. Have to get you over to Kongsberg. Tomorrow maybe. As far as I can find out the Jerries have given up looking for you. They figure you're under a couple of tons of snow in the gorge and won't come up until spring. How do the feet feel now?"

"They've stopped hurting."

"Good. Hungry?"

"Starving."

"I've got hold of some eggs. We can pop them into the tin and boil them. Eggs and bread will have to hold you. Think you can walk?"

"I can try." Then, "You really think the Germans have given up the search?"

Skinner chuckled. "They're fat and lazy. They don't enjoy tramping around in the snow and cold any more than the next fellow."

But privately he was not so sure.

Michelle was surprised to find Max Richardson waiting for her at the BBC. She had met him a few times through Peter Guthrie, but he had never displayed any particular interest in her. For a moment when she saw him standing there waiting for her outside the glass booth, she had a flash of hope. Perhaps he had heard something about Jens. She rushed through the end of her story which had to do with a little boy who had somehow gotten himself lost in a chocolate factory, and hurried out to meet him.

"Max!"

"Hello, Michelle. How are you?"

She searched his face. "I'm all right."

"I was in the neighborhood and thought I'd drop in."

"Time for a drink?"

"I suppose so," she said.

"We could go round the corner to Gino's, if that's all right with you."

"Fine."

Gino's was not too busy at that hour and reasonably quiet. He offered her a cigarette.

"Thank you."

"I've been thinking about you," he said, "wondering how you might like to have a job."

"What sort of job?"

"Special Operations."

"I've tried repeatedly to get into one of the services, Max, but I've been turned down by them all."

"For what reason?"

She shrugged. "Usually some fishy excuse. In the end it comes down to the same thing. I'm a foreigner and considered a poor security risk. They're very polite about it, of course, but I've learned to recognize the signals."

"Yes, well, for the job I have in mind I believe you would do very well. You speak French, don't you?"

"My mother was French, and my grandparents lived in Versailles. As a child I spent half my time there. French would be as much a native language to me as German."

Richardson nodded. "Just what they're looking for."

"Can you tell me more about it?"

He shook his head. "Not here, I'm afraid. Can you come round to my office tomorrow morning?"

"Yes, of course."

"And I wouldn't mention it to anyone if I were you."

"I understand."

"I suppose you're familiar with Paris."

"Oh, yes. A second home, really." A little pulse of excitement had begun to beat in her throat.

"Good. We'll talk about it tomorrow. Now tell me about your father. And how's Peter? I haven't seen either of them for a long time."

In the large room in Baker Street where Naval Intelligence was centered, Richardson offered her tea. Behind them the green baize door that guarded the admiral stayed firmly shut.

"The thing is," said Max, "some of our people—another agency, actually, although we often overlap—are thinking of sending a team to France. The point of the exercise will be to contact the underground forces and to serve as liaison. The people who go over will be expert radio operators and will be required to transmit messages back and forth."

"I'm afraid I don't know one end of a radio from another."

"Of course not. You'll be taught."

"Why me?"

"Because you're at home in France and can pass yourself off easily as French. Naturally you'll be given all the documents you need. You even look French. There will be no reason for anyone to suspect you. But what I want to make quite clear to you before we go any further is that it's an extremely dangerous job. If you're caught you can hardly expect the Germans to be very merciful."

Michelle bent her head to the teacup. If her eyes reflected fear she did not want it to be evident. Her dark glossy hair shone softly in the sunlight pouring through the windows.

"I understand."

"Still interested?"

"Yes."

"Mind telling me why?"

"I think you know. I'm sick of telling fairy stories to children while other people are off fighting the war. I want to do something that will absorb me completely and that will be useful."

"It will be useful all right. I can guarantee that." He started to say more, then hesitated. Christ, she was so bloody young.

"Can you tell me something about it?"

"Not too much at this point. You'll be part of a team composed of people like yourself, all of them volunteers. If you decide to join—and I say 'if' because I want you to think this over very carefully— you'll have to undergo a whole battery of tests to determine psychological and intellectual fitness and motivation. Then, if you're accepted, you'll be sent to a training school somewhere out of London. A large part of the course will consist of a conditioning program in parachute jumping and landing. Do you think you can manage that?"

"Have other women done it?"

"Yes. Several."

Michelle's large dark eyes were steady. "Then I think I can do it, too."

"Good. As I told you, it's a volunteer program. If, at any point, you decide it's all rather more than you bargained for, you can drop out without too many questions being asked, and we'll try to find something else for you."

"Something less hazardous?"

"Yes."

"I don't think I would want that."

"Good. Now, there's one other requirement. Absolute secrecy. If the mission is compromised, many lives will be endangered, and an extremely useful information network will be blown. Therefore no one must know what you're doing once you've entered the training program. Not even your father."

"I understand."

"Right. Now I suggest that you go away and think it over, and if you're still keen on it tomorrow, come to see me again at the same time."

When she had gone he reached for the telephone. "Get me Colonel Brothers," he said.

TWELVE

Reichmarshal Goering regarded his typed list of appointments with distaste. First on the list was his old friend, Ernst Udet, who was now suspected of having cooked his books while serving as supply chief for the Luftwaffe. Dealing with Ernst would not be easy. Udet, who had been a greater World War I fighter ace than Goering (second, in fact, only to the legendary Richthofen), had always been a notorious womanizer and boozer. None of that had mattered so much while he had served in second-rate jobs, but now that he was responsible for maintaining the level of production for the Luftwaffe's badly needed fighters and bombers, he was endangering the future of his boss, Goering.

It was incredible really to think that Udet could have imagined he could get away with faked production figures. Yet it was now apparent that he had been getting away with it for months, perhaps years. Ernst, with his great personal charm and spirit of reckless gaiety, had thrown some of the best parties in town, and somehow the members of the investigating committees always got invited—along with the most beautiful and promiscuous women in Berlin. Few men turned down an invitation to one of his affairs. Goering had attended one or two himself until his doctor had warned him that the strain might be too much for his heart.

But now the Luftwaffe's dwindling reserve of planes and its faulty performance could no longer be kept secret. Ernst Udet the golden boy, Germany's greatest living ace, was in trouble. And if Udet was in trouble, then so, too, was Hermann Goering.

This time he would really tear a strip off Ernst. Simply firing him would only serve to bring the scandal out into the open. He would have to be quietly demoted. A sterner taskmaster, possibly General Milch, must be put in charge. All done very quietly. Let Ernst screw himself to death if he liked; the planes must be produced. Adolf Hitler was not noted for his patience.

Udet at nine, Canaris and Hauser at nine-twenty. What a morning!

He supposed the appointment with Canaris and the scientist must have something to do with the uranium bomb. Since that fiasco at Leipzig, Goering had pretty well forgotten about it. Trust Canaris to remind him.

He plucked the golden phone from its stand on the marble-topped desk and growled into it, "Is Udet out there?"

"No, sir."

"Any word from him?"

"No, Herr Reichmarshal, but Admiral Canaris is here along with Dr. Hauser."

"Give me five minutes and then show them in."

"Very well, Herr Reichmarshal."

He left the office and went into the adjoining bathroom. From his pocket he produced a small gold key with which he unlocked the medicine chest. He shook from the bottle four paracodeine tablets and gulped them down with water. The relief from anxiety, the sense of renewed confidence imparted by the morphine, was almost instantaneous.

Goering strongly distrusted the little admiral with his high starched collar and reptilian eyes. Who knew what went on behind that thin-lipped, expressionless face? And who knew what juicy secrets the old bastard kept in his files? With any luck he and Himmler would finish each other off in their struggle for power.

He relocked the medicine chest and returned to his desk. There was a knock and he said, "Enter."

Canaris inclined his head. "Herr Reichmarshal. I believe you know Dr. Hauser."

Hauser bowed deeply. "Herr Reichmarshal."

"Coffee, gentlemen?"

Canaris declined.

"What can I do for you?"

"We have had news from Norway. British commandos have mounted an attack on the heavy water plant at Vemork."

"Any damage?"

"Substantial. Explosives were planted under each of the heavy-water cells. Production has been halted."

"For how long?"

"Six months at least. Perhaps a year."

"Blast! What happened to the British?"

"All killed. One still unaccounted for. They believe he fell into the ravine and was buried by snow."

"Where does this information come from?" Goering felt piqued that he had not been told first.

"General Von Falkenhorst."

"What is the situation now?"

Canaris shook his head. "We have suffered a considerable setback. Meanwhile the Americans and the British will be at work on similar projects. If we lose a year now, the war will be over before we can achieve the atomic bomb. In your absence yesterday"—Goering had been off deer hunting. First Udet, and now this bastard of an admiral!—"I took the liberty of discussing the situation with various members of the scientific community, including Dr. Hauser."

"If I may be allowed to sum up . . ." Hauser began.

Goering looked pointedly at his watch. ". . . to *sum up* we have put all our damn eggs in the wrong basket."

"In a manner of speaking, yes. But there is still another possibility."

"What's that?"

"It might be called the plutonium alternative. Through sources in America," Hauser went on, "I have been privileged to receive copies of a scientific journal called the *Physical Review*. In a recent issue the decay products of uranium-238 were discussed. It was speculated that by capturing neutrons, the uranium-238 nuclei might be transmuted into a new element as fissionable as uranium-235—with one important difference. A *chemical* difference. According to von Weizsäcker's theory we have always believed this decay process would stop at element number 93, which is element neptunium, but the Americans have now revealed that neptunium will decay to yet another element, plutonium. We have reason to believe the fission process can take place in plutonium without the excessive demand for heavy water."

"And?"

"Unfortunately we have no one who understands the process." Hauser hesitated. His pale cheeks had taken on a touch of color. Surprisingly, he appeared to be blushing. "It may require an Einstein."

"Very funny," said Goering. "Unfortunately I have little time for jokes."

"I am quite serious, Herr Reichmarshal."

Goering smiled. "Are you suggesting that we ask Einstein to return to Germany to help us build an atomic bomb?"

"Of course not," Canaris said smoothly. "What Dr. Hauser is suggesting is that we go and get him."

The tide of pink which had suffused Goering's fat cheeks began to subside. His eyes narrowed. "Take him by force?"

"Yes."

"And then what? Turn him over to Himmler? He is an old man, and I think not in the best of health. If he is tortured he is likely to die."

"I wasn't thinking of torture. What I had in mind was more in the nature of an exchange. Jewish lives for information."

Goering picked up a gold letter opener and was twisting it reflectively between his thick fingers. "Shoot a hundred or so Jews before his eyes and then another hundred. And so forth. It might work. Fortunately we have no shortage of Jews. But what do you think the Fuehrer will say?"

"Perhaps the Fuehrer will not hear about it," said Canaris. "Or at least not until it is over and we have got what we want."

Goering leaned back in his chair. It was the kind of bizarre scheme that tickled his fancy. If it failed, no one but Canaris and Hauser need know about it, and they might not live to tell the story.

"Go on," he said.

"Einstein is currently employed at the Institute for Advanced Studies at Princeton University. He has lived there since his flight from Germany in 1933 in a small private house on Mercer Street. Number one hundred twelve to be exact. Because of his fondness for sailing small boats, he also maintains a cottage at a place called Peconic Bay on Long Island. This bay is almost directly on the coast. It would be a comparatively simple matter for a U-boat to land a shore party there."

"What if he is guarded, or what if he decides not to go sailing on that particular day?"

"We have considered that," Hauser said. "The guards could be overcome by force if necessary, and Einstein could be abducted from his cottage, but there is a better way. Someone Einstein trusts completely must be allowed to make all the arrangements to deliver him to the submarine."

Goering snorted. "Easier said than done."

"I already know of such a man," Canaris said, letting his gaze flicker briefly to Hauser's face and then back to Goering's. "His name is Stern, and he lives in London. Until 1933 he was Einstein's close assistant and friend. There is no reason to suppose that Einstein would question Stern's sincerity."

"And how do we get Stern to cooperate?"

"Stern has a daughter, an only child. Our people in London have had her under observation for some time. She has been recruited as a radio operator, owing to her fluency in French, she will be attached to what

they call their F Section. Since our agents have recently
been successful in penetrating the Prosper network in
Paris, it would not be difficult to arrest her when she
reaches France. Once the father is satisfied that his
daughter is in fact in our hands and that her fate depends on his cooperation . . ." Canaris shrugged.

Goering smoothed his sleek hair with a large moist
palm, considering. "It is well known that Jews have
an unnatural attachment to their children. The trick
will be to convince Stern that she is in fact in great
danger," he said finally.

"Once he understands the situation he will do as we
wish."

"We do not intend to actually harm the girl,"
Hauser interjected. "She will simply be held in Paris,
and then eventually her release will be arranged."

"Of course," Canaris said a trifle impatiently.

"And how do you get this fellow Stern to America?" asked Goering.

"There are ways," said Canaris. "Through Lisbon
for instance."

"And what if he should change his mind en route?"

"He won't."

They were interrupted by the flashing of a light
attached to Goering's desk phone. Goering picked up
the receiver.

"Yes? . . . I see." He hung up and turned back to
his visitors. "It will be necessary to terminate this
meeting, gentlemen. I have been called away on an
urgent matter to do with the Luftwaffe. Please contact
my secretary for another appointment. Meanwhile,
I will give it some thought and advise you of my decision at our next meeting. You know your way out?"

"Of course, Herr Reichmarshal," answered Canaris.

* * *

Goering's Mercedes drew to a halt in the street below Ernst Udet's apartment. Goering hurried into the building, ignoring a salute from the flustered doorman. He made his way to Udet's door and pounded on it. When there was no answer he paused to listen. Inside someone was weeping. He knocked again, more gently this time. After a moment the door was opened by a half-naked woman. She wore only silk panties and a frilly French-style brassiere. Her face was tear-streaked but still pretty. Nice tits, thought Goering.

The woman's eyes opened wider and she attempted to cover her breasts with one hand. Through the diaphanous silk of the panties the thatch of hair was clearly visible.

"Herr Reichmarshal!"

Goering brushed past her. "Where is he?"

She pointed to the closed bedroom door, then put a restraining hand on his arm.

"I'm afraid it's too late."

"He did it?"

"Yes, Herr Reichmarshal. Ernst is dead."

The body of Ernst Udet lay across the unmade bed. Blood seeped from a gaping hole in the back of his head. The pistol, still in his hand, rested on the white fur rug.

Goering shook his head as he looked at the body of his old comrade. Behind him the woman was still sniffling.

"You wait here," he said. "And don't use the phone."

She nodded and sank down on the couch with her head in her hands. Goering closed the door. It was the first time he had been in Udet's bedroom; it was largely what he might have expected. On the walls were glamor photographs of many different women, among them the faces of half a dozen film stars. One wall was devoted to Udet's pen-and-ink sketches; he had been a clever cartoonist. Among the sketches was one of Goering bent over a workbench which held a collection of tiny airplanes. The caption beneath it read: "And look as morning dawns afar, our man has built the Luftwaffe."

The night table held an empty bottle of brandy and an unlabeled pill bottle. He uncapped the medicine bottle and sniffed at the contents. Paracodeine. So Ernst had been hooked, too.

There was a gray metal filing cabinet against the wall. He tried the top compartment. Locked, of course. It could be pried open, but doing so would take too much time and attract too much attention. The whole thing was probably hopeless. Still, it was likely that Udet would keep such files at home rather than at his office. He would probably have the key on him. He looked with distaste at Ernst's hairy buttocks.

Udet's trousers lay crumpled on the floor. Goering searched the pockets and found a leather key-container holding a dozen or more keys. His heart began to beat faster.

It would almost certainly be one of the smaller keys. The fourth key fit. Goering grinned, his blue eyes blazing. He unlocked the drawer and opened it. Technical files mainly having to do with aircraft production. A series of blueprints for the proposed new fighter, the ME 262. Why did Udet keep such top-secret stuff at home?

The second drawer was more interesting. It contained personal letters and photos. In one of the pictures a naked man sat on what appeared to be an ordinary kitchen chair. A woman with her back to the camera knelt between the man's legs. The man's eyes were closed, his right hand tangled in the woman's blond hair. Goering felt a quickening of prurient interest. He studied the man's face more closely. It was Milch, General Erhard Milch, Udet's rival as head of fighter production for the Luftwaffe. Interesting. He wondered how Ernst had obtained the photo. Quickly he extracted it from the file and thrust it into his pocket.

The third and bottom drawer contained what he was looking for. Photos and memorabilia of the first war. Shots of Udet along with half a dozen other flying officers of the Richthofen Squadron, among them a younger and slimmer Goering. Behind the photos a yellowed diary covering the years 1917–18. He leafed through it hurriedly. There it was! A complete and utterly damning record of Goering's service as the squadron's last commander. Carefully documented notes challenged the authenticity of almost all Goering's "kills." Udet had guessed that Goering was claiming for himself the unclaimed enemy aircraft credited to his squadron. He had hinted at the possession of such knowledge just often enough to keep Goering from firing him. And to think that he had been blackmailing Milch, too! Well, now the bastard was dead, and Goering had the book. He thrust it into his pocket, locked the file, and returned the key to Udet's trousers.

He opened the door to the living room. The woman

was sitting there still in her underclothes. At least she was no longer blubbering. What a pair she had!

He touched her shoulder. She looked up at him. "I don't understand it. I was out of the room for only a moment when I heard the shot. He always seemed so . . . happy-go-lucky."

"He was in trouble. Serious trouble. It was probably better this way."

"What will happen now?"

He could see her nipples through the filmy lace. "I'll take care of it. You are to mention it to no one."

"The police . . ."

"The police will not be called in. My own people will handle it."

"We were so in love," she said brokenly. "He wanted to marry me."

Goering thought of the photo in his pocket, this slut with Milch. He sat down beside her on the couch and put his arm around her shoulders. "You mustn't take it so hard."

"What must you think of me, Herr Reichmarshal?"

"I think you are very sweet."

His hand probed beneath the shoulder strap of the brassiere and suddenly possessed her breast.

"Oh, no," she said, "not with Ernst in there."

He released her, stood and unfastened his trousers and undershorts, and let them drop to his knees. His penis, lost in all that great pink expanse of flesh, seemed remarkably small, like that of a child.

She shook her head as he thrust himself toward her.

"Go on," he said. "Go on, you bitch."

❈   ❈   ❈

When he returned to his office the Reichmarshal dictated a memo:

> While testing a new weapon, the director of air armament Colonel General Udet suffered such a severe accident that he died of his injuries on the way to the hospital.
>
> The Fuehrer has ordained a state funeral for this officer, who has departed this world so tragically in fulfillment of his duty.

THIRTEEN

Major General Sir William Guthrie's widow lived in a house surrounded by rolling heath. The living room held a collection of souvenirs and photos which told the story of the General's service in different parts of the world, outposts of empire as far off as India, Burma, and Singapore. There were photographs of the general reviewing troops, playing polo, pigsticking, and with his stern face showing out of the open hatch of a tank.

As a child Peter Guthrie had hardly known his parents. For most of his boyhood he had been at school in England while his parents were stationed abroad. He had learned to accept his feeling of loneliness and isolation. On the rare occasions when he saw them, usually during holidays, they were strangers; his father an imposing martial figure who treated him with a sort of bluff heartiness and seemed to take for granted that Peter would go on to Sandhurst and a career in the army. Lady Guthrie, a vague, sparrow-like little woman, had lived in her husband's shadow and seldom expressed an opinion without consulting him first. She had gotten into the habit of referring to her husband formally. "The general says . . ."

The general had never openly expressed the disappointment he felt when Peter decided against a military career. Physics and schoolmastering seemed as strange a choice as poetry or playwrighting. But the general had soldiered on.

As the hero of Arras who had won a posthumous Victoria Cross, the general's name had been, for a short while, a household word in England. His tank action had delayed the German advance on Dunkirk. It had been almost the only aggressive action of those black days when the whole of the British and French forces was in retreat before the onrushing German armor. Guthrie's counterattack had served briefly to plug one small hole in the crumbling dike.

Now Lady Guthrie greeted Peter and Zofia. "Peter, how good of you to come."

"Mother, this is Captain Lesniowska."

"So good of you to come, Captain."

"Please, Lady Guthrie, Zofia."

"Of course, my dear. My husband, the general, used to say . . ." Her comment was drowned by the furious barking of an ancient spaniel awakened from its position by the hearth.

"That's Flush," Peter said.

"Blind, you know," shouted Lady Guthrie. "Mustn't mind her."

"I don't," Zofia said bending down to soothe the dog.

The barking subsided.

Lady Guthrie busied herself with the silver tea service. "Peter tells me your father is a military man."

"Yes," said Zofia. "Polish."

"Ah, Polish."

"General Sikorski," said Peter.

"Of course," said Lady Guthrie vaguely.

There was a momentary silence broken only by the snoring of the old dog and the slight rattle of the teacups as Lady Guthrie passed them with a tremulous hand.

"My husband, the general, once attended the Polish war games as an observer," Lady Guthrie said. "Did you know that, Peter?"

"No, I'm afraid I didn't."

"Perhaps you were away at school at the time."

"Quite likely."

"The general thought well of the Polish cavalry."

"We all did," said Zofia. "Until we discovered that a horse was no match for a tank. I'm afraid we were some thirty years too late in realizing it."

"Quite," said Lady Guthrie. "And what do you do, my dear? Are you associated with Peter in this curious committee of his?"

"No," said Zofia. "I'm associated with the women's corps of the Polish Army in Exile."

Lady Guthrie's eyes swam in vague astonishment. "I don't think I've ever heard of that. But then there are so many foreign groups these days, aren't there? Do you know I've never exactly understood what Peter does. Can you explain it to us, dear?"

"No," Guthrie said. "I'm afraid I can't."

"Yes, well," said Lady Guthrie without much interest, "everything is quite different these days, isn't it? Do you know I believe I have some photographs of the general taken while he was in Poland. You come and sit here by me, Zofia, while I search for them."

*   *   *

After tea with Lady Guthrie they walked hand in hand along the country lane. A flight of rooks darkened the otherwise peaceful sky.

"Poor Peter," Zofia said. "You must have been a troublesome little boy."

"Yes, I'm sure I was."

"Do you want to tell me about it, love?"

"Not particularly."

"This Battle of Arras. What happened?"

"Something on the order of the charge of the Light Brigade," Peter said in a faintly bitter voice.

"My childhood was quite different from yours. My father took me with him everywhere."

"The Polish way?"

Zofia laughed. "Yes, the Polish way. The general always used to say . . ."

Looking down at her smiling face, Guthrie felt love clutch suddenly at his heart. He said in a suddenly serious tone, "You mustn't ever leave me, Zofia."

"Ah, love, in these times who can say? It's not wise to get too attached."

"Wise be damned."

"I'll have to leave you for at least a little while very soon."

"What's up?"

"We're going to America to see Mr. Roosevelt."

Guthrie didn't speak, but the expression on his face reminded her of the childhood photos shown to her by Lady Guthrie. Once again he was the little boy at school whose parents were going off to India.

"It's only for the one meeting," she said. "We'll be back in a day or two."

"It's damned dangerous, flying the Atlantic."

"It's being done every day by delivery pilots," she answered lightly.

"They go by way of Dakar. Quite different. Better weather."

"You mustn't worry. It will be all right. In any case there's no choice. It's imperative to have an agreement with Mr. Roosevelt as soon as possible."

"What's it got to do with you? Can't your father go without you?"

"Do you think I'd ask him to do something I won't do myself?"

"He's not in love with an Englishman. At least I hope not."

Zofia laughed. "No, but he's in love with my mother."

"And if he were leading a tank charge? Would you want to go along with him on that as well?"

"The analogy is absurd, but the answer is yes."

"That's the trouble with war," Guthrie said. "There are too many bloody heroes."

The Lockheed Hudson, boring westward against headwinds, was already more than halfway across the Atlantic. Zofia, huddled in her sleeping bag for warmth, dozed fitfully, but sleep eluded her. She looked across at her father. Using his black attaché case as a desk the general had been engaged for the past two hours in rewriting the draft of the agreement he planned to present to President Roosevelt. The small twin-engine bomber, flying low to avoid the jet stream, was tossed like a leaf by sudden updrafts. Zofia struggled to control her feeling of nausea.

Sikorski frowned in concentration. The meeting

with Roosevelt would be vital to his effort to restore a united Poland after the war. It was necessary to have a commitment in writing from the American President. The draft must be worded precisely and yet at the same time in terms that would not antagonize the Americans. Sikorski had already discussed the matter in London with the President's assistant, Harry Hopkins, and they had agreed in principle.

The bomber lurched again. Group Captain Klimenki, the general's aide, stirred in his sleeping bag. The vibration of the twin engines was merciless. How, Zofia wondered, could anyone sleep under these conditions? Yet Klimenki managed. Perhaps he had fortified himself with whiskey before the takeoff from Scotland. She had the impression that he was growing increasingly fond of the stuff.

It might ease the feeling of airsickness to move about. She unzipped the bag and went to stand in the cockpit behind the pilot's shoulder. Through the Perspex window she could see clouds penetrated now and then by flashes of moonlight. The pilot turned his head to look at her, grinned, and gave her a thumbs-up signal. Zofia's answering smile was weak. She felt rotten.

As she returned to the main cabin she saw that Captain Klimenki had left his sleeping bag and was talking to her father. Klimenki's lean face with its bright blue eyes and military moustache seemed agitated. He was gesticulating vehemently toward his sleeping bag. In one hand he held what Zofia thought at first must be some sort of oversized cigarette lighter.

Sikorski's face was grave. He had put down his attaché case and had taken the object from Klimenki's hand. Zofia moved toward them. She could see now

what her father held. It was a small black box about
five inches long and perhaps an inch and a half wide
bound with adhesive tape.

Leaning close to Klimenki and shouting above the
roar of the engines Zofia asked, "What is it?"

"Incendiary bomb."

Startled, she said, "Where did you find it?"

"Hidden under my sleeping bag. Don't worry, it's
safe now. We've disarmed it." He showed her the
wooden safety pin held down by the adhesive.

"There may be others," said Sikorski. "We had
better search the plane. Zofia, you go forward to alert
the pilot."

Zofia felt a moment of panic. Her last conversation
with Peter Guthrie flashed through her mind. He had
begged her not to go, pointing out how dangerous
such a flight might be.

She missed Peter. This sudden proximity to death
made her realize just how much.

Klimenki had already begun shifting various pieces
of heavy equipment in his search. Sikorski was un-
locking their luggage. Hopeless, thought Zofia, a box
five inches long could be hidden anywhere. Ah, Peter
my love, if I get out of this I will stick to you like
glue. Even during the Blitz she had felt comparatively
safe simply by virtue of being in the same city. Out
here over the icy Atlantic she felt as if she had fallen
off the edge of the world. If they went down it would
be without a trace, as if they had never existed.

The search of the aircraft produced nothing. Sikorski, who had been a soldier for most of his life and
was fatalistic about such matters, shrugged and said,
"We've done what we can. It's impossible to search

the entire aircraft while we're in the air. After we land we'll have it gone over thoroughly."

Zofia looked at the ominous little black box with its taped trigger and felt again a shiver of fear. "Can't we throw that thing out?"

Sikorski shook his head. "The Americans will want to examine it for evidence. Klimenki seems to think it's a standard RAF incendiary used to destroy grounded planes. In any case it's perfectly safe now. If there were any others we would probably have known it by now." He smiled at her. "I for one intend to get some rest. We'll only have an hour or two to spruce up before going on to the White House." He closed his eyes and in a moment was asleep.

For the remainder of the flight Zofia sat rigidly awake.

Despite his useless legs which made the wheelchair necessary, Franklin Roosevelt radiated energy and charm. He mixed martinis for them, and Zofia found herself giddy as a result of an almost lethal mixture of iced gin and vermouth. Harry Hopkins, the President's aide, was there, as well as FDR's secretary, Missy LeHand. The President apologized for the absence of Mrs. Roosevelt, explaining that she was away on one of her many trips. Missy kept her gaze riveted on the president's face while he talked. An aura of warmth flashed between them. It was at once obvious to Zofia that Roosevelt and Missy LeHand were lovers. She felt curiously shocked. Yet why should not this powerful, charismatic man have a mistress? Harry Hopkins, obviously cognizant of the relationship, treated Missy with deference.

Sikorski had produced the draft of the agreement and Roosevelt was studying it. At that moment Hopkins was called to the phone. He listened carefully, now and then asking a few low-voiced questions. When he replaced the receiver, he caught Zofia's eye and made a small gesture with his head to indicate that he wished her to step into the next room.

"Captain Lesniowska," he said when the door had closed behind them. "That was Mr. Hoover of the FBI. His people have searched your plane very thoroughly and could find nothing else of an alarming nature. The incendiary device was, as you suspected, standard RAF and might have been obtained at almost any RAF military depot. They don't offer much hope for clues in that direction. They have, however, questioned Group Captain Klimenki very carefully since he was the one who found the bomb, and they are not happy with his answers."

"I don't understand," Zofia said. "What could Klimenki have had to do with it?"

"Klimenki has confessed that he planted the bomb himself."

"But that's impossible!"

"Mr. Hoover is sure of his facts. Klimenki has signed a confession. He says he never intended any harm but wanted to show how easy it would have been for one of your father's enemies to attack him."

"What happens now, Mr. Hopkins?"

"That's entirely up to you and your father, Captain. I have advised Mr. Hoover to hold Klimenki but to take no further action until he hears directly from this office."

"Mr. Roosevelt is studying my father's proposal. I

don't think this would be a good time to interrupt. Must the President know about this?"

Hopkins gave her a tired smile. "The Boss always knows about everything in the end, but I see no reason to bother him with it now."

Zofia felt a sense of relief. If Roosevelt knew that her father was surrounded by enemies he might no longer regard him as the legitimate spokesman of the Polish government in exile. Roosevelt was a consummate politician; he would not wish to offend the millions of Polish voters in the United States. It would be best if Klimenki were removed as inconspicuously as possible and returned to England to be questioned by Sikorski's own security people.

"Where is he now?" she asked.

"Still at the airport."

"Would Mr. Hoover agree to hold him there and then return him to England with us?"

"I see no reason why not. Klimenki's action was certainly ill advised, but as yet he has committed no real crime. Conceivably an investigation of this sort could result in political repercussions." Hopkins again permitted himself the ghost of a smile. "I feel sure that Mr. Hoover would welcome the opportunity to have the investigation take place elsewhere."

As they returned to the Oval Office, Roosevelt was apparently telling a joke. His eyes sparkled with glee. Missy LeHand was laughing. Even General Sikorski was smiling. Looking at her father's face Zofia felt sure that the American President must have signed the agreement.

On the return flight Klimenki kept to himself. Normally an affable, easygoing man, he sat in stony silence. No attempt had been made to restrain him, but it was almost as if he had created bonds of his own. Zofia felt a touch of sympathy for the ordinarily dapper but now haggard-looking group captain. General Sikorski, ebullient after the successful conclusion of his meeting with Roosevelt, chose to ignore the incident, saying only that Klimenki would be subjected to a full interrogation.

As the Lockheed slowed to a halt on the ground at Edinburgh airport, Klimenki suddenly leaped to his feet and dropped down through the bomb bay. Zofia saw him running across the tarmac toward an opening in the wire fence. The gate was unlocked. Klimenki struggled with it for a moment and then swung it open. At that moment a bright red van started up from behind the hangar and swung at high speed toward the gate. Klimenki, with his back to the speeding vehicle, turned in alarm, but it was too late. Zofia saw the expression of panic on his face just before he was struck. He was hurled upward and thrown into the wire. The van swerved on two wheels, then righted itself and sped away.

Klimenki was dead when they reached him. No one had gotten the license number of the truck, and it had borne no identifying insignia. The Scottish police were unable to determine if the killing of Klimenki had been intentional.

Sikorski, clutching his attaché case, stood by with compressed lips and answered the inspector's questions in monosyllables.

Peter drew the blackout curtains and switched on the light. He saw that Zofia's eyes were filled with tears.

"What is it?"

"It's just that I keep remembering his face."

"Klimenki?"

"Yes. His face when he walked away from us. As if he knew."

"It could have been an accident, Zofia. Vehicles do go out of control."

"And then speed away without stopping?"

"Yes."

"You may be right."

He put his arms around her and she sobbed against his shoulder. "I knew his wife and children in Warsaw," she said. "He was a vain man and sometimes foolish, but I don't think he was a traitor. Now we'll never know. Oh, Peter, I'm so tired."

"Come and lie down."

He led her to the bed, and she lay face down clutching the pillow. He began to stroke her back and shoulders. The sobbing ended and she lay still. He moved his hands gently and carefully in softly repeated gestures.

"You're good to me, Peter."

"I love you. It's very simple, really."

"Is it? Is anything simple anymore?" She turned to face him, her dark eyes probing his. Guthrie continued to stroke her hair and brow and cheeks. He could feel her rigidity and tension beginning to drain.

"Yes," he said, "it couldn't be simpler. You're staying with me. You're not going away anymore."

She shook her head. "That isn't possible, love."

"We'll make it possible," he said still using his hands to soothe her.

She managed a sigh and the hint of a smile. "Isn't it nice to think so?"

"You'll see."

He unbuttoned her blouse and pushed it off one shoulder and bent down to kiss her breast. He felt the nipple stiffen. She pushed his head away.

"It isn't right," she said.

"Why not?"

"Klimenki . . ."

"Is gone. We are still very much alive."

She put her lips against his and let her tongue probe his mouth.

Guthrie began to undress her.

"You're a devil," she whispered.

The weariness of the long flight had begun to melt away. She moaned with pleasure as she felt his hard masculinity enter her body. There was no sound but his breath close to her ear. The heartbeat of the great city was still.

FOURTEEN

The old man did not come back to the barn that night, nor the next. Larsen obtained water by breaking icicles and sucking them, but he had been without food for more than thirty-six hours. Had the Germans caught Skinner, or had he gone off on a binge? Either way, he could not wait any longer. His shoulder was badly swollen and red streaks were beginning to appear along the underside of his arm. He remembered the story Skinner had told him about the man who had cut off his own toes.

By dawn of the third day he knew he must leave. It was a clear, cold morning, almost painfully bright. The sun sparkled off the snow. In the distance something moved, perhaps a German truck or one of the wood-burning autos used by a few Norwegians. Larsen made no attempt to conceal himself. It no longer mattered if he was caught; without medical attention he would die anyway.

The car, or whatever it had been, was gone. The landscape was empty. Larsen moved slowly along a road that seemed to lead nowhere, raising his good arm now and then to shield his eyes from the glare. How far was it to Kongsberg? The need to sleep was almost overpowering. Only the pain kept him mov-

ing. But why bother? He still had the cyanide cap-
sules. One bite and all this would be over. Surely
the momentary agony would be no worse than what
he was already experiencing.

He walked on. He had the impression that ice was
forming in his veins, moving upward inch by inch.
When it reached his heart he would die.

There seemed to be a mist in the air. Was it growing dark already? How many hours had he been on
the road? The light, which had been so dazzling for
so long, was fading. He rubbed his mittened hand
across his eyes. That helped momentarily. The bright
light flared up once more. He felt as though his eyes
were being scorched. He was suddenly aware of what
was happening to him. The retinas were being affected
by the glare. He was going blind.

He had the curious impression that he was no
longer alone. Hundreds of others marched with him,
all of them crippled and blinded like himself, marching on bare feet with legs like frozen sticks. He called
out to them, but they passed him by. Was he still on
the road or had he wandered off into the mountains?

Helberg was there making a joke of it: "Don't worry,
Jens, we'll get you a tin cup and dark glasses. You
can beg for pennies. Or one of those newspaper kiosks
run by the blind. Hell, they make a damned good
living most of them, better than you and I."

But Helberg was dead, along with Torsten. They
were all dead, all the commandos. Perhaps he, too,
was dead. He could remember falling into the gorge.
How had he gotten out of it?

Was it snowing again? There was something soft
and wet against his face. He licked his lips, sucking
in the moisture. He was no longer conscious of pain.

He supposed he was past all that. He felt warm. In a moment he would be asleep, beyond pain and cold.

He forced himself back to his feet. The other marchers, stumbling on their ruined limbs, were calling to him. He hurried after them. Was it night or day?

Michelle was early for her interview at SOE Headquarters, F Section. The building at No. 64 Baker Street was not overly impressive, a five-story structure with a dark, narrow hall off which could be seen the briefing and map rooms. People were passing through the main doorway, but none of them spoke. Was that a deliberate policy? Secret agents, she realized, were trained never to recognize each other in public.

She entered a wobbly lift which climbed slowly to the top floor. She opened the door to a sparsely furnished office and was told by an unsmiling lieutenant to wait.

She glanced now and then at her watch. It seemed she had been there for hours. Possibly they were observing her through a secret peephole. She took out a cigarette and lit it, doing her best to appear unconcerned. When she could bear it no longer, she left her chair and went to the window to look down into the street. How had Richardson put it? "French Section lives somewhere between heaven and Marks and Spencer."

Marks and Spencer, at least, was clearly visible.

She was interviewed by a psychiatrist, a diminutive, damp-handed man who continually popped sweets into his mouth. He offered her his definition of the ideal agents: "Men who plunge headlong into an undertaking of fast change and danger because they are discontented. They want to give worth and meaning to their otherwise futile lives."

Rubbish, thought Michelle.

"If we were not at war such men might very well be committed to institutions for the insane," the psychiatrist went on in his languid, high-pitched voice. "D'you see what I mean?"

"No, I'm afraid I don't."

"The formula, like any other dealing with so complex a matter as the human personality, is not one hundred percent true. There is, in fact, nothing really wrong with what might be considered a love of productive peril. It has been the motivating force for most great adventurers and explorers. Some of our best agents are those who in peacetime make good bankers, physicians, or creative artists. Their response to danger is positive. The good agent is one who chooses action over inaction, who learns to control his impulses and detach himself from a temporary reality in order to resume abstract thought. Do you see yourself fitting that formula?"

"I don't see myself fitting any particular formula," Michelle answered coolly. The moon-faced psychiatrist gulped another sweet. What neurotic compulsion, she wondered, drives him to such an excess of calories? Hardly reassuring. He might at least offer them around. She felt a desire to giggle. Nerves. Managed to turn the giggle into a simulated cough.

"Then what would you say was your motivation in wanting to join this branch of service?"

"I think that because of my European experience, I am suited for it."

"Nothing stronger?"

"The Germans must be defeated. I would like to contribute toward that end."

"The work you are doing now? You find it unsatisfactory?"

"Would you say that reading fairy stories to children was a vital part of the war effort?"

He laced his small white hands together and placed them over the bridge of his nose. "It might be considered so. After all, life must go on, war or no war, and the welfare of children is always a prime consideration."

"Welfare, yes. Entertainment, no."

"You could volunteer for work in a hospital."

"Carrying bedpans may be a necessary task," Michelle said, "but it is not my idea of the way to defeat the Germans."

"Do you think you could kill a man with your bare hands?"

"I have never tried." The man was a pompous ass. At this rate they would never take her.

"If you are accepted, you will be taught to do so. With your bare hands—or perhaps by inserting an ordinary needle into the back of his neck. In addition you will be given a supply of L pills. Do you know what they are?"

She shook her head.

The L pill, he explained, could be carried in the mouth. The capsule's skin was insoluble. If the pill was swallowed accidentally, it could be passed through the body without causing any harm, but if it was crushed between the teeth, the potassium cyanide would bring immediate death. Did she think she could manage that?

"It's a little like asking me how I would behave if I were drowning," Michelle answered. "How can I say?"

The psychiatrist nodded. "Certain agents have been forced to carry important objects in intimate parts of their bodies. With practice and regular exercise of the vaginal muscles a woman can learn to carry objects of considerable size. Naturally, the enemy understands such procedures, and if you are brought under even the slightest suspicion you may be searched in that area of your body by any German soldier or policeman. Could you submit to that?"

"Would I have a choice?"

"The L pill."

"I do not think I am suicidally inclined."

"So you would take your chances?"

"In war, everyone takes chances."

"But not everyone is turned over to the Gestapo, as you would be if you were caught."

"In that case, I would use the pill."

"You are Jewish?"

"Yes."

"That might make things even worse for you if you were caught."

She shrugged.

The doctor took his elbows off the desk and leaned back in his chair. Michelle did not think he was very good at his job and she felt sorry for him.

"Can you sum up for me in a single sentence your real reason for applying for this work?" he said.

"My mother died in a German concentration camp."

"You will be informed," the doctor said.

* * *

Larsen heard a dog barking. Where there was a
dog, there might be a house. For a moment the veil
seemed to lift, and he saw the outline of a structure.
He started toward it, but after a dozen yards the fog
closed in once more. Larsen groped with his hands
in front of him. He slipped and fell. After a while he
picked himself up again and staggered on. He had an
important message to deliver. What was it? He could
not remember. Christ, to have come all this way and
not be able to remember. Tears started from his
nearly sightless eyes and froze on his cheeks. He remembered now; the message had to do with Vemork.
The plant had been blown up, and he must inform
London.

Again the dog barked. The sound was ahead. His
outstretched hands encountered the corner of a building, then something that felt like a door, then a latch.
The door opened. He fell forward onto a hard, dry
floor.

Sigrid Berg was having dinner with her two small
sons when the awful-looking thing that had been a
man stumbled into the room and collapsed at their
feet. Outside the dog was barking furiously. The
children backed away in alarm, as Sigrid attempted to
shield them with her body. She thought of reaching
for the shotgun that hung on two pegs driven into the
wall, but after another look at the wretched figure
that sprawled before her, she knew there was no
danger.

The two little boys who clung to her skirts were
silent. She was proud of them. They had in them the

blood of their father, Johan, who had gone off to fight the Germans and had never returned. Johan, too, would have been proud of his sons.

She fetched the lamp from the table and bent closer to the man on the floor. From the way the cracked lips were drawn back, she thought at first he might be dead, but then she detected shallow breathing. His face, what she could see of it behind the ice-laden beard, had a corpselike pallor. His clothing was covered with dirt, and the shoulder of his uniform blouse was caked with dried blood. His hands looked bloated and discolored, and from the condition of his boots, she felt sure his feet must be frozen.

"Johan," she said to the older boy, "fetch a towel quickly and fill a basin with hot water from the stove. Amandus, you go out and quiet the dog. Take him a biscuit." The younger child let go of her skirts. She selected a knife from the rack above the sink and began to cut away the man's boots. His feet were dead white.

The uniform blouse puzzled her. She had thought first that he must be German or one of the Quisling people in Norwegian uniform. But this was unlike any uniform she had ever seen, and as she thought about it she began to realize who he must be. Even in her isolation she had heard about the commando raid on the hydro plant. There had been a sudden flurry of German activity on the road—staff cars and half-tracks carrying heavily armed troops. A corporal and two men had searched her house, tramping mud and snow across the floor. The two boys had stood in the corner scowling. The corporal had offered Amandus a square of chocolate, but the boy had declined with a shake of his head.

The corporal had looked at her, at her strong, full-breasted body.

"You're a good-looking woman."

She had shrugged.

"Where is your man?"

"Dead."

"From what?"

"From killing Germans."

"You need a man."

He had reached out and squeezed her breast. She looked down at his hand, but did not move. Her eyes had been like those of the boys, glacial. After a while the German had felt foolish and had taken his hand away. He had said something to the other two, and then all three had laughed, but the laughter lacked conviction.

"Why don't you send the kids out to play?"

She had remained dumb, motionless. It had been a dangerous moment, but she had not sensed any real purpose in the German. He had a weak face and watery eyes. He was showing off in front of the others like a schoolboy. At last they had gone away.

Now she worked steadily, cutting away the ruined blouse and the wool shirt. When she saw the man's shoulder, she drew in her breath with a hiss. She turned to the boy who was standing there with a basin of hot water.

"Johan, this man is a friend. He has come here to fight the Germans but he has been badly hurt. We will try to keep him from dying, and later you will go for Dr. Karlsen. But no one except the doctor must ever know he has been here. You know what the Germans would do to us if they found out?"

"Yes."

"And you must explain it to Amandus."

Johan nodded.

"Now help me and we will get him into the bed."

The man was surprisingly light. She took the shoulders, and the boy took the feet; they lifted him gently onto the bed. She opened the pinewood chest that held her husband's clothes and drew out a flannel nightshirt and pulled it on over the man's skinny frame. The nightshirt was far too big. He looked, she thought, like a child in it. A bearded, ancient, half-dead child.

Michelle's second interview took place in a room in the Hotel Victoria on Northumberland Avenue. It was in a dreary working-class section of London, and her heart sank as she entered the dingy old building. The man who interviewed her wore the uniform of an army captain, but did not introduce himself. He had a long, lantern-jawed face like that of a horse. An intelligent, if slightly sardonic, horse. He had horse's teeth, too: large, square, and yellow. But his eyes were kind.

His questions were general, but he referred several times to what might happen if she were captured. When she was asked how she felt about that, she answered frankly: "It terrifies me."

"You realize, of course, that you will not have even the protection of a uniform. However, you will hold an honorary commission from the RAF. It is hoped the Germans will honor the Geneva Convention regarding captured prisoners of war."

"If they do," said Michelle, "I should think it might be the first time."

"Your hatred of the Germans . . ."

She interrupted. "Don't you think it natural that I should hate them?"

"Natural, yes, but hatred is not necessarily the best emotion for this kind of work."

Michelle's large brown eyes shone with candor. "Why else would anyone want to do it?"

"Adventure, perhaps. Excitement."

She stood up. The horse face watched her. "I think I'm wasting your time, Captain. If you suppose that I regard this as some sort of game . . ."

He smiled and said, "Sit down, Miss Stern. Please."

She reached into her purse for a cigarette. "Do you mind if I smoke?"

"Not at all. Can you report to Bletchley Park tomorrow morning for the first phase of your training?"

With the match in midair, she answered, "Oh, yes!"

FIFTEEN

Larsen opened his eyes to see a bearded face bending over him.

"That hurts," said the man with the beard. "I know. I could give you a shot to kill the pain, but in your weakened condition, I don't think it would be advisable. Can you stand it?"

"This is Dr. Karlsen," said the woman's voice.

It was coming back to him now, the blindness, the snow, the cold, his wound.

He nodded.

"There is some debris in the wound. We must clean it before it is bandaged."

Larsen groaned.

"There," said the doctor. "Done. Beautiful."

Larsen was aware of sweat stinging his eyes. The woman leaned over him with a towel to mop his brow. She said in a soft voice, "It's all right. It will soon be over."

He had felt so much pain in the past few days that a little more did not seem to matter. He attempted a smile which came off as a teeth-bearing grimace.

The woman bent lower. "What is it?"

"I can see."

"Of course," said the doctor. "Snow blindness is only temporary."

The pain went on and then the doctor straightened and said, "That should do it. A clean wound but lucky we caught it in time. Do you have some brandy in the house, Sigrid?"

"Is he strong enough for that?"

"I was thinking more of the doctor than of the patient. A little brandy won't hurt either of us."

She brought the bottle and poured it out into tiny silver cups hardly larger than thimbles.

"He must on no account be moved for a few weeks," Karlsen said.

"And what if the Germans come?"

"You have risked so much already, it is a further risk to be taken. I leave it to you to invent a good story. Perhaps a long-lost brother."

"Without papers?"

"It is possible that something can be arranged. I will be returning in a day or two to inspect the patient, and I may have news for you then. Meanwhile the excitement seems to be dying down. Well, young man, whatever your name is, do you think you can manage here for a bit until your feet are in better shape? By the way, you may yet lose a couple of toes. Now, go to sleep while I examine my other patient, little Amandus."

"But he's perfectly well," said Sigrid.

"Of course. And with God's help may he stay that way. But if the Germans question me, I want to be able to tell them the truth. The truth is always more palatable. I came here to examine the child. Come, Amandus!"

The little boy approached cautiously. The doctor looked into his eyes. "Put out your tongue."

The child obeyed.

Karlsen took a piece of hard candy out of his pocket. "That's medicine, Amandus. Suck on it thoroughly before swallowing. I will leave a little more with your mother, and you are to take another in half an hour. And you, too, Johan."

Amandus took the candy and gravely put it into his mouth. The doctor closed his kit and picked up his heavy overcoat. "I will be back in two days, Sigrid. Meanwhile you are to continue the treatment of our friend here. That dressing on the shoulder will need to be changed tomorrow. Can you manage?"

"Of course."

"And the pills every two hours. Understood?"

"Yes."

When he had gone Sigrid returned to Larsen. His eyes were closed. The hollow cheeks etched with their lines of pain were covered with a scraggly beard. She opened the chest where her husband's things were kept and took out an old-fashioned straight razor and the wooden bowl of shaving soap. With warm water from the stove she worked up a lather and applied it to Larsen's cheeks. He mumbled something but did not open his eyes. She shaved him carefully. When she had finished, she was amazed to see how young he looked.

Two hours later she woke him to give him the medicine. After the pills she gave him a bowl of steaming potato soup.

"I've got to get out of here," he said.

"Certainly. Why not? What do you expect to use for wings? You surely can't walk."

"I'm endangering you and your children." His voice was weak, cracked.

"It is the Germans who are endangering us. Not you."

"They're looking for me."

"Of course. I know all about that, what you did at Vemork."

"There's an old man at Rjukan. His name is Einar Skinner. If you could get word to him. He has a horse and wagon."

She shook her head. "Not anymore. The Germans shot him."

Larsen groaned. "Poor old fellow. What happened? Was it because of me?"

She shook her head. "It had nothing to do with you. I heard about it from Pastor Lindstrom who was there. Old Skinner was drunk as usual—it was last Sunday. He pulled up in front of the church in his bread cart. There were a dozen or more Germans standing there looking at the girls going into church. They were making remarks and Skinner got into an argument with them. No one knows exactly what was said—it does not really matter. He was a poor old drunk man with a loose mouth—anyhow, one of the Germans shot Skinner's horse. Pastor Lindstrom along with several others came rushing out of the church, but it was too late. Skinner had reached into the back of the wagon and picked up a heavy timber he kept there and hit the German over the head. The other Germans seized him and took him into the school grounds and put him up against the wall and shot him. They say that before Skinner died, he used language such as has never been heard before near the church or in the school yard. So you see," she said, "it had nothing at all to do with you, and you must not feel any guilt. It happened. If it had not been that time, it would have been another. You are no more to blame for it than were the girls going into the church. Now you must try to sleep."

"Yes."

"I'll have to wake you in two hours to give you another pill."

"All right."

"We must get you well so that you can leave."

He did not answer. As she looked down at the sleeping face, she wondered why she was treating him like a child. They were probably the same age.

Sigrid Berg spent a restless night. She had to get up every two hours to give Larsen his pill. But there was more to it than that. The decision to save him had been given without reservation and, she now had to admit, without much thought. She had acted instinctively. But had she the right to endanger her children?

Like most Norwegians she had been taken by surprise by the quick German occupation of her country. It was ironic that Quisling, whose name would become an international synonym for treachery, should have been a Norwegian, while in fact so many of his countrymen had been fighting bravely against the overwhelming power of the Wehrmacht. The Norwegians were scattered so thinly (there were only three million of them) over such rugged country that many of them did not even know about the German invasion until it was over. Sigrid and Johan Berg had heard about the occupation of Oslo three days after it happened, and then the news was brought to them by a postman riding a bicycle.

Johan had reported at once to his army unit and had been sent into the bitter fighting around Narvik. He never returned. It was still possible that he was a prisoner of war somewhere inside Germany. Sigrid no longer allowed herself to hope for very much. As the German occupation grew more brutal, as more Norwegian hostages were seized and killed, it became less likely that he might still be alive.

The responsibility for raising the family was now on her shoulders. She had accepted the risk of sheltering Larsen because that was what Johan would have done. What she owed Johan's memory seemed clear. Both she and the children would have to take their chances.

Sigrid Berg did not know exactly what Larsen had been up to at Vemork. No one had explained to her the significance of the heavy-water production at the hydroelectric plant; if they had, she would not have understood. What mattered was that it had been a blow against the Germans. They had reacted sharply; therefore the blow must have been painful. Now, in her own small way, she would strike another blow.

In the cold light of dawn she felt Larsen's forehead. He seemed cooler. He opened his eyes and smiled up at her, and she could see at once that he was better. She gave him another pill and a cup of hot tea.

"I must leave here," he said.

"Impossible."

"If the Germans find me you know what will happen. When this is over, Norway will need her strong sons. She will need Johan and Amandus. And their mother, too."

"And what about Jens Larsen? Will Norway have no need for him?"

He shook his head. "I came here as a soldier. Soldiers take their chances."

"All right. We will do as you say. I will put you out in the snow and what then? How long will you last? You are too weak even to walk across this room. Stop talking nonsense."

"You're a bossy woman, Sigrid Berg. Perhaps there is someplace you can hide me."

"I could hang you on a nail like an old suit of clothes. That's what you look like."

"Perhaps a cellar."

She shook her head. "The first place they would look. You might as well stay up here and be comfortable." Then: "There is a place . . ."

"Where?"

"Perhaps a mile or two from here. In the forest. An old woodcutter's shack. Invisible from the road. No one who does not know about it would go looking for it. But you would freeze to death."

He shook his head. "Can you take me?"

"We could use the children's sleigh. Perhaps tomorrow. You will be a little stronger then."

"Today," he said firmly. "And what about tracks? The Germans will see your tracks in the snow."

"If they ask, we can say we were woodcutting in the forest and used the sleigh to haul logs."

"Good. And it would be better if the children did not know. It is too great a responsibility for them."

"All right," she said. "After they have gone to school. Go back to sleep now."

When the boys had left she got out the sleigh and half dragged him onto it, wrapping him carefully in an old blanket, then covering him over with a heavy canvas. It was snowing again, and the visibility was poor. In such weather the Germans preferred the warmth of their barracks; it was unlikely that they would be out searching the roads.

Tugging the sleigh behind her, she walked into the forest. There was no wind and it was eerily quiet. The runners sank into the snow. It was slow going. She stopped once and opened the canvas shroud and looked down at Larsen. His face was flushed and she thought the fever might have returned. When she reached the hut, she would give him another pill. The problem would be keeping him warm. There was an old iron stove in the hut, but even a wisp of smoke coming out of the woods would give him away. She would have to go back and forth as little as possible. Her excuse, if anyone asked, would be that she was fetching wood. Fortunately the woodshed was nearly empty. She might even be able to risk a small fire in the logcutter's cabin at night.

The problem would be Johan and Amandus. She could not bring herself to lie to them. Their father had drilled that into her. If you lie to a child, he had said, he will know it and will never again have complete faith in you. They would have to be told.

Having come to that conclusion, she experienced a sense of relief. The boys would be told the truth, and they would learn to keep a secret. Young as they were they must learn, and brutal as the Germans were she did not think they had yet got around to torturing children. At least not without some reason. At all costs she must avoid giving them that reason. So far

only Dr. Karlsen and the boys knew of Larsen's
presence. When he was well enough, he would try
to make his way to Sweden. She had no idea how.
Perhaps Karlsen would come up with something.

SIXTEEN

The locked door, kicked from its hinges, burst inward. Michelle, her heart thudding, sat up in bed. A powerful flashlight blinded her eyes. German voices were shouting orders and imprecations. A hand seized her naked shoulder and dragged her out of bed. She fell to the floor. A cold hand fumbled at her breasts. Another was thrust between her legs. Desperately she tried to cover herself. A voice in German shouted orders and the hands left her body. The flashlight was switched off, and the overhead light was turned on. There were three men in the room, beefy men wearing long leather coats and soft-brimmed felt hats. Through the snarls and curses being hurled at her, she heard over and over again the dread word *Gestapo*. Her heart seemed to freeze in her breast.

But how was it possible? She was still in England at the training center. She was sure of that. Had the Germans invaded?

"Your name?" a heavily accented voice said in English. "Come on, bitch! Stinking Jewish whore. Speak up!"

"Michelle . . ." she began.

"Ah, Christ," said an English voice, this time without the German accent.

Another voice said, "Here, luv. Better cover up." A blanket was placed over her naked shoulders and she huddled under it.

The three men left the room. The wrecked door still sagged from its hinges. A British officer in a captain's uniform came in without knocking and sat down on the bed. His long horse face was familiar; it was Captain Moore, who had been one of the first to interview her. Her blurred mind was beginning to cope with what had happened. This was one of the tests she had been warned about. She knew she had failed. In her terror she had given her real name instead of the code name that had been agreed upon.

Captain Moore said, "Sorry, Michelle. Perhaps they were a bit rougher than necessary, but of course it wasn't a patch on the real thing."

She got up off the floor and sat down on the small white chair that was, apart from the bed, the room's only furniture. Her hands were still shaking.

"Cigarette?" Moore said.

She nodded.

He took a cigarette out of a leather case, lit it, and handed it to her.

Moore said, "We gave you a sleeping pill. It was in the coffee you had before you went to bed. Had to make sure you were sound asleep, otherwise the test would have been meaningless."

"Yes." Even to her own ears her voice sounded cracked and thin. God, but she had been frightened.

"Well, now, what do you think?"

"What do you mean?"

"Still want to go through with it?"

"Do you mean do I still want to go to France?"

"Yes."

Her voice was stronger. "Yes, I do."

Moore smiled. "I was sure you'd say that, but all the same I want you to think it over. No one can blame you for being frightened. I'd be frightened myself if three gorillas broke down the door in the middle of the night and roughed me up. But this is just to give you an idea of what might happen. And you're still not really committed. You've had your radio operator's training, but you still haven't been trusted with any classified information. If you were to back out now, you would not be a security risk. There would be no harm done. Think about it, Michelle. Take tomorrow off. Go for a walk in the park. Go home, if you like. Just remember that you're not in a position to talk to anyone about anything that has happened here. But I urge you to think it over most carefully. Once you take the next step, which will involve operations relating to an actual network and real code names, it will be very difficult to release you. If you no longer cared to proceed after that, you might even be held in custody. Is that quite clear?"

"Yes, I understand."

"Good girl." He stood up. "Try to get some sleep now. Want another pill?"

She shook her head.

"All right, Odette." Odette Renie was the name they had given her, the name she had forgotten. Moore said, "Don't worry about all this. The easy part comes next, the parachute training."

The flat at Orchard Court was very pleasant. From the garden sunlight flooded the French windows. Colonel Brothers was lucky to have found the place. He was lucky, too, to have found Bates, the almost perfect Jeeves.

"Commander Richardson is here, sir," Bates announced.

"Give me ten minutes and then show him in."

"Yes, sir."

The colonel sat back in his chair to reflect on the problems surrounding Prosper, the largest operation the Section had ever attempted. Its main function was to organize the French Resistance. It was hoped that Resistance forces emerging from their hideouts behind the German lines and in Vichy could provide a powerful thrust against the German rear. But first the *résistants* must be armed. For that purpose tons of weapons and thousands of rounds of ammunition were being secretly dropped at night in predesignated collection areas. The trouble was they were not dealing with an organized group. SOE had been willing to recruit anyone who was prepared to kill Germans, and they had come up with a ragged underground army consisting of capitalists, communists, princes, clergymen, artisans, factory workers, housewives—almost anyone who could fire a pistol or lay explosives.

The Prosper network was growing at a fantastic rate. It stretched from the old battlefields around Sedan, through Paris, and all the way down to the Loire valley. At what point did a clandestine organization become an army?

The RAF was flooding the French countryside with drops for Prosper. In one month alone they had dropped 240 weapons containers, each container holding 6 Bren light machine guns with 1,000 rounds per gun, 36 rifles with 150 rounds, 27 Stens with 300 rounds per gun, 5 pistols with 50 rounds each, 52 grenades, 156 field dressings and 6,600 rounds of 9-mm parabellum and 3,168 rounds of '303 rifle ammunition.

The communications centers operating under the code names "Physician," "Donkeyman," "Bricklayer," "Chestnut," "Butler," "Satirist," "Cinema," "Orator," "Surveyor" and "Priest" were calling for expanding facilities from which they could handle intelligence, action, finance and medical problems. Prosper was already employing ten thousand people in its clandestine forces. More were being recruited every day.

It was all too big and unwieldy. Prosper, like some mythical snake, was beginning to consume its own tail.

Bates had the door open.

"Come in, Richardson. Sit down," the colonel said. "That will be all, Bates."

"Yes, sir."

"Well, how have you been, Richardson?"

"Well enough, sir."

"How are the new pianists doing?" The Colonel glanced at a slip of paper on his desk. "Yolande Beekman, Cecily Lefort and Michelle Stern."

"Lefort and Beekman are first rate. Absolutely solid."

"And Stern?"

"Her French is impeccable. She has the motivation."

"Well, then?"

"She's terrified of the Germans."

"Aren't we all?"

"I'm told they played a bit rough with her in a training exercise. She didn't do too well. Frightened out of her wits. She had been given the usual sleeping pill in advance, and that may have blurred her mind, so it's hard to say if it was a fair test or not. Being Jewish, she may be more sensitive than the others to the possibility of falling into German hands. Betty Chadwick, the case mother, seems to think Stern will pull herself together once she's in the field."

"And what do you say?"

Richardson shrugged. "With Prosper growing at such an extraordinary rate, signal transmission is our biggest headache. Everyone knows the pianists are in an exposed position. Not too many people are knocking on the door begging to be let in."

The colonel rubbed his pipe against the side of his nose and then studied the shiny briar. "For the moment we'll let her continue," he said.

When Richardson had gone, the colonel took out a file marked "Prosper" and studied it carefully. His stomach growled. He would go to Gino's for lunch. On occasion Gino could manage a passable chop.

He hoped he would not run into Richardson at lunch. He hated queers. Intelligence seemed to be full of them. It was one of the weaknesses of the Old Boy system.

One of these days, he decided, he must do something about Max Richardson.

David Stern, pale with anxiety, was furious. He tried to conceal the tremor of his hands.

"You could have called," he said.

Michelle shook her head. "I couldn't."

"I suppose it's some man."

"It's not a man. It has nothing to do with a man." She had circles of weariness under her eyes. She was wearing the FANY uniform they had given her, and it was poorly cut and too large.

"This uniform. What does it stand for?"

"First Aid Nursing Yeomanry."

"Is there anything secret about that?"

She shook her head.

"Then why couldn't you call?"

"I just couldn't. You mustn't worry. Come now and eat your dinner."

"I don't want any dinner."

"You're making yourself sick over nothing."

"Is it nothing when you disappear for twenty-four hours without a word? Am I supposed to laugh that off? Go to the theater perhaps? Have a good time?"

"Please," she said. "Don't shout at me."

"Who's shouting?" It was part of an old joke between them. She managed a smile.

"Everyone I know is involved in the war in some way," she said. "You are involved in it yourself, in a very big way. You can't tell me about your work, and I don't want to know. I respect the fact that there are certain things one must not talk about. If what you are doing will help to shorten the war by even one day, that is enough for me. Why can't you grant me the same respect? Or do you think I can go on inventing fairy tales for children while my friends are being killed?"

"But you're a child yourself."

"Am I?"

"Then that is the way it will be?"

"That is the way it has to be."

"And you will do all this without a thought for me?"

"Never without a thought. Believe me, Papa." There were tears in her eyes. She looked so young. So like her mother at that age. Surely they were not down to fighting a war with children. Why would anyone want to harm her? He had asked himself that same question about Denise when she had left for Germany. The Nazis were monsters, rabid dogs striking out at anything that moved. Why in the name of God had he not taken Michelle to America while he still had the chance? But he had been half out of his mind with grief for Denise. Then, suddenly, the war had caught them in England. And there had been his work.

"Michelle."

"No more, please, Papa."

"All right. All right. I just want to say suppose I could get us away from here. To America."

She shook her head. "I don't want to go to America."

"We used to talk about it."

"That was before the war. Before . . . Mama. This is where I am. It's where I want to be."

"You're still thinking of that fellow Larsen?"

She shrugged wearily.

"You still think he may come back?"

"No, I know he won't come back. Now please leave me alone. I want to rest. I have to go out again in a little while."

"To the same place?"

"Yes."

Her combat instructor was a tiny wrinkled sergeant who looked, she thought, like one of Snow White's dwarfs. She was astonished to see him throw two-hundred-pound men over his shoulder with ease. She practiced holds with him, but had no strength at all. He shook his head.

"Lass, if you meet a Jerry, there's only one thing to do."

"Yes?"

"Kick him you know where."

"Where is that, Sergeant?"

"God," said the sergeant. "Do you want me to show you?"

"No, no," she replied laughing. "I'll take your word for it."

"But go softly with the knife. The knife should be wielded as delicately as a paintbrush. Between the ribs and up into the heart with a flick of the wrist."

"Like that?"

"Aye. But with a bit more muscle."

"Did Delilah have muscles, Sergeant?"

"Eh?"

"Look what happened to Samson. All she needed was a pair of scissors."

"Aye," said the sergeant with a keen look, "but at the right time and in the right place. Off you go now to communications."

Her transmitter, she was taught, would be tuned to a particular frequency so that there would be no time lost in establishing contact, but all the same she would have to memorize schedules and coded abbreviations. QRB meant "Your message received and understood." QRM: "Interference is bad." QSLIMI: "Please acknowledge receipt of message number——." There were dozens of these code groups, but the one that was least forgettable was QUP: "I am forced to stop transmitting because of imminent danger."

The code letters were part of a system designed to speed up transmission and thereby minimize detection time. It was understood that with every transmission the danger to the operator increased. Radio direction finders were constantly being improved, and the Germans were now using mobile gear mounted on trucks. As a result the pianist would have to be prepared to move at once after each transmission.

As Odette Renie, a children's nurse living in Paris, Michelle would be issued forged identity papers and ration books. Even her clothing was skillfully faked. Her measurements were taken and sent to a "manufacturer" who managed an establishment in Montreal where her clothing was prepared. There were a half-dozen ways in which a hemline could be stitched or a button sewn, and the man in Montreal knew them all. His workers were sworn to secrecy as they busily prepared men's suits and women's dresses for the agents who would be dropped into France.

Michelle was furnished also with Parisian subway and bus tickets, concert programs, and crumpled French cigarette packs. Even her way of pouring tea was carefully observed to make sure she had not picked up any English habits that might betray her. Her hairstyle was changed as well as her way of applying makeup.

In the second week of her training she was obliged to make her first parachute jump, not from a moving aircraft but from a stationary barrage balloon. To Michelle this was more frightening than jumping from a plane. In a plane the roar, the speed, the vibration, the howling of the wind would override the fear, she thought. Jumping from the balloon was a far more deliberate act performed in eerie silence. But, she did it.

SEVENTEEN

Dr. Karlsen's ancient sedan, burning methane, left a trail of smoke. Sigrid Berg watched the doctor's car moving slowly along the road. She replaced the field glasses in their case and put the kettle on to boil. Karlsen could do with a cup of tea when he came in.

The doctor removed his woolen cap as he came through the doorway, letting his thatch of white hair fall down over his forehead. He had once been the cross-country ski champion of southern Norway, and although now well into his seventies, he was still square-shouldered and straight-backed.

"Watching for me, were you?"

She nodded.

"You knew I'd come when I was able. I had planned to come yesterday but there was trouble at the clinic, and the Germans were taking some interest in my movements."

"More than usual?"

"No, I don't think so. Still, it pays to be careful. Today was routine. I simply announced I had several patients to visit. No less than the truth, eh, Sigrid?"

She smiled. "I have water on for tea."

"Good. How is our patient?"

"Well enough, I think. As of last night his fever seemed to have gone down."

"He's a strong man. When I first saw him, I thought he was finished. Or at the very least would lose his feet. But I believe now he'll come through. Thanks to you."

A touch of color suffused her cheeks.

Karlsen looked at her speculatively. "You're very pretty today, Sigrid. Does attending that young man have anything to do with it?"

With downcast eyes she shook her head.

Karlsen said, "I've never seen you blush before. It's very becoming."

"Stop teasing me, Doctor."

"Of course. Come along now, and we'll go out to the hut."

"Very well. The tea will be ready in a moment."

"Good. And plenty of sugar with it, if you can spare it."

She smiled. "I don't give it to the children because of their teeth."

"It's one of the advantages of growing old. You no longer give a damn about cavities." He gulped the hot drink. "Do you have extra skis?"

"Yes, of course."

They buckled on the skis and set off across the open field to the woods. Karlsen skied vigorously, putting his arms and shoulders into short powerful thrusts with the poles. Sigrid had difficulty keeping up with him. She was breathing hard by the time they reached the protection of the trees.

Karlsen rested on his poles waiting for her. "Do you think anyone saw us?"

She shook her head. "It's doubtful. People here mind their own business."

"No one minds his own business and certainly not out here in the country. They'd be bored to death if they did. If anyone asks you, you can say we're lovers and were on our way to an assignation."

"In the snow?"

"Why not? Do you think I'm too old to remember what can happen in the snow?"

"You're a terrible one. Are any female patients safe with you?"

He shook his head. "Only the grandmothers. And not all of those."

Sigrid had been looking out across the snowfield in the direction of the house. Suddenly her face changed. She made an abrupt motion to Karlsen to get down. He saw it then, too, a German half-track moving along the road, the pot-shaped steel helmets glinting in the sun. The scout car slowed as it approached the house. Karlsen thought it might still go by, but then it drew to a halt. He cursed himself for having left his car exposed. Of course if he had made an attempt to conceal it, they would have been even more suspicious.

He saw one of the distant figures get out to examine the car. The soldier took out a notebook. Trust the Germans for that.

Karlsen kept his head down. One of the Germans, rifle at the ready, had gone up to the house and pushed open the door. He went inside and came out again a few minutes later carrying a bottle which he offered to the others. The man with the notebook had his binoculars out and was sweeping the fields and woods. Karlsen crouched lower. The Germans

were too lazy to search across the area of deep snow
into the forest, and in any case they had no specific
target. It had been coincidence that had brought
them along the road at this time. Now they would
go off to the warmth of their headquarters. Eventually they would check on the registration of the car,
and when they questioned him, he would say that
he had been visiting patients and had gone skiing to
get some exercise.

When the Germans had gone, Sigrid stood up,
brushing the snow from her jacket and long fair hair.
If she was frightened she did not show it. She smiled
at the doctor. He regarded her with admiration.

"A good job our friend wasn't in the house," Karlsen said.

"Do you think they're still looking for him?"

"Perhaps, but not that lot. I think that was a
routine patrol. My car has been checked any number of times. They're accustomed to finding it in
odd places."

Sigrid led the way in a long traverse down a small
open slope and then once again into the forest. In
five minutes they were at the hut. Sigrid whistled softly, and then opened the door. Larsen lay stretched
out on a blanket with his head pillowed on one of
Sigrid's fur-lined anoraks. His face was pale, but his
eyes were sharp. He grinned up at them. The doctor
put his hand on Larsen's brow. The skin was cool.
He checked the pulse. Regular enough. The wound
in the shoulder was clean, and the frostbitten feet
were at least no worse.

Karlsen nodded. "You'll do. You've had proper
care, I take it."

"The best."

Sigrid had been faithful in her attendance. She had slipped away to the hut at least once a day, sometimes more, to bring him food and to change his dressings. Lying alone in the hut he had wondered at the good luck which had led him to her door. She was one woman in a thousand.

"Am I well enough to travel?" Larsen asked.

"I can't give you a straight answer to that," the doctor said. "You can be moved, if that's what you mean, but you are hardly up to traveling on the open road in freezing weather. Try that and you'll be a dead man for sure. All the same I think with a little help we might get you away to the border."

"How?"

"As Johan Berg."

Sigrid's clear brow had creased. "As Johan?"

"Exactly. They're about the same size. Surely you have enough of your husband's old clothes to fit him out."

"Yes. I could do that."

"Good. We'll go in my car. If we're stopped they have only to look at him to see that he's been badly wounded. We'll be taking him home by way of a clinic belonging to some friends of mine where they can administer special treatment for frostbite. By coincidence that clinic is very near the frontier. If we leave him there, it will be no job at all for him to slip over the border."

"Hadn't we better travel at night, then?"

"I think not. Nighttime traffic is bound to be regarded with suspicion. We'll go in daylight as honest citizens who have nothing to hide."

Sigrid smiled. "When do we leave?"

"Why not right now? A patrol has just gone by. There's not likely to be another today."

Larsen said abruptly, "I don't like it."

"Why not?" said Sigrid.

"Because it will endanger both of you."

Karlsen had been looking from one to the other. He smiled and said, "The man is right. Put him out in the snow with a pair of crutches and let him make his own way to Sweden." Sigrid did not say anything and Larsen lay back with his head on the anorak. "It's only a couple of hundred kilometers," the doctor went on. "If you start now you might make it by spring. Anyway, we've got to get rid of you one way or the other. The fact is you're a menace to us all lying about here and expecting to be waited on hand and foot. You can see that, can't you?"

"Yes, I can see that."

"Then kindly shut up and leave the brainwork to those who have them. This is the moment to move. The car is here, the patrol has just gone by. Sigrid is ready to play the role of loving wife, and by tonight we can deposit you close to the border. After that you can be as independent as you like. Now, for God's sake, let's get on with it."

Karlsen had gone red in the face with the intensity of his speech. Sigrid said, "How shall we take him out?"

"You go back to the house and round up some clothing. Also bring along any documents that will help to identify him as Johan Berg—those without photos, of course. Now, what about the children?"

"There's no problem there. I can send word for them to spend the night at a friend's house."

"Good. On your way, then. I'll put him on the sleigh and bring him out as far as that clump of trees near the road. After that I'll come back for the car. You wait for me at the house. Understood?"

Sigrid nodded. Karlsen reached into his bag and drew out a hypodermic syringe.

"What's that for?" said Larsen.

"For you. The road will be long and bumpy. This will help you sleep."

"I don't want it. I'd rather know what's going on."

"Kindly shut up and let me get on with it. The shock to your system will be far less if you're properly sedated. The springs on that car are atrocious. We'll all wish we were knocked out with something before this trip is over. And if we're stopped I'd rather you were drowsy. That way when you answer questions you won't put your foot in it. Understood?"

"With a bedside manner like yours, I don't see how you stay in business," said Larsen as the needle went into his arm.

"Fortunately most of my patients have more sense than you."

Larsen was only vaguely aware of what was happening. The cold fresh air bit against his face. Sunlight worked its way through the leafless tree branches and dappled the snow. Karlsen, the towing rope over his shoulder, forged steadily ahead.

The doctor left Larsen in the shelter of the trees close to the road and walked back to the house. It was easier walking on the packed snow of the roadway. Sigrid was waiting for him.

"Is he all right?" she asked.

"Knocked out from the shot I gave him, but otherwise he'll do. I see you've packed some sandwiches. Good thought. It will probably be close to midnight by the time we get back here."

"Will you have enough fuel?"

"No, but I know where I can get more. And the boys?"

"I've left a note for them. They're to go straight to the neighbor's house."

"Do you trust them not to talk?"

"Yes."

"I've been wondering if you might not be better off staying here," Karlsen said.

"I don't understand. I thought it was agreed that I would pass as his wife and we would travel together."

"That was how I saw it at first, but now I'm not sure it's really necessary. Very likely I could pull it off without you."

"How? What would be your reason for taking him so far?"

Karlsen shrugged. "Special treatment at a particular clinic. You don't think it sounds reasonable?"

"It might sound reasonable to me, but I don't think it will to the Germans."

"And having you along will?"

"There is nothing," said Sigrid, "half so convincing to any man, even a German, as a weeping woman."

Karlsen sighed. Sigrid Berg, for all her calm blue eyes and silken hair, was made of iron. There was hope yet for Norway.

Larsen was stretched out on the back seat with his head in Sigrid's lap. She was doing her best to ease the jolting. Several times she had to grip him by the shoulders to keep him from being hurled off the seat. Once they passed through a knot of German military vehicles but no one questioned them.

Larsen was hardly aware of any of it. The injection Karlsen had given him induced not only sleep but confused dreams. He dreamed of Michelle, and called out to her. Sigrid smiled and stroked his forehead.

At the moment when Larsen called her name, Michelle Stern was also driving in an old car over a rutted country road, but in Sussex. With her was her supervisor, Betty Chadwick. Neither of them had much to say. Now and then Betty turned her head to look sideways at Michelle. The girl's creamy-skinned features were pale but composed.

Michelle knew what Betty was thinking. During the eight-week training program they had become close friends. Betty had been frank with her, had told her from the beginning that she was not right for the job.

When they arrived at last at the old thatched cottage, both women were tired and chilled. Betty led the way upstairs past an open room where a group of men sat talking in low tones. She took Michelle by the arm and hurried past them. What one did not know, one could not reveal, even under torture.

Michelle sat down on one of the straight-backed chairs and looked out of the window at the dusk settling on the hills.

"I'm going down to the kitchen to fix us some tea," Betty said. "It might be better if you wait here."

Michelle nodded.

"I suppose you could do with a sandwich. I know I can. I'm famished."

"Yes," Michelle said. "A sandwich would be fine."

"You might want to get your head down for a bit. There's no telling how long it may be. The moon is right and the weather is good, but the aircraft don't always come when we expect them. We don't have our own machines, you see, so it's up to the Air Ministry to supply one. Sometimes they have the peculiar notion that their own needs come before ours."

Michelle smiled. "There's really no great hurry."

"I'll go down for the tea."

"You're sure I can't help?"

"It's better if you remain here out of sight. It may take hours, or even days. I should warn you that we've had occasions when agents came here to the departure house, and then were sent away again because no aircraft was available. It's not likely, but it can happen."

But at midnight they were called. There was a knock on the door, and a low voice said, "Time to go."

"Michelle?" Betty whispered.

"Yes," Michelle answered. "I'm ready."

They had been lying down fully dressed. Betty insisted on a final inspection to make sure they had not overlooked anything incriminating—a London theater stub; a match cover. There was nothing. She gave the handbag, heavy with the weight of the .38 inside, back to Michelle. Michelle still appeared calm. Betty had sent off dozens of agents, but she could not remember any who had displayed such serenity.

The Lysander, high winged, painted black, looked, Michelle decided, rather like a flying hearse. She shrugged off the thought. It was frightening enough to be heading for France without letting her imagination run wild. One must accept, as the Buddhists did, the immutability of fate. If it had been decreed that she would die in France, then all her life to this point had been only a preamble for that moment.

She felt for the amulet containing the cyanide pill. She had practiced slipping the pill from its container into her mouth. It would take only a few seconds to die.

No one spoke. Betty pressed her arm in a gesture of comradeship and then was gone. The pilot, startlingly young looking, slipped into his seat and advanced the throttle. The plane turned and charged down the runway into the wind. Michelle gritted her teeth. She hated flying.

The flight was uneventful. The ordeal of parachuting was spared her. They were able to land at a strip near Le Mans. The pilot wished her a hurried "Good luck," then immediately took off. Holding her suitcase she stood alone on the patch of grass. She was to be met, she had been told, by members of the network. No light showed; there was no sound. Then, far off, she heard a train whistle. She was aware of the pounding of her heart. If she followed the tracks, they should lead her to the Le Mans railway station; from there she could catch a train to Paris.

As she bent to pick up her suitcase she heard the sound of footsteps. A man wearing corduroy trousers and a leather jacket materialized out of the darkness.

"Mademoiselle Stern, I presume," the man said in heavily accented English. Michelle's heart seemed to stop.

"Permit me to introduce myself. SS Hauptscharfuehrer Karl Langer. Your flight is an hour late." The

German chuckled. "The British are not so efficient, eh?"

She was reaching for the cyanide capsule when he seized her hand.

Stern regarded the letter with a sense of foreboding. His nerves were jumpy. Since Michelle had disappeared he had slept hardly at all. Four days had passed with no word. He did not think he could take very much more. He had asked Peter Guthrie for help in obtaining information, but Peter, too, had come up against a stone wall of official security. Max Richardson was apparently away and had not answered his calls.

The large yellow envelope lay at the bottom of the box where it had been dropped through the chute. Stern's name had been printed across the front in block letters, but there was no address and no postage; it had been delivered by hand.

He tore open the envelope. It contained four photographs but no written message. Each of the photos resembled the other, with just enough difference in the posing and background to show they had been shot over a period of time.

Michelle was the principal figure in each photo. She was naked. She sat on what appeared to be a stone floor. In two of the photos her hands were tied in front of her, giving the impression that she was praying. In the others her hands were free, and she was attempting to conceal her nudity. Her hair was in wild disorder, and her face was frozen in a grimace of fear. A man stood behind her holding her head toward the camera. His face did not show, but the shiny jackboots and death's head insignia of the SS were clearly visible.

Stern collapsed into a chair.

With trembling fingers he examined the photographs once again. It might have been some kind of monstrous joke, but he quickly discarded the notion. That the Germans had Michelle was clear. And that they wanted something from him was equally clear.

He stood up weakly. His knees had turned to jelly. He walked like an old man. He went to the window and stood looking out. Automobile traffic and streams of pedestrians continued to move at their usual pace. Incredibly, the world around him was going on as usual; his world was finished. With shaking fingers he fixed himself a glass of brandy. In the silence of the room the tick-tock of the clock sounded unnaturally loud.

BOOK II

1943

EIGHTEEN

"Peter, this is David Stern." The voice on the phone was almost unrecognizable.

Guthrie waited. "Yes, David. Anything wrong?"

"I am sorry to disturb you at this hour."

"That's all right." He could hear Stern's heavy breathing. "What is it?"

"It's Michelle. Could you come over?"

"Of course. I'll put on some clothes. Be right there."

The call for Stern came less than five minutes after he had spoken to Guthrie.

"Professor Stern?" A man's voice speaking English. Something stiff and formal about it. A carefully trained voice like that of a headwaiter or butler.

"Yes?"

"You received the photographs?"

"Yes."

"You are satisfied that she is your daughter?"

Stern's answer was a croak. "Yes. What is it you want from me?"

"You would like to save your daughter's life?"

"Where is she?"

"I don't mind telling you. She is being held at SS

headquarters on the Avenue Foch in Paris. She is providing amusement for several of the officers. Eventually she will be turned over to the enlisted men, and when they are finished with her she will go to a brothel for one of the Polish or Russian brigades. If she is still alive when that is over, she will be taken to Belsen and shot. Do I make myself clear?"

"Who are you?"

"That is of no consequence."

Stern fought for control. The voice on the phone said, "You see, we knew all about her projected visit to France. The Lysander landing at Le Mans, all of it. Naturally we had a reception committee waiting for her. She attempted to swallow a cyanide capsule, but we were prepared for that and managed to prevent it." A pause. "Well, now that I have filled you in on the general picture, we can get down to facts. We would like you to take a little trip to Lisbon."

"Is this some kind of joke?"

"If you think those photographs of your daughter were a joke, wait until you see the next group."

"But I don't understand."

"Of course not. You will understand more as we go along. Meanwhile I suggest complete silence. If you were to be so foolish as to report this matter to your British hosts, we would know about it at once, and the game would be up. In that case your daughter would surely die after she had served her purpose in the program I have outlined. Now, I suggest you think it over, Dr. Stern. I advise you to stay close to the telephone. You will be contacted again some time tomorrow."

There was a click. Stern said into the dead line, "No. Wait!"

He sat, head down, immobile, until his doorbell rang. It was Guthrie.

"Sorry to be so long, David. I was unable to find a cab."

"Come in."

The blackout curtains had been drawn and only one lamp was shining, but even in that dim light Stern looked awful. His lean face was gaunt. He moved with the stiff-jointed shamble of an old man.

"A drink, Peter?"

"Whatever is handy." Guthrie shrugged out of his dripping raincoat and hung it on a peg in the entrance hall.

Stern poured them each a measure of brandy, gulping his down in one swallow.

"What about Michelle, David?"

Stern wanted desperately to tell him. The envelope of photographs still lay on the table where he had dropped it. He avoided looking in that direction. He could trust no one; the Germans apparently knew everything. They had even known when and where Michelle would arrive in France.

"Perhaps I dragged you out into the night for nothing. I am sorry."

Guthrie shook his head. "You're a key figure in the program, David. It's my job to try to keep you happy. You told me you were concerned about Michelle. Do you want to talk about it?" Stern shook his head. There was a hint of moisture in his eyes. "I'll say good night, then," Guthrie said, thinking what the hell.

In the morning there was another envelope in the drop. It had been delivered some time during the night, but Stern had not heard it fall. He ripped it open. It contained a single photograph.

It was of Michelle, naked again, but this time bent over a rough wooden table with her feet on the ground. Two uniformed men held her down by the shoulders, but her head, twisted sideways, and her face were clearly visible. Her eyes were squeezed shut, but her mouth was open in what appeared to be a scream of agony. The camera had been set up from the side and showed a man standing behind her, a fat man who still wore his SS uniform jacket, but whose trousers hung down around his ankles. In one hand he held his erect penis which he was forcing between Michelle's buttocks.

Stern had not dared to leave the house for two days, afraid of missing a call. Each time the telephone rang, he snatched it up. "Hello? Yes?" Twice it was the wrong number. The third time it was Peter Guthrie.

"They told me you hadn't come into the laboratory this morning," Guthrie said. "I hope you're not ill."

"No, no. A little cold. Nothing."

"Perhaps a doctor . . ."

"No, no. No doctor. I tell you I'm all right!" It was imperative to clear the phone. "It's nothing, Peter. Thank you. You must excuse me now."

Stern slammed the receiver into its cradle. He sat waiting, listening to the pounding of his own heart.

When he dozed he dreamed he heard the phone ringing. He lunged to pick it up, but it was dead.

He was in the bathroom when the call finally came. This time it was the real thing. In his haste to answer he slipped and fell, cracking his elbow painfully against the tub. Afraid that the ringing might stop, he slithered naked and helpless on the tile floor, at last gaining his feet and reaching the phone. God, don't let it stop. Don't let them go away.

"Yes? Yes? Hello?"

"Dr. Stern?" He recognized the voice at once.

"Yes."

"This is that friend of Michelle's." Friend! My God!

"Is she all right?"

"How she is remains up to you, Doctor."

"Anything! Tell me what you want. Is it information? Classified information?"

"As I told you in our last conversation, we want you to go to Lisbon."

"An exchange? Is that it? An exchange on neutral territory? You will release Michelle and take me instead? Yes, yes, of course. I am willing. Only release her, and I will tell you everything. I know what you are after. I'll tell you, I swear I—"

"You are to be in Lisbon on the twenty-fourth of this month," the cool voice cut in. "The Spanish ship *Concepción* leaves Ireland on the eighteenth for Lisbon. A room has been booked for you at the Hotel Alegría. Wait there for further instructions.'"

"Wait! Listen to me! I'll go back to Germany with you. Only leave her alone! Don't hurt her any more."

He was speaking into a dead phone.

The twenty-fourth. Less than a week. They would want notes, diagrams of the reactor. If he were caught by the British, Michelle would be finished. It was important not to give grounds for suspicion. He must return to work. When he disappeared from London it would be without baggage. Perhaps just an attaché case. As if he had gone to the laboratory. A Spanish ship to Lisbon. It would mean bribes for customs agents and passport officials.

As for his fate in Germany, that did not matter. Once the exchange had taken place, they could do with him what they liked.

NINETEEN

General von Lueger's bomb proved to be another dud. He had approached Colonel Heinz Brandt, a member of Hitler's staff, to ask if he would mind taking along a small parcel containing two bottles of Cointreau as a present for General Staff in Berlin. Brandt had been only too happy to oblige his fellow general.

Lueger murmured his thanks, and after seeing that the package was carefully placed in the FW-200's luggage compartment, strolled back to the administration building. A heavy Baltic mist was rolling across the Prussian lowlands, and Lueger hoped it would not delay the takeoff. He reached for his gold cigarette case bearing the Wartenburg crest and lit a cigarette. He was pleased to observe that his fingers were steady.

Hitler, accompanied by a party of some thirty staff officers, including his physician and personal chef, was saying good-bye to General Kluge. Wrapped to the ears in a greatcoat, his face sallow and unsmiling, the Fuehrer made an abrupt farewell and mounted the steps leading to the aircraft.

Lueger thought about the staff who would die with Hitler. Some of them, like Brandt, were men he had known for years. It was regrettable, of course, that innocent men should die along with the tyrant, but their deaths would save the lives of millions. Brandt, seeing Lueger standing by the window, gave him a salute before boarding. The FW-200 took off and disappeared almost at once into the grayness. Lueger glanced at his watch. In less than forty-five minutes Hitler would be dead, and Germany would be under the control of Valkyrie.

He turned away. His Mercedes and driver were waiting for him. He got in and was driven back to his headquarters, where he dismissed his secretary and placed a priority call to Captain Ludwig Gehre at Canaris' headquarters in Berlin. Lueger spoke casually about certain staff matters and then mentioned that the Fuehrer had seemed to enjoy his visit to General Kluge's headquarters—most particularly the apricots that had been provided for him.

Captain Gehre thanked the general for his call and immediately began to send out a stream of messages putting the Valkyrie forces on the alert.

At eight thousand feet, nearing Rastenburg and with twelve minutes yet to go on the bomb timer, the FW-200 was flying through heavy clouds. There was considerable turbulence. In order to spare the Fuehrer's delicate stomach any discomfort, the pilot decided to go up to fifteen thousand feet. The aircraft rose above the cloud cover. It was bitterly cold at that altitude but smoother, and the Fuehrer, who had been feeling queasy, settled back and looked with satisfaction at the sunlight sparkling through the windows and at the accompanying escort of ME-109 fighters.

According to General Lueger's calculations Hitler now had four minutes left to live. He waited by the phone. Pacing nervously he smoked one cigarette after another, his long thin fingers displaying a distinct tremor. Something had gone wrong.

At the end of an hour a teletype message was received reporting Hitler's safe arrival at Rastenburg. A study of the weather map told Lueger what had happened. Hitler's pilot had flown at higher-than-usual altitudes. The acid which had been expected to eat through the detonator wire had frozen in the unheated baggage compartment. Once again the dictator had enjoyed the luck of the devil.

How long would it be before someone got curious about the parcel General von Lueger had placed on the plane?

He sat motionless for several minutes, then reached into the top desk drawer and took out a pistol and a small silver-framed photograph of his wife and children. He slipped both objects into his pocket and left the office.

The Mercedes was waiting for him.

"Wartenburg," he instructed the driver.

They had crossed the Peene River and were approaching the little village of Wolgast when they saw the roadblock: two armored half-tracks close together blocking the road while machine-gun nests on either side eliminated any possibility of a high-speed dash. SS troopers were stationed behind the barrier.

The Mercedes drew to a halt. Lueger sighed. There was still time to put a bullet through his head. He had his hand on the weapon before deciding against it. There was a possibility, slight to be sure, that the roadblock had nothing to do with him.

He sat very erect in the back seat of the car staring

coldly at the SS major who was approaching. The major bent down to peer through the window. He straightened and saluted.

Lueger rolled down the window and said in a bored voice, "Yes?"

"Your papers, sir."

"I am General von Lueger."

"Yes, sir."

"What seems to be the trouble, Major?"

"A routine check, sir. Your papers please, Herr General."

The major's holster was unbuttoned. Lueger handed over the pigskin wallet containing his identification.

"I'm traveling on official business, Major."

"Of course, Herr General."

The SS officer glanced at the wallet and then returned it with another salute. Lueger's spirits began to rise.

"Are we free to proceed?"

"I am afraid not, sir."

"Dammit! What now?"

"I must ask the Herr General to step out of the car."

They stripped him naked; his elegant uniform was rolled into a ball and tossed into a corner. They tied him to a kitchen chair in a small house on the outskirts of Wolgast. A ragged hole had been cut in the bottom of the chair through which his genitalia hung down. It was freezing in the room. He was shivering uncontrollably. Nearby stood an SS lieutenant colonel and two technicians. The room was brightly lit. A photographer with a hand-held movie camera focused on the general's face.

A length of iron rod had been forced up the general's rectum. From it a copper wire led to a bank of automotive-type twelve-volt batteries. Another wire was fastened to a battery clip which was clamped to the head of the general's penis. Two additional battery clamps with attached wires were fastened to his nipples.

Lueger was trying hard to remove his mind from what was happening to him. He had told himself that he would concentrate on the estate at Wartenburg, his wife and children, his favorite mare Empress and the velvet nostrils and warm sweet breath with which she nuzzled his hand. In the end he would talk—in the end everyone talked—but his honor as a Prussian officer demanded that he hold out as long as possible.

Perhaps by the time he broke some of his fellow plotters would have had a chance to get away.

A knife switch had been set into the main wire leading to the batteries.

His eyes were closed. At Wartenburg, in summer, the sun came up red and heavy over the hills and meadows. The horses would begin to stir. The air was soft and sweet . . . .

As the switch closed he screamed. He felt as if his insides had been pulped. His body seemed to liquefy. A stream of watery excrement poured from his loosened sphincter. His penis had gone rigid under the shock. A foul odor filled the room. The general sat limp in his bonds, his head hanging loosely to one side. The lieutenant colonel made a hurried motion with his hands and the current was shut off.

The lieutenant colonel stepped gingerly around the evil-smelling puddle and bent down to put his ear to the general's chest. When he straightened up he glared at the sergeant who had been in charge of the switch.

"The son of a bitch is dead," the lieutenant colonel said grimly.

"He must have had a weak heart, Herr Colonel. How was I to know?"

"You stupid asshole."

The general's body was transported to the family estate at Wartenburg and there hung naked from a meat hook in the central courtyard to serve as a warning to his family and friends.

Goering was at his country estate when the summons from Hitler reached him. He was alone in the great dining hall (Emmy was spending the evening in Berlin). The Reichmarshal was enjoying a superb meal of caviar from Russia, duck and venison from the Schorside forests, Danzig salmon, and French pâté-de-foie gras, all washed down with vodka, claret, champagne, and brandy.

Despite the excellence of the meal and the fact that on the walls around him hung many of the world's greatest art treasures, the Reichmarshal was not happy. Word had reached him of the bombing of Hamburg. Eight hundred heavy RAF bombers had crossed the North Sea from Britain, passed over Lübeck, and arrived over Hamburg from the northeast. Hamburg was Germany's most important port. Its docks, central harbor, and inner city had been bombed with acute and devastating precision.

The Luftwaffe had been outmaneuvered. The fault, Goering tried to tell himself, lay not so much with his pilots as with the operators of the German radar. The British had employed a simple but effective trick.

By dropping millions of strips of tinfoil they had completely "blinded" the radar defenses. After the tinfoil had come the bombs.

Now there was a summons from Hitler. The Fuehrer expected him at the Wolf's Lair.

It had been months since there had been any personal communication between the Fuehrer and himself. Not even the paracodeine tablets were able to put the Reichmarshal to sleep that night.

The Fieseler-Storch flew low under a heavy cloud ceiling. The Prussian skies were cold and gloomy as always. Goering shivered as he stepped out of the aircraft. He entered the waiting car and was driven to the Fuehrer's headquarters.

Along with Goering there were fifteen or twenty other guests at Hitler's table that night, among them his three female secretaries and Eva Braun. The Fuehrer seemed in an expansive mood.

After dinner a movie screen was brought into the room and a projector set up. The guests turned their chairs to see better. The lights were dimmed. A picture flashed on the screen. It showed a naked man bound to a chair. Goering's jowls trembled with amazement and fear as he realized that he was watching the execution of General von Lueger.

The doomed man struggled, his face contorted, his limbs seeming to fly out in all directions. There was no sound in the room but the labored breathing of the viewers. Goering turned his head. In the greenish light of the projector he could barely make out Hitler. The Fuehrer looked squarely back at Goering.

Hitler's secretary, Christa Schroeder, rushed out of the room with her hand over her mouth.

*   *   *

Canaris had received a phone call from Lisbon. The caller had not identified himself. He simply said, "X factor is here."

"Very good," said Canaris.

"Shall we proceed?"

"But of course," said the admiral with unusual good humor.

The failure of the latest assassination attempt had hit Canaris hard. Lueger had been an old friend and one of the original plotters of the Black Orchestra. The news, therefore, that Stern had reached Lisbon provided a lift to his spirits.

"Come in, my dear fellow," he said to Hauser, who stood tentatively in the doorway. "I have just received a call from Lisbon. Stern is there. All is well."

If he had expected a smile from Hauser, he did not receive it.

Hauser said, "I am concerned about the girl."

"What about her?"

"It was not in our agreement that she would be placed in the hands of the SS."

"The SS has jurisdiction in Paris," Canaris answered mildly.

"They are perverts, torturers. God knows what they may be doing to her. Is she still being held at Avenue Foch?"

"I believe so."

"Perhaps she could be removed," offered Hauser.

"On what pretext?"

"Interrogation by the Abwehr."

Canaris pursed his lips. "A dangerous game. Herr Himmler might begin to wonder. Even in your own case I have been forced to sail close to the wind to protect you from the SS. Just why are you so concerned for the girl?"

Hauser's normally ruddy look had faded. His cheeks were pale. The scar which slightly disfigured his upper lip was prominent. "She might have been my own child."

Canaris whistled soundlessly, but said nothing. More nervous now, Hauser spoke in a rush. "I was on intimate terms with the girl's mother. From the moment she met Stern, our relationship ended. They were married less than two weeks later. I wish to know what treatment she is receiving at the hands of the SS. It is common knowledge what goes on at Avenue Foch."

Canaris' expression had not changed. "Your role in the affair begins to smack of a personal vendetta against this man Stern. We cannot afford such petty emotionalism. One life is nothing when weighed against the future of Germany. I must warn you, Dr. Hauser, that your own position is none too secure."

"I am aware of that, Herr Admiral."

"I will take the matter under consideration," Canaris said coldly, reflecting that it might not be a bad idea after all to have the girl placed under the control of the Abwehr. Her stay at the Avenue Foch headquarters had produced the desired results. Stern had gone to Lisbon. She would not last long in the hands of the SS; no one did. Hauser's suggestion that she be removed for Abwehr interrogation was not bad at all.

Michelle lay on the stone floor. There was no bed in the cell, no furniture, no light. No hook from which to hang herself. Even her hair had been chopped off to keep her from using it to strangle herself. Her fingernails, too, had been cut to the quick to keep her from opening the veins in her wrists. She had tried to use her teeth to kill herself, but had only succeeded in mangling the flesh. Now her torn wrists were tied behind her back.

The nightmare persisted in her mind. The men who had used her in unspeakable ways. The photographer with his flashbulbs. She had already told them everything she knew. If only God would let her die.

Was this what it had been like for her mother—that gentle smiling woman? Or had death been mercifully swift? To think that one could long beyond all else for the firing squad or the gas chamber.

The cell door opened. A shaft of light. God, not again. Of what use to them was her poor body?

She was being taken out. Forced into the back of a van. Total darkness. The van sped over cobblestone streets and then to what felt like country roads. They must be taking her to a place of execution.

She breathed a prayer of thankfulness.

Dr. Dopel, who had been associated with the failure of the L-IV pile at Leipzig, was both depressed and mystified by the current state of atomic research in the Reich. Professor Hauser appeared to have removed himself from the project. It was rumored that Hauser was in hot water with Bormann and was lying low. So be it, thought Dopel, but why this curious silence from Reichmarshal Goering, who had been appointed director of the Reich Research Council? It was not surprising that Goering should have lost interest after Leipzig, but all the same, one would suppose that, as director of the project, he would be on the lookout for new methods.

Dopel felt that he was currently onto something promising. Since the sabotage of the Vemork plant it had been necessary to look elsewhere for a source of atomic energy. A promising avenue of research had emerged from the intense temperature created by spherical or cylindrical shock wave in a gas. As far back as 1936 Dr. Hund had written a paper on the behavior of matter under extreme pressure. Dopel had calculated on the basis of this and Bethe's theory regarding the energy production processes in the stars, that if he could generate a temperature of about four million degrees at a pressure of 250 million atmospheres, a number of fusion processes must follow.

To demonstrate his theory he had devised a hollow silver sphere about two inches in diameter, and this was filled with heavy hydrogen. Around the sphere was packed a quantity of ordinary explosive. The explosive would be detonated at several points simultaneously. The silver sphere would be liquefied under the intense pressure and forced in toward the center at fantastic velocity, perhaps twenty-five hundred meters per second. Thus, all the energy contained in the conventional explosives would be focused on the trapped hydrogen at the center. The conditions would approximate those at the center of the sun. The Einstein equation would be used to measure the release of energy.

The experiment was conducted by CPVA, the German Admiralty's explosives research establishment at Dänisch-Nienhof, near Kiel. Once again Reichmarshal Goering had been invited to attend but had pleaded the press of urgent business elsewhere. As it turned out, no traces of radioactivity had been observed.

Dopel was puzzled. In his report to the Reichmarshal he had said that it was a mystery why the Allies had gone to so much trouble to destroy Germany's source of heavy water since it now appeared it was impossible to produce bombs with hydrogen. He had expected to earn a reprimand for having wasted time and money. To his surprise he received instead the copy of the report he had sent the Reichmarshal. Scrawled across it in Goering's hand was the message, "Keep up the good work."

It proved one thing only to Dopel: Goering had other fish to fry.

TWENTY

Richardson took another pull at his brandy and soda and regarded the nude portrait of Nell Gwyn which hung above the general's head. The lush outlines of the king's mistress, which had long been a fixture of the Army and Navy Club, were agreeable to the eye. What was not so agreeable, decided Richardson, were General Brownlee's lipless mouth and hooked nose which gave him the appearance of a cock salmon rising to the fly. Richardson was not in the least grateful to his admiral for assigning to him this necessary but unpleasant briefing. It was one of the consequences of being the custodian of the green baize door.

The admiral had been guarded in his appraisal of the information that was to be relayed to the other services. Richardson knew his boss well enough by this time to be able to read between the lines of his instructions.

Full but not fulsome. Forthcoming but not outgoing. Remember, some day the war will be over, and awkward questions may be asked.

Richardson pulled out his cigarette case. "Mind if I smoke, sir?"

The general shook his head.

"Care for one, sir?"

Another shake of the head.

Surly bastard, thought Richardson, transferring his attention to Mistress Gwyn's celebrated tits.

"This plan of yours . . ."

"Hardly mine, sir," said Richardson modestly.

"Quite. But conceived, I take it, by Special Operations Executive."

"Yes, sir."

"I have advised Colonel Moorhouse to prepare a memorandum on the subject."

Richardson raised an eyebrow but said nothing. Damned navy fop, thought the general. Bloody fruit.

"I take it then you don't actually want the French Resistance to rise." The general had a reedy voice which did not match his massive frame.

"No, sir."

"The project is to be entirely diversionary?"

Richardson nodded.

"But the Resistance won't know it."

"No, sir."

"Seems a bit underhanded. . . ."

If he says anything about breaking eggs, I'll hit him with the bottle, decided Richardson.

"But I suppose one can't make an omelette without breaking eggs," the general continued.

"Quite, sir."

"I have the C in C's directive," said the general, reaching for his briefcase.

Bloody careless security, thought Richardson. Old bugger should be shot.

"Who exactly is to coordinate these plans?" the general asked.

"Controller of Deception, sir."

"These operations," the general read, "will be directed towards territories where the expectation of early liberation is at present the main sustaining factor in resistance. The effect of these operations will be to heighten to flash-point expectations of relief, and then ultimately to disappoint the population of western Europe."

The general lowered the sheet of paper and removed his reading glasses, which had left a pinched white look above his beaky nose.

"Your phraseology, Richardson?"

"Hardly, sir."

"Whose then?"

"I'm sure I couldn't say, sir."

"It seems unnecessarily flowery, but then so does much else of this operation. Has it occurred to you that not only French *résistants* may be sacrificed in this operation but our own agents as well?"

Richardson nodded. "Certainly it will be hazardous for some of the people we have already sent in to staff the networks. But of course they are all volunteers."

"Do any of them know the truth?"

"I should hope not, sir. Security would be finished if they did."

"Very well." The general stuffed the papers back into his briefcase. "Colonel Moorhouse will be in touch. My compliments to the admiral, and I suggest that everything be held in abeyance until my staff has had a chance to go over this in greater detail."

"I'm afraid that's impossible, sir."

"How so?"

"The operation is already under way. Several of our people were sent in last week with the express purpose of stirring things up."

The general's face grew a shade redder. "Damn it,

Richardson. You people have no right to take matters into your own hands like this. No right at all."

"Yes, sir."

"I shall see that the C in C hears of this."

"Yes, sir."

The general buried his further irritation in a long swallow of brandy and soda. Richardson rose to his feet. The general had picked up an old issue of *Tattler* and was ignoring him. Richardson said, "Thank you, sir, for the brandy and soda."

Richardson stood at attention before the admiral's desk. "The disappearance of this fellow Stern has created a tremendous flap, Richardson," the admiral said.

"Yes, sir."

"It seems he got away from Ireland on a Spanish ship bound for Lisbon. Did you know that?"

"No, sir."

The admiral frowned. "Word has come down from the Prime Minister's office. Winston himself has been asking questions. There was even talk of sending a destroyer after him to arrest him at sea. Winston decided against it. Might be all that was needed to bring the Spaniards into the war. Can't chance that. Some connection with what happened to the girl, don't you think?"

"Yes, sir."

The china-blue eyes had turned colder. "Your name has surfaced in that connection."

"I was involved only to the extent of cooperating with Colonel Brothers, sir."

"Brothers seemed keen on her, did he?"

"Yes, sir."

"Good man, Brothers. Wouldn't like to lose him."

There was a longish pause. Richardson, who knew his admiral, waited. At last the admiral said, "Anything else?"

"My meeting with General Brownlee, sir."

"How did it go?"

"He doesn't seem particularly enthusiastic, sir."

"Not surprising. The man's a fool."

"Colonel Moorhouse will be preparing a memo for the C in C."

"Moorhouse is an ass." The admiral considered for a moment. "This chap Guthrie. Asking awkward questions. Friends in high places, has he?"

"His father was Major General Sir William Guthrie. The PM called him in on the Hess affair. Sent him up to Scotland with Lord Beaverbrook."

"Look here, Max." Richardson blinked. The admiral called him Max only when he was about to use him for something sticky. "How well do you know young Guthrie?"

"He was a year behind me at Oxford, sir."

"If he gets too pushy, you might remind him that this was the PM's cockeyed scheme in the first place. Devised it for the benefit of Uncle Joe now that Stalin has begun pressing for the opening of a second front. The PM offered him this instead. Thin soup perhaps, but Stalin seems to be buying it for now. I don't think the PM will appreciate any criticism at this late date."

Richardson had never known the admiral to be quite so discursive. The old man obviously felt himself to be on infirm ground.

"You take my point, do you, Max?"

"Certainly, sir, but Guthrie was more or less responsible for Stern. It's natural for him to be in something of a snit."

The admiral coughed dryly and touched his lips with his handkerchief. "Well, unsnit him."

TWENTY-ONE

Anthony Eden smiled a gracious English smile beneath his short military moustache. "My dear General Sikorski. Do come in."

"Thank you, Mr. Secretary."

Eden, a tall, handsome man, was impeccable in morning coat and striped trousers. Sikorski briefly regretted having shaved off his own moustache. He had informed Zofia that he had done so because it made him look like Hitler. Actually he was now clean shaven because he had begun to feel that his graying moustache made him look older than his sixty years.

"And this must be Major Lesniowska," said Eden.

Zofia smiled but continued to stand at attention. "Yes, sir."

"A strong family resemblance."

"I like to think so, sir," Zofia answered.

"Do sit down, General. And you, too, Major."

When they were all three seated Eden said, "Tea?"

Sikorski managed the briefest of winks in his daughter's direction. He had wagered Zofia a pound that the English foreign secretary would offer them tea in less than thirty seconds.

"Thank you," said Zofia.

"And you, General? Tea or something stronger?"

"Something stronger if you have it."

"Scotch?"

General Sikorski considered Scotch a nauseating drink, but to decline might offend. One never knew.

"Scotch will do nicely," said Sikorski.

When the tea had been served and the Scotch splashed into glasses, the foreign secretary said, "I have been looking forward to this meeting for the longest time." It was a lie. Sikorski had requested the appointment on several occasions, but Eden had always managed to postpone it. He had known all along that Sikorski might prove to be a hot potato. Not nearly so intransigent as the stiff-necked de Gaulle, but still dead set against the Russians. When the so-called Sikorski-Stalin pact had been proposed, Sikorski had asked Stalin for information on fourteen thousand missing Polish officers. The enigmatic Russian had stroked his moustache and said with a straight face that it was more than likely the missing Poles had fled to Manchuria. Even Eden, trained in diplomatic double-talk, had felt the blood leave his cheeks on that one. Sikorski had swallowed his rage. A scene with the Soviet ruler would not bring dead men back to life and might impede the progress of the war. It had been a shameful moment for them all, and Eden would not soon forget Stalin's sly glance and arrogant look.

"I thought it best to advise you in person of my forthcoming journey," said Sikorski. "I intend to travel to the Middle East."

Eden raised an eyebrow. There were thousands of Polish troops stationed in the Middle East, and it was not unusual that their commander should see fit to inspect them, but all the same he suspected there might be more to it than that. Rumor had it that General Anders, the Polish commander in the field, had quarreled with Sikorski. Was there trouble brewing between the two Polish leaders? Eden made a mental note to take that one up with Churchill. The Prime Minister would be furious. He was inclined to regard all the leaders in exile as prima donnas. Certainly, Eden felt, that was true of de Gaulle, who was already locked in a life-and-death struggle with the communists in the Resistance. Sikorski was a likable chap, and Polish fighter pilots had distinguished themselves in the air battle over London; yet in a showdown Churchill would sacrifice the Poles without a qualm for what he considered the greater good.

"A general inspection of your forces in the Middle East?" Eden asked now.

Sikorski nodded without comment.

"Returning by way of Gibraltar?"

"Yes."

Eden stroked his moustache. "Well, then, my dear General, perhaps you would permit me the pleasure of lending you my own Liberator for the flight. I can strongly recommend my pilot. He is a Czech and one of the best transport pilots I know. In fact he is, I believe, one of only five pilots certified to land at Gibraltar at night."

Sikorski's weathered features lit up in a smile. "That is most kind of you, Mr. Foreign Secretary. I accept with pleasure."

"Consider it done, then. Now let me see what we can arrange to make your stop at Gibraltar more comfortable. Do you by any chance know our governor-general there, Sir Frank Noel Mason-Macfarlane?"

"I know him well. We are old and good friends."

"Splendid! Of course he will wish to offer you the hospitality of Government House. And if I am not mistaken, you have a representative of your own at Gibraltar."

"Count Lubienski."

"Better and better, General. Between the two of them they should be able to make your stopover quite snug. And what about you, Major?" Eden said turning to Zofia. "Will you be accompanying your father?"

"She goes everywhere with me," said Sikorski.

Eden glanced at his desk clock. Gone were the days when war had been a reasonably straightforward business. The levels of intrigue were becoming too complex. Stalin was accusing Sikorski of being a German agent and was threatening to break off relations with his government in exile. A sticky wicket all around.

Sikorski had not missed that glance at the clock. He rose and put out his hand. "We must not keep the foreign secretary any longer."

Eden stood up. "It has been a great pleasure to see you, General. I regret that our visit has been so short. Perhaps when you return from Cairo we can have a longer one. I shall be most interested in receiving your impression of conditions there."

"Of course."

"Good-bye, Major."

"Good-bye, sir."

The foreign secretary watched them leave. He then placed a call to Ivan Maiski. He had promised the

Soviet ambassador to keep him abreast of Sikorski's plans.

Jens Larsen limped down the gangway of the destroyer that had returned him to England. The hospital in Sweden had done wonders, but from time to time his feet still hurt. It had seemed at first that he must lose the badly frostbitten toes of his left foot, but after two months of treatment they had been saved.

During his stay in Sweden he had written to Michelle nearly every day but had received no answer. He decided to go straight to the apartment to surprise her.

He rang the bell repeatedly. At length a sour-looking individual with a three-day growth of beard appeared from the basement.

"What's all this now, mate?"

"I'm looking for the Sterns."

"Well you'll have to look elsewhere, won't you? No one home, is there? Haven't been for days. Bloody gone, ain't they?"

"What do you mean?"

"What I bloody said. Gone."

"But where?"

The man sighed. All these foreigners had begun to bore him. "Never said. Went out for a walk and never come back."

"They left no message?"

"Not with me."

"You're sure Miss Stern isn't here?"

"You been ringin' the bloody bell, ain'tcha?"

"When did you last see the doctor?"

"I ain't 'is bloody social secretary, am I? I don't keep track of the tenants."

Larsen's bewilderment was being replaced by anxiety. "Have you notified the police?"

The man looked at him with contempt. "Police? Not bloody likely. I'll police you if you don't stop ringing that bloody bell."

The door slammed in Larsen's face.

TWENTY-TWO

There had been occasions in the years before the war when General Fleming had come down to the country to spend a summer weekend with his friends, the Guthries. Teen-aged Peter Guthrie had been particularly impressed by the general's ferocious backhand. He was able to hit it down the line with awesome power.

Nowadays General Fleming was far too busy for tennis.

The general, an urbane man, had his headquarters at Norfolk House in St. James's Square, a pleasant backwater off Piccadilly where, in the days before the war, the peak of excitement had been a display of Josiah Wedgwood's famous china.

The general studied Peter Guthrie's face. "You think the Germans may have the girl?" he asked.

"There is reason to think so," Guthrie answered.

"And might be using her to influence Stern?"

"I think it's possible."

"You've queried F Section?"

"They won't talk to me."

"They will to me," said the general.

* * *

At his desk, Max Richardson was busy composing a handwritten letter to the editor of the *East Anglican Times*. The notepaper bore no letterhead. The missive contained phrases which Richardson thought might have been penned by what he liked to refer to as a "livid vicar." He wrote about the "moral collapse" that had occurred since the area east and west of Dover had been "invaded by ever-increasing numbers of foreign troops, particularly American paratroopers and French and Polish tank units." He then launched into a spirited discussion concerning the "immense number of rubber contraceptives" found around "the American bases at Marham and Coggeshall."

Richardson let his imaginary vicar ramble on a bit further before concluding with a final statistic regarding the alarming incidence of "foreign-inspired" venereal disease among his parishioners. He signed the letter with a name and address drawn from the Dover directory of parsonages.

Lounging back in his chair he reread his missive with satisfaction. He had made it just spicy enough to guarantee publication, perhaps even a series of rebuttals. Best of all would be the apoplectic fury of the unfortunate vicar whose name had been taken in vain. Never mind, some day he might know that he had been an unwitting hero who had made a contribution to the war effort. The information contained in the letter would find its way to Germany, where it would serve to reinforce the enemy's belief that an invasion was forthcoming.

Another scheme involved the construction of a false oil dock along the Dover foreshore. They could get Spence, professor of architecture at the Royal Academy, to design it; the whole vast structure could be built of camouflaged scaffolding, fiber board, and old sewage pipes. The final touch would be wind machines to kick up enough dust to give the impression that hundreds of trucks and thousands of men were busily at work.

A touch of genius, thought Richardson. Perhaps his greatest coup since the invention of exploding elephant dung to be placed on the jungle paths of Malaya.

His euphoric mood was interrupted by the unannounced arrival of Jens Larsen. For a man returned from the dead Larsen wore a singularly long face.

"My dear fellow," Richardson said with a broad smile, "it's good to have you back."

Larsen did not return the smile. "I want to talk with you."

"But of course. Have a seat. Tea?"

"No tea. I didn't come for a tea party."

"So you pulled it off after all. Congratulations."

"The congratulations belong to Torsten and Helberg, except that they're dead."

"I'm sorry about that."

"Yes, I suppose you are."

"Look here, I know you've had a rough time, but why take it out on me?"

"I haven't come to talk about Norway."

"No?"

"I want to know what has happened to Michelle Stern."

"Not my department, old boy. But I can tell you this. She thought you were dead. She was desperate for something to do. I simply suggested she talk to certain people at SOE."

"But anyone could have seen in five minutes that she was wrong for that kind of job."

Richardson leaned back in his chair. "Let me tell you some of the facts of life in relation to the work of this office. A handful of incidents out of thousands going on right around the rim of the war. A German general kidnapped in Crete. An SD officer murdered in Lyon. An attack by the Greek Sacred Heart Boat Squadron on a radar post on Rhodes. Five German aircraft crashed in flames outside Athens after abrasive grease had been placed in their engines. A dozen German soldiers killed by a commando unit near Savvaag in Norway. Three compressors in a liquid-oxygen factory at Boulogne-sur-Seine blown up by F section agents. Luftwaffe repair shops at Klover-marksvej in Denmark blown up by saboteurs. A German leave train derailed in the Ardennes. Three hundred thousand liters of petroleum products destroyed in a fire at Boussens in France. A ball-bearing factory at Aubervilliers burned to the ground. I could go on and on, but what's the use? I think you get the picture. Take your own operation. You were not a professional soldier, not trained for it. But somehow you pulled it off. It's that kind of war, Larsen, a war fought to a considerable extent by amateurs. A great many of them get hurt. I don't want to sound heartless, but that's the way it goes."

"There are people in Norway who believe the British will sacrifice the Resistance anytime it becomes expedient to do so," Larsen said bitterly.

"I don't think that rates an answer. Good day to you, Major."

Larsen stood. Richardson appeared to be having second thoughts. His tight-lipped expression changed to a smile. "Oh, do sit down! There's a good chap. Nothing to be gained by flinging gauntlets, you know."

Larsen resumed his seat.

"I don't suppose you'll change your mind about tea," Richardson said.

"No."

"There is something you ought to know. Deception is becoming very nearly the biggest business of the war. No one has ever before fought a war of deception on a global scale. Codes are being cracked right and left, agents turned. There is double-crossing and triple-crossing. Believe me, Larsen, when I tell you we now have the means of placing a deceptive message on Hitler's desk within twenty minutes of the time of its origination at Churchill's headquarters. It's absolutely the biggest bloody chess game in history. For every move there's a counter-move. And everyone, absolutely everyone, can be considered a legitimate piece to be moved, or sacrificed if necessary, in order to win."

"These are human beings you're talking about," Larsen said angrily, "not pawns on a damned chessboard."

"Those are human beings, too, who are shot down in aircraft or burned in tanks or blown up by bombs. But we can't afford to think of it that way or we should never be able to get on with the war. They become statistics. I'm sorry, but that's the way it is. The only difference is that some of the pieces on the board are of greater or lesser importance. Substitute admirals and field marshals for knights and bishops and you begin to get the picture. Do I make myself clear?"

"What is perfectly clear is that you are a cold-blooded bastard."

Richardson smiled. "I'm so glad you understand, old boy. If you felt otherwise, I shouldn't be doing my job."

TWENTY-THREE

General Fleming looked across his desk at Peter Guthrie. "It would appear that the Stern girl was seized almost immediately after landing in France. The SS treatment in her case has not followed the standard form. If it had, they would have shot her after the initial torture and interrogation. So far as we now know, she has been transferred from the SS headquarters to a political prison. Two other F sector agents caught the same night were also interrogated at Avenue Foch but then shipped to Buchenwald where they were executed.

"May I ask, sir, where this information comes from?"

The general shrugged. "Why not? You know too much already; you might as well know the rest. You've heard of 'Jade Amicol'?"

Guthrie nodded. "Jade Amicol" was the code name for the headquarters of British intelligence for Occupied France. Hidden in a tiny convent in Paris close by the high stone walls of the asylum of Sainte-Anne, Colonel Claude Ollivier—a balding giant with brilliant blue eyes—had for years been concealed from the Gestapo by the nine sisters of the Order of the Passion of Our Blessed Lord. Although "Jade Amicol" seldom ventured out from behind the convent walls, his intelligence unit—through contact with Prosper and other resistance networks—provided reports on the activities of the Germans.

"No word on where they may have taken her, sir?" Guthrie asked.

"Amicol thinks she is still being held somewhere in the south of France. I don't know just what that information is based on, but one supposes he must have his reasons. In any event you may be right about the girl; she appears to have a special significance for the Germans."

"I want to try to get her out, sir."

The general shook his head. "We don't even know where she is."

"You said the south of France."

"An area somewhat larger than the British Isles. Be reasonable, Peter."

Guthrie stood up. "Thank you very much, sir."

A smile touched the general's lips. "If you get killed, I don't want your mother to hold it against me. I'd prefer you didn't mention my name."

"Of course, sir."

"You might want to see Admiral Bowater, an old friend of mine. He has a lot of submarines he plays about with. Do you know him, by any chance?"

"No, sir."

The general scribbled a few lines on a sheet of notepaper. He put it into an envelope and handed it to Guthrie. "They call him the Giant Panda. You'll know why when you meet him."

With his immense frame and shock of white hair and large, dark, lustrous eyes the admiral did indeed resemble a panda. Guthrie thought he had hardly ever before seen a man so huge. He stood in front of a wall-mounted chart and stabbed a forefinger the size of a sausage at the French coastline. "Damned fine place to fight a war. If the casinos don't break you, the Frenchwomen will. I might just go along with you on this little caper. Sailed along that coast once or twice on a small boat and always came away without a sou. Grand sort of place."

Suddenly Guthrie remembered where he had seen the admiral before. The mention of small-boat sailing had done it. Gibraltar. Years before the war. Guthrie had been there single-handing on his small ketch when a disreputable-looking black-hulled schooner had come in puffing smoke rings. With its stubby masts and cluttered decks and the old spare tires slung over the side for fenders, it had created a jarring note in the otherwise immaculate torpedo basin. At the schooner's wheel was a bear of a man sporting a full beard, wearing only a pair of grease-stained shorts.

To Guthrie's surprise half a dozen ratings under the command of a petty officer had leaped aboard to help the bearded skipper secure his craft to His Majesty's seawall.

Now the reason was clear. It had been the admiral himself—the Giant Panda.

"I believe we nearly met once in Gibraltar, sir."

Bowater snorted. "Nearly met once in mid-Atlantic for that matter. You were crossing in some damn fool little boat . . ."

"*Sopranino.*"

"That's the one. I was on a forty-thousand-ton carrier at the time and that contraption of yours looked not much bigger than a canoe."

Guthrie smiled. "She wasn't very much bigger at that. Twenty feet overall, five-foot beam."

"Suicidal type, are you?"

"Not really, sir."

"Hmmp. This little game you're up to now—paying social calls on the SS in France—doesn't sound healthy."

Guthrie didn't say anything. The admiral pressed on. "And so now you want one of His Majesty's submarines to ferry you off to riotous living on the Riviera. You must be mad."

"Yes, sir. Mad, sir."

"Well I'm damned if I'll endanger one of His Majesty's vessels on this sort of Scarlet Pimpernel idiocy, but considering your background in small sailing craft, I do have a suggestion for you. You know, I suppose, what a felucca is?"

Guthrie nodded. "Small native sailboat used principally around the North African coast. Generally a lateen rig like the dhow. I saw several of them in Gibraltar before the war."

"No doubt. Murderous gang of smugglers. Fine sailors though. Killed many a bottle with them. Most of the feluccas are diesel powered these days and they operate over to the coast of Spain and even up to Marseille and Toulon. The fact that there is a war on doesn't seem to worry those devils. Always a market for the stuff they're carrying. Cut your throat and drop you overboard more than likely, but at least it will save the Gestapo the trouble of shooting you. I have one particular chap in mind. Dukov. If he isn't dead, he might take you. What do you say?"

"You're on, sir."

"If you ever mention my name officially in connection with any of this, I'll deny everything. Unofficially, I believe a man is entitled to go to hell his own way."

"Where do I find him, sir?"

"You don't. He'll find you. Leave it to me."

"Thank you, sir."

"You can thank me if you come out of it alive. Which I very much doubt you will. *Sopranino,* eh? I don't suppose you have a set of her plans?"

"I certainly do."

"Like to see them sometime. After the war, that is."

"Of course."

"What did she weigh, this cracker box of yours?"

"The hull weighed 450 pounds."

"Good God! Mast height?"

"She had a cruising and a racing mast. The racing mast was twenty-seven feet above deck."

"Too much sail area for an ocean passage?"

"Partly that, sir. And partly that when you had to climb the mast, the boat would tip over."

The Panda raised an eyebrow as thick as a caterpillar.

TWENTY-FOUR

It was nearly midnight. Anthony Eden's personal plane—an American Liberator bearing the markings, AL 523—stood on the airstrip at Bristol, engines ticking over. Eden's pilot—a Czech flight lieutenant—was at the controls. He was impatient. Sikorski had scheduled their departure for midnight and now, with less than ten minutes to go, there was still no sign of him.

In fact the general was, at that moment, on his way to the airport. He sat gazing out of the car window at the dark landscape rushing by. The delay had been unavoidable. Less than an hour before leaving London, Sikorski had received a letter signed by two of his ministers and delivered by hand:

> Personal—Top Secret.
>
> Your Excellence!
>
> For some time now you have been intending to travel to the Middle East. This intention corresponds with your intense preoccupation with affairs of state and particularly with your interest in the Polish fighting forces stationed in the Middle East.

It has become known that some of the Polish refugees in the East have become exceedingly agitated through the criminal incitement set in motion by certain circles; this renders the journey highly dangerous to you, General. The possibility that provocation from enemy quarters has had a hand in the matter cannot be ruled out. We, as members of your government, and as men sincerely devoted to you, appeal to you most earnestly to desist from traveling to the Middle East under the present circumstances.

Sikorski handed the letter to Zofia. "I think it only fair to let you know what you are getting yourself into," he said.

"Do you really think there is some danger?"

"There is some danger in everything. Even in eating oysters."

"Be serious."

"Very well. Yes, there is some danger. Which is why I have to go. If there is disaffection, it is always better to confront it directly. As a stateless head of state, I have to go where our people are, and at the moment they are in the Middle East. There is, however, no real reason for you to go."

She smiled at him. "No, of course not."

"You'll stay here, then?"

"No."

"And if I were order you to stay?"

"Then you'd have disaffection in London as well as in Cairo."

"There's a streak of stubbornness in you."

"I wonder where it came from?"

* * *

The Liberator, under a full load of fuel, took off slowly, using up nearly all of the runway until it gained at last a solid grip on the sky. In the early morning hours they touched down briefly at Gibraltar for refueling and then flew on to Cairo.

The next day telephones rang in several Polish ministries in London. Horrified ministers heard a voice say in Polish, "Have you heard the news, Minister? General Sikorski's plane has crashed at Gibraltar."

For several hours British officials were unable to confirm or deny the report. At last it was learned that Liberator AL 523 was safely on the ground in Cairo and that General Sikorski and his daughter were alive and well.

The mysterious calls were never explained.

The letter to Guthrie had arrived that morning. It had been posted from Bristol. He had read it three times already.

> My darling Peter—
> I regret our quarrel. Let us save our fighting for the Germans. The time will go quickly until I return. You have many things to do, and so do I. Please do not worry. We are traveling in the foreign secretary's personal plane this time and with his own crew. No unfortunate Captain Klimenki. Even so, I promise to check all the sleeping bags.
> Remember that I love you and want to come

back to you. Would you like to move to Poland
after the war, or should I plan to stay on in
London?

> Written in haste,
> Your Zofia.

Peter's heart sang. He was glancing for the fourth
time at the letter when he stepped off the curb. He
was aware briefly of the screech of brakes and the
shape of the ancient Daimler. Then the shock of the
impact and feeling himself tossed over the hood of the
car and back onto the curb.

He did not lose consciousness entirely. He was
still clutching Zofia's letter when they placed him on
the stretcher.

The light on Max Richardson's desk phone blinked.
The admiral did not like bells. When Richardson answered, the admiral said, "Come in, Max."

Richardson opened the door. Admiral Brooks, a diminutive man with a narrow head and a face like the
blade of a hatchet, indicated a chair. Unusual, that.
Bad sign?

"Word from Paris," the admiral began.

"The resistance people are raising a hullabaloo
claiming they're being used as some sort of sacrificial
lambs in connection with the Second Front scheme.
All rubbish, of course, but someone will have to get
over there to reassure them. Try to pick up the pieces.
Needs the right man, though. Someone who speaks
the lingo."

"Whom did you have in mind, sir?"

The bleak gaze never wavered. "I was thinking of you, Max."

Richardson allowed himself one long look of undying hatred. "When, sir?"

"Almost anytime. Say tonight?"

TWENTY-FIVE

In his gloomy Wolf's Lair at Rastenburg, Adolf Hitler lowered his trousers and bent over a chair. His personal physician, the piggish Dr. Morell, plunged a needle into the Fuehrer's buttock. Morell had shots for everything. This one—Prostakrinum hormones, prepared from an extract of young bulls' testicles and prostate—was designed to alleviate the moods of black depression to which the Fuehrer was subject.

In addition to his emotional upheavals, Hitler was now suffering from physical complaints—splitting headaches and a tremor of the left arm—which Morell privately diagnosed as being largely hysterical in nature. Hitler had increased his consumption of Dr. Koester's Antigas Tablets which had first been supplied to him in 1936 by his SS doctor, Ernst Grawitz. These apparently harmless black pills produced a temporary sense of euphoria. With things going poorly on the Eastern Front, Hitler was now taking from eight to sixteen pills a day.

The label on the small tin of antigas tablets read: "Extr. nux. vomic. 004; Extr. bellad. oor." Neither Morell nor Grawitz had bothered to translate that label into layman's language for the Fuehrer. What it meant was that the pills were made up largely of two poisons, strychnine and atropine. Over the years the Fuehrer had consumed enough of both to kill a horse.

The poisons manual has this to say: "Atropine acts on the central nervous system first as a stimulant, then as a paralyzer. In humans it primarily affects the forebrain, manifesting itself in a state of psychic exultation. A state of cheerfulness develops, coupled with vivid flights of ideas, talkativeness and restlessness, visual and aural hallucinations, and fits of delirium which may be peaceful and serene but may equally degenerate into acts of violence and frenzy."

On the subject of strychnine the manual states: "Accumulates in the body, acting on the nervous system to increase all the senses' acuteness. After heavy doses the accentuated sensitiveness to light may turn to downright aversion to light, and the other senses show similar changes. The senses of hearing and touch are accentuated, and for a time the senses of smell and taste may become more acute."

Hitler had great faith in his antigas tablets. He had been taking them at the time he had conceived his brilliant master plan for out-flanking the Maginot Line and crushing France. He had been taking them, too, when he had sent Rommel to Africa. And he had been taking particularly large doses before the invasion of Russia.

The portly Morell was not without a sense of the whimsical. He sometimes privately speculated on how the course of history might have been changed if his patient had never discovered Dr. Koester's little black pills.

Dr. Morell's rubber-encased forefinger had now entered the Fuehrer's rectum. Hitler groaned as the physician massaged his prostate. The sensation was both painful and pleasant. A drop of fluid appeared at the tip of the Fuehrer's penis. The prostate was soft and spongy. Flaccid like all the rest of Hitler's body, thought Morell looking down at his patient's skinny white shanks.

The Fuehrer complained that the light hurt his eyes. In addition he was suffering from shortness of breath. For these complaints Morell had added an ever-increasing variety of prescriptions, among them the heart tonics Strophanthin and Prostrophanta and the stimulants Cardiazol and Coramine. The Fuehrer had become obsessed with the state of his health. He could never get enough of the quack medico's pills and injections. Each new drug seemed to him a miracle cure for something. "Dr. Morell is expanding the frontiers of medical knowledge," Hitler would announce smugly to his assembled guests at luncheon. The atropine circulating through his veins brought a flush to his cheeks and a glitter to his eyes.

Morell was making the most of the opportunity while it lasted. Privately he had reason to believe that Hitler's time was limited. Shortly after his first meeting with the Fuehrer, he had performed an electrocardiogram study of Hitler's heart. The graphs, analyzed at the heart institute at Bad Nauheim under a pseudonym, showed beyond a doubt that the patient was suffering from an incurable heart disease and might be expected to suffer fatal consequences at any time. Having been present while the Fuehrer frothed at the mouth during one of his frenzied tongue-lashings of subordinates, Morell would not have given him a snowball's chance in hell.

Morell had withdrawn his finger. He handed Hitler a piece of tissue. Hitler pulled up his trousers.

"Well?" Hitler said, gazing sternly at Morell out of bloodshot eyes.

"The Fuehrer has the prostate of a sixteen-year-old," said Morell. "Quite remarkable for a man of your age."

"How, then, do you account for my general feeling of weakness?"

"The Fuehrer is bearing an intolerable load. You are carrying on your shoulders the whole future of western civilization. No man in history has ever borne such responsibility, my Fuehrer."

Hitler nodded. "True. You see then nothing in my physical condition that will prevent my carrying this war to a successful conclusion?"

"Nothing, sir."

Hitler gave him a piercing glance. "Even though I am surrounded by traitors? Even though treachery is in the very air I breathe?"

Morell felt a clutch of fear. Had Hitler discovered the true nature of the pills he had been gulping? Or had he seen the reading of his electrocardiogram? If Hitler thought his doctor was lying, he would have him shot in five minutes. He had ordered generals shot for less.

"I do not know to whom the Fuehrer is referring," Morell said in a low voice.

"To that swine Goering, of course. Not since that rotten homosexual Roehm have I been faced with so bitter a choice. Goering is following the same dissolute, profligate pattern. Thank goodness he has not yet openly displayed homosexual tendencies, although I am not even sure of that anymore. Think of it, Morell—while so many of our people are on short rations in order to bring this war to a successful conclusion, that fat swine has the gall to travel around the country making speeches in which he demands that people choose guns before butter. I tell you if he had not been loyal to me in the old days, I would have the pig dead before the sun goes down!"

Hitler's voice had risen. His eyes began to glaze. Flecks of foam appeared on his lips. Morell had seen the performance many times before, but still found it frightening. Hitler was whipping himself into a rage which might take his life. The last thing Morell wanted was to be found alone with a dead Fuehrer. Who would believe that he had not killed him? All his diagnoses had declared the Fuehrer to be in perfect health.

"Calm yourself, my Fuehrer. You must preserve your strength for the difficult tasks ahead. All Germany prays nightly for your good health."

Morell was already preparing a syringe full of Prostakrinum. The drug itself was probably useless, but if the Fuehrer believed it was having a beneficial effect, it might help.

As Morell approached him with the needle, Hitler waved him brusquely aside. "Get me Bormann!"

"Certainly, my Fuehrer."

Almost at once Bormann appeared.

Listening at keyholes again, thought Morell, finding it hard to conceal his distaste for the Fuehrer's brutish secretary. Bormann was short and wide with a massive head and a neck that bulged over his collar. Since the defection of Hess he had become the Fuehrer's closest confidant and adviser, even handling Hitler's personal checkbook and household expenses. With the decline of Goering in the Fuehrer's esteem, Bormann was now unquestionably the second most powerful man in Germany. If anything were to happen to Hitler, Bormann would take over the reins of government.

It was said of Bormann that he had once been imprisoned for bestiality. All court records pertaining to the case had vanished in a mysterious fire. Morell was inclined to believe the charge was true. The man had the look of a sexual degenerate.

If anything happens to Hitler a sheepfucker will rule the world, thought Morell.

"Where is Skorzeny?" cried Hitler.

"On a training exercise with his commandos," replied Bormann. "Due to return this afternoon."

"Contact him by radio and inform him that he is to report to me personally."

"Very well, my Fuehrer."

"All other appointments to be delayed until after I have seen Skorzeny."

"Field Marshal Kesselring is here."

"Let Kesselring wait."

"As you say, my Fuehrer." Bormann stood irresolute, waiting for further clarification. When it did not come, he saluted and left the room.

Morell guessed that Bormann was feeling a touch of anxiety. As Hitler's closest confidant, he was in the habit of being included in all Hitler's meetings with his officers. Why was Hitler letting Field Marshal Kesselring wait until after he had consulted with the SS officer? And why had he said nothing to Bormann about this sudden change in scheduling?

Morell tried to reconstruct the sequence of events which had led to Hitler's demand to see Skorzeny.

There had been the sudden rage at Goering. Hitler

seemed to have come to some decision. The hulking
Skorzeny with his immense frame and scarred features
was a killer, the kind of man to do the Fuehrer's dirty
work. Was it possible that Hitler had now decided to
rid himself of Goering? They had been friends for
years, but, so, too, had Roehm and the other Brown-
shirts marked for death on the Night of the Long
Knives.

The Fuehrer had finished dressing. Although there
was still a noticeable tremor in his left arm, the pills
were beginning to take effect. He held himself
straighter and his bloodshot eyes glistened. With a
curt nod to the doctor, he left the room.

Skorzeny, still in combat uniform from the training
exercise, and with his boots muddy, was conducted at
once to the Fuehrer's office. Topping six feet six inches
in height in his black death's-head uniform, he made
an imposing figure as he rendered the party salute.
Hitler responded with a flick of the wrist. "That will
be all, Bormann."

Bormann left the room. Hitler gestured Skorzeny to
a chair. Even seated, the massive Skorzeny seemed to
dominate the room. Hitler gazed at him for a long
moment out of heavily pouched eyes.

"I have an assignment for you."

"It is an honor to serve the Fuehrer."

"This matter is to be treated in utmost confidence.
No one, not even Himmler, is to hear a word of what
I have to say to you. Is that understood?"

"Of course, my Fuehrer."

"I want a full and confidential report on the activities of Reichmarshal Goering. I want to know with
whom he meets and when. More particularly, I want

to know of any meetings he may have with Admiral Canaris. And if there are such meetings, I wish to be informed concerning the topic of discussion."

Skorzeny permitted himself a small frown to cover his surprise. "Such a procedure would require the installation of listening devices, my Fuehrer."

"Of course. That is why it must be undertaken in absolute confidence."

"Very well, my Fuehrer."

"You have my authority to draw on any personnel and equipment you may require. Nothing is to appear in writing. You are to report to me personally once a week. Understood?"

Skorzeny lumbered to his feet. "Heil Hitler!"

TWENTY-SIX

The felucca lay close to the pier, her black-painted sides scraping the tarred pilings. Her decks were piled with nets, floats and the rusty odds and ends common to any fishing boat. Her bedraggled canvas was heaped untidily around the boom. A seaman in a blue jersey picked his teeth with the tip of a sheath knife and scowled at Larsen. Larsen heaved his seabag onto his shoulder and stepped on board. The stench was overwhelming. Larsen sighed. In an age of aircraft carriers it seemed to be his fate always to go to sea on some old tub stinking of fish guts.

"So you're Larsen?" said the bearded pirate on deck. Jens nodded.

"I'm Dukov. Where's Guthrie?"

"Got run over."

"Dead?"

"Busted ribs."

"So what happens now?"

"I'm taking his place."

Dukov shrugged. "Makes no difference to me. We get under way in half an hour."

The felucca—an ex-sardiner built for heavy weather —fled westward before the Levanter, its single lateen

sail taut as a drumhead. Dukov grinned, his teeth a
slash of white against the bronze-colored skin. A Levanter was no joke, but Dukov seemed to be enjoying
it. He had manned the wheel hour after hour, trusting
no one else to hold the vessel dead on course and to
take the giant seas precisely on the quarter. Each
time they came off a crest with a rush and swoop,
the felucca tried to broach sideways and to bury itself in the next wavetop. Larsen thought that if he
were responsible for the vessel, he might by this time
have had all the sails off and be dragging warps, but
if Dukov was afraid of broaching or pitchpoling, he
never showed it. His two crewmen, Bretons in black
berets and red fishing smocks, huddled in the shelter
of the wheelhouse. They had sailed with him before
and knew it was useless to question his methods.

Now Dukov grinned at Larsen and bellowed something that was lost in the wind.

"What?"

"A good sail, eh? Jolly good."

"Oh, yes. Jolly good."

"The admiral says you are also a sailor."

"After a fashion."

"What do you think? Maybe we should get the sail
off her, eh?"

Larsen managed to look unconcerned. "Why?"

"The Levanter. It will blow stronger."

"This bit of breeze?"

Dukov reached out a hand as big as a ham and
gave Larsen a slap on the back that nearly drove him
to his knees. "We let her run, eh?"

"Till the keel comes through the deck."

"By God, I like you, squarehead. Bowater says you
blew up a lot of Germans in Norway."

"Just a hydroelectric plant."

"And with a baby face, too. I'll bet you are a devil with women."

"Fantastic," Larsen said. "Absolutely fantastic."

"I'll tell you what. Why don't we just skip this shitty war and go off to Estoril together? The Portuguese are getting rich. We could make a fortune there, you and I, spying for both sides. You spy for the British and I will spy for the damned Germans, and then we will compare notes and exchange information and screw them both. What do you say?"

"Sounds like a lovely idea," said Larsen with a smile. "Perhaps after we do this little bit first."

"Bowater did not tell me much. Only that you are crazy enough to stick your head into the lion's mouth. You wish to be put ashore on the French coast. Something about a woman." Dukov nearly fractured Larsen's ribs with a dig from his elbow. "She must be very beautiful, eh?"

"She was."

"Until the lousy Krauts got her." He smiled broadly. "You know what they will do to you, those Gestapo bastards? They will cut off your balls in little pieces and make you eat them. Want to go back?"

"No."

"Good. Then take the helm for a while. Wake me when you see France."

Dukov padded away on salt-scarred bare feet that looked as tough as blocks of wood and lay down on a pile of tarred rope. He closed his eyes. The two Bretons watched with some alarm as Larsen took the wheel, but were reassured by the ease with which he handled the vessel.

Larsen had never before sailed with the antiquated

lateen sail. As he expected, the craft developed a
pronounced weather helm, but once he got accustomed to the feel, he enjoyed it. The whole rig looked
as though it might blow away at any moment, but
somehow it did not, and he began to realize that the
unstayed mast and yard were designed to bend under
pressure rather than to break.

He looked across at the black-bearded Dukov who,
even in sleep, presented a formidable appearance. A
pirate undoubtedly, but that was what the work
called for. He was inclined to think that Dukov had
been only half joking when he had suggested they take
turns working for both sides.

The coast of France was in sight, low and almost
hidden in the haze, although the offshore islands of
Hyères were clearly visible. Far beyond the coast he
could make out the snowcapped peaks of the Alpes
Maritimes. A crewman reached over to touch Dukov
on the shoulder. He came instantly awake, his expression so ferocious that the Breton stepped back in
alarm. Dukov grinned and clapped the man on the
back. The Breton grinned sheepishly.

"Son of a bitch," the captain roared at Larsen. "You
were supposed to wake me when the coast was in
sight."

"I hadn't the heart. You were sleeping like a baby."

Dukov spat to leeward, then pulled off his heavy
wool sweater and stood half naked in the wind. His
upper arms and his barrel chest and back were covered with an astonishing profusion of hair. He tossed
a canvas bucket attached to a rope lanyard over the
side and hauled aboard a foaming bucket of seawater
and splashed it over his head. He bellowed. The
Bretons grinned and shook their heads.

"Cognac!" Dukov roared. "For God's sake!"

One of the Bretons reached into the wheelhouse and pulled out an almost full bottle of brandy. Dukov uncapped it and poured a third of its contents down his throat. At that moment the wheelhouse window exploded, hurling fragments of glass into the air. A line of bullets stitched a row of holes across the roof of the wheelhouse and down the deck. Cursing, Dukov and the Bretons scrambled for whatever cover they could find. Larsen turned to see the Heinkel coming down out of the sun. The plane dived low over them, then shot upward in preparation for another run. It was only after it had passed that they heard the roar of its engines.

Larsen put the wheel hard over, risking a jibe that might pull the mast out of the vessel. It would not do to hold a steady course in the face of another strafing run. Looking up he could see the German swinging around in a circle behind them. The Heinkel appeared unhurried. The felucca was obviously defenseless, the strafing was hardly more than target practice.

Dukov had emerged from behind the coil of anchor line, the brandy bottle in one hand, the other clenched into a fist which he shook at the approaching bomber.

The great yard of the lateen sail came over with a roar and a crash. The boat shuddered under the impact, but the mast held. Almost at once the felucca's bow paid off and she ran off on a new course at right angles to the old one. The machine gun bullets this time were wide of the mark, stitches of foam a dozen feet from the hull. As the plane swept low, Dukov hurled the bottle at it.

The Heinkel was gone, disappearing toward the distant coast.

"Bloody bastards," bellowed Dukov.

The two Bretons slowly untangled themselves from the coils of rope.

"Anybody hurt?" asked Dukov. "No? Good. That's the second time with that bastard. I recognized him."

"How do you know?" said Larsen.

"He gave me the finger. Both times."

"Then he wasn't really out to sink us?"

"Not necessarily. He works on coastal patrol and he likes to shoot up the odd felucca. Two or three of our lads have been killed that way, but none of the boats has been sunk."

"Are you serious? He just uses you for target practice?"

"Thinks we're French fisherman, I suppose. Jolly good sport."

"The rotten bastard."

"One of these days I'll scrounge a Lewis gun and give him the surprise of his life."

"What happens next? We're not going in in daylight, are we?"

"Not unless you can't wait for the Gestapo to get their paws on you. That will happen soon enough anyway. No, now we catch a few fish." Dukov turned to his crew. "Get that sail down, lads, and we'll put the nets over the side."

They fished throughout the remainder of the day, coming up with a mess of sardines. Enough were kept for appearance's sake and a handful of the rest were fried in oil and consumed along with two bottles of rough red wine.

To Larsen there was an air of unreality about the scene. The bullet holes in the boat, the two grave-faced Frenchmen, the wild Hungarian, the strong wine and heavy loaves of bread and small silvery fish. A picnic within sight of an enemy-held coast. And his own fantastic quest. Had the reports from Jade Amicol any real foundation? The asylum of Sainte Anne, Colonel Claude Ollivier, the nine Sisters of the Order of the Passion of Our Blessed Lord. How credible was any of it?

Dukov said to him in English, "So you think you know where the girl is being held, eh?"

"In a house outside Antibes."

"Is that what Ollivier says?"

Larsen did not answer.

"Panda told me the whole story. I would not have taken you otherwise. Panda says it is important to find the girl. He wanted someone to back you up. That was why he chose me. I am the best man for the job." Dukov gulped his wine. "I am an old hand. I have been doing this for almost two years now. Nobody can stay alive in this line of work for two years without being good at it."

"So?"

"So I am going in with you. We will start by going to see my old friend Christine."

"Who is Christine?"

"She runs a beauty salon in Antibes. When you want to know something that is not generally known, you go to a beauty salon. A woman with her head in a towel and with grease on her face will sing like an angel. All those sluts who are fucking the Boche come to Christine's."

TWENTY-SEVEN

At almost the same moment that Jens Larsen was preparing to disembark near Antibes, Max Richardson was approaching the northwest coast of France on board an American PT boat.

He had never before ridden on a motor torpedo boat. Having now done so, he had little desire to repeat the experience. They had bashed across the Channel at thirty knots and his gut felt as though it had been used for a football. Now they rolled mercilessly in the swells, the three great engines throttled down, but still growling like leashed tigers.

A procession of sailing ships, ghostly reminders of the past as they sailed slowly across the path of the moon, was visible through the binoculars.

"Part of the French fishing fleet," explained the American lieutenant. "They're usually shepherded by an E boat. There has been no radar report, so he's probably just over the horizon. The Jerries know we head this way and they may be laying for us. Probably best not to hang around. You about ready, Commander?"

Richardson felt far from ready. It had all happened too fast. Less than twelve hours had passed since the admiral had stunned him with the announcement that

he was being sent to pick up the pieces of Prosper.
Bastard. Hanging back like a cobra waiting to strike,
and all the while giving him the impression that it
was Brothers whose neck was being readied for the
block.

The ritual gift of the gold cuff links had been almost more than he could bear. Agents going into the
field always got links bearing the admiral's signature,
crossed anchors. Crossed X's would have been more
appropriate. Did he buy them by the gross?

And what the bloody hell was he supposed to do
with cuff links while dressed in this *apache* outfit of
scuffed leather jacket and frayed flannel shirt and re-
volting fish-stinking corduroy pants? His skin crawled
with distaste as he wondered what seedy character
had worn the clothes before him. The first order of
business when he got ashore would be to arrange a
hot bath and change of clothing. No matter how dis-
organized the *réseaux* might be, surely they could
manage that. If the Gestapo got their paws on him,
he wanted at least to die in the dignity of clean
linen.

"Aren't we awfully far out?" Richardson said in
response to the skipper's question.

"Not particularly. A thousand yards, more or less."

Richardson looked down at the fisherman's dory
which had been launched from the PT's deck and
was now being held alongside by two enlisted men.
He knew he was only delaying the inevitable. The
Yanks were anxious to get the hell out of there and
back to the protection of Dover.

"I'm a rotten rower," he said.

The American did not say anything.

The hatchway to the wheelhouse was open. Richardson caught a glimpse of ghostly faces in the red glow of the battle lamps and then the green tail of the radar sweep crawling across the screen.

The radarman said, "Two E boats, Skipper. No more than six miles off and closing."

Richardson nodded with an air of resignation. He crossed the deck to the side where the dory was being held. He reached into his pocket and took out the admiral's gold cuff links. "Here," he said to the lieutenant. "A present for you."

The dory looked incredibly unseaworthy. Bilge water sloshed along the bottom and soaked his feet.

He had not taken more than a dozen strokes with the oars before the PT roared away. He was now conscious more than ever of the cold and the dark. Even the unsophisticated, gum-chewing Rover Boys had helped, but they, too, were gone, leaving him alone with his fear.

A wave of panic engulfed him. He wanted to row madly back to England. Fifty miles. Perhaps five miles an hour? Ten hours. But E boats roamed the Channel like wolves. And even if he made it, what then? Live the rest of his life in disgrace?

He remembered how smugly and coldly he had told Larsen that agents were pawns in a bigger game. Statistics. But now at last he knew how those trembling wretches must have felt. He was close in. At least there was no heavy surf running on what appeared to be a sandy beach ahead. He was no seaman; he would surely capsize.

Would Bouillard and Dédé le Basque be waiting for him as arranged? It had all happened so quickly; there had hardly been time to set things up properly. His brain was in a whirl. The Pessac group. Sabotage group Bouscat. Group Georges would carry out railway demolitions. They had done well in the past. Place names and figures flashed across his mind. Railway line cut between Le Puy and Jonzac. Railway bridge at Montendre blown up. Bridge on Route Nationale 137 destroyed. German troop train derailed near Pons. Destruction of railway bridge near Fléac. Railway line cut at Soulac. Statistics. Even the inevitable losses had been hidden behind code names —Alain, Albert, Alice, Lise, Lancelot. From the security of Baker Street none of it had seemed real. Larsen, in anguish over the loss of Michelle Stern, had seemed vaguely melodramatic. That fish-faced old bastard Brownlee at the Army and Navy Club: "One cannot make an omelet without breaking eggs." They weren't *his* bloody eggs.

Buoyed by anger he rowed harder for the shore. When he grounded on the shelving beach he felt the dory pushed sideways by an incoming wave. He stepped out into knee-deep water and dragged the skiff further inshore. His suitcase and documents were in the bow. He got them out and walked over the sand to a clump of sea grass and sat down to wait. Footsteps or the wind rustling the sea grass? He crouched lower. A solitary whistler. Surely the Germans would patrol with more than one man. What did he expect, an infantry division goose-stepping up the beach?

The tune of the whistler was now recognizable. The opening bars of *Je tire ma révérence*. To be acknowledged with the second phrase. But his lips were suddenly dry. Impossible to whistle. Absurd. A comic opera war. The man had paused and was looking expectantly in his direction.

"Dédé?" he whispered, his voice hardly more than a croak, sounding foreign to his own ears.

A chuckle from the whistler. Then suddenly there were other men rising from the dunes. Half a dozen or more, Sten guns blackly menacing in the moonlight.

"So you are Aristide," said the deep French voice. "Come along, then. Whose idea was that idiot recognition signal? *Révérence* my ass."

Marching across the sand toward what appeared to be a cluster of abandoned shacks, he felt his uneasiness compounded. Why were they all surrounding him so closely? Why the feeling of menace in the Stens even though they were not pointed at him directly? Surely they had been warned to expect him.

It was black inside the windowless hut. There was the damp smell of moldering netting. A press of bodies. He heard a muttered command and then, in the guttering light of a candle, a dozen or more hostile faces.

"Look here . . ." he began.

"Shut up!"

He had not been warned to expect hatred from the *réseaux*. The trial-like atmosphere inside the shack startled him.

"London understands your feelings. . . ." he began again.

"We of Prosper have no feelings. How can dead men have feelings?"

"Major Suttill . . ."

"Major Suttill is dead, Englishman. Betrayed by London."

"That's ridiculous. Why would London betray its own agents?"

"Why indeed? You tell us," said another voice.

Despite the damp and the cold, Richardson felt a trickle of sweat along his rib cage. "I have been sent to take Prosper's place," he said in what he hoped was a commanding voice. "To re-form the *réseaux*."

"Oh, is that why you have been sent?" a mocking voice answered. "We thought you were the first wave of the invasion. Isn't that what London has been promising us? An invasion any day now?"

"Give him a drink," another more kindly voice said. "He looks as though he could use it."

A bottle of rough red wine was passed to Richardson. He waited for a glass but none was forthcoming. His throat felt dry and scratchy. Was he coming down with something? He wiped the mouth of the bottle with his hand and drank deeply.

"Why are we wasting time?" a voice from the back of the room demanded. "Kill the sonofabitch and be done with it."

Richardson felt a shiver of fear along his backbone. They had it all wrong. It could be explained. The PM's Second front charade had never been meant as a deliberate betrayal, simply a legitimate use of deception to confuse the enemy. And yet . . . and yet . . . lies came sweetly to the tongue. It was truth that was bitter as gall.

How callously he himself had sacrificed others. Now it was his turn. His mind beat helplessly against the cage of his skull like a trapped bird. The admiral's words came back to him. ". . . An unspeakable flap over this man Stern. Questions being asked . . . good man, Brothers . . ."

Brothers!

It was Brothers who had first mentioned Michelle

Stern. Casually. "Running short of pianists, you know. Need people. Preferably someone who has lived in France. Young women have a way of blending in. Someone unhappy . . . perhaps the Stern girl."

Unhappy.

Christ, yes! Why hadn't he seen it before? She had been picked up within minutes of landing in France. Who but Brothers . . . ?

And now himself.

He fought down a feeling of nausea, reaching instead for the wine.

A voice from the crowd called out, "Enough of this farce. Finish it."

The gravel voice of Dédé le Basque commanded, "Quiet! We have to consider. Take the prisoner outside while we deliberate."

Prisoner! "Now wait just a minute . . ." Richardson began. Before he could complete the sentence he was jostled out of the hut and into the cool black shadow of a clump of trees.

He felt a little drunk from the wine. He could not believe any of it was really happening. Strong hands held his arms while a blindfold was tied around his head. He struggled but there were too many of them. When he tried to claw away the blindfold, a length of rope was knotted around his wrists.

"Allies!" he cried in English. "We are allies."

"For the betrayal of Prosper," the gravel voice said behind him, "and for the betrayal of France."

He was being forced down onto his knees, his head lolling forward like that of a sick dog.

He heard the click of metal. Smelled gun oil. Felt something hard thrust against the back of his neck.

* * *

It was nearly dawn when the men of the *réseau*, moving in solemn procession, trooped back to the beach carrying the body of Max Richardson on a slab of wood. Rough justice had been administered.

The body was dumped unceremoniously back into the dory. Half a dozen *résistants* dragged the boat out into deeper water. An offshore wind was blowing. Perhaps, in time, the little boat and its cargo would find their way back to England.

TWENTY-EIGHT

Soon after dark Dukov's felucca entered a quiet bay to the west of Cannes. The normally busy stretch of beach and the hotels beyond were deserted, although a cluster of lights indicated the center of the town.

Latour, one of the two Bretons, brought the felucca in until her keel was almost touching the sand, and Dukov and Larsen dropped over the side. The water was bitterly cold. They waded ashore and then waited until they could make out the dim outline of the felucca turning out of the bay.

"We'll have to go through the village of Théoule before we catch the bus in the morning," Dukov said. "There's a curfew on and we don't want a bunch of Vichy cops asking questions. We'd better lay up somewhere. How about a nice warm hayrick?"

"Hayricks mean farm dogs," Larsen said between chattering teeth.

"True enough," Dukov agreed. "We'll just try for the woods, then."

It was midnight when they reached a slight rise above the village of Théoule. The wind bit through their wet clothes and seemed to turn their sodden flesh to ice. From their high point they could look down the deserted main street of the village. One feeble red light shone out of the blackness.

"Either the whorehouse or the police station," Dukov said. "Maybe both. We'll get up into the woods here and lie up until morning." Moving around during the curfew was too dangerous. In the morning, with their rough clothes and unshaven faces, they would not stand out among the French peasants and fishermen on their way to work.

During the night it hailed. They crawled into the woods but found little shelter. Fed up, Dukov grumbled, "None of those Vichy bastards will be on the roads on a night like this. Let's go!" They scrambled out of the woods and hurried through the town.

The activity made them a little warmer. Suddenly, as they skirted the tiny railway station, they were caught in a cone of light. Nearly blinded by the glare and expecting at any moment to be challenged, they dropped to the ground and lay there while a freight train thundered through the station and vanished into the darkness. A few minutes after the train had passed, Théoule was again in blackness.

The hail had turned to rain. Two sopping kilometers farther on they reached another small village, this time La Bocca. It was growing light. Cyclists were beginning to move along the road in the direction of Cannes. People were already starting to queue up in the market square and outside the food shops. Occasionally a French policeman gave the two strangers a hard stare, but none of them was inclined to leave the shelter of his doorway long enough to examine papers. Dukov and Larsen, heads down against the rain, looked no less surly and unhappy than the crowds of workmen hurrying on their way to the factories. After a conference they decided that even if it meant capture, it would be worth it to stop at one of the neighborhood cafés for a coffee and brandy. The proprietor behind the zinc bar took their money with a muttered comment about the lousy weather. Dukov growled something in return and they gulped their drinks and left.

"You can't stay long in any of these dumps," Dukov said. "The flics are doing the Gestapo's dirty work for them and they are even better at it than the Germans."

Larsen, with the combination of coffee and brandy lighting a pool of warmth in his stomach, said, "What do we do about food? I'm starving."

Dukov grinned. "Christine will give us breakfast. You will love Christine."

Christine was a slender, elegant woman who appeared to be in her early thirties. She was not at all what Larsen had expected. She looked at the two sodden figures on her doorstep and said, "What do you two want?"

Dukov nudged Larsen in the ribs and said, "Not bad, eh? I'm looking for Joseph. Joseph Charbonnier."

"Well, there's no one here with that name."

He thrust a foot inside the door. "Hold on. Isn't this number eleven?"

"It's eleven all right, but there's no Charbonnier here."

"Rue Pasteur?"

"No, you idiot, Rue du Canada."

Dukov let his jaw drop. "Well, I guess that explains it."

"Rue Pasteur is around the corner. In back. Through the alley. Even an idiot like you ought to be able to find it in half an hour or so," the young woman said in acid tones. She let her left eyelid droop for a moment and with the slightest gesture of her head, she indicated the two women who sat under hair-drying machines.

Dukov said, "How about a date sometime? Would you like to . . ."

The slamming door cut him off.

"Merde!" Dukov complained loudly. Then, with a shrug, he turned to lead the way into the back alley.

They found a place out of the wind behind a collection of dustbins. The blind alley was long and narrow with no windows looking down on it and only one doorway, the back door to the beauty shop. Unless someone deliberately came looking for them they were invisible from the street.

"Who is Christine?" Larsen asked. "She's not French, is she?"

"Polish. The Countess Krystyna Skarbek, actually. We first met while she was in Hungary working for British Intelligence. After that, she was gathering information in Yugoslavia, Istanbul, and Athens. When she came here she came by way of Algiers. I brought her on the last leg of the journey on the felucca. Despite our little exchange we are really old friends."

"A beautiful woman."

"Yes, but don't get any ideas. Better men than you, including myself, have tried and failed. Perhaps one day when the war is over . . ." his voice trailed off. "Meanwhile, she is interested in only one thing— killing Germans. She is more dedicated than any of us."

The back door had opened a crack. Dukov nodded toward it and said, "You first. Fast."

The entrance to the alley was clear of passersby. Crouching low Larsen slipped around the dustbins and in through the partially opened doorway. He found himself in darkness. A hand touched his, and Christine's soft voice said, "Be still."

A moment later the door opened and Dukov slipped inside. As soon as the door had closed behind him, Christine put her arms around his neck and kissed him soundly.

"Dukov, my love, how goes it?"

"Ça va. And you, Countess?"

"As you see. By the way, you stink horribly of fish."

TWENTY-NINE

They had eaten and bathed, and now Larsen was explaining the purpose of his mission. When he had finished, Christine said, "The girl could be in the Petite Mahal, a villa between Cannes and Antibes. It was built by an Indian prince along the lines of the Taj Mahal. It is remotely situated. It has been used by our German guests to keep political prisoners who may one day be useful. Do you intend to take her out by force, the two of you?"

"Why not?" said Dukov.

Christine smiled. "Why not indeed? Except that it is impossible. There are watchtowers all around the perimeter except on the cliff side, which is considered unscalable. You would need a regiment."

"What about the Resistance? A little outing might do them good. Give them a chance to fire off some of those fancy new weapons."

"It is possible, but first we must find out if the Stern girl is truly there. I will speak to one of the guards at the villa. I have done some business with him before. But he is expensive. Very."

"How much?" Larsen asked.

"For something like this, I should think ten thousand francs."

Larsen opened his jacket and rolled up his sweater. Around his waist was a black money-belt. He opened a zippered compartment and pulled out a thick wad of thousand-franc notes.

"My God!" said Dukov. "If I had known you were carrying that, I would have knocked you on the head the first day out."

From the window of the small bedroom above the beauty salon, Larsen could see Christine returning. She walked rapidly, her slender body held very erect, her dark hair blowing in the wind. A gendarme on the corner nodded to her, and she favored him with a smile, teetering for a moment on her high heels as though made giddy by his attentions, and then continued on. Larsen chuckled.

Dukov, lying on the bed with his eyes closed said, "What's up?"

"The gendarmes are taking an interest in the countess."

"Those abominable flics."

They heard the door open, then the sound of Christine's steps mounting the stairs. She used her key to open the bedroom door and after she had entered, locked the door behind her.

"Good morning, gentlemen."

"You took your own sweet time," growled Dukov.

"I must remember never to have anything to do with you before breakfast." From her handbag she drew out half of a loaf of bread and a package containing garlic sausage. She split the sausage in two and made a sandwich for each of them. "I'll make coffee, such as it is, and bring it up."

"Thank you, Christine," Larsen said.

Dukov, his mouth full of bread and sausage, gave her a baleful look.

When the door had closed behind her Larsen said, "Why are you so hard on her?"

Dukov belched heavily and wiped his mouth with the back of his hand. "Do you really want to know?"

"Yes."

"Because I don't want her doing this lousy work. Sooner or later those Gestapo pigs will get their hands on her, and you know what will happen to her then. Why don't these damned women stay home and leave the war to men? Never before has there been such a thing as women going to war."

"Never before has there been such a war."

Christine returned carrying a red enamel tray with three small cups of coffee. It tasted strongly of some artificial essence and very little of coffee, but at least it was hot and steaming.

"About the girl?" said Dukov. "You're sure it's the same one?"

Christine shook her head. "Not absolutely. She was described to me by the guard, but I'm not sure."

Larsen took a photograph from his wallet. "Did his description fit?"

"I think so, although I gather she has lost a good deal of weight. I will meet him again tomorrow in the Rue du Canada to show him the picture."

Karl Hauser stepped from the train's washroom with an expression of distaste. The French, never noted for their cleanliness, seemed to have surpassed even their own standards of filth in the wartime con-

dition of their trains. What a stink! No wonder their
vaunted army—the largest standing army in the world
—had crumbled in a matter of weeks.

He returned to his seat to watch the countryside
sliding past the window. Another fifteen minutes to
go. His briefcase, with the topcoat neatly folded over
it, was already on the seat.

He sat rigidly erect, his face reflecting none of the
disquiet he was experiencing at the thought of seeing
Michelle. Even when the train approached the sea
and he saw the great expanse of the Mediterranean
spread before him, he was not really conscious of it.
Why, he wondered, had the old fox Canaris so readily
agreed to his visit? A moment of compassion? Another
strand in his web of intrigue? Impossible to say. Canaris in his wing collar and with the gold stripes on his
arms looking like a kindly grandfather. It was said
that he and Heydrich, who hated each other and were
deadly rivals in their battle for control of the intelligence services, had gone riding together every Sunday
in the park and visited each other's homes for dinner.
Heydrich—young, keen, predatory—a hawk who might
very well have some day inherited the mantle of the
Fuehrer. How different he was from the little admiral
with his secret smile.

Canaris sat in his office on the Tirpitzufer and made
his arrangements. Devious. Ever devious.

The sun had come out, and the sudden bright glitter of the Mediterranean and the long curving coast
reminded him of the harsh glare of Africa and the
city of Mogadishu as seen from the sea. In his twenties
he had gone away to Africa because his heart was
broken. His own true love had married that Jew
Stern and there was nothing to be done about it. The

thought of Denise in Stern's arms had made him feel suffocated. He had hoped that the excitement of visiting strange places would help. But nothing had. When he saw the long-bodied sharks along that coast twisting in the thin blue skin of water that foamed onto the yellow sands, it did not distract him; all he could think of was how he would have loved to show it to Denise.

The train jolted on. Railway beds were in poor repair all over Europe. Yet this part of France remained comparatively untouched by the war. There were no tourists, and the few cars ran on charcoal, but the fields seemed peaceful, the cattle grazed as before.

He felt strange returning to Cannes. Denise and Stern had selected Cannes for their honeymoon. Hauser had followed them. He had stood in the street in front of their hotel. He had moaned like a dog.

When he left the train there was a car waiting for him with an Abwehr driver in civilian clothes. The driver had a pistol beneath his jacket and a submachine gun on the floor beside his feet.

"Herr Dr. Hauser?"

Hauser nodded.

"May I ask for some identification, Herr Doctor?"

Hauser showed him his papers.

"Very good, Herr Doctor. I will take the Herr Doctor straight to the villa."

The driver kept the car moving fast, whipping the heavy Mercedes around the bends of the Corniche. Hauser understood why. Any one of those curves might have concealed an ambush. It was not considered good practice for a Mercedes to dawdle on French roads.

The sky had clouded over; cold, dank fog rolled in

from the sea. The car slowed. They were leaving the
main road and were climbing sharply. The car drew to
a halt before a wooden barrier. A guard, also in civilian clothes but carrying a submachine gun strapped
to his back, stepped out of a wooden shelter to chal-
lenge them. The driver showed his papers and muttered a password. The guard waved them on.

The villa was a miniature edition of the Taj Mahal,
but done in wretched taste and painted a vile shade of
electric blue. An architectural nightmare, but suitable
for its present use. Remote, protected by abrupt hills
and high cliffs, unapproachable from the sea and although under Abwehr control, offering a pretense of
Vichy French supervision. No one would have supposed from its appearance that it was a prison.

Major Schroeder, the commandant, greeted him in
the reception hall with a firm "Heil Hitler!" Hauser
responded with the Nazi salute.

"Your bedroom is on the second floor, Herr Doctor."

"Thank you, Major."

"I will have your bag taken upstairs. Perhaps you
would care for something—tea or coffee?"

"Tea," said Hauser. "But later."

"How long do you expect to be with us, Herr Doctor?"

"Not long. Perhaps a day or two."

"You are here only to interrogate the prisoner
Stern?"

"Yes."

"That can be arranged at your convenience."

Schroeder wore a black patch over one eye. His left
hand, although gloved, was held with the rigidity that
could only be achieved by metal. His green whipcord
uniform fit his lean frame to perfection, and around

his throat he wore the Iron Cross first class. It was not unusual, Hauser knew, for badly wounded combat officers to be placed in charge of detention camps.

"Would it be possible to see the young woman now, Herr Major?"

"You wish to begin your questioning immediately?"

"No, only to observe her."

Schroeder nodded. "As you wish. There is a peephole for that purpose."

The small room was stark white under the naked bulb shining from behind a metal grid. There were no windows and no furniture, only an iron cot set against one wall. The cot had a wooden slab over its framework and on top of that a thin mattress. There were no springs. Prisoners had cut their throats with bedsprings.

The woman lay on the cot with her face to the wall. She was painfully thin. She wore a shapeless cotton hospital gown. Her feet were bare.

She turned over and opened her eyes. Hauser gave a grunt of surprise. This was not Michelle. The woman on the bed must be at least forty. Great dark eyes and a gaunt face. Skin the color of old parchment. She got up and began to move back and forth four paces in each direction like a caged animal. Hauser wondered; there was something familiar there after all, something in the way she carried herself, still a hint of pride in the squared shoulders.

Michelle.

THIRTY

Dukov, mounted on Christine's bicycle, rode the nine
kilometers along the coast road to Antibes, past the
house where the Duke of Windsor used to stay, and
then over the railway bridge and around the shimmer-
ing expanse of the Golphe-Juan. Only a handful of
people. Boring.

The bicycle wobbled. He was trying to appear
drunk and was succeeding. He had a bottle of *vin
ordinaire* sticking out of the pack on his back. He
stopped every mile or so to take a pull at it.

The prospect of action pleased him. In the meeting
with the Resistance leaders he had said little. They
were a talkative lot, and in Dukov's estimation they
knew nothing of real war. Their forays against the
Germans had so far been limited to blowing up the
occasional freight train or slicing the throat of some
corporal riding home on his bicycle after a night of
whoring. The collapse of the French armies still
mystified Dukov. Powerful as the German thrust
around the Maginot Line had been, how was it possible for one of the world's great military machines
to fall apart like wet newspaper? There had to be
more to it than that. They had been betrayed by
that fish-eyed Laval and that old bastard Pétain and

an officer corps that had been rotten ever since the Dreyfus case.

Nor was the Resistance entirely to be trusted. It was too easily infiltrated. Who knew how many were working for the Germans?

The meeting with the Resistance leaders had seemed more like a cocktail party. All of them standing around in Roger Renaudi's shop in the Jardins Fleuris. The place had an entrance into the gardens, and another leading to the street behind. Renaudi considered it ideal because it furnished him with a view both ways through a dividing curtain. Thus he could carry on his business of selling fancy buttons while keeping open house for the Carte group. His young wife, Germaine—a hot number from the looks of her—sold buttons during the day and acted as a courier for the organization at night. Dukov did not approve. People coming and going through the button shop and hardly any of them buying anything. And the worst part of it was that all of them knew each other. If the Gestapo put the screws to any one of them the entire organization would be blown.

He pulled over to the side of the road, leaned the bicycle against a tree, and sat down to finish his wine. It would not do to arrive too early. Larsen and Christine could not move until he had finished off the guard at the barrier gate, and he could not do that until after dark. The Germans did not move around much after dark. It was unlikely that German vehicles would be encountered on the road to the villa. And even if there were, he would hear them in plenty of time.

Disposing of the sentry would not present too many problems. First a convincing imitation of a drunken fisherman and then the double-edged gutting knife taped to his leg to finish the job.

What if the sentry shot first and asked questions later? The whole thing was a gamble. Who knew how many of those Vichy bastards were prepared to double-cross him? In the meeting at Renaudi's, that stiff-necked Vautrin had tried to reassure him, but Dukov still had his doubts. Vautrin was a Gaullist and made no secret of the fact that he resented SOE penetration into what he considered to be his own territory.

"You can trust our observations," Vautrin had said. "Our men are quite capable of covering the ground, and besides I've had a team of French airmen living nearby for the past couple of weeks. They ought to know what's up."

Dukov had smiled. Vautrin was entirely too well dressed for his taste—cashmere sweater, sport jacket, well-pressed flannel slacks. And besides the bastard stank of cologne. Dukov thought of his own sweat-stained clothing and the chunk of garlic sausage he carried in his pocket. It had amused him to offer Vautrin a bite. The starchy colonel had declined with a grimace.

"If you insist on looking the place over, you must get there under your own steam. I've got no petrol to waste on unnecessary journeys," Vautrin had said.

Dukov grinned ferociously. He bit off another chunk of salami and said in an easy, conversational way, "I'll tell you, *mon colonel,* what you can do with your precious petrol. You can shove it up your ass."

Christine stepped between them. "Will you excuse me, Colonel, if I take Dukov away for a few moments?

Instructions from London have come through on a matter that concerns him."

Vautrin bowed stiffly.

Christine steered Dukov in the direction of a buxom redhead who seemed to be bursting out of her tight black dress. Only hours away from the attack on the villa and already they were squabbling among themselves. The trouble was, Dukov reflected, that in such a climate of intrigue and fear, it was impossible to know which side people were on. Pro-Allied? Pro-Vichy? Pro-Nazi? Gaullist? Communist? Black Market? Collaborator? Informer? Resistance?

The redhead gave him a broad smile and accepted the last bite of salami. Cat ragout was the subject under discussion. She showed him an article clipped from the local paper:

CAT EATERS, ATTENTION!

In these times of restrictions, certain hungry persons haven't hesitated to capture cats to make a nice "rabbit stew." These persons don't know the danger that threatens them. In fact cats, having as their useful mission the killing and eating of rats, which are carriers of the most dangerous bacilli, can be for this reason particularly harmful. . . .

Dukov handed it back. He was more interested in the shape of her buttocks as outlined by the black satin. Ten minutes later they were on their way to her flat.

For Larsen, too, the cocktail party at Renaudi's had seemed frivolous and time-consuming.

"Don't worry," Christine had told him, "when it comes to killing the Boche they will be serious enough. As for Dukov, this is part of his performance. It pleases him to play the role of the *apache*. Actually he was brought up in respectable bourgeois surroundings. I knew his sister, a lovely child before the Gestapo got her. She was seventeen, slender, beautiful. She was caught in the St. Germaine des Près quarter distributing the underground paper *Combat*. She was turned over to the Geheime Feldpolizei, real experts at their job. Before that she was in the hands of the Milice. The Milice, as you know, are Frenchmen trained by the Gestapo. If anything, they are more vicious than their mentors. Scum. But skillful. She had expected to be kicked, shoved, and punched, but instead she was ushered politely into a room where the music of Bach came from loudspeakers. She was seated in a comfortable chair and offered a cigarette. She was asked to reveal the location of the printing presses that had produced the copies of *Combat*. She told them she did not know. A fellow student had pressed them into her hand and asked her to distribute them. They asked for the name of the student. She replied that she did not know. To every question her answer was the same, '*Je ne sais rien.*' 'I know nothing.'

"They stripped off her clothes. It was the first time she had ever been naked before a man. They prodded her with their fingers in all parts of her body to humiliate her. Then the one who had so politely offered her a cigarette began to beat her with a riding crop. They beat her until she was covered with blood and her skin hung in strips. She screamed and screamed, but to every question she still responded, '*Je ne sais rien.*' "

Christine's voice had grown hoarse with suppressed emotion, and her face was pale. Larsen felt a shiver along the nerve ends at the back of his neck.

"After the whipping," Christine went on, "they treated her to a bath. Standard procedure. The tub is filled with ice water and the subject, hands tied behind his back, is knocked into the tub face forward. He is held under until he begins to go limp and is then pulled out, revived, and thrown into the tub again. As a rule the panic accompanying the sensation of drowning is enough to make almost anyone talk. Between periods of unconsciousness the girl kept repeating, '*Je ne sais rien.*' So they varied the technique. They applied electrodes to her nipples and the genital area. The shocks were enough to start her screaming again and to leave deep burns in the skin. Even so, she still denied knowing anything.

"The electrodes were followed by hot irons applied to the soles of the feet, cigarette burns, a savaging by police dogs, and injections of ice water.

"She clung to life and the shreds of sanity, repeating over and over the one undestroyable thought, '*Je ne sais rien.*' After that it almost seemed as though they had given up on her. For several days she was left alone in her cell. They removed her handcuffs and even applied an ointment to her wounds which had become infected.

"On the third day they brought in a sixteen-year-old boy from her neighborhood. She recognized him as the son of a Neuilly doctor. The boy was strapped into what looked like an electric chair. They told her that if she revealed the location of the printing presses they would do nothing to the boy, and that both of them would be released. 'If not,' they said, 'then everything that happens to him is your fault. You can stop it any time.'

"They broke his fingers one at a time. He screamed. At intervals she was asked if she was ready to talk, but she could only repeat what she had already said over and over. They broke the boy's wrist. Then his arms, his legs and his ankles. The boy, of course, was unconscious by that time. They questioned her one last time and shot him through the head. She fainted.

"When she revived, she was back in the small room near the entrance. The loudspeakers again played Bach. They said she had been sentenced to death and would be taken to Fresnes prison and shot."

Christine paused. Her hands were trembling with emotion. "You may wonder how we know all this. One of the Milice who interrogated her later defected and revealed the entire story. Dukov was present when he told it. It required no less than five of our people to restrain him."

"Did they take her to Fresnes?" Larsen asked.

"Yes."

"And the Milice?"

"He was knifed that night in an alley near Les Halles." Christine had herself under control again. She managed a smile. "The story is not so unusual. It has happened to many. It can happen to any of us. I have told it not because I am morbid, but only so that you will have a little better understanding of our friend Dukov."

"He is in love with you, you know."

"I know. It is to be regretted."

"You don't like him?"

"I like him very much. I even could love him.
But not until this is over. I will not permit myself
the luxury of such an attachment." She looked across
at Dukov who was leaving with the redhead in the
black dress. "In any case, it does not appear to be
cramping his style too much."

Dukov leaned his bicycle against a tree and sat
down to wait for darkness. A juicy piece, that Renée.
She was not as young as she appeared—somewhere on
the wrong side of forty. But what the devil, it had
not been hard to get her to slip away with him. She
was as hot as Tabasco sauce. As they walked back to
her place, a patrol of two Vichy police had displayed
more than a passing interest. Renée had promptly
put her arms around him and thrust her tongue
halfway down his throat. She had felt him getting
hard. She swung her belly against him. The flics had
laughed and moved on without checking his papers.
It was no longer safe for a Frenchman to move around
the streets even on this side of the demarcation line.
The Germans were beginning to tighten the screws.
But Renée could deal with the flics. She'd had plenty
of experience. And she had proceeded to prove it in
bed. He hoped he would not be too weak in the knees
for what lay ahead.

He uncorked the bottle of *vin ordinaire* and tilted
it down his throat before dropping the empty bottle
into a refuse can.

His life, he thought with a grimace, had been
marked by a trail of empty bottles. Christine had not
resented the redhead. If anything she had placed the

bird in his snare. "Get on with it," he told himself.
"You are a little drunk and you have recently been
well and truly fucked. What more can a man ask?"

It was getting dark. He whistled as he mounted
the bicycle.

The Abwehr sentry came out of his box when he
saw the shambling figure pushing a bicycle up the
road. He carried his machine pistol loosely in his
left hand.

"Halt!"

Dukov threw up his hands in mock terror. "Kama-
rad!"

"What the devil do you want?"

Dukov lurched closer, singing as he came.

"Get out of here," said the sentry. "Back the way
you came."

Dukov reached into his pocket. The sentry raised
the machine pistol. Dukov chuckled slyly and withdrew a pack of Gauloises.

"*Zigaretten?*"

The sentry shook his head. Dukov put a cigarette
between his lips and fumbled for matches. The box
of wax tapers fell at the sentry's feet, spilling out onto
the ground. Mumbling to himself Dukov bent to re-
trieve them. When he came up the knife was in his
hand, held with the blade as an extension of the
forefinger—the knife fighter's grip.

The tip of the gutting knife caught the German just
under the rib cage, penetrating the man's leather
jacket and driving deep into his belly. Dukov's powerful wrist completed its sweep with the same motion a
man might use to shuck an oyster out of its shell. Dis-
emboweled, the dying German sagged backwards, his

finger tightening in a spasm on the trigger of the machine pistol, driving two shots into the ground. Dukov wrenched his knife out of the man's guts and let him fall.

THIRTY-ONE

Skorzeny was making his second report. Hitler listened with somber attention, only his eyes seeming alive in the pallor of his face. The Fuehrer found himself slightly repelled by Skorzeny's brutish size and scarred features. In many ways he reminded Hitler of the Brownshirt thugs who had served under Roehm.

Skorzeny reminded him, too, of Emil Maurice, the ex-convict who had been his bodyguard and chauffeur at the Haus Wachenfeld on the Obersalzberg, and who had seduced Hitler's niece, Geli Raubal, the only woman Hitler had ever really loved.

He studied Skorzeny's report. The SS officer had done his usual thorough job. In the past month Goering and Canaris had met twice, each time at Carinhall. Why? The commanders of the Luftwaffe and the Abwehr had nothing in common, nor had they ever been part of the same social circle. Their conversation had been guarded. Lisbon had been mentioned several times. Also, New York. It was Skorzeny's supposition that someone known to both Goering and Canaris was going to New York by way of Lisbon.

Hitler nodded. "No names were mentioned?"

"None, my Fuehrer."

"And since then?"

Skorzeny shook his head. "We have heard nothing. Obviously both phones have been swept clean of listening devices. Routine, one presumes, customary with high-ranking officers. But earlier there were other calls to and from Canaris that may be of interest to the Fuehrer even though they did not concern the Reichmarshal."

"The names?"

Skorzeny withdrew a slip of paper from the breast pocket of his uniform. He had begun to read aloud when Hitler interrupted him with an impatient gesture. Skorzeny handed over the paper. Hitler put on his glasses to study it. Beck, Olbricht, Goerdeler . . . nothing too unusual in that. There was no reason why Canaris, as head of the Abwehr, should not be in touch with various members of the armed forces.

Hitler frowned. He had come to the name of General Fromm, C in C of the Home Army. The Abwehr's concern was with international spying—the Gestapo took care of matters at home. Why then should the head of the Abwehr be in touch with the commander in chief of the Home Army?

Possibly there was nothing to it, and yet . . . Hitler had never really trusted the wily Canaris. He did not trust any of the old-line officer corps. Plotters all, who had been opposed to the invasion of Russia from the start, ostensibly because they remembered 1914 and the lessons taught by a two-front war. Yet, if Goering had not made a botch of the air war over Britain, England would have come to terms, and there would have been no two-front war. Always he was betrayed by fools or traitors. Himmler had been after him for months to get rid of Canaris and to turn the apparatus of the Abwehr over to the Gestapo. Perhaps he was right. Himmler was a plodder, but he was loyal. Perhaps it was time to give the investigation of Canaris to Himmler.

"I will keep this list," Hitler said.

"Of course, my Fuehrer."

"And I will want to know more about what is going on in Lisbon."

"It may be necessary for me to go there myself, my Fuehrer."

"Do as you see fit, Skorzeny. You have my complete confidence." Hitler waved his hand in a gesture of dismissal.

THIRTY-TWO

Michelle Stern opened her eyes and stared into the darkness. The staccato bark of gunfire had penetrated even her windowless room. It was a sound she had gotten to know well at the Gestapo headquarters on the Avenue Foch. Sometimes at dawn, but more often at odd hours of the day or night. Firing squads did their work in the courtyard where the chestnut trees were now riddled by bullets. At other times a single shot in the back of the neck was administered while the prisoner sat tied to a chair.

The sound of firing continued, punctuated by a series of heavier explosions.

Her knees were trembling. She heard shouts and then the thud of running feet. Someone banged on her door and bellowed something in German. She stood waiting, her heart pounding. She was quite sure she could smell smoke now, even hear the crackle of flames. The thought of being burned alive was almost more than she could bear. She wanted to scream but she had learned that screaming was accepted in such places; her captors paid little attention to agony. Nor would she give them the satisfaction. She had sworn never to cry out again.

She did not hear the door open. It was only when

the narrow beam of a flashlight dazzled her eyes that she knew she was no longer alone in the room.

A voice said, "You will come with me, please."

She moved forward, obeying automatically. There was always pain, but perhaps less pain if one obeyed.

The unknown man gripped her arm. As they emerged from the building there was gunfire all around them. The hand on her arm drew her to a halt. Someone was shouting at them in German. The man beside her replied. Then she was urged forward again but in a different direction.

Half crouching, half running, they crossed the outer courtyard, making for the small iron gate that led to the garage. Ordinarily two armed men guarded that gate, but they were otherwise occupied now, firing back at the attackers. The hand gripping her arm urged her on.

They went through the gate and bent low behind the shelter of the garden wall. The firing seemed to have slackened. Or the focal point of the battle had shifted elsewhere. "Now!" said the voice beside her. They ran down the steep, gravel-surfaced drive that stung her bare feet, her guide moving ahead. In the flash of gunfire she could see him. He was tall and thin, wearing civilian clothes and a gray felt hat pulled low. If he carried a weapon it did not show. Then they were across the drive and out on the main road. The villa was behind them, hidden by the abrupt crest of the hill. Her guide pulled her off the road and down into the scrub. She stepped on something sharp and gasped with pain. In another moment they had crossed the open ground and were crouched in the brush that bordered the side of the road. A truck, showing only narrow slits for driving lights, thundered by. In the silence that followed its passage, the man beside her said, "Michelle. Don't you know me?"

The voice triggered her memory, but she could hardly believe it.

"Dr. Hauser?" she said in astonishment.

Larsen was finding it increasingly hard to make sense out of the battle. All was confusion—sudden intense bursts of firing followed by periods of relative inactivity when each side appeared to be waiting for the other to make the next move.

It was during one of these lulls that he became aware that the man beside him with a machine pistol was Dukov. He knew that it had been Dukov's job to fix the sentry at the lower barricade. Obviously he had been successful. The felucca captain's features were visible in the orange glow of the gunflashes. He was grinning as he held up the Schmeisser. "Not bad, eh?"

"Are you hitting anything?" Larsen asked.

"Who knows? One I am sure of—the one who owned this."

"Where is Christine?"

"She has gone after the girl."

"That was not the plan," Larsen said sharply. "I was to go in with Claude."

"Claude is dead," Dukov answered, "and you appeared to be busy here. Christine made the decision herself. Besides, she knows the place. She was a visitor here before the war."

"When did Claude catch it?"

"At the beginning. Took a burst head on. He was dead when I came up the hill."

Larsen thought sadly of the brave young Frenchman with his trim moustache and shock of fair hair.

Firing had begun again, if anything heavier than before. Enemy reinforcements? Dukov unleashed a long burst which stopped when he came to the end of the clip. He reached into his pocket for the last one and held it up with a shake of his head. Larsen, firing more slowly with his semiautomatic rifle, still had a spare clip to go. He wondered how many of his shots had been effective. A head popped up above the wall and then was gone.

Dukov was slapping him on the shoulder. "Get down to the rendezvous point. I'll cover you from here."

Larsen shook his head. "You go first. I'll follow."

"For God's sake let's not argue about it. Go on!"

Springing suddenly into the open, Larsen made a dash along the garden wall. A storm of bullets followed him, sending chunks of masonry flying, but he had the advantage of surprise and in a moment was safely around the corner of the villa. He held up his rifle and waved to Dukov to come on. Dukov fired one long burst before scuttling to join him.

It had been assumed from the beginning that the Germans would be moving reinforcements along the road, and Dukov was the one who had suggested escaping by way of the cliff face. Several of the Maquis were montagnards from the Vercors area, accustomed to scaling rock walls. Ropes had been obtained from one of the sport shops in Antibes and anchored from the clifftop the night before. The problem would be to secure the ground at the base of the cliff.

So far things had gone well. From the volume of

firing it appeared that the Maquis had given the Germans a rough time.

The main thing was to get away before the enemy could bring up reinforcements.

Suddenly they heard Christine's voice. "Larsen?"

"Over here, Christine. Have you got her?"

Carrying her tommy gun by the stock, the barrel pointing down, Christine ran to join them. There was no sign of Michelle.

"What happened?" Larsen asked. "Where is she?"

"I don't know. The room where they were holding her is empty. We gave the other rooms a pretty good going over, too. She's gone."

"Christ! Are you sure?"

"Two of the Maquis reported seeing her escape by way of the garden gate. There was a man with her. They couldn't go after her because the Germans had them pinned down."

"My God, what a mix-up. Well, they can't have gotten far. I suppose the only thing to do is to spread out and try to find her. Who was the man who got her away? One of ours?"

Christine shook her head. "It doesn't seem that way. More likely one of theirs. Whoever he was, he was not in uniform. He wore a felt hat. Could be SS or Abwehr."

"The bird has flown," said Dukov, "and if we want to get our asses out of here, we had better start moving. There's something heavy coming up the road and I don't think it's a kiddie car."

They could all hear it now, the rumble of tank treads. Probably an armored car or personnel carrier. If the Resistance fighters were not to be trapped, they would have to get out now. Larsen could hardly conceal his bitter disappointment.

"All right," he said with a heavy heart, "let's go."

Christine had removed a small brass whistle from her pocket. She blew it and almost immediately the Resistance fighters with their blackened faces began to appear at the assembly point along the clifftop. Claude and two others were missing. Three men gone, Larsen thought with regret.

Christine read his mind. "It couldn't be helped. That is the way these things go. So much of it is luck."

"Damn luck," Larsen answered fiercely. "Good men are dead."

"Good men are always dead in a war. And usually the best are the first to die. If we don't go now, we will be dead as well."

"I'll go first. I've had some experience on ropes."

"Just as you please."

Larsen slung the rifle over his shoulder and formed a mountaineer's loop, running the rope between his legs. He lowered himself over the edge. A bullet hit the rock face close to his head, showering him with fragments. The cliff curved away, protecting him from above, but leaving him exposed to a marksman on the ground. He swung in, hugging the rock face. At the same moment Christine and Dukov opened fire.

A set of lights illuminated the cliff. Dukov shot them out almost at once, but in that brief moment Larsen saw the entrance to what appeared to be a sizable cave some twenty feet below the top. He let out more rope and swung back and forth in a pendulum action that brought him in close. His feet touched the ledge and he teetered at the mouth of the cave with the rope dragging him backward. There was another burst of firing. Splinters of stone bit at his face. He let go of the rope and fell forward into the cave.

"Hey, Larsen," he heard Dukov call. "Did those bastards get you?"

Larsen was too winded to answer.

Dukov called again.

"I'm all right. I'm in a cave here," Larsen answered.

Spasmodic bursts of gunfire issued from below. Larsen was safe enough as long as he stayed hidden, but he was trapped.

He heard heavy firing from above, and then Dukov called out to him, "Move over. We're coming down. It's getting hot up here. Can you keep our friends busy down below?"

"I'll try."

"Good. Christine is going first. I'll cover her from above."

Larsen moved to the outer lip of the cave. A ledge provided partial cover and kept the earth from crumbling away. The blind spot created by the angle of the cliff face prevented him from picking out targets. A beam of light probed upward. Someone with a hand-held torch. Dukov squeezed off half a dozen shots. The light went out, and there was a cry of pain. Larsen could make out Christine on the rope. He reached out, his fingers touching the cloth of her jacket before she swung away, a blurred shape illuminated by the reddish glare of Dukov's machine pistol. When her momentum brought her back he was waiting, his fingers grasping her own and pulling her onto the ledge.

She released the rope and stumbled forward.

A volley from below whined off the cliff face. Larsen fired a single shot in return. Almost immediately Dukov appeared at the mouth of the cave. Larsen gripped him by the legs and drew him in to safety.

Michelle had slipped going down the embankment. The soft clay, still damp from the rain, was slick. She lay with her ankle twisted.

Hauser said, "What is it? Get up."

"I can't go on."

"But you must. They will find us here."

"What difference does it make?"

"Let me help you."

"Don't touch me. Stay away."

"But my dear child, I came here only to help you."

"As you helped my mother?"

Hauser looked stunned. "What about your mother?"

"What about her?" Michelle answered in a bitter voice.

"I did nothing to harm her. It was the Gestapo."

"You could have saved her. When she came to your door, you turned her away. You were afraid for your own miserable skin."

Hauser was stung. "What are you saying? How do you know all this? It is rubbish!"

"She was arrested on your doorstep, Dr. Hauser."

"Yes! Yes! But there was no one there. I could not help her."

"You were there. You could have hidden her. They would not have searched the house of the eminent

Dr. Hauser. But you let them take her. A dangerous criminal. A threat to the Third Reich. So you remained shivering in your bed. And when they were gone, you peeked through the curtain. Brave Dr. Hauser. But you were seen. You were not the only one awake that night. And word was sent to us back in England. We knew then that you were responsible for her death. My father . . ."

Hauser exploded. "Your father! Your noble father. We will see how your famous father behaves when he and Einstein . . ."

"What about my father and Einstein?"

"Nothing."

"What do you want of me? Why have you come for me? Has guilt been gnawing at your heart all these years? Or do you want to murder me as well?"

He sank to his knees on the embankment. In the glow of moonlight that penetrated the fog, his face was ghastly. "Please believe me. I loved your mother. I thought they would take her only for questioning. I never wanted them to hurt her. I never wanted them to hurt you. . . ." His voice trailed away.

Michelle was sobbing. "What does it matter now? Let them kill me. I will welcome it."

"No, no, my dear child. We have only to get to the train station in Antibes. I will take you across the border to Spain. You will be safe there. I will tell them you are my daughter. I have papers for you. I beg of you, try to walk."

"My ankle is twisted."

"Soon it will be light. We must get you away from here before they begin to search. The highway cannot be very far off. Someone will be coming along soon—a farmer with a cart. I will find help. Stay here, Michelle. Don't move, I will be back very soon. Promise me that you will not move."

Michelle did not answer.

"Do you hear?" he said in a gentler voice.

"Yes."

No sooner had he gone than Michelle was on her feet. The ankle was not as bad as she had led him to believe. Limping, she set off in the opposite direction.

THIRTY-THREE

Captain Ludwig Gehre rendered a military salute as he entered the office of the Abwehr chief. "Herr Admiral."

"Come in, Gehre. Come in."

Canaris left his chair to close the door.

Gehre waited. On the bed in the corner the fat old dachshund snored. A box of snacks for the dog rested on the shelf. The Old Man is killing that dog, thought Gehre.

"I have an important task for you, Gehre."

"Yes, Herr Admiral?"

"I would like you to go to Lisbon." Canaris indicated a package on his desk wrapped in plain brown paper and tied with string. It bore no markings. "To deliver this."

"To whom, Herr Admiral?"

Canaris hesitated. When at last he spoke, his voice was very soft. "To the British embassy."

There was silence in the room.

"You have a right to know what the package contains," Canaris went on. "Among other things there are the plans and specifications for the rocket installations at Peenemünde."

Gehre was startled. The V-2 installations at Peene-münde were one of the top German secrets.

Canaris untied the package and drew out a large envelope labeled V-2. He handed it to Gehre.

Captain Gehre studied the drawings and sighed heavily as he slowly replaced the diagrams in the envelope.

"I do not have to tell you how important all of this may be, Gehre," said Canaris.

"No, Herr Admiral."

"Arrangements have been made for your departure this afternoon. You will leave from Tempelhof at two o'clock on the regular flight to Madrid. A car will be waiting for you there, and you will proceed at once by road to Lisbon. I have been in touch with our friends in London. A courier will be waiting for you at the British embassy. Any questions?"

"No, Herr Admiral."

"Very well, then." Canaris reached into his desk drawer. "One thing more. You will also deliver this envelope to Dr. David Stern at the Hotel Alegría. No response is required."

Gehre took the envelope without comment.

At Tempelhof airport a short, stocky man in a belted raincoat watched Gehre board the flight to Madrid. The aircraft taxied to the end of the runway and took off. The man in the raincoat walked unhurriedly to the nearest phone and called Gestapo headquarters.

Within fifteen minutes the news of Gehre's departure had been relayed to Skorzeny in Lisbon.

* * *

David Stern, pacing his hotel room at the Alegría, was growing more despondent as the days passed. His hopes for a quick exchange had faded. There had been no word from the Germans.

Afraid of missing a call, he had not dared to leave the hotel except to walk once or twice as far as the Avenida Da India. The fishing smacks gliding along the river made a pretty picture. Lisbon was an oasis of peace in war-torn Europe, but Stern was conscious only of the four walls of his room and the lifeless telephone.

On the morning of the tenth day he was informed that an envelope was waiting for him at the desk. He hurried down to the lobby. The clerk handed him a large manila envelope carefully sealed with heavy tape. A label bearing his name had been pasted on the front. There were no postal marks; it had obviously been delivered by hand.

The envelope was similar to those he had received in London.

Stern locked the door of his room behind him before tearing open the envelope.

Inside was another photograph of Michelle. This time she was standing in the courtyard of what appeared to be a villa. Judging from the clumps of cactus which grew along the wall it was somewhere in a warm climate. Her body was in shadow but her face was in bright sun. She was squinting against the glare. Her hair had been cut short and her features were so drawn he had trouble recognizing her.

But she was alive and obviously in an improved situation.

He was completing his part of the bargain, and the Germans seemed to be reciprocating. His spirits rose.

* * *

Captain Gehre had been followed from the time he left Madrid, but driving like a demon, he had managed, somewhere in the winding mountain passes, to lose his pursuers. It was not until his travel-stained Mercedes pulled up before the entrance to the Alegría that he came once again to the attention of the Gestapo.

Although Gehre was in civilian clothes, the desk clerk sized him up at once as a German, and an officer at that. Lisbon was a nest of spies. Hotel clerks had been ordered to report suspicious comings and goings to the police.

The clerk did his duty. His call was relayed to a police lieutenant named Fernandez. The lieutenant asked for and received a complete description of both Stern and the man who had left the envelope. Lieutenant Fernandez had been on the German payroll since the start of the war. Within minutes the information had been passed along to Skorzeny.

Skorzeny was pleased. He looked forward to his next report to the Fuehrer. He had been furious when the Gestapo had lost Gehre in Spain but now they had him again. And he had been seen entering the British embassy. Another nail in the coffin of that old fox Canaris.

The green lawns and shaded verandas of Cairo's Mena House were a welcome relief from the almost unbearable heat Sikorski and Zofia had experienced in Iran, Iraq, and Palestine. The meetings with General Anders and the other Polish officers had gone well, and a feeling of mutual confidence had been restored. Most of their desert traveling had been done by jeep,

and they were both burned brown from the sun and
exhausted by the hot dry winds. Mena House was a
refuge to which they returned gladly. Zofia was concerned for the general. For the first time he looked his
age, or more. Twin furrows had been carved from
his nostrils to the corners of his mouth. The once
merry eyes no longer twinkled, and the soldierly bearing was marred by a slight stoop of weariness. When
she proposed that they remain at Mena House to rest
for a week or two, he did not offer the objections she
had expected. But on the third day of their stay there
was a telegram from Churchill requesting that General Sikorski return at once for a conference. The
same Liberator was being sent to bring them back to
England. Churchill's request would have to be com-
plied with; Sikorski's badly needed rest must be cut
short. Mingled with Zofia's feelings of regret was a
surge of excitement. She would soon be in Peter's
arms.

THIRTY-FOUR

Sitting alone at the bar of the hotel Jour de Rève in Lorient, Korvettenkapitan Otto Kretschmer, skipper of the U-99, morosely downed his third Cognac and considered the inequities of fate. Although not yet twenty-eight years old Kretschmer was well on his way to becoming Germany's greatest U-boat ace. Known as "Otto the Silent" he was a thoughtful, disciplined young man with the face of a schoolboy and the brain of a master strategist. It was Kretschmer who had discarded the classic underwater attack and the "fan" shot and had gone instead to night attacks on the surface. He limited himself to one torpedo per ship. Using the new tactics, U-99, bearing the familiar golden horseshoe emblem on its conning tower, had already sunk the remarkable total of twenty ships.

Kretschmer ordered another Cognac and regarded his face in the mirror behind the bar. Unlike most of the other young U-boat commanders he had not taken to wearing a beard, regarding it as an affectation. He did not require a beard to make him look salty—the Knight's Cross at his throat spoke for itself.

Word had come from Halifax that convoy SC7 would shortly be sailing for England. A fat convoy of aged tramps ripe for the picking. Tubs, thought

Kretschmer, hardly able to get out of their own way. Let U-99 in among them and it would be like turning a fox loose in a hen house. What a slaughter there would be when the wolf pack surfaced among those waddling ducks. Kretschmer had figured on sinking at least ten ships himself, which would make him Germany's leading ace. Admiral Doenitz had as good as promised him command of one of the new snorkel-type boats as soon as they were delivered from the yard.

But at the last moment—when she had been fully loaded and ready for sea—U-99 had been ordered to remain at her pen in Lorient awaiting further instructions. The wolf pack had gone off without her. Then came the second blow: U-99 was to avoid combat. Her primary mission would be the transport of passengers.

A damn ferryboat, thought Otto in disgust as he read his orders.

He considered sending a letter of protest to Doenitz, but the orders had already been countersigned by the admiral.

As if all that were not bad enough, he was further instructed to wait in Lorient for the arrival of Reichmarshal Goering. Could it be that fat Hermann of the Luftwaffe was now reduced to inspecting submarines?

It was too much for Kretschmer. Stuck here in this pigsty of a French port where the fog never lifted and people glared at you on the street as though you were an animal. Whores and pimps. Jour de Rève. Dreamy Day indeed! One of his crew had already caught the clap in this dump.

Kretschmer was aware of the sudden silence which

had settled over the lounge. He looked up. Two Luftwaffe officers carrying machine pistols at the ready
stood in the doorway. There was no hint of friendli-
ness in their narrowed eyes. The group of Frenchmen
at a table in the corner had gone rigid. One of them,
looking for a way out, had begun to rise, but had
then sunk back into his chair.

One of the Luftwaffe officers remained in the doorway, his machine pistol covering the room, while the
other advanced toward the Frenchmen and demanded
to see their papers. He looked each man full in the
face to compare him with his photograph, and then
dismissed him. The Frenchmen picked up their
jackets and hurried out. The barman, seeing he was
not to be paid, began to protest. A wave from the
machine pistol shut him up.

Kretschmer returned his attention to his drink.
Fuck those flyboys.

"Korvettenkapitan Kretschmer?"

He looked up. "Yes?"

"Your papers please."

He was about to inquire acidly whether the Luftwaffe, having suffered such heavy losses to the RAF,
was now serving as a standby force for the SS, but
decided against it. He pulled out his wallet and
handed it over. The Luftwaffe captain examined
Kretschmer's identification papers, then handed it
back.

"Heil Hitler."

"Heil Hitler."

"You will come with me please, Herr Korvettenkapitan."

The tone of voice made protest unwise. He followed
the two Luftwaffe officers through the doorway and

out into the street. A six-wheeled Mercedes-Benz touring car was parked at the curb. One of the Luftwaffe officers opened the door and said, "Please." Kretschmer got into the car. An oversized shape in the uniform of a Reichmarshal was in the back seat.

"Good evening, Herr Korvettenkapitan," Goering said in an easy voice.

Despite himself Kretschmer was awed. "Good evening, sir."

"A foggy town you have here. No wonder people in this part of the world are so glum."

Kretschmer did not answer.

Goering chuckled. "I see it's not for nothing they call you Otto the Silent."

"Yes, sir."

"This is not to be a 'yes sir, no sir' conversation. I wish you to hear me out and then to speak frankly. Your assigned mission is of the highest delicacy and it is important that we understand each other. Do I make myself clear?"

"Yes, sir."

"To begin with you are probably wondering why we are meeting in such strange circumstances. It is because I do not wish to be observed visiting your U-boat, nor do I wish to have you seen at my headquarters. The fewer people who are aware of what I am about to tell you, the better." Goering sniffed the air. "Have you been drinking, Kretschmer?"

"Yes, sir."

"But you are not drunk?"

"No, sir."

"Good. Then one more will not hurt either of us. The air in these coastal towns is raw." Goering produced a bottle of Four Star Hennessy and two small glasses. Kretschmer shot the brandy down his throat in one gulp.

"I believe you have already received explicit orders from Admiral Doenitz?" said Goering.

"Yes, sir."

"You will be required to make a round trip to a point on the coast of the United States, returning with two passengers."

"Yes, sir."

"You are wondering perhaps why an officer with a distinguished combat record such as yours should be selected for such a mission?"

"Yes, sir."

"Then I will tell you, Kretschmer, that this particular voyage will be the most important one of your career, or that of any other U-boat commander. In a global war it is necessary to maintain a grasp of over-all strategy," Goering went on. "This war will not be won just in Russia or just in the English Channel, or for that matter in the Atlantic where you have been fighting. Your wolf packs have been sinking a great many of the enemy's ships. Fine. But I must tell you, Kretschmer, you will not win the war that way. For every tactical advance, the enemy will have a counter-measure—more powerful escort vessels, longer-range · aircraft. That has been the story of warfare since the Romans first conquered the civilized world with the phalanx and the chariot."

Goering poured himself another drink and offered the bottle to Kretschmer. The submarine commander shook his head. The Reichmarshal had not come all this way to give him a lesson in military history. He must keep a clear head. His stomach gurgled loudly. Damn that cabbage soup.

"For every weapon there has been a counterweapon," Goering continued. "Until now. Now the world will see at last the unanswerable weapon. A bomb of such magnitude that entire cities can be destroyed by a single explosion. Moscow, London, New York—wiped out in a flash. Do you understand what I am saying, Kretschmer?"

Kretschmer shook his head. He had told the Reichmarshal he was not drunk, which was not quite the truth. Perhaps it was Goering who was drunk. "Not really, sir."

"Of course not. It is almost beyond comprehension."

"You mean the Americans have such a weapon?"

"Not yet, although they may be working on it."

"You are to bring back the man who can build such a bomb for Germany. His name," Goering lowered his voice, "is Albert Einstein."

Kretschmer was stupefied. "Einstein is returning to Germany?"

Goering nodded.

"And the other man?"

"A Dr. Stern. Also a German. Also a scientist. Also a Jew."

The Cognac and cabbage soup were an unhappy mix. Kretschmer felt a desperate need for fresh air. Clenching his fists to control his stomach cramps he said, "Herr Reichmarshal . . ."

"What is it?"

"I must be excused to go to the bathroom."

Kretschmer opened the car door and rushed back into the hotel.

Dukov, his voice sounding hollow in the blackness of the cave, said, "We are in the shit. Germans above,

the Milice below and the devil looking to see which
way it goes."

"Cheerfulness has always been one of your better
qualities," Christine said.

"How much ammunition have you got left, Larsen?"
Dukov asked.

"Not much. Perhaps the better part of a clip."

"And you, Christine?"

"The same."

"Then there's nothing for it but to sit tight. They
can't get at us and we can't get away. Our Resistance
friends may return for a share in the fun. What do
you think, Christine?"

"I think you talk too much."

"Agreed. But what do you really think? Will your
heroic Maquis be back or are they already safely
tucked away in their beds?"

"I think quite possibly they are regrouping and will
be back," Christine said.

"Well, let us hope so. Meanwhile, we will have to
entertain these Boche by ourselves. From the sound
of it they are bringing up the panzers."

"I doubt it," Christine said. "One cannot conceal
tanks beneath flower stalls. If there had been panzers
in this area, our people would certainly have known
about it. And in any case why should the Germans
have panzers here? To shoot a few dozen Frenchmen
now and then? No, it is more likely to be an armored
personnel carrier from Antibes."

The clanking sound had stopped. Suddenly the
cave was illuminated by the glare of a powerful
searchlight. Dukov raised his Schmeisser but then
ducked back behind the ledge as a hail of bullets burst
from below. The three of them hugged the ground.

As soon as the firing was over Dukov raised himself on his elbows and let off a short burst. The light exploded in a tinkle of glass. From the darkness could be heard a volley of curses and shouted orders.

"Shitheads!" Dukov bellowed. "Shitheads!" The response was another burst of firing from below.

"Feeling better?" Christine asked.

"Much."

There was a faint sound from the outer ledge as of a small rock falling.

"Christ!" said Dukov. In a moment he was on his knees groping wildly in the dark and then hurling something away. There was a blinding flash and an explosion from below followed by the cries of wounded men.

"Bloody grenades," said Dukov crawling back inside the cave. "Play dirty with me, eh?"

Christine laughed. "Ten seconds more and you would have gone up in smoke, darling."

"Of course. But it's necessary to be ten seconds ahead of those Boche bastards. I doubt if they'll try that little trick again."

"And if they do?"

"We'll be ten seconds ahead."

"Look, you two, I'm sorry I got you into this," Larsen said in a low voice.

"Nobody got anybody into anything," Christine said. "No one was forced to participate."

"The swine are up to something," Dukov said. "Listen!"

They could hear whispered instructions from above. One of the ropes was being drawn up.

"Do you think they're stupid enough to use the ropes?" Larsen said.

"Even the Boche are not stupid enough for that. If they try it we have only to pick them off. No, it's something else."

Muffled orders in German. A flicker of light.

"A fused charge!" roared Dukov. "Get back quick!" They huddled against the rear wall. The blast, when it came, was shocking. Larsen felt himself hurled back like a candle blown out in the wind. Again the oppressive silence. Dukov picked up a fist-sized chunk of rock and tossed it out of the mouth of the cave. They heard it land. A burst of automatic weapons fire came from below followed by shouts of anger from the Germans above.

"Good," said Dukov, "they are killing each other. But I imagine there will be another little present coming our way."

This time it was Larsen who moved first, sensing rather than seeing the sputtering fuse and using his knife to cut the rope. The charge fell into the darkness. There were cries from the Milice below and then a tremendous explosion.

"Cocksuckers!" roared Dukov. His laughter echoed in the ravine. They could hear the cries of the wounded. He put his arms around Larsen and hugged him. "What a performance!"

There was increasingly heavy firing from above. Then another violent explosion, this one more spectacular than the first. A fireball of smoke and flame shot up almost to the mouth of the cave.

"My God," Dukov cried. "Come and see! You won't believe it!" The armored car at the base of the cliff had exploded with such ferocity that the entire face of the cliff and the ravine below were lit in a yellow glare. Dead and wounded Milice were scattered around the flaming vehicle. Others could be seen fleeing along the ravine.

"It must be Vautrin and the others," Christine said. "I knew they would come back."

"A good time then to leave this cozy nest," said Dukov. "What do you think, Larsen?"

"I'm ready."

"I will go first down the rope with Christine to follow and you to come last."

"They may have cut that rope."

"We'll soon find out then, won't we? In any case we have to chance it. Do you agree, Christine?"

"We're wasting time," said Christine.

Dukov slung the Schmeisser over his back and took hold of the rope with both hands, applying his full weight immediately. When he was down he gave two sharp tugs on the rope.

Christine said, "See you at the bottom."

She was away then with Larsen steadying her. The sound of firing from above had decreased, and he guessed that the *résistants* were being driven off. There was not much time left. He waited impatiently for Christine's signal. When it came, he let the rope take his weight.

Christine and Dukov were waiting for him. "What now?" he asked.

"Now," said Dukov, "we ride the train like gentlemen. But not to Antibes where they may be expecting us. We will work our way north toward Clermont-Ferrand. Up there in the mountains we will have our best chance."

Larsen shook his head. "Clermont-Ferrand is not for me. I came to find Michelle, and that is what I mean to do."

"Are you crazy?" Dukov exploded. "You want to put your head straight into the tiger's mouth, eh?"

Christine said, "I think Jens is right. Antibes will be dangerous, but we may hear something. I vote we go back."

"Back? You are even crazier than he is."

"You are free to go to Clermont-Ferrand if that is what you want, André."

Dukov's white teeth gleamed against the blackness of his beard. "The hell it is. I am crazier than both of you. Antibes it is!"

The Liberator carrying General Sikorski was due to land at Gibraltar, presenting Governor General Sir Frank Noel Mason-Macfarlane with a problem in diplomacy. The Soviet ambassador, Mr. Maiski, would also be stopping at Gibraltar that day on a return flight to Moscow.

In view of the strained feelings between the Soviets and the Polish government-in-exile, Sir Frank did not see any way to offer hospitality to both of these distinguished guests under the same roof. He thought it best to discuss the matter with Count Lubienski, Sikorski's representative in Gibraltar. Lubienski, who wore his two-star cap at a rakish angle, inserted a cigarette into his long ivory holder and grinned at the governor.

"I can see the difficulty of your position," Lubienski said. "It will be most awkward indeed to have them both at Government House at the same time. One will have to stay elsewhere. But which one? Mr. Maiski has ambassadorial rank, and General Sikorski is a head of state. Which one would you prefer to insult?"

"I don't intend to insult either one, my dear Count.

Maiski is as sourly suspicious as are all the Russians. On the other hand General Sikorski and his daughter are old friends, and it would be a pleasure to entertain them. But how am I to explain it all to London?"

Lubienski examined the ash on the end of his cigarette and seemed to draw inspiration from it. "May I make a suggestion, sir?"

"Of course, my dear fellow. That's the point of this meeting."

"Why not advise London that you already have a houseful of guests and that in any event, it might be better for security reasons if Maiski arrived from London during the night. One has to reckon with German fighter planes. After a few hours' rest Mr. Maiski can continue his flight to Moscow the same day. I will arrange to keep General Sikorski occupied in his suite until Maiski has departed."

Greatly relieved, Sir Frank raised his glass in salute. "Capital, my dear Count. Capital. The very essence of diplomacy. I drink to your health and to that of General Sikorski."

When the phone rang, Stern reached it in one bound.

"Stern?"

"Yes, this is David Stern."

"You received the photo?" It was a man's voice speaking German.

"Yes. Where is she? Is she here in Portugal? When will the exchange take place?"

"There are certain things you must do first."

"What things?"

"At seven o'clock in the evening on this coming Friday, you will report to the terminal of Pan American Airways. A seat has been arranged for you on the eight o'clock flight."

"Flight to where?" Stern said wildly. "Where am I going?"

"No questions, Stern. Do as you are told."

"But when will I see my daughter? How can I be sure you will honor your word?"

"There is one thing you can be sure of. If you do not follow instructions you will not see her again. Understood?"

"Yes."

"The photograph should demonstrate to you that her situation is much improved. I assume you would not like to see her returned to the Avenue Foch."

"No! No!"

"Then be on the eight o'clock flight."

There was a click as the caller hung up.

Several minutes passed before Stern picked up the phone again.

He asked to be put through to the offices of Pan American. When the connection was made, he said he wished to know the destination of the flight which left Lisbon at eight o'clock on Friday evening.

"That is our weekly flight to New York, sir."

"New York! Are you sure?"

"Quite sure, sir."

Zofia looked down at the great rocky mass of Gibraltar rising out of the sea. They had circled twice over the narrow landing strip that occupied the only bit of flat land between the rock of Gibraltar and the Spanish border. Landing or taking off from Gibraltar was like operating from the flight deck of a carrier, hardly the ideal place for a four-engine bomber.

Judging the crosswind, the pilot set the big plane down abruptly; there was no room for a long descent. The Liberator hit hard and bounced once but then hugged the ground. With the brakes set the plane slowed. Zofia found that her nails had been digging into her palms. She exhaled slowly. Her father glanced across at her and gave her a tired smile.

The governor-general and the count were waiting to greet them. Zofia was glad to see them both. Sir Frank was a superb host and the young Count Lubienski always managed to enliven an occasion. And Gibraltar was still untouched by the war. The honor guard appeared as stiffly starched as ever, and there were warships in the Royal Dockyard. At the fringe of the airstrip a band of apes watched curiously as the plane taxied toward them. Zofia knew the legend of Gibraltar—that the English would remain as long as the apes were still there. She smiled at the sight of the little creatures.

THIRTY-FIVE

Michelle's feet were bleeding, but the ankle was not as bad as she had feared. The sky to the east was growing pale. She must get away before daylight.

She slid down the side of a railway embankment into a grove of trees. She heard the sound of a dog barking. It came again, closer. She broke a limb from a dead tree. The animal was close behind her now. She saw him only when he was almost on top of her, a dark, raging shape. She swung at his head, feeling the wood crack and hearing the brute's yelp of pain.

The dog writhed for a moment among the dead leaves before regaining its feet. It backed away, and slunk off into the woods.

Michelle sank down trying to control her sobs. She must not give way to hysteria. Hauser could not be far behind. Certainly he had heard the dog barking. She must keep moving.

She was soaked and freezing. The shapeless cotton hospital gown was no protection against rain and cold. It was imperative to find shelter.

"Michelle!"

It was Hauser calling after her. She could hear him blundering through the woods. She turned away from the sound, moving back toward the embankment. It was growing steadily lighter. The stones of the embankment bit into her already lacerated feet.

Ahead was a meadow and the dim shapes of cattle grazing. She could make out a building of some sort, a shed where hay was stored. She ran toward it, stumbling into a wire fence. The barbs left streaks of blood along her thighs and back. She pulled herself free and went on until she found the shelter of the hayrick, burrowing among the warm odorous bodies of the cattle. They inspected her with bovine eyes and then resumed their feeding. She dug deeper into the hay, her heart pounding. She thought she could still hear Hauser calling.

She closed her eyes. The cattle radiated warmth; their breath was sweet. She heard the whistle of a train. The ground trembled.

A hand touching her shoulder brought her awake. A dark-haired child stood watching her, his eyes like coals in a pale, pinched face. When Michelle opened her eyes, the child stepped back staring at her gravely. She raised her hand to touch the boy's cheek. He shrank back and darted away.

Karl Hauser had never been entirely clear in his own mind about what he intended to do when he reached the villa after his trip from Berlin. He had not really thought of helping Michelle to escape until the shooting had started. With the villa under attack he could think only of getting her away. He had lied to her when he told her he carried a passport that would get her into Spain. But he carried money, and the Spanish border guards could be bribed.

Spain had been an afterthought. It would be warm

in Spain, and they would find a modest house surrounded by flowers. Perhaps a fishing village. An
image flashed across his mind—the lights of fishing
boats moving like fireflies across a tranquil bay.

In time she would forgive him. In time she would
learn to love him. Not even Canaris could find them
there. When the war ended most of Europe would be
in ashes. Let Stern, if he lived, try to hunt them
down.

The governor-general had provided a splendid
lunch for his guests in the cool dining room of Gibraltar's Government House. Afterward General Sikorski dozed briefly. He asked to be awakened at three
o'clock to complete his inspection of the troops. Zofia
went into the bedroom and shook him gently by the
shoulder. He awakened smiling and asked, "Yes, my
dear?"

"It's three o'clock."

"Is it? Well, then, I had better get up. We don't
want to keep the Polish Army waiting."

Sikorski seemed rested and in a happy mood. He
joked with the soldiers during the inspection. It was
obvious that he was looking forward to getting back
to London and the conference with Churchill. "I am
optimistic," he told Zofia. "Do you think that is
foolish?"

"It is never foolish to be optimistic."

"It costs nothing, eh? No, I am really looking forward to London. I think Stalin must have agreed at
last to sign the treaty."

Zofia was privately of the opinion that any treaty
with Stalin, signed or otherwise, was worthless, but
she did not say so. She did not often see her father in

a jolly frame of mind these days and she had no intention of spoiling it.

"You'll be glad to get back, too, eh?" he said.

"Yes, I suppose so."

"To see all your friends?"

She looked at him sharply. They had never discussed it, but she felt sure that he must have known she had a lover. He was a keen student of her moods. Her happiness had been hard to disguise.

"Yes," she said.

"Good. What time do we depart?"

"It has been scheduled for six."

"Then we have time to stroll through the town to buy a few little presents and to thank Sir Frank for his hospitality."

"I understand he's coming to the airport with us."

"Is he? Good. Lubienski too?"

"Yes."

"Splendid."

At the airport they were greeted with a strange request. Two British secret service officers had arrived unexpectedly from Cairo and wished to join them on the return flight to London. Sikorski had no objection. The two Englishmen voiced their appreciation, then strolled out to talk with the pilot. After a brief conversation they returned to the lounge.

When the time came for departure the two secret service officers could not be found. A twenty-minute delay ensued. Sikorski could no longer conceal his impatience.

"I don't understand it," Sir Frank said. "But I see no reason why you should wait any longer, General. If they miss the plane, it's their lookout. I'll wish you good-bye then."

The pilot came out of the control room carrying a briefcase. Zofia was surprised to see that he was wearing a lifejacket over his uniform. The flight was over open water, but she could not remember his having worn a lifejacket on the flight out.

They did not take off at once. The pilot ran the Liberator's engines up and down, testing each one separately and then all four together. By that time it was fully dark. Only the green flarepath lamps outlined the runway.

The governor and Count Lubienski stood watching the takeoff. They could see the plane's outline silhouetted against the ghostly greenish glow of the lights. When the big plane was still only a little more than halfway down the runway the pilot seemed almost to wrench it up into the air. With engines screaming at full pitch it became airborne.

They were still low as they swept over Gibraltar. Zofia could make out the lights of Government House, Catalan Bay, and the great mole that protected the submarine pens. Suddenly she felt the plane tilt. There had not been any change in the rhythm of the engines, but she was certain they were about to crash. She was sure of it. By her side her father still slept. She closed her eyes and clenched her fists and pressed her body back against the seat cushion. She tried to pray, but no words came.

After the crash the pilot was found floating in his life vest, alive but unconscious. He testified later that he had followed his usual procedure for takeoff from the short runway. He had gotten the plane into the air as rapidly as possible and then had made a shallow dive in order to pick up speed. The plane had never come out of the dive. The steering column had been unaccountably blocked. Yet it had been functioning when they had taken off.

General Sikorski was found a few hours later. He had died from a massive head wound.

Zofia's body was never recovered.

Guthrie stood on the quay in Plymouth watching the Polish destroyer *Orkan* tie up. The *Orkan*, traveling at flank speed and bearing the general's body, had taken less than a week between Gibraltar and Plymouth. The harbor was shrouded in fog. Spatters of rain slashed at Guthrie's face as he stood bareheaded while the coffin was lifted by the ship's crane and swung down to the quay.

The captain of the *Orkan* felt a sense of relief at having discharged his somber duty. Like all sailors he thought it bad luck to carry a dead body on board his ship. As the coffin was placed in a hearse and driven away, the captain lit a cigarette and turned to invite his number one down to his quarters for a drink. An unusual gesture for the captain; but then it had been an unusual and disturbing voyage.

Three weeks later the *Orkan* was lost at sea with all hands.

The requiem mass sung for General Sikorski at Westminster Cathedral was attended by many dignitaries, among them Winston Churchill. It was reported that Churchill wept. Later the coffin was taken to Newark and buried there. A handful of Polish earth was tossed into the grave before it was closed.

THIRTY-SIX

A man's voice yelled, "Come out of there!" The grating voice had a baritone quality achieved by a mix of cigarettes and Calvados.

Michelle opened her eyes. A barrel-shaped man held a pitchfork aimed at her breast. She managed a half smile. "I will come out gladly if you will be kind enough to point that thing elsewhere."

The farmer moved back a step, but his sullen, unshaved face still wore a look of intense suspicion. Michelle crawled out of the hay.

The farmer was looking at her body. The torn dress had left her breast exposed. He let his tongue slide over his lips. She tried to cover herself. He made a threatening motion with the fork. "Get on with it. Up to the house."

The farmhouse, which she had not seen in the dark, was no more than five hundred yards away along a path that skirted the woods. At the side of the house the dog that had attacked her was fastened to a chain, barking furiously.

A woman came out of the house and shouted something at the animal. When it continued to bark, she picked up a stone and made a threatening gesture. The dog slunk back whimpering. The woman started down the path toward Michelle and the farmer. She was tall and gaunt, with a beaked nose and the predatory eyes of a hawk. She stopped in the path and stood with her fists on her hips.

Michelle stumbled. The woman took in the blood-spattered dress and naked feet and moved to help her. She put a strong arm around Michelle's waist and then pulled off her shawl and placed it over Michelle's shoulders.

"Wear this," the woman said, "before that pig lets the eyeballs drop out of his head." She rounded on her husband. "So you have a pitchfork with which to defend yourself. Who do you think she is, General Rommel in disguise?"

"I know who she is," the man growled. "The one who got away from the villa last night. The one all that row was about."

"What of it? She's hurt. She needs help."

"They'll come looking for her, and when they find her they'll hang us."

"So what do you want? To drive her back into their hands? Are you a Frenchman or a shitty Boche? Maybe they'll give you your thirty pieces of silver." She spat on the ground at her husband's feet and led Michelle into the house.

"I am putting you to bed," the woman announced firmly. "Screw the Boche. By the way, my name is Lise Robert and his is Aristide. If he tries to lay a hand on you, the randy old goat, I will hang his guts out to dry like a row of onions."

Even more than he feared the Germans, Aristide Robert feared the whiplash tongue of his wife. Lise was a virago, but she knew more about what was going on in the district than the mayor himself. She had a

way of sniffing out profitable black-market deals in
exchange for a bit of bacon or a slice of ham. Aristide
prided himself on being as sharp as the next fellow,
but in his narrow peasant mind he was willing to
admit that of the two of them, Lise was the born
trader. She was as sharp and tough as a Marseille fish-
wife. He had yet to see the man who could come
out even on a deal with Lise. Without her the farm
would surely have gone under, and they would have
starved like so many others. Although there was hardly a day that passed when he did not feel like blowing her head off, he was not fool enough to think he
could do without her.

Squatting by the side of the barn in the watery
sunshine, he remembered the way the girl had looked
when he had first seen her lying in the hay with her
breasts exposed. At the thought of those marvelous
young tits with their delicate pink nipples, Aristide
felt himself becoming aroused. Lise's meager dugs
were leathery as sow's ears with great dark nipples. In
any case they had not slept together since the birth
of the child nearly five years before. But that young
one, the girl in the hay, how he would have liked to
get his teeth into that. He had been a fool to bring
her to the house. He should have taken her there
where she lay. Lise need never have known.

Aristide took a swallow of Calvados and put his
hand inside his trousers. Lise always went to the Antibes market on Tuesdays. She would leave the girl
alone in the house. He would tell her he was going
into the forest to cut firewood, and after she was gone
he would double back. The girl might resist at first
and if she did, why so much the better. She would

know soon enough what a real man was like, and after that she would not be able to get enough.

Preoccupied, his eyes closed, he failed to notice Lise until she stood in front of him.

"Pig!" she spat at him.

Hurriedly he began to readjust his clothing.

"Go on," she said, "don't let me spoil your fun. I'm going into Antibes and taking the girl with me."

THIRTY-SEVEN

David Stern knew he was being followed. Three times in the past twenty-four hours he had seen the same man, a scar-faced giant. An unmistakable SS thug. Now he saw him again standing near the newspaper kiosk pretending to study the headlines. He had been there for the better part of an hour.

It was nearly five o'clock. Soon it would be growing dark. In two hours he must report to the Pan American terminal.

The hotel account had been settled. His bag was packed and lay on the bed with his raincoat folded across it. The window of his hotel room was shuttered in the usual European fashion, controlled by a lead counterweight fastened to a cotton cord. Stern took out his pocketknife and cut the cord, weighing the chunk of lead in his hand. Satisfied, he dropped the lead into his raincoat pocket. Carrying the coat over his arm and with the bag in his other hand, he left the hotel.

He turned the corner of the Terreiro do Poço and paused to look into a shop window. Elegant luggage made of the finest leather and with silver buckles. Where did they find such stuff in wartime?

The huge man with the scarred face was in his usual place by the newspaper kiosk. Stern walked with purposeful strides along the Avenida Ribiera das Naus in the direction of the Avenida Da India. It was the way he usually strolled; his pursuer would see nothing strange in that.

The lead in his pocket felt heavy and lethal.

Late afternoon had formed shadows in the narrow streets, the clear Portuguese sky turning a darker blue as dusk settled over the city. He glanced at his watch. It was almost five. He was cutting it too fine.

He quickened his steps. He was in a mean district of trash-laden alleys and old warehouses. He turned a corner and then another. Risking a quick glance backward he saw that for the moment he was alone. It would take the pursuer at least five minutes to bring him into sight again. The man would be hurrying after him, thinking more of not losing him than of the possibility of attack. Ahead was a doorway leading to a deserted warehouse, the entrance largely concealed by giant wooden casks. The rotten casks, as tall as a man and twice as big around, offered a hiding place. His heart was beating fast. He could feel the adrenalin pumping through his veins. He reached into his coat pocket and drew out the lead weight. His hat hampered his vision. With an impatient gesture he pulled it off and threw it on the ground.

He could hear rapid steps now. The pursuer was running after him. The steps drew to a halt. Some instinct must have warned the huntsman that he was hurrying into a trap. Stern could hear ragged breathing as the unseen man sucked air into his lungs. A last sliver of yellow light from the setting sun started the long edge of the pursuer's shadow moving toward him.

Stern stepped from behind the cask and struck at the man's head. The giant staggered. He struck again. The huge man went down, lying motionless on the cobblestones. His hat had been knocked off, and there was blood on his forehead. Stern dropped the lead weight and ran.

The old Peugeot truck had a charcoal burner fixed at the rear. It had taken Lise Robert the better part of an hour to get it started, but after that it trundled sedately along the road at ten kilometers to the hour, its open bed piled high with baskets of turnips. As they neared the city a gendarme waved at them; Lise's truck was a familiar sight. Michelle sank back in her corner of the cab to avoid the policeman's gaze, but Lise only grunted. She feared no man, and particularly not these jumped-up flics who gave themselves such airs while kissing the asses of the Germans.

Michelle wore one of Lise's rusty black dresses. Her legs had been bandaged and covered with woolen stockings. Her dark hair was hidden by a faded blue scarf. To the casual eye she might have been a little old woman hunched in upon herself as the truck bounced unevenly along on its ancient springs.

"You had better know where I am taking you," Lise had explained. "I can't keep you at the farm because they will be searching all the houses close to the villa. But you are not as alone here in Antibes as you might think. There is an organization to provide help for British fliers trying to get to Spain. Sometimes they go by boat, other times they travel to Perpignan and then across the border to Bañolas. I have nothing to say about that. It will be up to Christine."

"Who is Christine?"

Lise chuckled dryly. "I am not sure who Christine is. She is a foreigner and Christine is not her real name. I think she must have been sent here by the British. But I don't ask questions. The less I know the better. What I don't know, the Boche can't make me tell. Anyway, you will like her. When she is not busy killing those German sons of bitches she is putting waves in the hair of French whores. Don't worry. If anyone can get you away, it will be our Christine."

THIRTY-EIGHT

The flying boat circled over the Tagus River and began to climb above the city of Lisbon. In his seat by the window Stern mopped his brow and looked down. Lights were coming on all over the city. His pulse no longer pounded so ferociously. Was that the Avenida da India and were those the deserted warehouses? He strained his eyes into the gathering darkness wondering if the body was still there.

Skorzeny had a blinding headache. He put up his hand and found his head encased in a turban of bandages. He was lying on a narrow iron cot. Uniformed Portuguese police hurried by. A few feet away sat a plump balding man wearing the stripes of a sergéant. When he saw that Skorzeny was awake, he signaled to a man in civilian clothing who came to the head of the cot and said in German, "Feeling better?"

"No," growled Skorzeny.

"You are lucky to be alive. You were walking in a bad section. Even for a man of your size. Permit me to introduce myself. I am Heiss, chargé d'affaires of the German embassy. They called me because you spoke in German. You have no identification."

Skorzeny reached into his breast pocket. His money and passport were gone.

He had made a bad mistake. He had not thought the Jew would have the courage to attack him. It would be difficult to explain matters to the Fuehrer. He raised his arm. His wristwatch, too, was gone.

"What time is it, Heiss?"

"Nearly midnight."

"Listen carefully, Heiss. I am Colonel Otto Skorzeny, SS."

Hess drew himself to attention.

"I was here in Lisbon on a personal mission for the Fuehrer. My papers have been stolen. You will have to provide me with new identification and a passport."

"That can be done, Herr Colonel, but not without authority from Berlin. It will take time."

"To hell with Berlin. You will receive your authority straight from the Fuehrer's headquarters. Get me to a phone where I can talk in private. I want to call Rastenburg."

"At once, Herr Colonel. My car is outside. Is the Herr Colonel well enough to walk?"

"Of course."

Despite the fact that it was after midnight, Skorzeny was able to get through to Gerda Christian, the Fuehrer's secretary.

"Yes, Herr Colonel?" Her voice was low, depressed.

"I wish to speak to the Fuehrer on a matter of urgency," Skorzeny said.

"The Fuehrer has had another one of his attacks.

He is taking calls from no one. Is there anything else, Herr Colonel?"

"No," Skorzeny said softly. "Nothing else, Frau Gerda."

The plane droned on through the night. Most of the passengers slept in their seats. Those with reservations for berths had retired behind drawn curtains. In the narrow beam of light from the reading lamp a sheen of perspiration was reflected from Stern's balding forehead. Dinner had been served earlier, but he had hardly touched the food. Instead he had drunk an entire bottle of sherry. The wine had done little to ease his anxiety.

Stern got up and made his way down the swaying passageway toward the lavatory. He closed the door behind him and splashed cold water over his face. He looked at himself in the mirror. The haggard features and anguished eyes were almost unrecognizable.

He returned to his seat. A slip of paper lying on the cushion caught his attention. A blank calling card. Certainly it had not been there a few moments before when he had gone to the washroom. He turned it over. Written in ink were two words: Hotel St. James. And beneath that: $E = MC^2$.

So they had someone here on the plane watching him. Only a few lights were on. Most of the passengers slept. It might be any one of them. Two seats to the rear sat a beefy red-faced man wearing houndstooth tweed. The man stared back at him, their eyes locked. Stern felt the sweat spring out again on his forehead. The man turned to the woman who sat beside him, and she gave him a sleepy smile. The red-faced man returned his gaze to the magazine he had been reading.

Aristide Robert was alerted to the presence of a stranger by the barking of the dog. The animal was lunging about at the end of its chain. Aristide shied a stone at the beast.

Aristide had made a considerable dent in the Calvados, but was only a little drunk. A man stood at the edge of the woods looking down at the farm. He wore a black leather coat and felt hat. He was tall and thin. Aristide did not much like the looks of him. Even from a distance he could smell a German. Fucking Boche. They were after the girl. If she had still been at the farm he would have given her to them. Fat chance of his risking his own neck for that little bitch. But Lise and the girl had gone off together in the truck. If they were found, Lise would be shot and the truck confiscated. If the girl were traced even this far, they might shoot him, too. He would deny everything. It was the only way.

The man at the edge of the wood was examining the ground. Picked up her trail right enough, thought Aristide. But why is he alone? Very brave or very stupid.

The German had left the embankment and started down the path. With a sly expression Aristide ducked inside the barn and reached for the shotgun he kept concealed behind the milking stalls.

It had been one of the minor victories of the Vichy government's deal with the Germans that farmers were allowed to keep their weapons. Rabbits had to be procured for the pot. Foxes sometimes got into hen houses. At first Aristide had approved of the way

Vichy was handling matters. The war was over. The
Germans had conducted themselves well. At first. But
then they had put the squeeze on. Men were seized in
the street and shipped off to labor battalions in Germany. Cream, milk, cheese, and butter were confiscated. Even horses and cows and supplies of hay and
grain were taken. Aristide's early admiration for the
Germans had turned to brooding hatred. It was not
a hatred based on patriotic fervor. De Gaulle's appeals
to Frenchmen to fight on had fallen on deaf ears so
far as he was concerned. He did not give a fuck what
happened to those Jew bastards in Paris. But when
they came onto his own land pinching his butter . . .

The German was at the side of the house now, peer-
ing toward the barn. Aristide slipped a shell into the
shotgun and cocked the weapon. He remained in the
shadowed interior of the barn with his gun held at
waist level. The Calvados had lent him false courage.
Maybe that bitch Lise would have more respect for
him when she learned how he had handled this
Boche.

Hauser had followed the faint trail of blood on the
stones. All night he had searched for Michelle in the
woods. He felt light headed, feverish. His legs ached.
The cold and damp were not helping. He was afraid.

He had not felt so frightened since the night Denise
had come to his door. There had been a brief moment
when he might still have saved her. With the full
weight of his university associations behind him, he
might somehow have gotten her away. He had let the
moment pass. And then it was too late. It still would
have meant endangering his own position at the university and weakening the close political ties with

the party which he had so carefully nurtured over the years.

They would do her no great harm, he had told himself. Later, through his influence with Hess, he could try to pull strings. But in the end there had been no strings to pull. By the time he was ready to try, she was already dead.

But had he not secretly wanted her dead as part of his revenge on Stern? And had not even the trap he had helped set for Michelle been dictated by the same need?

Why torture himself with questions that could never be answered?

He squared his shoulders as he strode down the path. The place seemed deserted but he could have sworn that a few minutes earlier, there had been a man squatting by the side of the house.

From inside the barn a voice said, "Stay where you are."

Hauser's French was not bad, but there was no way to disguise his accent. He said, "I am looking for a young woman."

"There is no young woman here. Move on."

Hauser drew himself erect. "My name is Dr. Hauser. I do not mean you any harm. It is necessary that this young woman be found. She escaped last night from the villa on the hill and may have come here to your farm. If necessary, I will call in the authorities to institute a search. I will . . ."

Hauser never finished the sentence. The concentrated shot fired at close range tore through the leather coat and smashed into his chest, penetrating between the ribs, killing him instantly.

Aristide had not meant to kill, had not even meant

really to fire the gun. It had all been too much, this
Boche bastard in his leather coat and gold-rimmed
glasses coming onto his land to steal his butter. Never
mind what the German had said about the girl; it had
been the butter he was after.

At the sound of the shot the boy came running from
the house and stood there wide-eyed staring down at
the dead man. Aristide emerged slowly into the daylight shaking his head. He let his gaze roam slowly
from the surrounding hills to the path leading to the
woods. There was no one. Aristide Robert, who could
almost feel the bite of the rope around his neck, might
still have a chance.

"Get me the shovel," he said to the child. "Quickly."

The boy ran to the barn. Aristide seized the corpse
by the legs and began to drag it toward the pigpen.
The dead man's hat fell off. He would come back for
it later. Everything had to be buried quickly, even the
gun. In the soft muck of the pigsty it would be easy
to scrape out a shallow grave. A matter of minutes.
What mattered now was to get the bastard into the
ground and out of sight. Even if a patrol came by they
would not want to soil themselves in the stinking
muck.

Lise brought the wheezing old Peugeot to a halt.
"We will walk the rest of the way," she told Michelle.
"Look in the shopwindows. Appear unconcerned. If
we are questioned, let me do the talking. I know these
Milice bastards. They buy butter and bacon from me
on the black market. I can handle them."

"I don't want to make trouble for you, Lise."

"My trouble is with the Boche, not with you," Lise

answered curtly. "But we will drive those pigs out yet. Now, come on."

The curfew was not yet in effect. The streets were crowded with bicyclists. Lise nodded to a few passersby, but spoke to no one. As they approached Christine's she led the way into the alley. The back door opened to her touch. The place was dark.

Lise led the way to the foot of the stairs and called up softly, "Christine, are you there?"

There was no answer.

"She cannot have gone far," Lise said. "I am sure she will return. You wait upstairs. Make no sound. No one will bother you. Trust Christine. She will arrange everything."

Michelle was seized by panic. "Are you leaving me?"

"I must," Lise answered in a softer voice. "I must return home before the curfew. You understand?"

"I understand."

Michelle embraced the older woman. "Thank you, Lise."

"For nothing." She gave Michelle a rough kiss on the cheek and then was gone.

The two Germans, one of them a private with a rifle and the other a corporal with a machine pistol, had come down the railway embankment and were following the path to the farmhouse. Aristide Robert did his best to look unconcerned. He leaned back against the pigpen and lit a cigarette. The familiar act of sucking the acrid smoke into his lungs steadied him.

The corporal—a small, ferret-faced man, behaved punctiliously. "Good evening, monsieur."

"Guten Tag," Aristide grunted in reply. He knew how to butter up these bastards.

"A nice place you have here. Pigs, cows, you are doing all right." The corporal had bright eyes like those of a rat. "We are looking for a man and a woman."

Aristide cocked a bushy eyebrow. He was aware that his pulse was beating faster. "Cigarette?"

"Thank you."

"One for your pal?" He held out the pack. The private took a cigarette and thanked him. Aristide took out his box of wax matches and offered a light. "A man and a woman, eh? We don't get many strangers in these parts."

"Then you would surely have noticed them passing by?"

"In daylight I would."

"Particularly this one, I think," said the corporal. "Distinguished-looking gentleman. Tall, thin, leather coat, eyeglasses, wearing a soft hat. Dr. Hauser from Berlin."

Aristide shook his head. "Nobody like that has been around here."

"Nor a young woman? Dark hair. Pretty. Bare feet."

Aristide chuckled. "I could use a pretty young woman with dark hair and bare feet. That one I would surely remember. No, I'm afraid not. Why are you after them, anyway?"

The corporal shrugged. "Apparently this Hauser is a big shot. If we have lost him there will be hell to pay."

"Well, if I hear anything I'll report it," Aristide said.

"That's the style. All right, then, we'll move along."

The corporal stubbed out his cigarette and tossed the butt over the fence in among the pigs. Pigs, he knew, ate anything, even their own young. An enormous black sow with mud-spattered flanks was routing about in the muck grunting with excitement. The others were moving to join her. The corporal, who had been raised not on a farm but among the smokestacks of the Ruhr, watched with interest. The big sow's ugly snout had turned up something that made his eyes open wider. He was looking at what had been a man's felt hat.

The sow had unearthed something else and was tearing voraciously at it. With a shout to the private to give him a hand, the corporal jumped over into the muck to drive the pigs away from the corpse. He was kicking the sow furiously in the ribs when he glanced up to see Aristide running for the embankment. With an oath the corporal unslung his machine pistol.

Aristide might have made it into the shelter of the woods had he not been slowed by the wire fence. In the moment that it took him to straddle the fence the first shots caught him in the small of the back.

With a shouted order to the private to keep the pigs off Hauser's body, the corporal climbed back out of the run and darted down the path. Aristide still clung with both hands to the wire. The corporal raised the machine pistol and pumped half a dozen shots into Aristide's head.

Michelle sat in the darkened flat above the beauty salon. She felt lifeless. Her emotions were numbed. The fragrance of hair lotions and colognes came from the salon below. She reached up to touch her stubble of hair. It was hard to remember what her once beautiful hair had been like. In some former life before the torment had begun, she, too, had been pretty. She could hardly remember.

She closed her eyes. It was better not to think of the past or the future. For the moment at least she was warm and dry and in a quiet place and that was enough.

Whether Hauser or the SS found her first no longer seemed to matter.

She was awakened by the sound of low voices and footsteps on the stairs. She clutched at the arms of the chair. A light was turned on and she saw a man standing in the doorway holding a pistol, a thin young man with fair hair.

It was Jens Larsen.

She screamed.

THIRTY-NINE

Morning penetrated the shutters. Michelle dozed fitfully. Larsen had spent the night sitting up listening for any sound that might signal danger. Dukov, having downed the better part of two liters of wine, was motionless on the other bed. Christine had gone out again before dawn. She returned now with hot coffee and croissants. Her face looked drawn and worried.

"It appears we've stirred up a hornet's nest," she said to Larsen. "The whole town is buzzing. The Germans are bringing in reinforcements from all along the coast. It's obvious they mean to search every mousehole they can find."

Larsen looked at the sleeping Michelle but did not answer. Her scream when she had first seen him had unnerved him. It had been followed by hysteria. Convinced at last that he was in fact alive, she had quieted. Christine had given her a mild sleeping pill.

"We've got to get you out of here," Christine said.

Larsen's head felt fuzzy. He shook himself awake. "What do you suggest? Up into the mountains?"

Christine shook her head. "I mean out of France altogether. Vautrin's people have contacted London. A landing near Dubáye and an exchange of SOE people for downed pilots will be taking place at midnight. With luck we could be there. The trouble is we will have to travel over some terribly rough country. I wonder if Michelle is up to it."

"Is there any choice?"

Christine shrugged. "Not much. It would appear that the entire Resistance is in danger. The Prosper network has collapsed and hundreds of his people have been arrested. They will be tortured before they are executed and some will talk. From this moment on none of us will be safe."

Christine began to rummage in her closet dragging out heavy boots, sweaters, and mitts. "Wake Michelle. Meanwhile I will try to contact an old friend who may help us along the way."

The trained voices of Father Paul's choir rose harmoniously toward the nave of the abbey. The singers attacked the notes with the precision of true artists, their rich young voices pursuing a theme of praise, swirling round the sturdy columns and surging up to the heights of the arched vault.

Father Paul was immensely proud of his choir. He was also proud of his charcoal-burning Ford V-8. Under cover of the harmony that flooded the church, the priest struggled to bring the old car to life. With Larsen's help a few feeble splutterings were induced through the pipe from the stern burner. The priest raised his eyes to heaven in a gesture of thankfulness and then jabbed his foot down on the accelerator. In a moment the garage was full of black smoke. Father Paul beckoned to Michelle, Larsen, Christine, and Dukov to get aboard. The wooden doors were thrown open. Amid the swelling chorus of the "Ave Maria" the Ford rumbled off into the night.

Michelle wore studded boots and a heavy sweater borrowed from Christine. Even so she trembled with cold. Larsen sat with his arm around her trying to give her the benefit of whatever body warmth he could muster.

"One good thing about charcoal," the priest called back over his shoulder. "It will make things warm after a while."

It was dark by the time the Ford, operating on only thirty percent of its power, had struggled halfway up the mountain road. With each kilometer the car traveled more slowly. At last it petered out altogether. No amount of coaxing brought anything but a wheeze from the engine.

Father Paul shrugged. "I am afraid it is shanks' mare for you from here on, my children."

"Will you be able to get back all right?" Christine asked him.

"With God's help and a steep decline, yes," the old priest said.

Larsen reached into his pocket and drew out a five-hundred-franc note. Father Paul shook his head.

"For the poor," Larsen said. "And for the training of the choir."

"Les Petits Chanteurs à la Croix de Bois. In their name I accept. Now if you will be so good as to turn me around."

They pushed the Ford around and watched it glide off with the priest hunched over the wheel like a racing driver. As it descended the curving road, they heard the engine sputter into life.

The village lay ahead up the stony track. The sky was clear and the air was cold. Patches of frost made the rocky path slippery. They had still three kilometers to go to reach the landing strip. With each step Michelle came closer to the final limits of her strength.

"Perhaps I should go on and leave Michelle here with you to rest," Larsen said to Christine. "I could be there when they land and get them to wait."

Christine shook her head. "They wait for no one. It is far too dangerous for them to remain on the ground. Down and up and that's that. We must all go on."

Michelle's breathing was ragged, but she struggled gamely back to her feet. Larsen felt a rush of compassion and admiration.

"Are you all right?" he whispered.

She reached out to touch his cheek with icy fingertips. "A picnic," she answered.

In that moment the feeling of strangeness between them seemed to melt away. They had violated her body, but her spirit was intact.

Dukov had already begun to move away up the track. "Come on," he called in a low voice.

"In a moment," Larsen answered.

He took off his belt, fastened it tightly around Michelle's waist, and took the loose end in his hand.

"I feel like a French poodle," Michelle said.

Larsen responded with a tug on the leash.

The moon, almost full, had begun to rise, illuminating the craggy peaks in a ghostly light. The track had grown steeper. Ahead lay the mountain village of Dubáye.

Perched precariously between rocky walls, the village had changed little since the thirteenth century.

The rough track which dead-ended in the town square was useable only by horse-drawn carts. Few tourists ever found their way to Dubaye. Looking up at the gray stone battlements, Larsen half expected to see archers in medieval helmets.

Dukov tried to muffle his steps on the rounded stones that paved the narrow street. What the villagers did not know, they could not tell. The silence and the blackness were eerie. Suddenly, as he turned the corner into the square, he saw a man standing in front of him holding a Sten gun. Dukov about-faced like a flash only to find two other armed men behind him. More men, moving catlike, had materialized from doorways. Not so much as the scuff of shoe leather on stone. They knew their business. He raised his hands above his head.

In a moment Larsen and the two women, ringed by armed men, had been brought to join him.

"Into the town hall where we can have a look at them," a voice said.

Dukov felt a gun's muzzle against the small of his back. He was shoved forward.

Moonlight silvered the square and its dominant architectural feature, a spired hall. Still the eerie silence. Where are the damned dogs, Dukov wondered.

A wooden door on creaking iron hinges was opened to let them through and they stepped into a roomful of armed men dressed in rough clothing. The room was lit by oil lamps. At a large table in the center sat a one-armed man in a leather jacket and military-style whipcord breeches. He had grizzled hair and a short white beard. By the light of a candle stuck in the neck of a wine bottle, he was eating chunks of bread and cheese and studying a tattered map.

He looked up when the door opened and took in the group ushered in by the armed men. He said, "What the devil have we here?"

The man who held the muzzle of his Sten against Dukov's back pushed him forward. "We found these four wandering around outside, Commandant. This one was in the lead. The others followed."

The one-armed man held the candle higher. He studied Dukov's features. "A proper-looking brigand. What the hell were you doing out there?"

"Searching for wild strawberries," Dukov answered. "They're supposed to be unusually good in these parts."

"Strawberries my ass," said the man with the Sten. "They could be Krauts. We should have plugged them right off. Anyway, it's not too late."

The commandant gave his follower a disgusted look. "You may be right. That one is obviously Rommel and the other is von Rundstedt. As for the women . . ." he peered searchingly at Christine. "Don't I know you?"

"Perhaps," Christine answered.

"My name is Bernicot. I command the Resistance here. Aren't you the one they call the 'Woman from Algiers'?"

Christine smiled. "Sometimes they call me that. At other times, Christine."

"Of course. I knew it. You look done in, the lot of you. Come and sit down. There is bread and wine and cheese. It will be an honor to set a place at my table for the famous Christine. But tell me first what brings you to Dubáye?"

"We are on our way to the airstrip. We have business there later tonight."

The commandant shook his head. "I regret to tell you, mademoiselle, that no one will be using the airfield tonight. In a little while"—he glanced at his watch—"say forty minutes from now, this entire area will be swarming with Germans. They have launched an all-out attack against the Republic of Dubáye as a preliminary step in throwing back the invasion."

"What the hell are you talking about?" said Dukov. "What is the Republic of Dubáye and what invasion?"

The commandant took a swallow of wine, sly self-satisfaction written over his features. He had a square, reddish face topped by heavy brows which half concealed his eyes. The empty left sleeve of his leather jacket was pinned to his breast.

A real old soldier, thought Dukov. If he is half as stupid as he looks, we are in trouble.

"The Americans and the British will be here in a matter of hours. Twenty-four at the most," Bernicot boomed.

Dukov scowled. "What gives you that idea?"

"I have already declared the liberation of the Republic of Dubáye."

"Damn the Republic of Dubáye! What's all this about an invasion?"

"Algiers radio has informed us that Allied landings are being effected at St. Tropez, Nice, and Cannes. The Germans are attempting to crush the Resistance before it can rise to strike them from the rear. Our scouts report that an enemy armored column is now less than an hour from Dubáye."

Christine shook her head. "No Allied landings have

taken place along the Côte d'Azur. We came from there only a few hours ago."

Bernicot exploded: "There were reports of heavy firing within the past few days to the north and east of Antibes. Why would Algiers give me false information?"

"Algiers is not Supreme Allied Command. It would not be the first time that rumor has been construed as fact. The firing you are referring to was not an Allied landing. It was a local Resistance attack on an Abwehr political prison."

"But this is a disaster," boomed Bernicot. "My command is in no position to fight a major battle for control of this region. It was my intention only to fight a delaying action until the Allied forces arrived."

"How many men do you have here, Commandant?"

"There are one hundred twenty men in the FFI of Dubaye, but only about fifty of them have weapons. There are no more than twenty rounds of ammunition per weapon."

Christine shook her head. "You have a very small force with which to face tanks."

"But what am I to do, then? I have been led into this trap by the abominable trickery of those bastards in Algiers."

"What about the FFI forces in Vercors? Can they do nothing to help you?"

Bernicot shook his head. "There are perhaps eight hundred Maquisards in that region and a few thousand more who have fled to escape forced labor and deportation. But their circumstances are the same as ours—only a small number are armed. If they, too, have responded to this false message from Algiers, then we are all in the same fix. What do you suggest?"

"Order your people to fight their way out. Preferably in small units. I'm against these full-scale engagements on principle; it's not what the Resistance was designed for."

Bernicot's brick-red face had gone pale. "Abandon the position?"

"It's the only way, Commandant. As it is, I doubt if all your people will get away. If the enemy is responding as fast as you say, then Dubáye is already cut off."

The one-armed commandant leaped to his feet. "We will give those bastards something to remember us by. What do you say, lads?"

A cheer went up from the ragged army of the Republic of Dubáye.

"The old coot is crazy," Dukov grumbled to Larsen. "A one-armed Quixote."

The commandant tilted his beret at a more rakish angle and said, "I will now prepare to address the troops. Certain formalities must be observed. Even if this is to be our final hour, we will not flee like rabble. Squad Commander, fall in your troops!"

Dukov, who had moved to the open doorway, put up a restraining hand. "Listen!"

They could hear the clatter of armored treads grinding up the rocky track. Spasmodic rifle firing came from the Col de Larche.

"Christ!" said Dukov. "Have you nothing but popguns to use against those battleships?"

"We have a Piat with about twelve rounds, but none of us is experienced in the use of antitank weapons," Bernicot said.

"Well, I am, mon Commandant. Bazookas or fucking Piats, it's all the same. Get it out."

The long tubelike weapon was produced. Dukov regarded it with satisfaction. "We will singe a few German assholes yet. Where they come around the corner of the church to enter the square might be the best place. What do you think?"

"Agreed."

"The rest of you clear out. You've got about five minutes to lose yourselves in the hills. Larsen, you and the women can still make it to the airstrip. I'll try to hold them here."

"I am going nowhere," Bernicot said.

"You had better get out while you can, Commandant."

"I do not need you to remind me of my duty, monsieur."

"There is not much a one-armed man can contribute to these proceedings."

"One arm or two, I can still set an example. As a Frenchman I have run away for the last time."

Larsen said to Dukov, "This isn't your fight, but if you stay, then I must stay, too."

"Bullshit! There is only the one Piat, and I am the one who knows how to use it. Your job is to get the women out. There's no time to argue."

Christine suddenly put her arm around Dukov's neck and pressed her cheek against his. He plucked her clear of the ground and brought her head around and kissed her mouth. When he released her, he said, "Now get going, all of you. Don't worry. I'll see you at the field. The Krauts haven't been able to kill me yet, and they're not about to now."

Within seconds they had disappeared up the narrow street that led to the brushy hillside.

He watched them go and then picked up the Piat. He slid a shell into the chamber. "I want this first round to go right up a panzer's ass."

"You really think you can stop one of those monsters with that toy?" Bernicot asked.

"Those Tigers have one weakness. In the gut. There is a plate that covers the underside, which is lightly armored. As they come over the rise near the church, we will give them a kick in the nuts they will never forget."

Bernicot drew himself erect. "Right, Monsieur Dukov. I will be your loader. Even a one-armed man can do that." He reached for the bottle of wine. "I give you the Republic of Dubaye. And for the Boche, as you say, a kick in the nuts."

The town of Dubaye, awaiting the onslaught, seemed to crouch behind its medieval walls. Riflemen and machine gunners were hidden by the town hall and its outlying buildings. At least half of Bernicot's small force had elected to defend the town. The commandant himself and Dukov had taken up a position among the gravestones.

As the tank arrived at the square, the defenders opened fire, their bullets bouncing off the armor.

The Tiger topped the rise before the square. Dukov stood up. He was no more than twenty yards from the tank. With the Piat held to his shoulder, he took aim and fired. The rocket struck the underside of the tank and penetrated its lightly armored belly. The monster lurched, seeming to feel itself mortally wounded. It

ground forward another yard and then stopped. Dukov fired again. The hatch was thrown open, and the
crew began to jump out into the street. They were
mowed down by a storm of small arms fire.

Bernicot leaped to his feet and pounded Dukov on
the back. In their excitement neither of them had seen
the swiftly moving armored car approaching from the
opposite direction. With gun ports open and machine
guns blazing, the armored car swept the square and
the churchyard. Dukov clutched at his leg and went
down.

Bernicot dragged him behind a headstone as the
armored car again raked the square. Despite his
wound Dukov was not out of action. With Bernicot's
help he was reloading the Piat.

A second tank, attempting to shove the destroyed
lead tank out of the way, struck sparks from the cob-
bles. The armored car roamed up and down the
square driving the defenders back into the shelter of
the town hall. With Bernicot supporting him, Dukov
was again on his feet, the Piat at his shoulder. He
fired at the car. At once the lightly armored car burst
into flames. Bernicot hugged Dukov, kissing him on
both cheeks. Still clutching the Piat, Dukov sank back
among the stones. German riflemen were now advanc-
ing across the square. A handful of the FFI fled before
them toward the rocky slopes of the Col, but the rest,
too badly wounded to move, lay behind the walls of
the Town Hall.

The battle was over.

At once the Germans began pulling the FFI out of
their holes. The wounded men were dragged out by
the hair and dumped on the cobblestones. They were

not considered worth a bullet. The Germans beat them to death with rifle butts. Most died hard. Bernicot, tears running down his cheeks, watched the slaughter of his men.

FORTY

The donkey was not much larger than a big dog. It braced itself under Dukov's weight and then moved, up the track away from the village. Dukov, his wounded leg dripping blood, sat astride the beast. He still clutched the Piat and its last two shells. Bernicot marched in front leading the way.

Such had been the blood lust of the German infantrymen engaged in slaughtering the wounded that they had paid little attention to the handful of survivors among the gravestones. Bernicot had found the donkey tethered behind the church, and after a struggle had gotten Dukov up onto its back.

Dukov groaned. When Bernicot looked back at him, Dukov managed a grin. "What an army," Dukov said. "A one-armed commandant, a one-legged gunner, and an ass."

"We may be small," answered Bernicot, "but with the Piat we are mighty. When the swine finish with the town, they will head for the airstrip. I was born in Dubáye and grew up here. I know this track like the back of my hand. There is a stand of trees just before the airstrip. A good spot for an ambush. We will be waiting there to give them another kiss from Mademoiselle Piat."

"Two kisses. The last two. We had better make them good."

Larsen felt the earth tremble. German armored vehicles were climbing the track. Ever since the fight at the villa the recurring nightmare of pursuit had grown closer. Now, when they were within reach of the airstrip, the enemy was closing the gap.

The forest was at last behind them. No more than a thousand yards ahead he saw a steep hogback, silvered by moonlight, rising against the sky.

He paused to examine the illuminated dial of his wristwatch. It was eleven forty-five. In fifteen minutes the plane would arrive and, as Christine had said, they would not wait. Nor could they hope to land without fires to mark the ends of the runway. Michelle sagged against him. Far off he heard something that sent a spurt of excitement through his veins—the thunder of aircraft engines.

Christine moved up beside him. "Did you hear?"

"Yes. Come on!"

"We're too late. Without the bonfires they can't land. They'll turn back."

Larsen's voice was sharp with urgency. "It's not yet midnight. They may circle. Where is the wood kept?"

"A little hut on the north side of the pitch." She looked back the way they had come. "I see lights."

"I know. The Germans are bringing up armored cars. They'll be slowed by the woods. We might make it yet."

Michelle had slumped down and was lying on her side. Larsen bent to touch her cheek. "You two come as fast as you can. I'll go on ahead to light the fires."

He sprang up the track, climbing desperately, listen-

ing again for the plane. As he mounted the hogback
it swept low overhead, enveloping him in the thunder
of its passing.

It roared on and disappeared.

Let them circle, he prayed. Dear God, let them
circle.

Finding the shed was not difficult. Dragging out
armloads of dry brush along with a tin of kerosene
took time. Beneath the tin was a glass jar containing
matches. Panting for breath, hands shaking, he ran
from one part of the field to the other scattering the
brush and soaking it with the kerosene. The wind
was up and his first two tries with the matches failed.
On his third attempt the brush caught and sent a pil-
lar of flame skyward. Larsen ran for the other end of
the strip and in a moment both fires were burning.

He waited, heart pounding, for some sign from the
sky.

Finally it came, an exultant roar from the Hudson's engines as it swept once again over the field.

Against the glare of the fires he could make out
Michelle and Christine. He ran to help them, realizing
as he did that the Germans were much closer than
he had thought. The lights of the armored car were
now visible as the car picked its way through the
trees. The enemy had only to surmount the hogback
to be upon them.

Other shapes were outlined atop the rise—two men
and a small horse or donkey. The rider of the burro
suddenly seemed to fall to the ground. As his companion turned to help him, Larsen saw with a shock
of recognition that the man who had been leading
the animal had only one arm.

* * *

Oberleutnant Schmitt, in command of the armored car, had read his Cervantes; it was thus with an expression of amazement that he surveyed, through his field glasses, the weird shapes caught in the glare of his headlamps. No more than one hundred yards ahead rode a bearded, lance-carrying Don Quixote guided by Sancho Panza. Schmitt, who had ordered a halt while he searched the track ahead, lowered his glasses to rub his eyes. He, too, had heard the British bomber looking for a landing and had been congratulating himself on the opportunity of catching an enemy aircraft on the ground. A burst of machine gun fire from the car would guarantee Schmitt's instant promotion to captain. But not if he were seeing things that did not exist. When he raised the glasses again, the track was empty. He ordered the car forward. It had not gone more than thirty yards when the bearded figure appeared once more.

Too late Schmitt realized that the apparition held not a lance but an antitank weapon. Before the startled *Oberleutnant* could order his gunner to open fire, a blossom of flame, as if tied to an invisible wire, shot down the track in his direction. Schmitt tried to duck but there was no time. The exploding rocket decapitated him cleanly and left his torso dangling from the open hatch. At once the car burst into flames. The driver and machine gunner died more painfully than had their commander.

Larsen had seen the lights of the armored vehicle wink out just before the car itself dissolved in a ball of flame. He heard the roar of the explosion and felt, moments later, the shock wave and the blast of heat.

He ran to Michelle and Christine. "It's Dukov! Dukov and Bernicot! Alive!"

His words were drowned in the thunder of engines
as the big plane swept only a few feet over their heads
and touched down on the strip. At once he started
the two women running toward the aircraft which had
come to a halt on the short runway and was now
turning to taxi downwind.

"Make them wait!" Larsen shouted. "I'm going for
Dukov!"

He ran to the hogback. Dukov, half supported by
the Frenchman and using the Piat as a crutch, was
moving up the track. He managed a grin as Larsen
reached them.

"The little major!" Dukov said. "Did you see that
bastard blow?"

"Yes! Yes! There's no time for talk. Put your arm
over my shoulder and for God's sake hurry!"

Propellers gleaming in the firelight, the big plane
was turning into the wind. Larsen heard voices shouting at him and saw hands projecting out of the open
bomb bay. First Dukov and then Bernicot were
dragged upward into the plane. Then it was Larsen's
turn, scrambling as the plane gathered speed. There
was enough light from the fires to give him a confused impression of Christine and Michelle gathered
around Dukov. A crew member warned him to stand
clear. The bomb bay doors closed with a bang. The
pilot seemed to wrench the aircraft up from the
ground by sheer strength. Even so they heard the
scrape of branches along the aluminum skin.

Larsen wiped the sweat out of his eyes. As he
crawled forward to the cockpit, the pilot, who had an
enormous RAF moustache but still did not look more

than twenty, grinned at him. He was pointing down-ward.

In the sputtering blue flame of the exhausts Larsen could make out a broken tree limb jammed into the landing gear. The pilot put his mouth close to Lar-sen's ear. "A bone in our teeth. Can't get the wheels up. Means a slow trip back."

"How will you land?"

The boy shrugged and rolled his eyes to heaven.

They hit with a bone-jarring crash, but the under-carriage survived, and the pilot fought the plane down to a manageable speed. Larsen could see fire trucks starting toward them. A group of uniformed figures stood beside the hangars in the chill light of dawn. Among them he recognized Peter Guthrie.

FORTY-ONE

"I know this is painful for you, Michelle," Guthrie said. "You're exhausted and you'd like to put it all behind you, and I promise you that after we have gone over it once more, Jens can take you home."

The smudges of weariness under Michelle's eyes were like blue stains against her pale skin. "I understand."

"I'm particularly interested in that reference Hauser made to your father. Can you give me that again, word for word, exactly as he said it?"

"I am not likely to forget. He said, 'Your father. Your noble father. We will see how your famous father behaves when he and Einstein . . .' I asked him what he meant, and he replied, 'Nothing.' "

"That was his only reference to your father?"

She nodded.

"Had there been any mention of Einstein earlier?"

"None." Tears welled up in her eyes.

Guthrie said, "Better take her home now, Jens. I've got a car and driver waiting for you. See that she gets some rest. We'll talk again tomorrow."

Guthrie watched them leave, then placed a call to General Fleming.

"I've got to see you, sir."

"Can it wait?" the general asked.

"It won't wait, sir."

There was a pause before the general spoke again. "I take it it's not something you'd care to tell me over the phone."

"It's too fantastic, sir."

A cold wind whipped the salt marshes as the taxi fought its way through the heavy traffic toward New York. Stern had slept hardly at all on the long flight over the ocean, and he now felt close to exhaustion. As they drove over the bridge, he gazed with little interest at the jagged skyline. New York had always been an architectural nightmare, its filthy streets strewn with rubbish. In the years since his last visit the place had not improved.

He settled back against the seat and closed his eyes.

Yes, the desk clerk at the hotel assured him, they had a reservation in the name of Dr. David Stern. Also a letter and a package, both delivered by hand.

The package was a little larger than a cigar box and heavy for its size. Pasted to the top was a label bearing his name.

Trying to conceal his agitation he put the letter in his pocket and carried the package with him to the elevator.

The bellboy who led the way to his room fussed interminably over the lights and curtains until at last Stern thrust a dollar at him and barked, "Yes, yes. That will be all."

When the boy had finally retreated, Stern closed the door and locked it. He sat down on the bed and opened the letter. It contained another photograph of Michelle, this time a smaller replica of the one he had received in Lisbon. There was the same high wall behind her and the semitropical foliage and the bright sunlight which did nothing to conceal the drawn look and the lifeless hair and the pain-filled eyes.

He felt the sting of tears as he looked at the picture.

Inside were two sections cut from ordinary road maps of the kind that were obtained at gasoline stations. Circled in ink was the town of Princeton, New Jersey. Beneath the circle was an address: 112 Mercer Street. Stern's jaw dropped. It was an address to which he had written fairly regularly over the past several years.

It was the address of Albert Einstein.

The second map showed an area of the south shore of Long Island. There was the deep indentation of Peconic Bay and the long narrow strip of beach which sheltered the bay from the Atlantic. A circle had been drawn there as well.

Beneath the circled area had been written: March 5. Beneath the date the time: 9:45 P.M.

The date was three days away.

The letter was in German written in stiff formal handwriting and in the same ink which had been used to circle the points on the map.

The directions were explicit, couched in military terminology. Beginning on the night of the fifth of March a U-boat would surface each evening at nine forty-five at the designated point off the coast of Long Island. Stern was to be there with Einstein. They would be taken off by rubber boat. U-99 would proceed to Estoril, Portugal, where Stern would be reunited with his daughter.

At Estoril Albert Einstein would remain on board the U-99.

If for any reason Stern and Einstein failed to make the rendezvous U-99 would return again the following night at the same time.

The submarine would remain on the surface for no longer than twenty minutes. The U-boat commander had orders to radio Berlin if Stern failed to arrive with Einstein. In that case Michelle Stern would be immediately executed.

The letter was unsigned.

He opened the package. It contained, wrapped in scraps of newspaper, a loaded revolver.

General Fleming stroked his graying moustache from time to time. "Most of what you are telling me is sheer supposition."

"Admittedly, sir. But consider what we know. The Germans captured Michelle Stern, but did not execute her. She was abused sexually and photographs were taken. She was transferred from SS headquarters in Paris to an Abwehr political prison near Antibes. She got away in the company of Hauser, who knew both Stern and Einstein in Berlin and had once been engaged to the girl's mother. Stern leaves England for Ireland and then goes on to Lisbon and New York. Hauser reveals to the girl that there is some business afoot between Stern and Einstein. Combine those facts with the destruction of the heavy water cells at Vemork and a pattern begins to emerge."

"You are seriously suggesting that Stern was sent to America to arrange for the kidnapping of Einstein?"

"I am, sir." The memory of Zofia had returned to

haunt him. The intensity of his grief had diminished slightly, but he was not yet ready to accept the finality of death. He was able for the first time to understand something of what Stern might be going through. If there had been some way to save Zofia, how far would he have gone? How far could a man's loyalties be stretched? It was impossible to put himself in Stern's shoes, but at least he could perceive the nightmarish depths of the quandary. When you gambled with the devil . . .

"What do you propose?" said the general.

"That you notify the American authorities to place a guard on Einstein."

The general shook his head. "Can't do that."

"Why not, sir?"

"Principally because of this chap Hoover of the FBI. He's a bloodhound for publicity and extremely jealous of his prerogatives. To begin with there is absolutely no guarantee that he wouldn't leak the story to the press, which of course is exactly what we don't want. Besides, he's apt to scoff at the whole thing and come down hard on our people in New York."

"Then forget him. Telephone New York and have our own people take over."

"Can't do that, either. Hoover knows every one of them and he's already making life difficult as it is. That man wields an unholy power. I'll tell you something in confidence, Peter. Mr. J. Edgar Hoover was largely responsible for the success of the Japanese attack on Pearl Harbor. In June of 1941 we had a double agent in New York. He received a request from his German masters for information which could assist the Japanese in a proposed attack on Pearl Harbor. The success of the British torpedo plane attack on the Italian fleet at Taranto had not been lost on the Germans or the Japanese. They made it quite clear to our man that a similar attack on Pearl Harbor was in the planning stage. The Japanese foreign minister was in Berlin working out the details and requesting data. Our chap turned the information over to Hoover, who promptly labeled him a sexual degenerate and had him thrown out of the country.

"As you can imagine," the general went on, "Mr. Hoover is still remarkably sensitive on the subject of British agents. No, we can't contact the Americans, and we certainly can't use our own people who are known and registered with the FBI. We'll have to send someone from London. Preferably someone who knows Stern on sight." Without waiting for a comment from Guthrie the general said, "Stay here." Ten minutes passed before he returned. When he did he said, "A Liberator will be departing for New York in two hours. As a courier you will be permitted to carry arms. A military car and driver will be at your disposal upon landing. Good luck."

Stern ordered a sandwich and a bottle of whiskey brought to his room. He ate half the sandwich and left the rest. The whiskey made his head fuzzy. His thoughts went round in circles.

He was being asked to betray the greatest scientific mind of the age, the man he revered above all others.

Could Einstein give them the bomb? Since his letter to Roosevelt warning of German progress in the atomic field, the old man had avoided further involvement, but he would certainly understand the plutonium alternative.

That brilliant mind might perceive in minutes what

had taken the rest of them years. How would the Germans unlock his brain? They had their ways. God knew they had their ways.

He was being asked to sign a pact with the devil.

Einstein was old. He was ill. His best years and his best work were behind him. The special theory of relativity had been published in 1905 when he was still a very young man. Since then he had been world famous. He had lived a long life full of honors.

But what if he gave them Einstein and they still failed to release Michelle?

He got up and went into the bathroom and looked at himself in the mirror. Ordinarily fastidious, he was still unwashed and unshaven after the long flight. The once clear blue eyes were bleary with drink. His face had always been lean, but now the remaining flesh seemed to have melted away. There were deep hollows at the temples. His cheekbones were clearly revealed. He was looking at a death's head.

He returned to the bedroom and picked up the revolver. He had not touched a weapon since his military service in Germany twenty years before. He had been a good shot then. Now his fingers recoiled from the blue steel.

He examined the six heavy bullets and then closed the revolver with a click and replaced it in the box.

He lay down on the bed and closed his eyes. When he woke he shaved and showered and rang down to the desk to ask the porter to obtain a schedule of trains going to New Jersey.

He hailed a cab outside the Princeton station. "One twelve Mercer Street," he told the driver.

The vehicle seemed enormous. Stern had forgotten how huge the American cars were. The elderly cabbie drove with exasperating slowness, turning his head from side to side, nodding at people on the sidewalk and at other drivers.

"How long is the trip?" Stern said.

"Depends."

Stern did his best to control his temper. The pistol in his raincoat pocket was heavy on his lap.

"Depends on what?" Stern said.

"On a lot of things. Mostly I guess on how fast we drive." The dry chuckle sounded like a last gasp.

"I haven't got all day."

The cabbie nodded but continued to maintain the same slow speed.

"You a friend of the professor?"

"Yes."

"Figured you must be, since you knew the address. Seems like every stranger comes to Princeton wants to know where the professor lives. Folks here in town don't talk much; they know the old fellow don't want to be bothered. Now, over there is Fuld Hall. In the wintertime you can find the professor over there every day at work on that relativity business. Folks ask me what it's all about, and I tell them I can't even understand my own relatives." Again the dry chuckle. Advanced senility, thought Stern.

They were passing the red-brick, ivy-covered buildings of Princeton University. Squads of naval cadets dressed in black raincoats marched by in rigid formations.

"Here's where the professor walks home from his office every day," the cabbie said. "Right along that street there coming from Fuld Hall. Folks around here set their clocks by him. Thirteen minutes past one every day you can see him passing that corner. Regular as clockwork. In the wintertime he wears that sloppy old wool hat. Always the same old baggy sweater. More often than not, no socks. Only man I ever knew goes without socks. Folks ask me about that, and I tell them he just forgets. Got his mind on more important things. Like that business about his phone number. When he first come here to Princeton the university people didn't want him bothered by nuts calling him to the phone so they give him an unlisted number. One day they get a call from somebody asking for the professor's home phone number. They tell him they can't give out the number without the professor's permission. 'But,' says the guy on the other end, 'I *am* Professor Einstein.' " Again the dry cackle of laughter. Stern shifted nervously on the back seat. Would this idiot never shut up?

Much, Stern reflected, had been written about Einstein's life at Princeton. Einstein, the theoretical physicist, had become Einstein the world citizen. The stories of his humility and serenity and kind deeds were legend. The myth had become the man. Yet Stern knew him well enough to know that Einstein remained an enigma. He had worked with him for years. He believed he knew Einstein the philosopher and scientist, but how well did he know the man? And faced with his, Stern's choice, what would that man do?

The cab had pulled up before the modest white clapboard house on Mercer Street. Stern got out. As he went up the path to the house he knew the driver was still watching him with undisguised curiosity. He rang the bell. He heard footsteps and then the door was opened by a diminutive white-haired woman. The resemblance to Einstein in the lustrous, wide-spaced, dark eyes was unmistakable, and there was the same faintly puzzled, humorous expression.

For a moment Stern did not recognize her. He had last seen Einstein's younger sister in Berlin in 1932. She had been petite and attractive. Now, only ten years later, she was a tiny, white-haired old woman. She seemed to move with difficulty, and her speech was faintly slurred. In one of his rare letters, Einstein had mentioned that Maja had suffered a slight stroke.

Her face lit up. "David! David, is it you?"

"Yes, Maja."

"I can hardly believe it. What are you doing here? You are supposed to be in London."

"I am here on a brief visit. Only a few days. I have appointments in Washington, but I could not come to America without seeing Albert and yourself."

Her face fell. "Oh, David, why didn't you let us know?"

"A surprise trip, Maja. Very unexpected."

"Come in," she said closing the door behind him. "Come in. Let me take your coat."

"No, no, it's quite all right. You see, I don't have much time. Where is Albert?"

"That's just it, David. He's not here."

"Not here?"

"He has gone away for a few days. Out to the cottage on Long Island. You know Albert and his sailboats. When it comes to boats he is still a little boy. He says many of his best thoughts have come while sailing. I was tired and so he went alone."

"This cottage you speak of. Where is it?"

"A little town called Peconic out toward the eastern end of the island."

"I have heard of it," Stern answered remembering the map with the circled reference.

An act of providence, thought Stern. The decision has been taken out of my hands.

"I must go," he said abruptly.

"But David, a cup of tea . . ."

"No, no," he said cutting her off. "Another time."

He left the house walking with rapid strides in the direction of the train station.

FORTY-TWO

The dun-colored car came to a stop in front of the Mercer Street house. An army sergeant got out to open the door for an officer wearing a foreign uniform. The officer mounted the steps and rang the bell.

"Professor Einstein's residence?" Peter Guthrie asked of the white-haired woman who opened the door.

"Yes, but I'm afraid he's not at home," Maja said.

"My name is Guthrie. Actually I was looking for Dr. David Stern."

She nodded. "David was here for a little while yesterday. He only stayed a few moments and then left."

"I see. Might I come in?"

"Yes, of course."

"Are you Mrs. Einstein?"

"Miss. I am Albert's sister."

"I am sorry to intrude, but I think it may be a matter of the greatest importance."

A puzzled frown touched her brow. "I don't understand."

"I don't want to worry you, but I think your brother may be in some danger."

"From David Stern?"

"Yes."

Maja smiled. "Oh, come now, is it Major . . . ?"

"Captain."

"You are English, are you?"

"Yes."

Maja said in her slow, careful way, "David Stern is one of Albert's oldest friends. They were associates at the Institute in Berlin."

"I know."

"Why would David want to harm him? Why should anyone want to harm him? Albert has no enemies."

"In fact he has a great many enemies. He and every other Jew."

"Where?"

"In Germany."

"Of course. That is terrible. A tragedy. But what has it to do with us here?"

"Perhaps I had better identify myself. Here are my credentials. And here is a letter of authorization issued to me only yesterday in London and signed by Mr. Churchill."

Maja examined the documents and then returned them. Her hand trembled. "Mr. Churchill . . . sent . . . you?" She was having greater difficulty with her speech.

"Yes."

She made a noticeable effort to pull herself together. "David went out to Long Island yesterday to . . . find Albert at the . . . cottage."

"Is there a phone there?"

She shook her head. "It is only a summer cottage and Albert . . . does not like to be disturbed while he is there."

"The neighbors, then?"

She shook her head. "Too late in the season . . . the other cottages are closed."

"There must be some way to reach your brother in an emergency."

"There is a caretaker who lives a mile or two away. . . . He comes to look after things when . . . Albert leaves."

"He has a phone?"

"Yes."

"Call him, please."

He watched while she fumbled through an address book at the desk and then slowly gave a number to the operator. In the quiet of the house he could hear the phone ringing at the other end. Maja shook her head and held out the receiver for him to listen.

"No answer," she said. "Perhaps the police . . . ?"

He shook his head. "No. No police. Any story involving Professor Einstein and the police would almost certainly be leaked to the press. We don't want that. I'll get there as fast as I can. Meanwhile I want you to keep trying the caretaker, and if you get him tell him to go to the cottage and to stay there until I arrive. Can you do that?"

Maja's illness was intensified by stress. Unable to speak she managed only to nod. Guthrie pressed her shoulder reassuringly and then ran for the car.

FORTY-THREE

The flat, uninspiring Long Island scenery hurried by, but Stern was oblivious to it, sitting with his gaze locked squarely ahead. It was a poor railway; the car was filthy and reeked of tobacco smoke. He wanted badly to wash his hands, but was repelled by the condition of the lavatory.

As the train drew into the tiny station Stern saw a mail truck waiting. He descended the steps and asked the driver the way to Einstein's cottage.

Following directions he found himself in a country lane that led toward a scattering of cottages on the shore. Most of them seemed deserted.

Would Albert be greatly changed? Perhaps not. That massive head with its shock of white hair had always made him seem older than his years. The loss of Elsa must certainly have been a blow, but those bright eyes with their puckish quality would not have changed. Denise had remarked on Einstein's eyes. Great lustrous orbs full of intelligence and sadness. The windows of the soul. Christlike in a way . . .

He forced his mind back to the image of Michelle. Michelle as a child. The delicate face framed by her mother's long dark hair.

He felt his resolve strengthen.

He walked rapidly until he came to a white-painted cottage set closest to the water and some distance apart from the others. There was a dock and beside it a sailboat. A white-haired man in a shapeless gray sweater and faded khaki trousers was standing on the dock.

The setting sun cast a reddish glow over the bay. The air was turning chill.

Einstein adjusted his glasses and took an uncertain step forward.

Stern smiled. "Hello, Albert."

"David?"

"Yes."

The old man moved forward and threw his arms around his friend, then he backed off and held him at arm's length and stared into his face. The great dark eyes were wet with emotion.

"Why didn't you let me know you were coming?" Einstein said.

"There was no time. It all happened too fast."

"Have you left London, David?"

Stern shook his head. "No, no. I am only in this part of the world for a few days. Actually, I am on my way to a meeting in Chicago."

A frown crossed Einstein's brow. "I suppose to see Fermi and the others . . . Oppenheimer and Szilard."

Stern nodded.

Einstein said, "You know how I feel about what you are doing, David."

"I know, but it cannot be stopped now. If we don't do it the Germans will. London has decided to integrate its research with the work being done by Fermi and the Americans."

Einstein shook his head. "Let us not discuss it. I am glad to see you anyway. You will stay the night?"

"Yes, Albert."

"And Michelle? Is she well?"

"Very well."

"Not married yet?"

"No, but there was a young Norwegian . . ."

Einstein's eyes lit up with the old puckish merriment. "Norwegians are very fine people," he said in a serious voice. "Most of them, anyway. But stubborn. Very stubborn."

As they entered the cottage Einstein said, "We will have some wine to celebrate your arrival."

"Good."

"And tomorrow, if you have a little time, I will take you sailing. Would you like that?"

"Very much."

"The weather forecast for tomorrow is fine. It will be my last day. After tomorrow I go back to Princeton."

"You are here all alone, Albert?"

"Not entirely."

"Oh? Who is with you?" Stern tried to keep the anxiety out of his voice.

"Mozart. Always Mozart," the old man said placing a record on the phonograph. "But you? You still prefer Beethoven?"

"I think so, yes."

Einstein shook his head. "Beethoven created music, but the music of Mozart is so pure, it gives me the feeling it has always been present in the universe, only waiting to be discovered by the master. Do you realize, David, that if you succeed in what you and

Fermi are attempting, the world may never again hear Mozart?"

When Stern did not answer, Einstein sighed. "But enough of this. Come, give me your coat. Don't sit there like a stranger."

Stern jumped to his feet. "I'll hang it up, Albert. What can I do to help?"

"The wineglasses are in the cabinet. And the corkscrew. We will talk again later. For now we will listen to the voice of the universe."

U-99 closed the shore in heavy fog. The moonless night was as black, Korvettenkapitan Kretschmer thought, as the inside of a boot. The sea was calm. An almost perfect night for a rendezvous on an enemy coast. And the navigation had been right on the button, off by less than three miles. Kretschmer felt well pleased with himself.

He ordered the boat to the surface. The hatch dogs were opened and the hatch fell back with a clang. Kretschmer stepped out onto the tiny bridge and sucked in the fresh air. Submarines stink of sweat and oil and unwashed bodies. The first breath of salt air after a boat has surfaced is like the first sip of good champagne.

He could smell the land. A creepy feeling to be in that close. The Americans would shit blue if they knew a German U-boat was less than a quarter of a mile from the beach.

But it wouldn't do to hang about. He listened for the sound of engines but heard nothing. Only the gentle lapping of the surf. All the same a patrol vessel might blunder into them.

Satisfied as to his position and that the reconnaissance had been successful, Kretschmer stepped down onto the rungs of the ladder and ordered the hatch closed.

With her tanks blown, U-99 sank back into the sea to wait for the appointed hour.

In the morning there was heavy fog and drizzle. A cat, looking for shelter on the porch, cried softly. Stern heard Einstein padding to the door in his bare feet with a saucer of milk for the unhappy animal.

Einstein gazed out at the rain and said to the cat, "There, there, my dear. The rain makes you miserable, eh? I know what is wrong. The trouble is I don't know how to turn it off."

Stern, coming out of his bedroom, said, "So much for your weather forecasts, Albert."

"Perhaps it will burn off later, and we can still get our sail. Do you have time, David?"

"Of course. I have all day."

"Good. In the meantime we will play a little chess to keep from talking about your terrible bomb."

By noon the drizzle had ended, and the fog was beginning to lift. Einstein became more animated. The last sail of the season would be possible after all. He felt a little sorry for his friend. It was obvious that Stern was under great tension. His cheek muscles twitched and his eyes were sunken. Stern had never really enjoyed sailing, never had gotten the hang of it. Einstein found the gliding motion more relaxing than anything else he knew. He felt at one with the elements, riding the slants of the wind. To Stern it was no more than an uncomfortable way of getting from one place to another. Einstein had felt a bit guilty about subjecting his friend, on this brief visit after so many years apart, to an experience he did not really enjoy, but to his surprise Stern had seemed almost eager.

Einstein laced on the mainsail of the little sloop and pushed off from the dock. When they were away from the land the breeze caught them and the boat heeled over and began to move. Einstein held the sheet in his fingers, tuning the boat as he did his fiddle. The chuckle of the bow waves at the forefoot brought delight to his soul. Life after all was still good. He noted with amusement that Stern, visibly tense, had brought his raincoat with him and held it in his lap.

Cautious David.

FORTY-FOUR

Sergeant Murphy had been an ambulance driver before the war. Now, chauffeuring Peter Guthrie, he
demonstrated his skill by outrunning three police cars
on Long Island's Sunrise Highway. Guthrie had advised him to break all the speed limits, and although
Murphy was not at all sure how much weight an
English officer's word would carry in Suffolk County
Traffic Court, he was prepared to accept that they had
not flown the captain over from London by special
plane just for the purpose of sightseeing. Then, too,
Murphy simply enjoyed driving like a bat out of hell.

It was turning dark as they ripped down the country
lane to the water's edge. Murphy brought the car to
a halt. No lights showed in the cottage.

The mailbox bore the initials A.E. Guthrie
mounted the steps and knocked on the door. There
was no answer. From somewhere under the porch a
cat mewed.

A woman's voice said, "No use knockin' down the
door. Professor's not home."

A middle-aged woman in a chenille bathrobe, her
hair in pin curlers, stood on the path in front of the
house staring disapprovingly at Guthrie.

"'That's my cat," she said. "Likes to wander over this way. Professor spoils her."

Guthrie essayed a smile. "Do you know where the professor might be?"

"Might be anywhere," the woman said in the same stone-faced manner. "Happens he's off in his boat."

Guthrie gestured toward the bay. "Out there?"

"Don't know where else you'd go in a boat. Need water, don't you?"

"Do you know what time he went out?"

"'Bout noon."

"Was he alone?"

"Had a friend with him. Friend spent the night." Obviously she was the neighborhood busybody.

"Does he often stay out this late?"

"Don't know. If he's becalmed he might."

"But there's a good breeze this evening."

She shrugged. "It's not my business where the professor goes, and I don't rightly know that it's any of yours."

"Forgive me. I'm Captain Guthrie and this is Sergeant Murphy."

The woman had scooped the cat out from under the porch. "Uniforms don't impress me much," she said spitefully. "Awful lot of nobodies in fancy uniforms these days."

"You're Mrs. . . ?"

"Potter." God help Mr. Potter.

"Well the thing is, Mrs. Potter, I've got to find Professor Einstein as soon as possible. I've got an urgent message for him. Is there anywhere we could get a boat?"

"I've got a boat. Boat with an outboard motor."

"That would be fine. May we borrow it?"

"Cost you," she said thoughtfully, "twenty dollars. In advance. If it's so all-fired important, I guess the government can pay."

"Agreed."

"And fifty dollars deposit," she added shrewdly. "Never saw you two before."

He gave her the money. "Where is the boat?"

"Over there on the beach," she said indicating an unpainted flat-bottomed skiff with a battered-looking motor. "Sure you know how to drive it?"

"I can drive anything," Sergeant Murphy said.

They boarded the boat and found a half-full can of gas in the oily bilge water.

"That ought to do us," Murphy said. "Get us across the bay anyway. That is, if this contraption runs. Twenty dollars. What an old bitch."

FORTY-FIVE

The sun sank low on the horizon and, although the little sloop still ghosted gently across the water, the breeze was beginning to die. Einstein sighed. The last sail of the season. Would there ever be another? At his age one could hardly be certain.

It had been pleasant to have his old friend with him although, if he were to be honest, he would have to admit that David made him nervous. There was an atmosphere of tension that Einstein could not understand. They were far from the war here in these peaceful surroundings. Was it the awesome significance of the bomb?

"It is getting late," Einstein said. "I think we will go back now while we still have the breeze."

"Would you mind if I steer?"

Einstein smiled. Was Stern at last beginning to enjoy sailing? "Of course you may be the helmsman if you like. Be careful how we change places. You first."

Stern moved aft and placed his hand on the tiller.

"You have it?" Einstein asked.

"Yes."

Einstein worked his way cautiously forward. "You

are doing very well, David, but we are heading the wrong way. Home is back there."

Stern did not answer.

"Did you hear me, David?"

Stern was tight lipped. He kept his eyes averted. "Yes."

"Then why don't you turn?"

"Because we're not going back to the house."

"I don't understand," Einstein said in a gentle voice. There was something alarming in Stern's averted gaze and the intensity of his expression.

"Perhaps then you will understand this," Stern said reaching into his pocket and taking out the revolver.

Einstein's eyes widened. "It seems a poor sort of joke, David."

Keeping one hand on the tiller to steady the boat, Stern pointed the revolver at Einstein's head. "It's no joke, Albert. Believe me. Now stay very still and don't speak anymore."

The sailboat grated gently on the shelving beach.

Stern said, "You will please step out."

Einstein began to speak but then thought better of it. If his old friend had suddenly gone mad it seemed wiser, for the moment, to do as he said. Perhaps the fit would pass.

Stern's bright blue eyes were like chips of ice. "Walk across to the ocean side," he said gesturing with the revolver.

It was only a few hundred yards across the loose-packed sand. Einstein did not look back, but he was sharply aware of Stern holding the revolver and following close behind.

The little sloop, its sails still up, began to drift away from the beach.

Guthrie spotted the sail far off against the western shore in the afterglow of sunset. He shouted to Sergeant Murphy above the clatter of the outboard and gestured in the direction of the sloop. Murphy swung the boat around to the new heading.

It took them fifteen minutes to reach the sloop, which was forereaching slowly, sailing itself on a course parallel to the beach.

Murphy cut the motor as they came alongside the empty boat. He said, "What now, Captain?"

"It's not likely they would both have fallen overboard, so they must have gone ashore."

The sergeant shrugged. "It's getting dark and there's miles of beach. Where would you begin to look? Maybe we'd do better to go back to the house and wait until morning."

Guthrie shook his head. "Morning may be too late. They can't be very far ahead of us now. My guess is they left the sloop grounded on the beach and then it drifted away. If we go in as close as possible and cruise along the beach, we may see something."

"Okay, Captain. East or west?"

"East."

"What about the sailboat?"

"Let it go."

The sergeant was able to maneuver the outboard within a dozen yards of the shore. In the failing light the land seemed uniformly gray and featureless.

After ten minutes of slow traveling Murphy said, "There's something up ahead, sir. On the sand."

"I see it. Pull in."

Barely visible in the fading light a blue woolen watchcap lay on the white sand. Guthrie had seen photos of Einstein wearing a similar knitted cap. He felt sure now they must be on the right track.

"We'll look around," Guthrie said.

"Those look like footprints over there."

"Bring your light."

Even in the dark it was not too difficult to follow the footprints. But as they neared the other shore the prints faded, washed out by the rising tide. Looking out to sea with the slow roar and tumble of the waves at his feet Guthrie said, "There's no way to know which way they went from here. We'll have to split up. You go west while I continue east. Do you have a watch?"

"Yes, sir."

"Go west along the shore for an hour. If you have found nothing by that time, return to the boat. I will do the same in this direction."

"And if I find them?"

"Stay with them. Try to draw my attention. Flash your light, start a bonfire on the beach, anything. Just don't leave them."

Guthrie paused once to catch his breath and to look at his watch. Half an hour had passed. It was entirely dark, but the horizon bore the hint of an orange glow as the early-rising disk of full moon thrust its way up from the sea. He strained his eyes into the blackness. His nostrils had caught the stench of diesel fumes carried in by the night wind. Only a sizable vessel could create such a stink, and it was unlikely that a seagoing ship would be maneuvering close to the shore after dark. Above the thunder of the surf he became aware of the rumble of powerful engines. Only a submarine on the surface could make that particular noise and stink up the air so with its passing.

Disregarding the pain in his side he broke into a desperate run.

Kretschmer had brought the U-99 in as close as he dared. Collar turned up against the dank night air, he studied his chart in the narrow beam of a hand-held torch. On this featureless coast it was difficult to pinpoint his precise location, but according to his depth sounder he appeared to be within half a mile of the designated area. He had less than two fathoms under his keel now. The moon was rising behind him. He was not too worried about being observed. The Americans were too lazy and complacent to patrol a deserted beach.

U-99 rumbled on the surface like a great-bellied whale. The sea was calm. The rubber boat would have little trouble getting to shore and returning with the passengers.

The port lookout said in a low voice, "A light, Captain. On the beach."

Kretschmer studied the shore. It came again—three short blinks from a small flashlight.

He ordered the rubber boat lowered.

Einstein saw the monstrous shape of the U-boat lying across the silvery path of moonlight. His heart seemed to freeze in his breast. So Stern was not mad after all.

"Why are you doing this, David?"

"Because they hold Michelle."

"And they have sent you for me?"

There was no panic in Einstein's voice, only in-credulity. "What do they think I can do for them? I'm an old man."

"It doesn't matter. They want you."

"And you think they will keep their word to you? What guarantee do you have?"

"Only the guarantee that they will kill her if I fail."

Einstein shook his head. "I am not going with you, David. You can shoot if you like. I would rather die here than in Germany."

"Don't move, Albert. I am younger and stronger. If you try to run I will stop you, and then you will be tied and taken aboard like an animal."

Einstein saw the black shape of the rubber boat moving down the path of silver with the two men paddling. After all the years and the thousands of miles that had separated him from the Nazis, they were at last upon him. The nightmare had become reality. He could no longer speak.

Stern, waiting for the Germans to land, felt light-headed, a little dizzy. A beautiful night, the air soft, the evening stars beginning to show. It would be nice, he thought disjointedly, to sit here upon the beach with Albert to chart the progress of the stars across the sky and to play their old game.

Remembering he smiled to himself. Albert would look at him gravely and then say in his quaint English, "I will now a little tink." Then would come the dreamy, faraway look—the twirling of a lock of hair around his forefinger the only outward sign that the great mind was working at its highest pitch—and finally with a smile but not so much as a hint of the reasoning—the solution.

"God help me," Stern groaned aloud.

Once again the image of Michelle's face as a child flashed across his mind—the pale face, the great dark eyes. In those days he used to refer to her as a rabbit or chipmunk. Always some small, soft animal. The grave little face would study his as she peeked in at him. "Are you busy?"

"Not too busy."

"I have a message for you."

"Please give it to me."

"I love you," she would say.

"I love you, too, liebchen," Stern answered softly under his breath.

The rubber boat was close in now.

Stern raised the revolver and fired five shots in rapid succession at the men in the boat, the pistol spurting flame and making a devastating noise above the whisper of the surf.

He could not see if his shots had taken effect. It is too bad, he thought, that I am out of practice.

He raised the pistol again and put the muzzle into his mouth. The steel had a warm, oily taste. He pulled the trigger. "Liebchen," he started to say in his mind, but there was no time to finish the thought.

Guthrie, three hundred yards away, heard the shots. He yanked his pistol out of the holster and fired at the U-boat now clearly visible against the moonlight. A hopeless gesture, but all he could do.

* * *

To Korvettenkapitan Kretschmer and the men in the rubber boat it appeared that they had been caught in a trap. Someone on this hostile coast was shooting at them. Kretschmer's only thought was to save his ship. The men in the rubber boat considered only their own skins. They had barely time to clamber aboard before U-99 fled to sea, leaving the empty rubber boat bobbing in her wake.

Guthrie was badly out of breath. At last he was able to say, "It's all right now, sir. They're gone."

Einstein regarded him somberly. Guthrie put away his pistol. Einstein turned to look down at the body of his old friend. An incoming swirl of water touched Stern's shattered head.

"Poor devil," Einstein said.